Involuntarily Immortal

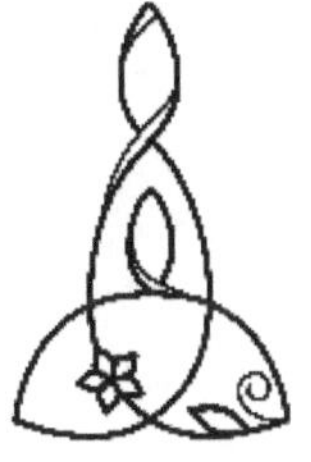

Emily Barlow

ISBN: 979-8-9998233-3-5

Printed in the United States of America

For my husband, whose patient support is everything to me.

AN ENDING...OR A BEGINNING?

It was an old curse, and a keen one at that. But she'd borne it a thousand years and more; what was another day? A week? A month? It couldn't be much longer now. She could feel her body shutting down, giving in to the crushing press of the years behind her as they caught up hundreds at a time. *Soon.*

She shuffled her ever-lighter frame across the sparse living room and into her cozy kitchen. It was the one portion of her tiny cabin in which she kept any extraneous comforts, mostly in the form of exotic ingredients; food was the one creative pleasure left to her, and she'd be damned if she'd give up that last bastion of humanity. Opening a cabinet, she hefted a cast iron pan onto the eye of her rickety gas stove and started the heat.

Thirty minutes later she sat down in the small kitchen nook with a plate of chicken covered in mashed potatoes and a dark, thick gravy. A dry white wine graced a stemless glass to her left, which she sipped appreciatively as she savored the dish before her. As she watched the sun set through the small, louvered window to her right, the crickets took up their nightly serenade, leading the bullfrogs in a cacophonous evening concerto.

She finished her meal and the accompanying wine and cleaned up the dishes, setting them out to drip dry in a wire rack by the sink. The few plates she owned never inhabited the cabinets, instead moving from the rack to the table and back. Taking one last look around the kitchen she switched off the light and retired to her bedroom. *Pretty good for a last meal,* she thought as she changed into her favorite cotton night shirt, an oversized holdover from the late 1990's with a band logo on it. The fact that it was pocked with holes never bothered her. It was comfortable, and she'd always valued function over form. She crawled into bed and sighed with contentment, for once not bothering to set the wards she usually kept around her house before falling asleep to the sounds of the night.

Pounding on the door awoke her after what seemed like mere minutes of rest. Covered in a cold sweat and with her heart thudding erratically she grabbed the second pillow on her bed and willed the banging to stop. *I'm not here…I'm not here… Who could have found this place?* Even now she could feel the life leaching from her body and curled up on her side, hoping fervently she would expire before her unwelcome visitors broke down the door. A muffled voice called through the sturdy wood. "Ms. Montgrief? Ms. Montgrief?" It was vaguely male and sounded desperate. *Not my problem. Not anymore.* She hugged the pillow tighter over her ears, not minding that it made breathing more difficult.

The pounding stopped. It was followed by a few louder thuds and a great crash as the front door hit her living room floor. She'd never taken the time to install a heavy lock; her wards were plenty to keep prying eyes, ears, and feet far enough away that no one had found her cabin in over eighty years. And she herself commanded enough power that the thought of a break-in held no fear; if someone was powerful enough to find her home, they were powerful enough to best her, and that meant the possibility of an end to her endless existence.

Heavy footsteps trod a circuit of the front room and kitchen, a voice calling her name as they explored. She pulled the blankets further up and hid beneath her pillows like a child, breathing shallowly in the hopes that they would think her already dead when they arrived at her bedside. *There's still time!* She was already so weak…but as the footsteps entered her room, she felt the ebb of her life stop abruptly, as if the curse was waiting to see what would happen.

"Ms. Montgrief?" The questioner whispered as if uncertain of whether or not he wanted an answer. She heard him approach the bedside and laid perfectly still, her back to the intruder. He lifted the pillow from atop her wizened head and a few greasy strands of bone-white hair trailed along with it. "Are you well?"

She squeezed her eyes shut. "Go away." Her little-used

voice sounded small, rough, and hollow, even to her own ears.

"I must speak with you," the man persisted, stepping back further into the darkness of the bedroom to maintain a respectful distance.

"No." She grabbed the pillow and re-covered her face obstinately.

"My daughter, Ai–"

"No names!" she shrieked from beneath the pillow. "I cannot help you. Leave my house." Then more quietly, "Leave me be."

"I have nowhere else to turn." Deep pain resonated in the man's voice as he pleaded with her. "Please. There is no one else who can help her."

"There is always someone else. Now go."

She could feel the man's hesitation as he shifted his weight toward the door, then settled in where he stood. "No." He crossed his arms in the shadows between her and the door.

His mistake. Squeezing her eyes shut, she sat up in the bed, heedless of the holes in her nightshirt and the unkempt state of her thin, white hair. "You will leave my house." As she opened her eyes light flooded the room, blinding the man. He snapped his eyes shut, wincing, as a great wind gathered between them, shoving him roughly toward the bedroom door. A large framed pack over his back slammed into the door frame and she heard a high-pitched grunt. Suddenly, everything stopped–the wind, the glare, all movement in the room–all at once. As Sable sat in bed, stunned, a thin, shadowy figure crawled out of the pack on the man's back. It moved cautiously, like a wild animal uncertain of what it saw, as it approached the bed and climbed onto the foot. It was human, and looked young, from what she could see. Then her steel-grey eyes met bright hazel ones and she was pulled into a maelstrom of thought and emotion. It tossed her about until she got her feet under her, but in that moment she saw a short lifetime of information–names, places, faces, and emotional reactions to all of them seared into her mind, and before she could stop herself she whispered a name.

"Ailith."

The mental vortex spat her out as quickly as it had sucked

her in and the small figure fell limp across the bed.

Stillness enveloped the room. No sounds of nature intruded through the thin walls of the cabin, as if the world waited. Then in a rush all the years that had piled on fled Sable's body, leaving her gasping for air as her lungs filled properly for the first time in years. Her heart beat strong and fast once again and she felt strength flow into her limbs, straightening her spine as it passed. When the rush subsided she was able to hear the ragged breathing of the man in the doorway, along with the shallow, light breathing of the child–*Ailith*–on the foot of the bed.

A single, bold cricket broke the spell in the room as it resumed its nightly performance. In answer the man in the doorway flicked the light switch, flooding the room once more with light. He shielded his eyes as they adjusted, then looked from the unconscious girl to the stunned woman sitting on the bed. "Who are you?" he demanded, a quizzical look on his brow as his mind attempted to reconcile what he'd seen moments before with the raven-haired woman before him.

"Sable Montgrief, at your service," she replied, then burst into tears.

WHERE TO?

S able sat with one leg underneath her in the breakfast nook in her kitchen, her antique dressing gown incongruous with her youthful appearance as she sipped a cup of tea. She'd donned extra clothing at her visitor's reaction to her standing up from the bed half naked in a holed t-shirt. It still irked her; the one thing she'd hung onto from her childhood was that human bodies need not be hidden for the sake of modesty. So when he'd swiftly turned his back, she'd pulled on a dressing gown and made a trip to the bathroom to dry her red, puffy eyes. She'd never quite gotten the hang of graceful crying.

He sat across from her in the breakfast nook, a steaming cup of tea untouched before him, looking more uncomfortable by the minute. His rich hazel eyes–a perfect match for his daughter's–scanned the room systematically at measured intervals from beneath a strong, dark brow; the rest of the time they studied his host in an attempt to discern what he could about her. Periodically he would shift in his seat in a vain attempt to create more room on the cramped bench he occupied before accepting that his bulk would allow for no further comfort. Being a head and shoulders taller than the house's owner, and broad-chested besides, he resigned himself to sitting sideways in the nook and continued his silent observations. They'd left Ailith on the bed to rest after her episode in hopes she would wake on her own.

Sable finally broke the silence. "Adem, is it?" she asked, resigned.

Her visitor's head whipped around to face her. "How do you–yes. Adem Ozturk." He stared down at his now-over-steeped tea as if seeing it for the first time.

"*Nice to meet you,*" she replied in Turkish.

"*And you as well,*" he answered reflexively before his

squared jaw went slack in surprise.

"Let me guess: first generation American," Sable posited, nonplussed, as she took another sip of her tea.

"Yes," he answered warily. When no more information was forthcoming, Sable moved on.

"With a name like that and zero accent, there's no way you could be otherwise. Put that next to the tanned complexion, black hair and beard, and hazel eyes and it's Turks all the way down." She chuckled at her own pun, not caring if her guest appreciated the humor in it. "So, Adem Ozturk, why the hell did you break down my door and completely ruin my chances at ending my curse?" Despite the puffiness of her eyes her expression was flat and deadly, and he leaned back as he met the steel of her stare.

"I did it for Ailith," he began. "You've seen her power. I have no idea what happened in there–" he gestured vaguely toward the bedroom where she lay–"but it's not unusual for her. Ever since she turned eleven a few months ago she's been in and out of consciousness at random. One moment we're having a conversation as we walk; the next I'm catching her before she crumples onto the sidewalk. I put together this frame to carry her here in case she had another episode on the way." He indicated that hiking frame he'd worn inside, which had supports for a seat and straps for safety. Sable also noted there was precious little room in it for provisions.

"That doesn't tell me how you found me." Sable's expression hadn't moved throughout his explanation, and she noticed with perverse satisfaction that it discomfited her guest.

"That was also Ailith. The morning all of this began, she woke up for school, looked me straight in the face and said, 'Dad, Mama said we have to find a lady named Sable Montgrief as soon as we can.' And she drew a complete map from memory that had this location marked with an X, then passed out." He hesitated, choosing his words before continuing. "When she woke up I asked her about it, how her mother could possibly have asked her to draw a map or send a message. You see, my wife, Irene, died giving birth to Ailith eleven years ago."

Sable showed no outward reaction, but the cogs of her mind, dusty though they were, turned rapidly. *Ozturk...Irene...*

Then she had it.

"Irene Ozturk the seer?" she asked.

"The same." Adem absently twisted a plain gold wedding band around his left ring finger. "She seemed healthy, and everything went fine throughout her pregnancy, but when it came to birthing…I still don't know what happened. The doctors couldn't explain it; it was like she simply couldn't exist at the same time as Ailith."

"Maybe she couldn't." Sable paused as she considered that last, not out of sympathy, but out of professional curiosity. She'd only known Irene Ozturk by reputation, and that only through scrying, but she'd been one of the best; maybe she'd seen something coming. *Best to watch my back, then.* "So how long do you think we have?"

Adem shook himself, surprised by the quick change of topic. "Until what?" he asked.

"Until whoever's chasing you catches up," Sable replied as she downed the last of her tea. She'd have to bring some with her wherever they were headed, as she'd come to rely on a calming cup of something warm to help her nerves when they got ragged, as they were now. *Guess that means I'm back in the game, at least for the time being. Time to set some boundaries, then, so I have some hope of coming out of this without losing too much ground.*

Adem's eyes narrowed. "How do you know anyone is chasing us?"

She leveled a look at him that was much older than her outward appearance. "I read people well, Mr. Ozturk, and you have the look of a man who is hunted. My guess is that you've spent the last–I don't know–three months on the run?" His eyes widened, but he still regarded her with the wariness of a caged dog. "I applaud you for making it this long without losing your shit, especially since you have a child involved. Or maybe because of that." She rose fluidly and slid from the breakfast nook, drawing herself to her full 5'1" of height so that she could look her visitor in the eye from where he sat. "But if Irene Ozturk thought you needed *my* help, you must be in absolutely dire straits. As in, world-ending straits. And I want to know why, but I need to know if that's something you should tell me right damned now or if we don't have enough time and need to get on the road. My bet is it's a tale." She held his gaze an uncomfortably long time until at last he broke the stare.

"They were three days behind us, at most, when we entered the national forest," he answered as he glared holes in the tabletop.

"Then we talk on the way." Sable spun on her heel and headed for the bedroom.

"But where will we go?" Adem's voice drifted from the kitchen as she sifted through clothes, looking for some that would fit her newly-refreshed figure. *Been a long time since I was twenty five; what's even in here that I can wear?*

"We'll figure that out when we get there," she yelled back. Five minutes later she was dressed in jeans, hiking boots, and a tank top beneath a sensible flannel shirt, with her waist-length hair braided efficiently down her back in a thick tail. Plain gold studs sat in her earlobes and a few small hoops climbed the outside of each ear, none large enough to catch on anything. They echoed the heavy torc-style bracelet that circled her left wrist, its stylized lions challenging each other from millimeters away, and a necklace was tucked safely under the tank top. Thus kitted out, she grabbed a duffel bag from the depths of the small closet and slung it over her shoulder. She couldn't be sure, but she could've sworn it sighed in contentment when she picked it up.

Sable paused as she passed Ailith, still sleeping peacefully on the bed, her chestnut brown hair spilling over the shoulders of her spare frame. *So small and young…and yet, so powerful.* She still felt a heavy resentment toward Adem and Ailith for ruining her chances at ending her curse, but long-stifled curiosity was waking within her, and she found herself reaching out toward the girl. Her finger hovered over Ailith's forehead as she sat, uncertain how far she wanted to commit herself to their cause.

"What are you doing?" Adem had appeared in the doorway as Sable gathered wool. She glared at him from her seat on the bed, then deliberately laid a finger right between Ailith's eyes.

Once again she was dropped into a swirling storm of color, images, and thought. It was less organized than before since the girl was unconscious, but Sable was prepared this time and wrenched her own awareness around much faster. Soon she wandered purposefully through Ailith's mind, sifting warily through the surface thoughts and emotions that sought to buffet her about, careful not to displace anything as she passed. The last thing they needed was for Ailith's stability to deteriorate further through Sable's meddling.

There was a method to the madness, and before long Sable found what she was looking for: a window into what Ailith saw at that very moment. Peeking out from around pre-pubescent detritus, she felt Ailith's attention directed at a bleak landscape of lifeless shadows and crawling darkness. A shiver ran up her spine as she recognized what the girl was seeing and she created a semblance of herself, reaching out a mental "hand" to Ailith. The girl appeared to her right, staring blankly at her outstretched hand.

"I'm waiting for my mom," she said calmly. "She'll be here eventually. This is where we meet."

"Ailith." Sable took a small step toward the girl, who seemed not to notice the closing distance between them. "I am Sable Montgrief. Your mother, Irene, sent you to me for help, but I can't help you if I can't talk to you. Your father and I are getting ready to leave, and we need you with us–back in our world. Can you come with me?" She took another step, and another, until she was close enough to touch Ailith's ephemeral frame.

The girl turned toward her. "Mama did say to find you," she replied, the ghost of a doubt flitting across her face as she made a decision. "I'll try, but it doesn't always let me back in." Looking to her left, Sable followed Ailith's gaze to a large stone gateway covered in ancient writing. It glowed faintly, and on the other side she could see her bedroom, where Adem Ozturk stood next to the bed, staring intently at his daughter and Sable.

"I can help there," Sable answered as she took Ailith's hand. Together they stepped toward the gateway, which glowed brighter the closer they stood. Sable pushed a hand easily through the shimmering image before her and felt her hand twitch through her physical body, then drew Ailith along behind her. The instant the girl's skin touched the portal the image turned to molasses, dragging at her skin as if to keep hold of her indefinitely. Sable narrowed her eyes, then laid a hand on Ailith's shoulder, lending her some of her essence for a time. The image cleared and both were able to walk through with minimal resistance.

Sable exhaled and removed her finger from the girl's forehead as she sat up on the bed. Opening her eyes, she encountered a large shoulder directly in front of her face as Adem scooped up his daughter in a giant bear hug. "Welcome back, sweetie," he whispered as she threw her arms around his neck. Sable waited a long, uncomfortable moment before clearing her throat.

"We should really get going," she pointed out to Adem before turning to Ailith. "I have a theory on why this is happening to you, but I need time to research it. In the meantime, I can anchor you to someone here so that it's easier for you to come back when you slip through the gate. Is that all right?" Ailith nodded mutely as Adem put her down. "Good. Mr. Ozturk, your hand, if you please." Sable held one hand out expectantly, palm up, as she dug through her forgotten duffel with her other. She produced a fine-point red Sharpie with a triumphant "ah ha!" before shaking her still-waiting hand with impatience. "Today?"

"It's okay, Daddy," Ailith said, reaching up to pat him on the shoulder. "I've felt her mind. She's safe." Brows furrowed, Adem turned to Sable and laid his right hand into hers, palm down. She turned it palm up, held it steady as she sketched an intricate Celtic knot onto his palm with the Sharpie, then let it drop without ceremony.

"Your turn, Ailith." She held her hand out and immediately found it filled with Ailith's. "You'll have to be still," Sable admonished, and Ailith stopped bouncing on the balls of her feet just long enough for Sable to sketch a matching knot onto her left palm. "Now take your father's hand." Ailith bounced over to Adem and slid her tiny hand comfortably into her father's large, calloused mitt. As soon as the symbols touched there was a flash of light that blinded everyone in the room. Blinking, Sable turned to Ailith. "Your father is your anchor now. Anytime you find yourself stuck on the other side, you can call to him and his essence will answer. It will help you get back." Ailith nodded, smiling.

"Time to go, then." Sable turned without further comment and strode toward the living room and the still-broken door. She'd taken two steps before a heavy hand descended on her shoulder from behind.

"You still haven't told us where we're going," Adem said as he leaned down closer to her level. Sable froze for a moment, still unused to physical contact, then whirled around, breaking his grip. The fury etched on her fine-boned face set him back a step.

"Do not. Touch me. Again. Without. Permission." A cold wind kicked up and lifted her braid and the tail of her flannel shirt in a menacing fashion as she continued. "I am helping you only because in doing so, I help myself. Do not forget that. For now, our purposes are aligned, but as soon as this is over I go back to my way of life and forget about the world again. In the meantime, I intend to have as little contact with people as possible. The fewer attachments I have, the easier it is to end my own endless curse. But if the world ends the way I think it's headed, I'll be even more doomed than you." Her rage spent, the wind died at her back and she turned, deflated, to walk through her mangled cabin door one last time. She never looked back.

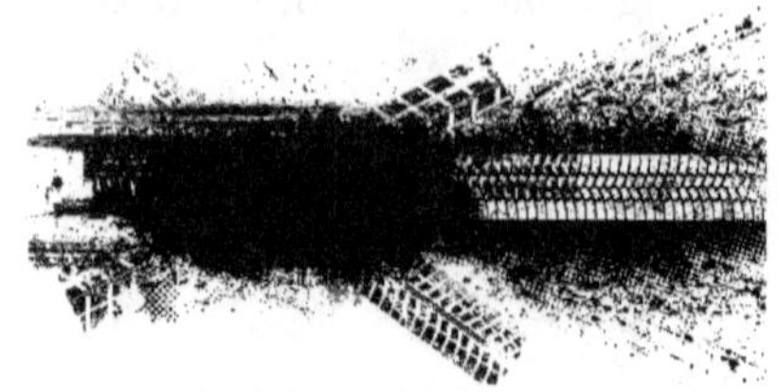

ROAD TRIP BACK TO REALITY

The forest beyond the door was pitch dark. They'd turned off all the lights before they left and Adem had propped the door back up to keep up the illusion of occupancy, so no man-made light illuminated the small clearing outside. Sable unconsciously set her own vision to drink in the small amount of starlight available and took stock of her surroundings. It was a new moon—no help there—and they were miles from any sort of civilization, so ambient light was nil. It was one of the reasons she'd picked this area when she'd settled down eighty years prior. But her own trails were familiar to her practiced feet, and she started confidently down a beaten path to the north.

"Dad?" Ailith's voice broke the relative quiet of the deep night. "I can't see a thing." Sable hung her head in annoyance and crossed back to stand before the girl and her father. Both were straining to see anything in the deep shadows of the trees. Rolling her eyes, Sable passed a hand in front of each of their faces and watched them blink rapidly as their eyes adjusted to their new vision, then stalked back toward the path. Adem and Ailith followed, picking their way between brier bushes and huge tree trunks. The large man moved without making a sound, a fact Sable filed away for later consideration.

After a few minutes she called back, "Did you drive to the park?"

"We left our car at the public lot back in Colville," Adem replied. "It's a rental under a pseudonym." Another point to consider on her ever-growing mental pegboard.

"You never told me that," Ailith shot back. *So she has some fire in her. Good. She'll need it.*

"You didn't ask," Adem replied grimly. The group fell silent for a few more yards before Sable spoke again.

"We're close to the edge of my glamours," she began,

pulling up short as they approached a wide intersecting path that showed more signs of regular passage. "From here on out we're on public trails and out from under the protections I've spent the last eighty years building. Keep your eyes and ears peeled; as long as that spell lasts you'll see things coming before they see you, but it won't matter if you sound like a herd of elephants crashing through the brush. The vision spell will last until dawn, which is about how long it will take us to get clear of the park." Adem and Ailith nodded, the former standing with his hands clasped behind his back as he listened. Ailith hung on her every word. It was disconcerting; her eyes went from focused to unfocused, but Sable was certain the girl had every bit of her attention on the conversation before her. She was also seeing things the rest of them weren't.

She leaned toward Ailith, who watched her with alternating focus as she approached. "What do you see?" Sable asked. In response, Ailith's eyes unfocused completely and gazed around the forest near the intersection.

"I see two woods," Ailith answered after a moment. "It's like there are two images on top of each other. One is the woods as they are now, and in the other there are more people. They have packs like they've been hiking, and they're looking at the ground really hard. They're tracking something."

"How bright is it? Is it daytime?" Sable asked, her tone edged with urgency.

"No; it's still night, but there's more light. I think the moon is brighter."

"Can you see it? Is it full?"

"I don't think so," Ailith answered uncertainly. Her eyes refocused on Sable. "They're looking for me, aren't they?"

Sable nodded. "I think that's a safe assumption. But it sounds like they're at least a week behind us." She stood and started toward the public trail. "It concerns me that they have someone who can see through my glamours…" Her voice trailed off as a thought occurred to her. "No. I should take them down." She raised both hands toward the night sky and dragged the air as if she were pulling down a window shade. When her hands reached the ground there was a popping sensation, as of pressure equalizing in the group's ears, and then nothing. Nodding in satisfaction, Sable motioned the other two on toward the trail.

"One of our greatest assets right now is the fact that whoever is chasing you doesn't know you're with me. I am entirely certain that no one knew about my cabin, and I left nothing identifying there, so even when they come across our path all they'll know is that you've picked up another person. That element of surprise could come in very handy later on.

"Now, Mr. Ozturk, please elaborate on exactly what we're up against." Sable glanced up at him expectantly as they continued onto the larger path and toward the park's exit. Adem ran a hand through his wavy hair as he calculated before replying.

"I'm honestly not sure," he began as they trekked through the darkened woods. "They come in threes, and they always have a strange symbol either drawn or tattooed on their skin somewhere. The first set showed up about a week after Ailith's first episode and was carrying kidnapping gear, so best guess is that they want her alive. Me…not so much." He fell into silent consideration long enough for Sable's patience to wear thin before continuing. "It's never the same three; two different groups came after us at home, and ever since we started running we haven't seen the same group twice. Whoever it is must have a lot of resources and extensive reach."

"Where have you run so far?" Sable asked when it was evident there was no more information forthcoming.

"We started in Indianapolis, where we live," Adem answered. "From there we headed west, zigzagging north to south through Illinois, Iowa, Nebraska, Colorado, Wyoming, Utah, Idaho, and now Washington. We've stayed ahead of our pursuers, for the most part, but they've caught up with us once or twice, usually around cities and large towns. It's been about a week since we caught wind of them in Boise and rented the car."

"Do you have family anywhere they might track you to?"

"My wife's family is spread across the country–California, Florida, Ohio–but mine is either in Indy or across the Atlantic."

Sable considered for a moment. "Seattle is the closest jumping-off point for us. If we pick up the car and drive there we can catch a boat, bus, or plane just about anywhere."

"It's a start," Adem agreed, "though we'll have to watch our backs closely; big towns are where we've had the most run-ins. Where are you thinking from there?"

"I'm not yet." Sable's light steps barely displaced the damp leaves beneath them as she trod. "There's safety in unpredictability, and we have some time to consider on the way. You said these people bore a symbol?"

Adem nodded, growing more accustomed to her sudden conversational shifts. "Ailith has a sketch of it in her sketchbook if you'd like to see."

Sable stopped mid-stride. "I would most definitely like to see," she said as she turned to Ailith, who produced a pad of thick paper from somewhere within the frame Adem wore. She flipped through the pages until she found what she was searching for, then held it up in the dubious light. Lines flowed across the paper from right to left, reminiscent of Arabic writing, but simpler. Sable took the sketch pad and turned it this way and that, flipping the book upside down before dropping it as if it had burned her. She picked it up by the corner with a distasteful expression before handing it back. "Ailith, I'm going to need to destroy that sketch," she said warily. "Please remove that page and hand it to me." Eyes wide, the girl ripped the page from her sketchbook and handed it to Sable, who pinched the corner between her thumb and forefinger. She whispered a word and the paper turned to ash.

Dusting off her hands, Sable started back down the path, digging in her duffel bag while she walked. Adem jogged to catch up with Ailith trotting ahead of him. "What was that?" he asked. "What do you know of it? I searched every public library we had time to stop in, the Internet, everywhere I could think to look, and that image never came up."

"I need to check something," came the distracted response from halfway inside the duffel. Sable had one hand shoved through the opening up to the shoulder and appeared to be sorting through things by feel. "No…not it…not that one, either… come on, useless bag…ah ha!" She drew forth a thick, antique leather-bound volume and held it aloft. It smelled musty, like old paper and saddle soap. "You won't find this in any public library." Despite the poor lighting she paged through the book confidently after checking the table of contents. "Indo-China… South America…the West Indies…here it is: Persia." Her finger hunted through the table of contents impossibly fast before settling on its quarry: an exact replica of the symbol Adem and Ailith had seen on their assailants. "I thought I recognized it, but I've only ever seen it upside down. Most Zoroastrians write it that way." Snapping the book closed, she tossed it carelessly back into the duffel bag and continued on as if that settled the matter.

"But what is it?" Adem demanded, his worn nerves fraying. His hands reached forward to shake Sable by the shoulders before he thought better of it and settled for shoving them into his pockets.

"It's the symbol for the Zoroastrian embodiment of chaos and evil thoughts," Sable replied, "whose name I will not utter here, not until I know more. I need to scry, but that's best done from a safe location." She fell silent, and as they walked she searched the twisted pathways of her own memory for tidbits that might help. Adem seemed content to let the conversation lapse and turned his own attention outward, alert for signs of pursuit or danger as he shepherded Ailith down the trail. Before long they turned onto a different path and headed southwest for a time, then turned due west. The sun was teasing the horizon before they realized it was dawn thanks to Sable's spell, which died as she'd promised just as the sun crested the treeline. As the sky reached the full brightness of day they were deposited into a field bisected by a dirt access road. Sable pointed at the obvious exit. "That will take us into Colville proper, which should get us to your car," she explained as she made her way toward the middle of the field.

Adem cleared his throat. "We should stick to the tree line," he suggested, "to draw less attention." Sable ground her teeth, but had to concede the point; she angled off toward the nearby trees and around toward the road as Ailith piped up.

"Dad knows all about how to be sneaky," she said conspiratorially. "He's really good at it–they taught him in the Army."

"Ailith." Adem's tone held a warning. "That's enough."

"What? She's helping us; she should know what we do well so we can all work together." Ailith kicked at a few dandelions as she passed, sullen eyes cast onto the path before her.

"That may be, but let me decide what gets shared. We still don't know much about her." This last was directed at Sable, who smirked in reply.

"Your father's right, Ailith," she said as she winked at the girl. "You don't know the first thing about me."

"We know your name."

"You know a name for me, yes."

"But that counts as a first thing." It was Ailith's turn to smirk.

"I think I preferred her comatose," Sable muttered under her breath. "Look, kid," she replied, "in this business it's best to share as little as possible. Knowledge of a person is power over them, especially when it comes to names. The only living creature on the planet who knows mine is me, and I intend to keep it that way, both for my safety and everyone else's." They walked in blessed silence for about thirty seconds as Ailith digested this information.

"How old are you?"

Sable exhaled sharply. "Never ask a woman her age. It's rude."

"But you don't look old," Ailith persisted. "How can it be rude if you're young?"

"What if you don't want to be young? What if you're sensitive about the fact that you're only fifteen, but your sister is sixteen and already out in society and entertaining suitors?"

Ailith snorted. "You sure don't sound young," she said around giggles. "I don't think I've ever heard anyone use the word 'suitors' before."

Sable's cheeks burned. "Well, now you have. So stop asking questions." She picked up her pace to put more distance between herself and Ailith, fully aware of the smile Adem repressed behind her.

Once they reached the access road they were able to make better time, though the exposed, straight lines of the dirt track made all of them nervous. Ailith complained of hunger after the first hour and Adem promised her something to eat when they got back to civilization. In the meanwhile Sable dug around in her duffel bag and produced three large, shiny apples, two of which she distributed before taking a satisfying chunk out of the third. Thus fortified, they completed the trip to the outskirts of town by midmorning.

Colville was nothing like Sable remembered it. When she'd first moved to the area it had been a tiny waypoint on the road north that contained a hotel, one restaurant, and a few shops for necessities. Now it had grown to accommodate a hospital, a movie theater, multiple chain grocery stores, and a golf course, among other things. She stopped at the edge of town for a moment to take it all in and found the effect overwhelming. *Just breathe. You've seen pictures of all of this; it's not news to you.* But seeing places in articles and films and scrying was a very different thing from experiencing them firsthand, and she'd been away from society for so long that the changes still came as a shock.

Ailith noticed her change in demeanor and slipped her hand into Sable's, who was too surprised to protest. "It's a lot, isn't it?" Ailith ventured. "You've been up there for so long…" She trailed off and squeezed Sable's hand before drifting back over to Adem, who looked sidelong at their travel companion.

"You all right?" he asked.

"I'm fine," Sable snapped in reply, straightening her spine and striding forward with a purpose. *Fake it 'til you make it.* "Let's find your car."

Fifteen minutes later they arrived at the public lot on the north side of downtown. A few cars peppered the space, but none had parked close to the nondescript gray sedan Adem had rented. He took a few moments to inspect the car and its surroundings before unlocking the vehicle and allowing Ailith and Sable to approach. Ailith nudged Sable toward the passenger side. "You take front seat," she said as she clambered into the rear bench seat. "The backseat's more comfy for sleeping, and the view is better up front." By the time Sable reached for the passenger side door handle Ailith was strapped in and comfortably ensconced with a pillow against the window.

Sable took a moment to feel the handle of the car beneath her fingers. The metal was cold and smooth, and the handle responded to the slightest tug. The door itself was lighter than she'd expected, and she set herself off balance as she dragged it open with more force than was necessary. Recovering her balance, she slid into the bucket seat on the passenger side of the car and pulled the door closed. Adem was already in the car and buckled. Securing her own seat belt she found herself wondering how such a small thing could make a difference in safety should they wreck at speed. The engine hummed to life and Sable's heart rate increased—she had never ridden in something that could go more than about 30 miles per hour, but she wasn't about to admit fear. After all, she'd faced down worse things than hunks of plastic and metal hurtling down the road faster than a hellhound on a chase. And people rode in cars every day, going to and from all sorts of places.

Just not Sable. As they pulled into traffic she felt her stomach do a flip. *You've seen this in movies and Internet videos and scrying and fifty other places. Suck it up, woman!* Closing her eyes, she slowed her breath and felt the car around her, the vibration in the frame, the shifting of its weight as they turned, the press of her own weight into the seat as they accelerated. She opened her eyes and drank in the sights of modern Colville as they drifted from light to light, passing shops and a police station and little cafes with outdoor seating. The seed of yearning for human company stabbed like a needle into her heart, and for a moment Sable closed her eyes to shut out a deep sadness; a part of her had desperately missed wandering amidst the throng of humanity, delving through shops for items and having tea with friends. She walled it back up behind decades of pain and loss, shoving human enjoyment aside to defend against further heartache.

If Adem noticed anything, he stayed silent about it as they drove. She decided they might be able to work together after all as they sped south out of town and away from the only safe haven she'd ever known. Sable wondered if she would ever find its like again.

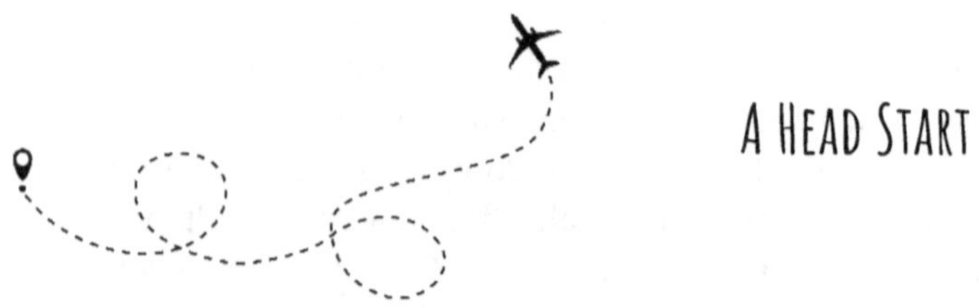

A HEAD START

They drove through the day, Ailith dozing in the back seat while Sable watched the world go by. Renewed wonder at its beauty flowed over and through her as the mountains rolled past; after all, if she was going to make one last venture into the world proper she could at least try to enjoy it. She watched as the sedan climbed Snoqualmie Pass, thankful they were traveling in the spring and not a month earlier as the still-snowy peaks heralded the beginning of their descent. By the time they pulled into the parking lot of a hotel in Snoqualmie all three of them were exhausted. Adem seemed the least worse for wear despite having driven the entire way but Ailith was visibly wilting and Sable felt as if she hadn't slept in a week. Two hours of sleep while aged several hundred years apparently didn't count for much.

The only hotel they could find was one of the more expensive ones in the country club section of town, and Sable noticed Adem checking his wallet as they walked in. Pushing past him in the lobby she produced a sleek silver credit card from the depths of her duffel and asked for a shared room for the three of them. The attendant's eyebrow rose as he took in the sorry state of their attire, but he ran the card and handed them a key, directing them to the top floor. Adem managed to stay quiet until the elevator door shuffled closed, then turned with a questioning expression toward Sable.

"I kept myself busy by learning finance and investment for a while," she said to preempt the questions on his face. "Might've made a few long-term investments that paid off. Played the stock market for a few decades, too, and got pretty good at it, especially once the Internet made trading easier." She shrugged. "Was purely academic at the time, so I took some big risks thinking it didn't really matter if they paid off. Turned out they did." The elevator chimed to announce their arrival on the fourth floor and deposited them into a quiet hallway that ran a good distance in each direction. The informational signs on the wall pointed them to the right, so they followed the numbered doors until they found their room. It faced the front of the building, where they'd parked, and had a fantastic view of the mountains.

Sable pulled the keycard from her pocket and held it up. She'd seen these in movies; people either swiped them through slots on the door or held them up to a pad next to it. This appeared to be one of the latter type, and as she held it up uncertainly before the raised rectangular box on the wall she heard a soft beep and the snick of the lock disengaging. Before she could reach for the handle Adem opened the door and strode through on cat's feet, checking the entire space before calling out for them to join him. The room contained two beds, one king sized, one queen; a bathroom just inside the door to the right; a television; heavy, room-darkening curtains; and a thermostat. Two bedside tables sat against one wall near the headboards with a lit lamp on each one.

"I don't know about you, but I'd love a shower," Sable said as she dropped her duffel on the queen bed. Adem grunted in what she thought was assent, and Ailith stretched out on the king bed's coverlet with the TV remote. "Guess I'll grab one first," Sable muttered and pulled the duffel bag into the bathroom behind her. She chose not to lock the door in case something happened while she showered. Somewhere in her subconscious she realized that showed a measure of trust in her new companions despite their short acquaintance, but she chose to ignore that little epiphany for the time being.

She turned on the shower and waited for the hot water to kick in, stripping off her hiking clothes and standing naked in front of the mirror. It had been decades since she'd last seen more than her wizened face in a reflection, and she took a moment to readjust her self-image to match the youthful figure looking back at her. She had never considered herself beautiful; her short stature, while solidly average for the time she was born, felt like it had diminished in consequence as the rest of humanity grew. Her squared shoulders, no longer bent with age, stood proudly over her moderate hips and trim waist, which was topped with perfectly adequate breasts. Legs accustomed to walking for transportation supported the rest of her frame in a balanced stance above wide feet. Her face was no more remarkable than any other part of her, with high cheekbones and a soft nose set into an oval face, but it was evident even to her that her eyes didn't belong in the face of one so young. Their level gaze peered out from beneath finely-shaped black eyebrows that offset the grey of her irises, penetrating everything she beheld with lifetimes of gravitas.

This is you again, she told herself. *It's not what you wanted, but it's what you've been handed. Accept it and move on or you're going to have more problems than even you can manage.* Nodding to herself, she brushed out her waist-length hair and stepped into the steaming shower.

Fifteen minutes later she was out and dry, reaching into the duffel bag for something to wear. It turned up more well-fitted jeans and a distressed t-shirt with skate sneakers and a denim jacket, then a pair of soft shorts and a tank top for pajamas. She slid on the pajamas, then folded and stacked the rest of the clothes and wrapped a towel around her still-drying hair before rejoining the others.

Adem sat on the foot of the king-sized bed, eyes glued to the television as Ailith slept on top of the coverlet beside him. His eyes flicked to Sable as she emerged, then back to the screen as she settled her things by the queen bed. A newscast rattled off information about a string of violent protests that had plagued many of the US's major cities for over a month, citing an unknown anarchist group as the cause. "That's them," Adem said softly, his strong tenor voice barely carrying above the sound of the television. "None of the newscasts have mentioned it, but you can see the tattoos on the ones who've been arrested." He gestured at the screen, where a bald man was being escorted by police into the back of a car. As he ducked into the vehicle the symbol from Ailith's notebook was visible on his forearm before disappearing behind the car door as it closed. Sable cocked her head to one side as she considered this new information, adding it to the moving pieces on the board.

"Your turn if you want one," she said as she dropped her folded clothes on the chair next to her bed. "I'll set wards on the room and stay awake until you're done. We can order some room service if anyone's hungry." She flopped down onto the queen-sized bed and tucked her feet underneath her, savoring the softness of the mattress. By way of response Adem tossed the remote onto Sable's bed, grabbed his own pack, and headed to the bathroom, grumbling something about not answering the door as he passed. He left the door cracked and started the shower.

True to her word, Sable went to work warding the room as unobtrusively as possible. The first ward she set to mimic the sound of a cell phone ringing if someone attempted to open the door from the outside, either with a key or through forced means. Second she set the window to sound like shattering glass if it was tampered with from the exterior. Her last ward was more esoteric: if any other being occupied the room, either physically or psychically, she would know. As she finished setting up this last ward she felt the weight of someone else's attention. Ailith had awoken and was watching her with an intense gaze.

"What did you just do?" she asked, tilting her head and looking around. "The room feels…different. Quieter."

"I set wards," Sable replied. "Can you see them?"

Ailith shook her head. "No, but I think I can see another version of this room." Her eyes unfocused and she studied things only she could see for a time. "It's night, and there are people here. They're looking for something…they're frustrated. Whatever it is isn't here." She refocused on the television, which Sable had muted, but left on. "Ms. Montgrief…"

"Call me Sable."

"Sable," Ailith echoed with only a little discomfort, "these things I see…they're real, aren't they?" Sable nodded. "They just haven't happened yet." Another nod. "Then how do I know about them? Why do I see them?"

"No one really knows how the sight works," Sable began. "We do know it runs in families, so it makes sense that you would be a seer since your mother was such a strong one. For that reason there's usually a family member nearby to help train a new seer when their gift starts to manifest–a parent, aunt, uncle, or grandparent–someone who can help the child make sense of what they see and take control of their power. Unfortunately for you, it sounds like you don't have that luxury."

"Can't you help me?" Ailith asked plaintively.

Sable shook her head. "The sight is one thing I've never had, and it's not a burden I would want. All I can do is help you sort through what you've seen; I can't help you control when or how you see it." Twisting herself around, she reached into her bag and dug around for a bit, coming up with another dusty, ancient volume from its depths. "This, on the other hand, might help. It's dry reading for an eleven-year-old, but it should give you a better idea of what you're doing." She handed the book to Ailith, who opened the blank, fabric-bound cover with round-eyed care. *At least she appreciates books.* It creaked ominously as it settled onto the bed in front of her.

"What is it?" she asked in wonder.

"It's a book," Sable replied drily. She chuckled at Ailith's eye roll response, then continued. "It was written a long time ago by one of the greatest seers of his age. He was attempting to write a manual of sorts for situations just like yours, where a seer finds himself or herself short a mentor, but he never had a chance to finish it."

Ailith picked up the first page between two fingers and turned it. "'A Treatise on Second Sight, by John'–what's this funny *f* in the middle of his last name?" She held the book out to Sable, who didn't need to look to know what she was talking about.

"It's an *s*," she replied. "John Sussex was the author. Wonderful academic, but extremely boring to speak with for long periods." She busied herself digging around in her duffel absently as she waited for the next question. The dry susurration of pages sounded once, then twice before Ailith made a noise of confusion.

"'As a litel child, I were given'…what even is this word?" she asked, stabbing a bony finger at the first page of the text.

"'Understonden,'" Sable replied without looking. "It means the understanding of a thing." She dug further into the duffel.

"'Understanding' means the understanding of a thing," Ailith retorted. "Half of these words are complete nonsense!"

"Not if you lived in England around 1400 CE." Another book thumped onto the bed next to Ailith. "Here's a Middle English dictionary you can use to help suss it out. I can't spend every moment helping you work through it, so you'll have to learn it on your own."

"But…but…" Ailith sputtered. About that time Adem reappeared from the bathroom, freshly showered and dressed in pajama pants and an undershirt. Sable sized him up quickly as he passed, adding physical conditioning and a few scars to her mental notes. One in particular stood out on his forearm; she could see signs of stitching on either side of a long, jagged mark that ran nearly the full length of it. Another, smaller mark peeked out from under the sleeve of his shirt, and his knuckles bore multiple signs of old lacerations. *A fighter, then. Ailith said Army, but I think there's more to that particular story.* She filed that away as he sat down next to his daughter.

"Middle English, eh?" he asked, picking up the dictionary and read the spine. "'Whan that Aprille with his shoures soote/ The droghte of March hath perced to the roote,/And bathed every veyne in swich licóur/Of which vertú engendred is the flour.'" He chuckled at Ailith's dropped jaw. "Chaucer's Canterbury Tales, prologue. You haven't studied it yet in school, but you will."

Sable smirked to hide her mild surprise. "Your pronunciation is a bit rough, but that's a good approximation," she remarked. "Need to work on your r's, though." Turning back to the bedside, she rearranged her things in an attempt to look busy instead of meeting her companions' stares. "Wards are up. You taking first watch?"

"I can," he replied as Ailith cracked open the dictionary, holding it open next to the older text.

"I can do it," she said as she pored over the books before her. "I slept most of the way here, so I'm not really tired. Plus I want to read some of this."

Adem looked dubious. "I don't know…are you sure you can stay awake for a while? And wake me when you're sleepy?" Ailith nodded, engrossed in her studies. "Okay, we'll give it a shot, but I'm setting an alarm on my phone for two hours. After that you're getting some sleep. Wake me if you hear or see anything, do you understand?" Another nod and the furious thumbing of dictionary pages were the only answers he got.

"Wake me for the graveyard shift if you need to," Sable tossed over her shoulder as she rolled onto her side, facing the door, and dropped into a deep and dreamless sleep.

It was still dark when Sable awoke. She cracked one eye and peered across the room before shifting so that she could see more of her surroundings. Adem's silhouette sat by the window where he could peer through the curtains, while Ailith's small form was just visible beneath every blanket the king-sized bed could offer. Stretching languorously, Sable threw her feet over the side of the bed and picked up her clothes from the bedside table before heading to the bathroom to relieve herself.

Having answered nature's call and dressed, she moved across the room to where Adem sat. He nodded his acknowledgement as she sat down at the small table. "Get some sleep," she said without preamble. She'd turned on her night vision and could see the lines on his face and bags beneath his eyes. "You have to drive in the morning. If you pass out now you'll get at least another three hours. You can use my bed if you don't want to wake up Ailith." Having left him with no excuses, Adem nodded, then crept past Ailith's bed and into the queen. Before long Sable heard his breathing even out as he drifted off to sleep.

She peeked around the corner of the curtains and found nothing obvious amiss in the parking lot or beyond. *Time to do some thinking.* The girl was a seer, though how powerful she was—or would become—was anyone's guess. She needed a teacher, but attempting to contact anyone in her family who might could help would only put more people in danger. Sable knew of a few seers who fit the bill, but she'd been out of the game long enough that her knowledge was dated and untrustworthy, and even if any of them happened to still be alive she wasn't sure they'd be willing to help train a child with whom they had no connection. Then it hit her: she did still have a connection with a powerful seer, one who would help train a youngster and who, on a completely selfish level, wouldn't count against her curse for purposes of getting back to where she could break it. Mind made up, she pulled a tablet out of the duffel and began researching flights out of Seattle.

The sun rose red and vibrant over the Rocky Mountains as Sable watched from partway behind the curtains. Behind it the sky was a riotous backdrop of color heralding uncertain weather. *Red sky in the morning, sailor take warning.* Letting the curtain drop behind her, Sable turned and found Ailith awake and staring at her from the king-sized bed. "Where's Dad?" she asked, blinking sleep out of her eyes. "I thought he was sleeping on this bed."

"I gave him the queen when we swapped watches," Sable answered, tossing her head in the direction of the humanoid lump in the other bed. Adem stirred at the sound of voices and sat up, peering around the room until he was satisfied nothing was amiss. "Not a peep from anywhere all night. Don't get used to it, folks. Today we're heading into Seattle."

"Did you come up with a destination for us?" Adem asked muzzily.

"Yep!" Sable busied herself gathering up the few things they'd strewn about the room.

"And?"

"I hope you have passports."

Adem snorted. "Of course we do. Do you?"

"Do now. Get dressed; we're flying out this afternoon."

"To…?"

"Our next destination." Sable stuffed the Middle English dictionary and the seer manual back in her duffel bag. "Are you going to use the bathroom or can I brush my teeth?"

"You're not going to tell us." It wasn't a question.

"Nope." A toothbrush and toothpaste appeared in her hands from within the duffel.

"You don't trust us?"

"You can't give away what you don't know," Sable answered. Adem shrugged and headed for the bathroom. "And I don't trust you." She fired this parting shot as the door closed and heard a muffled "Of course not" from beyond.

Turning, she met Ailith's wide-eyed stare. It was a little watery, and it made her realize just how young the girl really was despite her penchant for sarcasm. "You really don't trust us?" Ailith asked in a quavering voice.

"I don't trust anyone," Sable replied gently, "and right now, neither should you. It's a hard lesson to learn, but most people are only out to help folk when it aligns with their own purposes, like mine do with yours right now." She leaned down to put her face on a level with Ailith's, her eyes taking on a harder cast. "I'm here to prevent the end of the world so I can end the curse that's on me, no more, no less. Once that's done I'll go right back to living in obscurity. So don't go getting attached." Straightening up, she grabbed the duffel and hauled it onto the bed as Adem emerged from the bathroom dressed in jeans and a nondescript t-shirt. Ailith pushed past him and into the bathroom, clothes in hand. Sable heard a sniffle as the door closed.

"What was that about?" Adem asked with narrowed eyes.

"Hard life lessons," Sable replied. "I simply reminded her of why I'm here." She grabbed her bag and moved toward the door, deciding she didn't need to brush her teeth that badly. "I'll go ahead and check us out. Meet me downstairs when you're ready to go; I need some coffee." Grabbing the door handle, she slipped through and closed it against Adem's protests. She'd be damned before she explained herself further to anyone, especially him.

By the time Ailith and Adem appeared downstairs Sable had procured two lidded cups of coffee and a cup of orange juice from the continental breakfast bar. She presented them without ceremony to her companions, noticing that Ailith's eyes were puffy and red. *Oh, hell.* "There's breakfast if anyone wants it, but we're already checked out and good to go," she said by way of apology. Ailith mumbled something about not being hungry, but at her father's urging they each snagged a few foodstuffs before following him out the door.

The drive into Seattle proper didn't take long, and before they knew it Adem was turning in the rental car at Sea-Tac airport. Sable was thankful when they debarked from the vehicle; the drive had been filled with sullen, uncomfortable silence stemming from her last conversation with Ailith. She wasn't quite sure what to do about that particular problem despite her centuries of experience with human nature, so she did what any sensible adult would do: she ignored it for the time being, fully aware that it would bite her if she didn't address it.

All three were traveling light, which made checking in easy. Sable's duffel bag had mysteriously shrunk to the exact size necessary for carry on luggage when she pulled it out of the rental car and Adem had ditched the hiking frame at her cabin in favor of the backpacks both he and Ailith currently held. As they approached the counter to get their tickets, Adem leaned in closer to Sable. "Two tailing us, twenty yards," he whispered as he took Ailith's hand.

"Of course we have everything, honey," Sable answered with a significant look as she snaked a hand into the crook of Adem's unoccupied arm. "I'm so glad they let you pre-check bags now; things go so much faster." Once they approached the counter, Sable showed her identification–a blank card that showed whatever it needed to show to whomever perceived it– and they were ushered toward the security checkpoint, carry-on bags in hand. She saw Adem lean down to kiss Ailith on the head and thought she heard him whisper something to her, but the girl didn't bat an eye as they took off their shoes and set their bags on the conveyor belts. Ailith and Adem both peered at the console's screen as Sable's duffel went through the x-ray machine, but when it revealed only a hodgepodge of everyday items they both deflated with an endearingly similar gesture. Sable crossed her fingers that their pursuers had no tickets and couldn't pass the checkpoint.

Once they'd passed security they regrouped by one of the many news kiosks around the terminal. "Are they still behind us?" Sable asked, risking a glance behind them. Adem nodded.

"They badged their way through the checkpoint," he said quietly. "I think we can assume security at the airport is compromised as far as we're concerned."

Sable swore under her breath. "Okay, what are our options? We have another four hours until our flight leaves, three until it starts boarding, and I made sure we were in one of the first zones to board. I can change our appearance for a while, but if they have someone who can see through glamours it'll be no good." She looked around, taking in whatever advantages their surroundings might give. "This whole place is windows and glass, which makes it hard to find a dark corner to blend into."

Adem looked around casually, as if he were simply looking for a restroom. "There appears to be some construction going on by those bathrooms," he pointed out. Sure enough there was a "keep out" sign right next to the closest men's room. "We could use that to find a hiding place until it's time to board."

Sable considered for a moment. "Ailith and I can go in the ladies' room long enough to change appearances, then join you by the men's room and change yours," she suggested. "From there we can try to find someplace quiet to mask our presence–or even hide in plain sight, if it looks like the glamour is working."

Ailith scowled. "How do I know you're not going to just ditch me in the ladies' room and let them find me?" she asked melodramatically. Sable grinned in response.

"Now you're thinking along the right lines! You know I won't ditch you because I still need you. You're the key to all of this until we figure out how to stop what's happening. So even if you can't trust me, you can trust my motives." Ailith raised a dubious eyebrow, then shrugged.

"You got a better idea, Dad?" she asked. Adem shrugged in response, looking both preoccupied and uncomfortable as he sought out signs of pursuit. Deflating, Ailith shrugged. "Guess we go with Plan A," she said, moving closer to Sable. "Lead on." She trudged behind Sable around the first turn into the ladies' room. By the time they reached the bank of mirrors and sinks Sable's hair had changed from black to platinum blond and her features were entirely different. She was the same height, but had put on a good thirty pounds and was wearing high-waisted jeans with a sweatshirt. Ailith was also about the same height, but had also gained some weight and was wearing ripped black jeans with a flannel shirt over an anime tank top. Her hair was a dyed shade of black with blue and purple streaks. The look on her face said she might actually like the look.

"Okay, little sis, I'm going to use the restroom," blond-Sable said. "Then we can find something to eat." She winked at Ailith, who was still staring at her own reflection. "If there's one thing I've learned, it's to take advantage of a bathroom whenever you find one. You should do the same." She entered one of the closer stalls. Shrugging, Ailith occupied the one next to her.

Sable heard the door to the stall next to her open and watched a pair of sensible work shoes head toward the sinks. She finished her own business, then exited her stall to see a woman in a security uniform washing her hands. Her hair was pulled up into a severe bun at the back of her head, and peeking out from beneath the collar of her uniform was the edge of an all-too-familiar tattoo. Sable moved one sink down to wash her own hands, keeping one eye on the mirror and one on the woman two sinks down as the water turned off automatically. "How you doing in there, sis?" Sable called as the woman crossed behind her to use the hand dryer, never once glancing her way.

"Fine," came the exasperated reply and the flush of a toilet. Ailith reappeared just as the security guard turned out of the restroom and washed her own hands while Sable dried hers using the electric hand dryer. The warmth from the machine counteracted the chill in the airport and made her fingers tingle pleasantly.

"You done?" Ailith asked from beside her. She nodded and left the hand dryer to the girl with a grandiose gesture. It earned her another eye roll. *At least she's good at staying in character with her look.*

"Got your bag?" Sable asked. Ailith nodded, hefting her carry-on, which now took the form of a black backpack covered with patches and pins. Sable was nothing if not thorough. "Good. Let's go find someplace to wait." They strode confidently out of the restroom and right past Adem, who peered at them with narrowed eyes for a moment, then let them pass at Sable's wink.

"What about…?" Ailith asked as they passed the men's room, her concern written on her face before she noticed Sable's mouth moving. Looking behind them, she saw a man about her father's height, but slighter of build and much lighter of skin and hair detach himself from the wall and follow behind them at a discrete distance. "Oh."

"They're looking for a group of three, or at best, a man with a daughter," Sable whispered as she put a sisterly arm around Ailith. "We'll do better split up while we wait in the terminal. Don't worry; our seats are right next to each other!" This last she said brightly as they turned into the main concourse. Ailith rolled her eyes in response, but let herself be led around the concourse.

They spent the next three hours bumming around the airport in an attempt to feign tourism. Sable, genuinely excited by the prospect of wandering the shops, dragged her unwilling counterpart through every kiosk and store they passed, picking up a few items at random. They wound up in a small café in the exact middle of the concourse, having pastries and overpriced coffee. Adem shadowed them in an impressively unobtrusive fashion as they flitted between storefronts. At one point Sable noticed him occupying a stool in one of the bars with a good vantage point, sipping something fizzy out of a tall glass as he watched the travelers pass in front of him. Their eyes met briefly and he nodded, then returned to his scanning. *Not his first rodeo,* Sable thought as she chattered away to Ailith about something else she'd found in the duty-free store. They noticed an increase in the number of security guards floating around the concourse the longer they were there and a tightness crept into Sable's shoulders; more guards meant more scrutiny, and that could lead to someone who could see through their disguises. But luck was with them; the loudspeakers announced boarding for their flight before the heat cranked up too much and Sable took Ailith by the hand, steering her toward the correct gate.

"Japan?!" Ailith asked as she saw the destination for the flight.

"I know—it's so exciting, isn't it?" Sable gushed, willing the girl to play along.

"Totally," Ailith agreed with genuine relish.

"I have some friends we can stay with in Tokyo and see the sights there for a few days. I know you're going to love it!" Sable presented their IDs and boarding passes to the gate attendant, who scanned them and waved them on. Adem had finagled his way into the line so that he was two passengers behind and caught up as they walked down the jet bridge. He continued to ignore them as he passed and boarded the plane just in front of them, nodding to the flight attendant and checking his ticket for his seat. Sable had booked them business class seats three across at the front of the section so that she and Adem could sit on the aisles with Ailith between them. As she stepped onto the plane the sensation of closed-in, recycled air hit her and she steeled herself for yet another new sensory experience. They shuffled with the rest of the passengers down the aisle and into their seats and stowed their carry-on luggage in the compartments above the window seats. Sable's duffel had changed form and now was the size of a large purse, so it fit comfortably beneath her seat; there was no way in hell she was putting it anywhere out of reach. Ailith pulled her headphones and a cell phone from her bag before stowing it with help in one of the upper compartments, then plopped herself into the middle seat on the row, popped in her headphones, and proceeded to ignore the world. Sable and Adem watched the rest of the plane's occupants board, their nerves mounting as the aircraft filled with humanity. Once the trickle of passengers stopped a group of airport security personnel did a walk-through of the plane accompanied by an announcement of a final safety check. Sable held her breath for a moment, then let it out in relief as the last security guard debarked without incident and the hatch was closed.

Settling back in her seat, Sable was free to turn her attention to the motion of the plane as they taxied away from the terminal. The sound of the engines spinning up to push them down the runway as they waited for takeoff sent a thrill of adrenaline through her body, and she found herself gripping the armrests on either side of her as they bounced down the asphalt. She peered to her right across the aisle to catch a glimpse out of the window as they pirouetted around the final turn and saw nothing but grass and painted lines on concrete. "Looks like we're number one for takeoff," the captain said over the intercom. "We're having some great weather for SeaTac today and are set to arrive in Tokyo in about nine hours and fifty-four minutes. Please sit back and enjoy your flight." As the mic keyed off the plane's engines roared to life and they accelerated down the runway. Sable fought the forces shoving her back in her seat as they gathered speed, leaning forward with effort to watch the runway pass by as they hurtled toward its end. The moment the wheels left the pavement her stomach dropped into her feet. She let out a small squeak at the disconcerting sensation of having all the blood in her body pulled downward at once, then again as they banked and turned west toward their final destination.

Looking to her left, she caught Ailith giggling. "Don't like flying, big sis?" she asked with wide-eyed innocence. Sable took a break from her deep breathing exercises to stick out her tongue, earning another chuckle before she went back to focusing on lowering her own stress levels to something approaching normal. As the plane continued to climb at a gentler rate Sable found herself better able to relax, and by the time the attendants came through the cabin with hot towels she felt she could almost enjoy herself. Someone handed her a small bag with convenience items and headphones for the in-flight movie, so she put them on to see if it was worth watching. By the time they hit cruising altitude she found herself dozing and leaned her seat back comfortably, considering only for a moment before letting herself catch up on some much-needed rest.

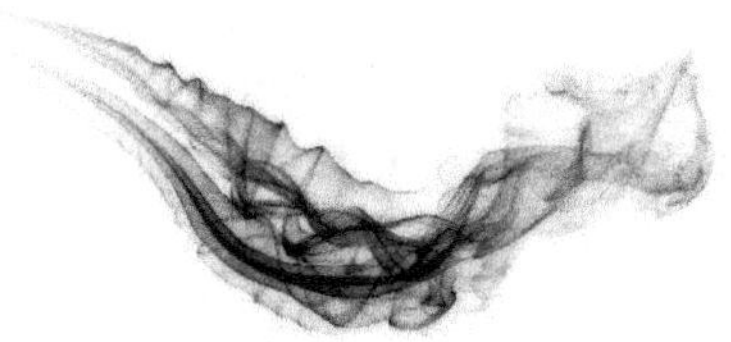

Portal to Nowhere

W"hy haven't you found them yet?" a guttural voice demanded from beneath its obscuring hood. "It's been three months! They're two people with limited resources. How difficult can it be to track them down?"

"With due respect, Great One, Adem Ozturk is no ordinary human," a smooth, oily voice answered. "And the girl…"

"The one on which all of this rests."

"Yes, her–she is coming into her power. I can taste it on the ether. But it means they may have another advantage at their disposal if she is learning to control it."

Long fingers drummed loudly on the armrest of a red leather chair. "You make a good point, Nanghait," the hooded speaker begrudged. "Bring me Indar." Nodding, the smaller man strode from the room, disappearing behind a wooden set of double doors at the far end. The hooded figure waited silently atop his dais, fingers steepled in front of him, until a dark-haired woman opened the doors and entered the room. She was strikingly beautiful in a western European sort of way, and when she spoke her velvet-dark voice swept the room with power.

"You called, Great One?" she asked as she bowed before the leather armchair.

"You are needed, Indar. The troops are finding it…difficult to apprehend Adem and Ailith Ozturk." The woman nodded, waiting for more. "They were sighted at SeaTac airport in Washington State, but as soon as they crossed the security checkpoint they disappeared. We own SeaTac; we should have been able to catch them, but no one recalls seeing them beyond that point. I think they've gained the assistance of someone with the ability to hide them from mortal eyes."

"Who would aid them against us?" Indar asked, her brow furrowed in confusion.

"I don't know…yet. But I intend to find out. For now,

I want you in Asia. I have a feeling they're heading there instead of staying in the States." The woman nodded. "Be ready to move; we have eyes on every airport and transportation hub around the world, so as soon as they surface, we'll know."

"As you command," Indar intoned, bowing low as she backed toward the door.

The hooded figure rubbed his temples. They were so close to victory, so close to achieving everything they'd worked so hard for. They must not lose faith. He dragged his body upward, stretching it to its full height yet still feeling constrained by it as he exited the room through a small door set behind the dais. The hallway beyond was pitch dark, but his steps never slowed as he approached a metal security door and touched a panel to its side, which lit in response to his hand. Metal hinges sighed as the door swung outward and soft light flooded the hallway as he stepped into the open room beyond. His eyes swept every surface, checking each item present to be sure all was in order, from the large, bronze bowl set atop a wooden table near the door to the great stone archway dominating the room's center. Mounting the steps to the archway, he leaned into it, closing his eyes as his forehead touched the cool surface of the rock. Carvings flared to life around and above him as the huge structure responded to his presence, the air between its pillars shimmering and humming with power.

"Almost," he whispered, reaching a hand toward the surface of the disturbance. Voices whispered in a thousand forgotten languages just beyond the barrier, each calling to him in their own way. He yearned for their release just as he yearned for his own, but as his fingertips met the power before him it turned to rubber, repelling his touch. He leaned back, hand still outstretched, and watched the portal dim. One last voice shoved its way through the veil as it winked out of existence, whispering a single word:

"Ahriman."

Whirling on his heel, the figure strode from the room with a renewed sense of purpose. He had to find the girl. For them. And for himself.

 A Murder of Pigeons

Psst!" Sable woke to a prodding in her left shoulder and batted the finger away. Ailith was staring at her from the next seat over. The stare alone should have woken her; it seemed she had gone soft in her years as a hermit. "I'm bored," the girl explained. "Do you still have that book with you?"

"Of course," Sable replied, reaching gingerly below the seat for her bag before realizing that bending over didn't hurt anymore. In fact, she wasn't at all stiff despite having been stuck to a seat in an aircraft for–she checked her phone–about three hours. A brief venture into the bag produced both book and dictionary, which Ailith balanced on her inadequate tray table.

Sable peered across at Adem, who was industriously reading the in-flight magazine for what she guessed was about the seventeenth time, based on the speed at which the pages flew by. *Probably doesn't want to put headphones on for security reasons.* Taking pity on him, she dug around once again in the duffel-purse and pulled out another book with an image of a man on the cover, wings extending to either side of his waist and a feathered tail blending into the bottom of the thigh-length tunic he wore. She reached around Ailith, who was bent over her work, and tapped Adem on the shoulder with the book. "Here," she said as his brow furrowed at the offering. "Some light reading for the trip that may come in handy later." He accepted the book with a nod and mumbled thanks before cracking the cover.

Turning to Ailith, Sable leaned over to see how much progress she'd made. "How've you been feeling?" she asked without preamble, keeping her voice pitched low to avoid eavesdroppers. "Any more faintness? Loss of consciousness?"

Ailith shook her head. "Not since the cabin. Every now

and then I'll start to feel a little weird, but then I think of Dad and it gets better." Adem's expression softened; he'd been eavesdropping himself, but he didn't join in the conversation. *Have to keep up appearances.*

"Good," Sable replied, nodding. "Did you notice it was worse anywhere in particular? Trying to work out triggers for your, um, condition." Ailith pondered for a bit before answering.

"Well…there was this one time we went past a really old cemetery that it got pretty bad," she admitted. "But there have been other places it just randomly happened as we drove." Sable produced a pad of paper and pencil from the ubiquitous duffel-purse and handed them to the girl.

"I want you to write down where you are and what's around you every time you feel weird," she instructed. "That way we can correlate based off better data."

"Or I could just make a list on my phone so it's easier to update," Ailith replied in her best adults-know-nothing-about-technology voice as she waved the device in front of her.

"Only if you want me to keep your phone in my purse from here on out," Sable retorted. "We don't want that list available to anyone who might pick up your phone, do we?" She could see the wheels turning as Ailith attempted to form a response, then failed. She took the paper and pencil and sullenly began to write.

Silence stretched across the seats and Sable felt she should be doing her own research or preparing something to help them once they landed, but was at a loss as to what else she should do. Scrying was out of the question; it was too public an area, and she needed water or a mirror, besides. She'd given Adem the book she would most likely need to reference about whoever was after them, which had surprised her a little; it meant that on some level she was starting to trust him. That probably wasn't a bad thing, since they would all need to rely on each other to get through this alive. But trust was a two-way street, and she couldn't go getting attached–or letting them get attached. She wasn't sure she could handle the loss of another close relationship on top of the mountains of friends and lovers she'd left behind across the years. As soon as this was over she was heading right back into obscurity to live out her years alone and finally beat her curse.

A pad of paper appeared in front of her face with a pencil shoved through the coiled spring binding it together at the top. "Done," Ailith announced and went back to her studies in Middle English. Sable took the pad and scanned the surprisingly legible list of places: home, her mother's grave, the beginning portion of the trail they took to get to Sable's cabin, various locations on the road to Seattle, the old graveyard they'd passed.

"Have you run into any of these since we left the airport?" Sable asked, waving the list.

"Nope." Ailith didn't even look up from her book. "Being in the air has actually relaxed a lot of the pressure on it." Sable added a scribbled note to the bottom of the list: "Proximity from ground helps." Then she stuffed it back into the duffel-purse and began to formulate a plan for their arrival in Tokyo.

"Adem." Sable's voice whispered right next to his ear. He twitched and glanced across Ailith to see Sable still reclined against the seat, seemingly engrossed in a book. Her lips barely moved as she continued. "When we land, can you rent us a car and meet us at baggage claim?" He nodded as if to himself. "We'll go straight there and wait, but I'll change our appearances again once we're off the plane." Another nod. "We still need a bolt plan in case things go sideways. I'm working on it, but coming up dry; all my resources and contacts around the world are eighty years out of date, so money is about all I've got. You have anything in this neighborhood?" The barest head shake. "Then I guess we wing it." She sighed, then realized she'd made a pun. "Ha, 'wing'–get it? It's an airport?" Adem passed a hand over his face, though she wasn't sure if he was hiding a smile or rolling his eyes. Chuckling to herself, she went back to the book in her hand.

The rest of the flight consisted of more book passing (Adem finished the volume she'd given him and politely asked if she had more she could lend him) and helping Ailith with her Middle English. She was picking it up quickly; they approached it like homework she needed to work on, which was innocent enough. At some point a meal was served and they broke long enough to eat before going back to their respective studies.

Sable found she enjoyed teaching Ailith, who was precocious and soaked up knowledge with the desperation of someone who needs a distraction. They even worked on pronunciation so that by the time the plane began final approach they could exchange short greetings and phrases. The antiquated language brought back memories Sable had thought long buried, which she shoved aside in favor of situational awareness in the present. They were landing in Tokyo, and while she didn't have the sight, something about it made the hairs on the back of her neck stand on end. She couldn't shake the feeling that someone was waiting for them.

Sable couldn't decide if landing was better or worse than takeoff. The sensation of losing her stomach every time they dipped in altitude was nauseating to her, but as they pulled into the gate she decided that despite its discomforts, flying was something she could grow accustomed to. They grabbed their carry-on bags from the compartments and beneath their seats, stretched legs that had barely seen use for a full day, and followed each other down the jet bridge, Adem in the lead as he ignored Sable and Ailith once again. "Eyes open," Sable whispered to Ailith. "Something's amiss."

The girl paled and nodded, swallowing hard. "I'm having trouble staying on this side of the gate," she replied. Sable squeezed an arm around her shoulders reassuringly, having no other way to encourage her; she could either hold her own or she couldn't. Time would tell.

As soon as they were out of sight of the flight crew on the plane she shifted their appearances again; Ailith became a boy of about her same age wearing jeans and a polo shirt, while Sable masqueraded as his mother and Adem became a dumpy middle-aged businessman wearing a button-down shirt and slacks. They strode toward the waiting area outside their arrival gate, eyes roving the massed crowd waiting to board, sensing nothing out of place–until their feet left the jet bridge, and Sable felt a sweep of power. "Jig's up," she said under her breath. Someone had just seen through their glamour. It was still in place, but she knew with certainty they'd been detected; it was only a matter of time before they were found. "Get ready to move," she whispered to Ailith. Using the same whisper trick she'd used on the plane, she warned Adem of their impending need to flee, fight, or hide. His steps picked up speed and he headed straight for the closest exit sign, Sable and Ailith in tow. No one seemed to be following them yet, but they felt the pressure of outside scrutiny as they wound through the crowded terminal. Haneda Airport was huge and impressive; multiple floors shone with gleaming, polished stone and brass banisters, stores crowding the expansive walkways as shoppers wandered in and out. They wove between the other travelers in their beeline for the rental car kiosks, but before they were out of the terminal proper a large man stepped out in front of Adem, reaching toward him. Two more appeared behind the first as Adem sidestepped easily and took the man's arm, folding it into two ninety-degree angles impossibly fast and shoving him into his companions. All three tumbled to the slippery terminal floor, floundering for their footing as Adem led the group down another pathway. Sable threw up a hasty illusion behind them that mimicked the hallway's occupants minus them in hopes that it would throw off pursuit a bit longer while they found a different escalator to take to the ground floor.

Once they were on the escalator, she took a moment to check on Ailith, who had dropped behind as they ran through the terminal. The girl was pale and sweating beneath the still-in-place glamour, and Sable knew she was fighting on two fronts: one they could see, and one they couldn't. "Stay with us," she mumbled, leaning close to Ailith to support her, both physically and mentally, and earned a nod and a weak smile in response. Sable was touched by the girl's resilience. She hoped it would be enough to get her through.

"There's someone there," Ailith whispered back. "On the other side. She's close, and I don't want her to catch us." The girl's eyes lost focus and her head lolled back, then snapped forward. "You're gonna need your bag. Keep it close." Sable nodded and concentrated on keeping the girl from tumbling down the moving staircase.

Movement in the crowd at the bottom of the steps caught her eye as they approached the bottom. Three more people in suits were making their way to the escalator, two women and a man this time, shoving through the travelers at the bottom. They reached the last step just as Adem stepped off. He grabbed the first woman just as she reached toward him and used her own momentum to push her into the escalator. Her face bounced off of the handrail and she fell to the floor, where the edge of her suit coat was caught by the mechanism and drawn into it. Turning toward the rest of the group, Adem motioned for Sable and Ailith to use the opening he'd just created to get past, then engaged the other two. One hit the ground quickly, while the other—the second woman—gave him a few more seconds of trouble, but before long he was right behind Ailith and Sable, who had almost disappeared into the ground floor crowd of shoppers. "We need a vehicle," Sable cast over her shoulder toward Adem as she changed their appearances once again. "They'll be watching the public transit."

"Can you make us look like security or employees?" Adem asked as they slowed in an attempt to look innocuous.

"Either," Sable replied. A few security guards had already appeared at the site of the second fight and were helping the woman by the escalator off the floor; she'd managed to take off her jacket in time to avoid injury.

"Flight attendants, then," Adem said, and suddenly all three were perfect representatives of the company they'd flown with into Tokyo. They hurried toward the rental car desk, which had just appeared around a corner. The woman working at the desk greeted them without batting an eye, and just as they got the keys to the rental—another sedan, if smaller than the last—a woman appeared from around the corner behind them and pointed.

"That's them!" Her voice carried power, though not nearly as much as Sable was capable of wielding. Still, it wasn't worth the risk.

"Time to go!" she said as they sprinted for the exit to the rental lot. As they passed through the doors she waved a finger to engage the locks in hopes of slowing their pursuers and was rewarded with the sound of a body hitting the door full force. *Score one for me!* She smiled grimly as they searched for the correct parking spot, then piled into the rental car just as the doors to the terminal opened, admitting six people in matching suits and two security guards. They watched all eight grow smaller in the rear view mirrors as they pulled away from the terminal and into the Tokyo morning rush hour.

As soon as she was buckled in Ailith passed out in the backseat of the rental car, one hand resting atop her backpack, head lolling back onto the headrest at the kind of angle only children can maintain without semi-permanent injury. Sable glanced back long enough to check her for signs of distress, then shot her eyes forward again as they pulled into traffic. The cars on the thoroughfare were densely packed, but moved at a regular, if slow, rate. It made their pursuers easier to spot when they ducked out from behind a waiting service van in an attempt to catch up.

"Adem," Sable warned.

"I see them," he growled. "Can't you hide us somehow? Or can they see through it?"

"Only if that woman is with them or they have some sort of trinket or device that negates the illusion," she explained. "I feel her power in the car that's chasing us, so it's no good– you'll have to lose them. Head north; it's the way we're going anyway. Maybe we can ditch the car somewhere and take the train or something."

"We should avoid public transit," he replied, weaving through the traffic as quickly as possible. The car following them gained. "Isn't there anything else you can do?"

"Most of what I can do is either too subtle or way over the top for this situation." Sable shifted in her seat, remembering the duffel on the floorboard. It had returned to its original size sometime after they'd reached the car. "Hang on, I might have an idea." She dug through the bag as random sounds escaped from its depths–metallic clanking, a gentle chime, something that sounded like a bird–and eventually came up with a small whistle. "Okay, let's see if this thing still works!" Rolling down the window she blew an ear-splitting blast. Immediately the sky began to darken ahead of them.

"Gah, and I thought nothing else could damage my hearing…what did you do?" Adem asked. "And what on earth is that?" He pointed to the horizon before them, where a shifting mass of something dark rapidly approached.

"Just keep driving," Sable advised. "It'll pass over us, don't worry." As she finished speaking the air in front of them filled with a boiling mass of feathers and beaks as hundreds of pigeons descended upon the traffic, which was now at a standstill. Adem continued to weave into and out of whatever spaces he could find, eyes wide but trained on the road, as the largest concentration of birds mobbed the car that was chasing them, pecking at the windows and perching on the roof as if it was no more than another building for them to sit on and survey their territory. Before long the vehicle was slathered in so much bird feces the occupants could no longer see through the windshield. One tried to open the door, but the birds flowed in as soon as it was open, conquering the interior as well as the exterior and driving out the prior occupants with triumphant coos.

By the time they were able to see twenty feet down the road Sable, Adem, and Ailith were long gone.

Cleansing Waters

The rental sedan slid down the Tokyo freeway alongside the regular morning traffic looking just as innocuous as its counterparts. They paralleled the river for a while and Sable enjoyed the intermittent view as they headed northwest toward the outskirts of town. In most places the road was walled in on both sides as they passed through densely-populated sprawl, making it feel more like a well-lit tunnel than an open highway. Eventually they turned away from the river to head more north than west and Sable lamented the loss of the running water as a travel companion. Trading views for more walls, they drove in silence until they reached the outskirts of Tokyo proper. Adem broke the stillness first.

"How did you know they saw us?" he asked.

"I didn't know they saw us, per se," she replied, "just that we had tripped something that was there to detect glamours like ours. And nobody would take the time to set up one of those if they weren't looking for something in particular." Sable chewed on her lip as she pondered, an old habit that was surfacing in her new-found youth. She wondered what other habits would creep back into her personality as it woke up.

Adem turned to glance at Ailith in the backseat, who was still unconscious despite having shifted enough to avoid a neck cramp. His eyes narrowed as he turned back toward traffic. "Who–or what–are you, Ms. Montgrief?" he asked in a dangerous tone.

"A very pointed question, Mr. Ozturk," Sable replied in kind. "I could ask the same of you."

"I've trusted your advice up to this point solely at the direction of my deceased wife," Adem replied. "We've now crossed an ocean and immediately been chased again by the same unknown group that's been after us for three months, and

I don't even know where we're heading despite the fact that I'm driving. I have zero–zero!–information or leads on who wants to kidnap my daughter or why, and the only person who might be able to help is a cryptic woman who hoards information like it's her job." His voice rose as he continued. "I know you wanted nothing to do with any of this, Ms. Montgrief, and I'm sure you have your reasons for that. But now that you're involved, I need to know how far I can count on your assistance and what kind of shape it might take if we're ever going to get ahead of these people." His grip on the steering wheel was white-knuckled as he fell silent.

Sable's lips drew together into a tight line as she considered. He'd asked a fair question, to which she wasn't at all certain how to respond. On the one hand, it was better for all of them if she kept her involvement minimal; that way, her curse would have less to latch onto. Plus they'd be less disappointed when she disappeared again after all was said and done. That said, she wasn't sure it was in her to be as rude and unkind as she would have to be to effect that sort of stilted working relationship. And then there was the girl. Sable found she actually liked the sullen little thing despite herself. She'd never had children of her own for fear her curse would truly become unending, and something in the girl's plight spoke to her in ways that were unfamiliar to her.

"We're going to Fukushima," she began in a gentle voice, surprising even herself. "There we will hopefully meet with the spirit of one of the world's greatest seers, who should be able to give us a better idea of how to get a handle on Ailith's abilities." She paused before plunging forward. "As for me, I'm exactly what you said: a cryptic old woman who hoards information like it's my job. In a way, it is; I've spent most of my very long life gathering as much magical and occult knowledge as I can, including artifacts like the bird whistle I used earlier." She patted the duffel between her feet and it seemed to sigh with pleasure. "This bag carries the most important pieces, along with whatever else I need it to.

"As for who we're up against, I'm still not sure myself; it's been eighty years give or take since I left the woods around my cabin, so despite having access to news and movies and television I'm still a bit out of date on matters concerning the occult world. It was always much smaller than what people like to think of as the 'real' one anyway." Sable looked down at the smooth skin of her hands, which she'd folded in her lap. She'd never expected to see them again without gnarled joints or yellowed nails, and she still wasn't comfortable in her own much-younger skin. She hoped it wasn't as obvious as it felt.

Adem was silent for a long moment. Just as the silence stretched into a new kind of discomfort–as Sable wondered if she'd been right to put even the smallest bit of trust in him–he asked quietly, "You hadn't left that cottage for eighty years?" His furrowed brows carried confused concern instead of the anger they'd supported moments ago.

Sable nodded, then remembered he wouldn't notice as he drove and squeaked out a "yes" in a more pitiful tone than she'd intended.

"That's why you've had me drive everywhere. It's why you didn't have a passport, and why flying was so new." She nodded again, unable to find her voice. "You've lived the last eighty years understanding society at an academic level through the lens of the media you've seen, but you haven't lived any of it." The weight of this last statement constricted itself around Sable's heart and squeezed harder than expected, as if giving it voice had brought it to life. She sucked in a deep, unsteady breath, then blew it out through pursed lips as Adem ran a hand through his hair, either unaware of the effect his statement had on her or too polite to remark on it. The acknowledgment within the silence between them supported the weight of Sable's newfound emotions, easing them to a dull, but tolerable ache. Just as she decided she should respond, Adem's soft tenor voice settled on top of the heavy atmosphere in the car.

"I spent eight years in the Army," he began. "Two of those were boots down in Iraq, right at the start of the war. I'd wanted to go special forces when I joined; already had a martial arts background, was in great shape, checked all the boxes–and then they looked at my test scores and decided I didn't get a choice. Intel it was." His expression was stony as he recounted his history. "It kept me from a lot of the front line fighting, but there's no such thing as a non-combat MOS, and I always felt like I could have done more, given more, saved more lives if I'd been put somewhere else. Regardless, I served my country, then came home and started a family. And the rest, as they say, is history." Judging by his face as he buttoned up that topic there was enough there to write several books. Sable afforded him the same courtesy he'd shown her and let the particulars go.

"War will always be hell," she said by way of acknowledgment as images from her own past flashed through her mind: charred bodies before her, the smell of blood and excrement and burning hair clinging to her nostrils even now before she shut off the mental parade of horrors.

A slow clap sounded from the back seat. "Bra-vo!" Ailith exclaimed sarcastically. Both adults jerked around at the sound of her voice, Adem looking relieved and Sable alternating between extreme annoyance and relief at the interruption. "Now that we've gotten the first group therapy session out of the way, can someone explain to me where we are and what's going on?" She peered out the rear windows, craning her head to see as far as the ubiquitous barriers would allow.

"Saitama, last I saw," Adem replied. "How are you feeling? What happened?"

"I don't know," Ailith replied, running a hand through her hair in a gesture not unlike her father's. "As soon as the plane touched down it hit. I was able to stay this side of the gate until we got in the car, and then I just…couldn't anymore." She looked forward without seeing what was ahead of them. "It pulled me in harder than anything I've ever run across."

Sable produced an antique atlas from the depths of the duffel, paging through until she found Japan, then poring over it intently. "Ew, I can smell that thing from here," Ailith announced, wrinkling her nose.

"If you'd been through as much as it has, I'd be smelling you, too," Sable replied as her finger drifted across the page, then stabbed at a location. "Yep, found it! Ailith, I think I know why you feel drawn to the gate at certain times and places. You mentioned it got stronger as we passed the large cemetery on the way into Seattle, and now you've had a hard time staying conscious landing in Tokyo–which has been the site of numerous disasters, natural and otherwise, that have cost a great number of lives. Tokyo has seen its fair share of death, especially near the coast. I think that calls to you, weakens the barriers between this world and that."

Ailith looked like a light bulb had turned on in her mind. "You're right," she breathed. "It's gotta be related!"

"Have you had any more visions since we touched down?" Sable asked.

Ailith shook her head. "If I did, I couldn't pay attention to them; I was too busy trying to keep up and stay conscious." She hung her head.

"Hey," Adem's voice was soft and encouraging. "You did great back there. I'm proud of you, squirt." Ailith smiled a little, blushing at the childhood nickname. "Hopefully we shook them for a while, though we'll have to keep a sharp eye out, so if you see anything–I mean, like, See anything–" Sable could hear the capital letter in the word–"you let us know, okay?" The girl nodded, mumbling something about doing her best before pulling out her headphones and ubiquitous cellular device.

"So." Adem shifted, settling his bulk into the too-small bucket seat as comfortably as was feasible. *Nothing in Japan is going to fit him.* "Fukushima, then. How close do we have to get?"

"To the city? Not sure; haven't been here since the Edo period, truth be told, so I don't know if she's still close by or if she's high-tailed it into the mountains to the west."

"You don't know, then?" Adem's eyebrows shot up before he remembered himself. "I suppose you missed that piece of news; there was a reactor on the eastern coast that was damaged by a tsunami a few years back. They've set up an exclusion zone around the site."

Sable frowned. "Was that somewhere between 2010 and 2013?"

"Think so," Adem replied.

"Explains why I missed it," she said, nodding. "Spent those three years studying the effects of psychotropic drugs on physical manifestations of magical constructs. Might've even tried a few myself. Nothing to lose at that point." One side of her mouth curled up in a mischievous grin. That was one expression she'd never lost through all her long years; it had gotten her into trouble as a child, then a young woman, then an old woman and everything in between. Another cerebral cog slipped into place as she remembered some of the scrapes she'd gotten into–and out of–and wondered again where this one would lead.

Adem cleared his throat. "Um, so how do we get there? My phone doesn't work here, and I don't see an atlas in the car that I can read." He picked up a travel book on Tokyo and a map in Japanese by way of illustration. Sable took the map from him and opened it, peering at its contents.

"Man, they really simplified their characters a while back, but I'm pretty sure we take the E4 until we get up around Shirakawa, which is well outside the exclusion zone. From there we can figure out where to head next and hopefully get a hot meal and some sleep. My circadian rhythm just isn't used to globetrotting anymore." Re-folding the map, she set her hands back down in her lap and fell silent as the road rushed by underneath them.

Walled roadways gave grudging way to house-dotted fields and townships as they traveled north. Occasional natural areas bordered the expressway on either side and made Sable long for the solitude and silence of their canopied depths in a bittersweet way. Adem had put her last eighty years into a perspective she had avoided until now, and that realization stacked itself right on top of the growing heap of emotional issues she was hoarding. *Much like the knowledge I keep, only this could be more deadly. And that's saying something.* She hoped, but didn't expect, that they would soon get a breather long enough for her to sort a few things out.

Two hours and very little small talk later Sable pointed at a road sign as they approached an exit. "Hot springs!" she exclaimed. "Great for the body and the soul, and this one has a hotel attached. You ever been to an onsen?" Adem raised an eyebrow and shook his head. "First time for everything. Let's go!" Too tired to argue, Adem eased the sedan off the highway and onto a smaller road that wound through the countryside a ways

before shoving them around a sharp hairpin turn into full view
of a magnificent wooden structure. It was built in the traditional
style, with broad roof lines tiled in dark green sweeping over
the edge of a hillside. White and dark wooden paneling stood
out from the natural greens surrounding the premises and an
archway proclaimed the entrance to the drive. The sedan joined
a scattering of other vehicles in the parking lot as they disem-
barked the vehicle, stretching muscles too long unused before
walking through the simple, yet elegant front doors and into a
tiled hall containing small cubbies for shoes. Sable took off her
own and slipped them into a cubby, trading them for the soft
slippers she found there. "No shoes indoors," she admonished,
and Adem and Ailith followed suit. Stepping up onto a tata-
mi-covered landing with a desk to one side, Sable wiggled her
toes in the comfortable, plush slippers.

"Irasshaimase," said a quiet voice behind the counter.
"Tourists?" Adem nodded and opened his mouth to answer, but
was superseded by Sable's rapid-fire response in fluent Japanese. The woman behind the desk smiled and exchanged a few
more sentences with Sable, who produced the same credit card
they'd seen before in return for a room key.

"We've got a room on the second floor," she explained as
they followed the hostess through the building. It was well appointed, with plush carpets in the hall acting as dampers for any
noise that might drift down them. Tasteful art hung on the walls,
all in traditional Japanese styles, and the doors they passed were
all made of wood and polished until they shone. They ascended
a set of steps covered in the same red plush as the hall, then
turned down an identical hallway and stopped. The hostess
gestured them inside, smiling, then left them to their accommo-
dations, closing the door behind her.

Two futons lay on the floor of the modest room, which
was also equipped with a low table and floor cushions. A china
set was laid out on the table with four teacups and a teapot, and
bags of green tea sat at the ready nearby. A small informational sheet sat next to the tea set to let guests know when dinner
would be served and how to get to the hot springs to bathe. On
one side of the room stood a small closet containing robe-like

garments in a calm taupe color.

Sable flopped the duffel down onto the nearest futon. "I don't know about you guys," she said, "but I'm ready for a bath. Ever been to a hot spring?" Adem and Ailith, who had been settling their own packs on the second futon, shook their heads. "Well, you're in for a treat. They're wonderful for both physical and spiritual well-being." She crossed the room in a few strides and took a robe from the closet, disappearing behind a rice paper wall into the bathroom. "Grab a yukata and let's go!" When she emerged she'd wrapped herself in the yukata and re-donned the slippers, looking perfectly at home in the ensemble. She threw her dark hair up into a messy bun and looked expectantly at her companions.

Ailith shrugged and grabbed a yukata. "When in Rome… so how does this work?" she asked on the way to change. "Do we need bathing suits or something? What do I wear underneath this? Are there separate baths for girls and guys? Do I have to put up my hair, too? Dad, are you coming or is it just me and Sable?" By the time she ran out of questions she'd finished changing. Sable chuckled.

"Answers in order: no, you don't need a bathing suit; in fact, they're not allowed. Japanese culture is very open about nudity, so everyone hits the baths in their birthday suit. This place doesn't have separate baths for the genders, but some do. Ooh, almost forgot!" She turned to Adem, who had frozen mid-stride at the mention of nudity. "Do you have any tattoos?" He shook his head dumbly. "Huh, would've thought a military guy like you would. That's good; many onsen don't allow them."

"I didn't want any identifying marks beyond what I already had in the way of scars," Adem answered as he made his way to the bathroom.

"When we get there, make sure to wash up before you get in; they'll have a spot where you can do that and ditch your robe before getting into the hot springs. And bring the small towel they give you with you so you can dry off a bit when you get out."

"So everybody's naked?" Ailith giggled.

"'Course," Sable replied. "I've never been able to understand modern hang-ups with nudity. We've all got basically the same parts, minus a few differences, and not learning about those parts is a disservice to everyone." She grumbled under her breath as Adem finished changing and joined them. "Any prudish objections now that you know the rules, Mr. Ozturk?"

"Of course not," he answered, standing taller and assuming the mien Sable was becoming familiar with as Dad Mode. "We practice sex-positive parenting at our house."

"Yeah, I know what a penis looks like, thanks," said Ailith, rolling her eyes as she twisted the soft wave of her hair into a bun.

"Anyone want tea before we go?" Sable asked blithely. Ailith and Adem both shook their heads. "Then let's go soak!"

Sable led the way back down the hall and onto the first floor, where they passed other guests in similar dress. They smiled and greeted the other guests politely, Sable in Japanese and Adem and Ailith in English. The lobby floated past as they crossed through a comfortable sitting area with large windows containing a few more guests, who were enjoying the stunning view of the springs themselves. Steaming naturally-carved pools of white water cast clouds across the vista, making it more like a living painting than reality. Small shrubs and artfully-placed trees added puffs of dark color to the landscape, and the gurgle of the water sluicing from one pool to the next was audible through screened panes placed regularly across the room. A sign pointed bathers further down the hall and to the left, where a large doorway opened into a locker room with showers on one side and wooden benches on the other. An attendant handed out small towels to bathers leaving the locker room without their yukatas, which were folded neatly and set next to larger towels on shelves above the benches. Most of them were empty, but there were a few folded robes scattered across the long shelves.

Sable wasted no time in doffing her own garment and heading to the shower to wash, glad of the packaged soaps available for use. Ailith followed her example, looking around furtively before scooting over to the closest shower and washing up. Adem shrugged off his yukata in an attempt at an unself-conscious fashion, folding it with precision before finding his own stall. Sable glanced over a few more times than was strictly necessary before he disappeared around the wall of the next shower over, noting more scars than she'd been able to see previously. *Bet those have a lot of stories to tell.* She decided they didn't diminish her estimation of his physique, though; if anything, they made it more interesting. She snapped a lid on that particular line of thought and chastised her newly-young body for its overactive interests, then strode confidently out to the hot springs, small towel in hand.

The water was warm against her skin as she slid into the mineral-rich soak up to her neck. It pervaded every pore as the steam opened her sinuses and eased her breathing. At the same time she could feel the part of her that stayed in touch with her magic open up, refilling and refreshing itself in ways she hadn't experienced in a century or more.

A sloshing sound next to her announced Ailith's arrival. Sable opened her eyes–she'd closed them without realizing it–and glanced sidelong at the girl, who sank in chin-deep and sighed. "Feels good, doesn't it?" Sable asked.

"Mm hmm," Ailith replied, smiling. Her heart-shaped face relaxed more than it had in the few days since they'd met, and Sable found a tension leaving her she hadn't realized was there until it was gone.

"How are you feeling otherwise?"

Ailith cocked her head to the side. "Good," she said after a moment's contemplation. "Everything here feels…balanced, like there are equal levels of things on both sides, if that makes sense." Sable nodded encouragingly as Adem slid into the water on the other side of Ailith. She did her best to ignore the little voice telling her there were interesting things to look at as he did.

"That's because they are in balance," she replied, refocusing her mind. *Good thing I've had years of practice at that.* "That's why I wanted to bring you here. Onsen are places of balance and equality, where good and evil, yin and yang, life and death all exist, but in a natural and harmonious way." She inhaled deeply, savoring the odd fumes of the hot spring. "This is how the whole world should feel."

"Why doesn't it?" Ailith asked, her brows drawing down in thought.

"Because once the balance is tipped, righting it is a very delicate thing. Picture a scale, one of the old-timey ones with two sides that have to balance each other out. What happens when both are weighted equally and you take all the weight out of one side?" Ailith raised her hands out of the water, palms upward, balancing them evenly, then dropped one into the water as the other shot upward. "Exactly," Sable nodded. "And once that happens it's not easy to stack the sides evenly again." Nodding, Ailith took this in and contemplated it, her gaze drifting out across the nearly empty pool. The only other inhabitants were diametrically opposite them, where an older couple soaked in silence about ten yards away. Occasionally one would look over at the other and smile, then go back to simply existing nearby. Sable watched them with a very strange, but powerful mixture of emotions. In many ways she could relate better to the older couple than either of her companions despite her appearance. She glanced at Adem and found him studying the couple, his expression one of deep sadness.

"They don't have long," Ailith whispered, her expression slack and her eyes unfocused. Sable's eyes locked back onto the girl.

"What do you see?" she asked, not wishing to disrupt Ailith's sight, but curious nonetheless.

"It's not a vision," she replied. "I see…people. Beyond the gate." She reached out as if counting heads. "I think they're loved ones waiting for them; they look happy." She smiled a little, turning toward Sable. "They're there to welcome them home." As her gaze settled beyond Sable's left shoulder her smile faded. "You have people waiting for you, too. Lots of them, but they don't all look happy." Her expression shifted through wariness and into fear. "I don't like some of them."

Sable grabbed her hand and squeezed it under the water, pulling Ailith away from the gate and back into the here and now. "Don't you worry about my ghosts," she said as she let go. "They're my own to worry about. But while we're talking, I believe I owe you an apology." Ailith's eyebrows shot up in disbelief. "I said some things before we left for Seattle that weren't entirely called for. They were the words of a bitter old woman who is unused to people and far more jaded than she ought to be. That doesn't excuse them, though." She looked down, studying the whorls and eddies of the water as she shifted around in the space between her apology and Ailith's answer.

Just when she thought she'd have to say more, the girl responded. "It's cool," she said, a little too diffidently. "You were stuck in the woods for, like, ever. People probably take getting used to. I'm not a huge fan of people in general, so I get it." Nodding in reply, Sable studied her fingers through a thin film of milky water. The skin on her fingertips was starting to look like it ought to for her age; it was time to get out. She lifted herself onto the edge of the pool and grabbed the small towel she'd left close by, toweling off before heading toward the locker room. She felt eyes on her back as she reached her folded yukata and glanced backward to see both Ailith and Adem heading her way. She'd figured it was Ailith's strange gaze that had settled between her shoulders like a burning itch she couldn't reach, but the girl was preoccupied with something no one else could see; it was her father who studied Sable. She drew herself up and met Adem's intense gaze, daring him to break eye contact. Instead he reached down for his own robe and donned it in one fluid motion without looking away, then nodded once before placing a hand on Ailith's back and leaning down to remind her to put on her yukata. That small gesture broke the spell on the entire group and they exited the locker room in silence, Sable leading the way to dinner, now with two curious gazes boring holes in her psyche.

Dinner was a multi-course affair consisting of varied seasonal dishes served in their room at the low dining table in the back. Green tea and sake were available, along with a small selection of beer, though Sable chose not to indulge herself there in favor of keeping a clearer head. By the time they had finished eating and the dishes had been cleared away, all three were nodding in their seats. "So, what do you think of Japanese hospitality?" Sable asked as Ailith brushed out her hair.

"It's awesome," Ailith sighed. "This is the best I've felt in weeks. Is it really the hot springs that do that?"

"Mm hmm," Sable replied as she pulled her own hair down from its earlier loose coiffure. "I haven't yet been able to figure out what exactly it is about them that does it, but they always refill every bit of mojo I have available and help with aches and pains. It's a win/win. Speaking of which, have you seen anything since we got here? Besides what you saw while we were soaking, that is."

"No," Ailith replied, "but I haven't really tried. Do you want me to?" Adem looked up from the latest book Sable had lent him as she asked, waiting for Sable's answer.

"I think it's a good idea," Sable replied, sitting down on the edge of the futon Ailith occupied. "Whoever is chasing us is operating with a hell of a lot more information than we have right now, so anything we can do to find out more about what's happening will give us an edge." Ailith nodded, then crossed her legs, straightened her back, and closed her eyes.

"The book says sitting like this and breathing will help me focus my energies," she began. "At least, I think that's what it meant." Her breathing slowed and her eyes drifted open, heavy-lidded, to look around the room. "It's working," she said dreamily, eyes scanning the room. "I see more guests in this room—not us, not someone looking for us. It's…tomorrow?" Her eyes darted around until they rested on something Sable and Adem couldn't see. "Yep, tomorrow, according to the date on that person's phone." She peered around the room once more, then closed her eyes again. "Hang on, there's something else…" Her voice trailed off as her delicate eyebrows furrowed. "It's not here, and it's not them…I see…a snake?" The orbs behind her eyelids darted about. "Woods…a trail of some sort… and…danger!" Her eyes snapped open, unseeing, a look of terror on her face.

Adem rushed over to the foot of the bed and took her by the shoulders. "Ailith, come back to us," he beckoned. "Come back to here and now. Listen to the sound of my voice and follow it home." As he spoke, Ailith's frail body melted into his arms and she rested her head on his shoulder, eyes closed.

Sable was already in motion, hands flying over the keyboard on her phone as she searched for something nearby with trails and snakes. Unfortunately, with all the wilderness in Fukushima Prefecture the results were entirely nonspecific. She continued to search, using the map feature to view the terrain around the area via satellite imagery and car-mounted camera. Eventually she grumbled to herself, dropped her phone face-up on the futon in front of her, and grabbed her duffel, rummaging in its depths for a full half minute before pulling up a small crystal hung on a length of fishing line. She wrapped the line around her finger until the crystal sat an inch or so above the map still visible on her phone, then began to swing it in small circles.

The screen on her phone dimmed, then went dark, displaying the lock screen. "Keep forgetting to set the timeout longer," she muttered, unlocking the phone and returning the crystal to its path around the phone. It began to dip toward the screen, passing in an increasingly elliptical orbit until at last it stopped right above an area covered in the green of mountainous woodlands. Sable let the crystal drop onto the phone, where it brought up a place marker as if she had tapped the phone with her finger. The crystal went back into the duffel and she picked up the phone to study it, oblivious to Adem's steely gaze as he tucked the now-sleeping Ailith into bed. "Ah ha! There it is," she crowed in triumph, stabbing a finger at the screen and looking up at her companions for the first time since Ailith's pronouncement. Adem lifted both eyebrows in a stern, fatherly expression, and she recognized his displeasure with how the exchange had gone.

"I hope whatever you've found is worth it," he replied before retreating to the bathroom to change into his pajamas.

When he returned a few minutes later he found Sable seated at the foot of her own futon, waiting patiently. "Mr. Ozturk, a word, if you please." Adem set down his bag and nodded, taking up a spot opposite her on the foot of the futon he and Ailith shared. "I can't say I fully understand your concern, given that I have never had a child of my own, but I do understand that you love your daughter and want to protect her from whatever life is throwing at her right now." Sable stared at her hands, twisting the torc bracelet she had re-donned as soon as they'd returned from the springs. "Truth be told, I'd like to do the same; she's growing on me, and it pains me to see her struggle so. But we have neither the time nor the luxury of ignoring any of the assets we have at our disposal. If there is a chance she can see something that will help us on our way, I don't think we have any choice but to take it. Do you disagree?" Sable met Adem's gaze cooly as she asked, confident in her assessment, but gauging his reaction.

Frowning, he broke eye contact. "No," he admitted, "but I don't have to like it." He glanced back up at Sable as a host of microexpressions flitted across his face, settling on a concerned frown. "Is there nothing else we can do? I've read all the books you've given me–" he indicated the small, but growing pile next to his futon–"and while I can tell you *all about* Zoroastrianism, I feel no closer to any sort of answer to who's looking for us."

Sable's lips pursed as she thought. "There may be one thing I can do, but it's risky; if someone detects it, it could give away our location," she warned. "I've been holding onto it until we got well and truly stuck, or until we were in a position we couldn't get out of. We're not stuck just yet, so I'd like to keep that card in the deck, if you don't mind." Adem nodded, his frown deepening. "For now, let's get some sleep. Between Ailith's vision and my warding, I think we can all afford to get some shut-eye tonight. I'll put out extra wards just in case, if that will help." Nodding again, Adem yawned and crawled into the blankets next to his daughter, settling all the way to one side of the futon so as not to wake the sleeping child. Sable slid between the covers on her own futon and shut off the light after setting up extra wards, as promised.

"Ms. Montgrief?" Adem asked as she shut off the lights.

"Please, call me Sable," she answered before she could stop herself. There was a pause before he responded; she could feel him turning over words, discarding some, starting over, before giving up and moving on.

"Wake me if you hear anything," he said finally.

"Will do," she replied.

"And please, call me Adem." This last utterance held a note she didn't recognize.

"Good night, then, Adem," she replied, liking the feel of his name on her tongue. Just as she drifted off, she heard him

respond almost too quietly to hear.
"Good night, Sable."

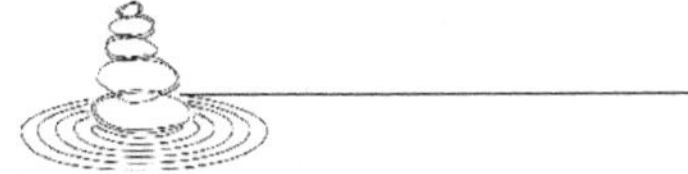

Paying Respects

They rose early the next morning feeling refreshed. A good night's sleep swept away most of the cobwebs jet lag had installed, and a solid breakfast in their room removed the rest. Ailith piped up as they finished eating and prepared to leave. "So where are we going now?" she asked around her last mouthful of egg.

"Not far," Sable replied, wiping her own mouth as she finished her tofu. Few places could boast proper preparation of tofu, but Japan was one of them. "Turns out the place I was looking for isn't far from here–about an hour drive, plus thirty minutes or so of walking."

"How did you find it?" Adem asked. He'd kept to himself all morning. Sable wiggled her fingers and waggled her eyebrows mischievously as she answered.

"Divination…and an Internet search," she replied anti-climactically as she stood from the low breakfast table. "I find that when technology just isn't enough, magic is there to step in and finish the job. They actually work quite well together if you have half an idea of how to use both." Retrieving her cell phone from the foot of her futon, she unlocked it and showed its contents to her companions, stabbing a finger at the middle of a satellite map of the area. "Right here," she indicated, "is a shrine where I believe the spirit of a seer I once knew resides. She was closer to the coast last time I met with her, but I think the reactor failure east of here forced her to move off her chosen location. We'll grab some snacks for the trail and a bottle of sake and head up to the shrine. If all goes well we'll be done by mid-afternoon and can find another place to stay."

"Why the sake?" queried Ailith. "And can I try it?"

"Legal drinking age here is 20, kid," Sable replied, "but that's up to your dad."

"Absolutely not," he replied, "and I think the rest of us

should abstain for now, as well. We need to be on our toes."

"Agreed," said Sable. "Besides, Tsuna will probably want the entire bottle to herself, especially if we bring her the good stuff." Packing the last of her few incidentals back into the duffel, Sable rummaged around for a change of clothes. Sensible jeans and a fitted, long-sleeved shirt appeared, along with her hiking boots, which she used to replace the sneakers she'd been wearing when they arrived on the shoe rack just inside the door. "If you'll excuse me, I'll go change and we can get going." The others had changed shortly after waking; Sable was the last to give up her yukata, which she did grudgingly. They were just so comfy.

Five minutes later they had cleaned up from breakfast and were checking out of the hotel. Adem preceded them to the car, wanting to check it to be sure no one had tampered with it during the night, and Sable made a mental note to extend her warding to their vehicle when next they stopped. He gave the all-clear and they piled in, Sable in the passenger seat, Ailith with her feet across the back seat, headphones in. She'd taken to studying the seer's manual in the car as they drove and seemed to have made good progress; she would ask the occasional question about a word or contextual reference, but otherwise she plowed through it on her own. Sable found it remarkable how quickly she was learning and mentioned it to Adem as they settled in for the drive.

"She's always been precocious," he responded. "Gifted classes at school, teachers who run out of ways to challenge her…we've heard from every single school how intelligent she is. None of them have measured her IQ, but that's mainly be-cause we've asked them not to; we feel it's limiting."

"You say 'we,'" Sable asked. "Is it just you and Ailith, or do you have some help with her?"

"Her aunts on her mother's side have been helpful over the years, and her maternal grandmother, as well. My family is too far geographically to be of much assistance, though they've offered often enough." Adem shifted in the bucket seat, uncom-fortable in a multitude of ways. Sable nodded in response and let the matter drop.

Sharp hillsides rose on either side of the roadway as they sped toward the park they'd chosen as their destination. The area was mountainous, but each facet was covered with trees and bushes, leaving very little within sight that wasn't green and verdant. Occasional boulders dotted their view. In a way it reminded Sable of the woods outside her cabin, and another sharp pang of homesickness pulled at her. She shook it off, attributing it to Stockholm syndrome given how long she'd imprisoned herself there, and shifted her mind to the task at hand. How long had it been since she'd seen Tsuna? It had to have been the spring of 1790, before her friend joined the spirits in their realm. They'd spent time together on the coast east of here, enjoying the fine weather and abundant fruits of the season in what would become their last few weeks together. Tsuna, a well-known seer and mystic and one of many daughters of the shogun, had lived in style in a large house with many attendants–until the townspeople had decided she was responsible for a string of unfortunate events. Sable had seen it time and time again across the world: when people had no explanation for tragedy, they found the closest outlet. In this case, it was Tsuna. Sable had returned from shopping in the market district to find her friend lifeless on the tatami inside the door, covered in blood. Next to her was the headless body of one of the samurai responsible for protecting her. As Sable watched, Tsuna's spirit had risen from her body, wailing in mourning for her bodyguard; they had been lovers, and Sable had suspected they would soon be married if her father gave permission. The sound of Tsuna's aggrieved keening echoed through the halls of Sable's memory as they turned off the main highway and onto a smaller access road.

Shaking herself from her reverie, Sable realized Adem had been speaking. "I'm sorry, I was woolgathering–what was that?"

"I was asking where we should park," he repeated patiently.

"Oh. Ah, wherever is fine; there's probably a trail to where we're headed." Adem nodded and parked in the first available spot. It was midmorning on a weekday, so there were few cars in the lot and none of them were occupied, giving Sable the opportunity to shift the appearance of their vehicle. It became a dark blue four-door instead of its original black and she placed a glamour on the license plate to keep anyone from noticing it or remembering what it contained.

Satisfied, she took stock of the trailhead before them, taking the time to memorize the map it provided before heading west toward the shrine, Ailith and Adem in tow. The trail was immediately swallowed by the tree line, giving them a sense of privacy as they switchbacked their way up the side of a mountain. Birds called as they passed, flitting from branch to branch above their heads, and squirrels chittered at them from their perches. The light filtering through the leaves danced with every shift of the wind.

Ailith was the first to break the relative silence. "This place is beautiful," she said with reverence. "It's a lot like where you used to live, Sable."

"It is," Sable agreed, and some of the many emotions floating through her mind must have leaked out into her speech; she heard Adem elbow Ailith in the ribs and get a muttered, "What?" in response. The group fell silent again as they approached the ridgeline above and began the first descent into a steep valley. From their vantage on the opposite side of the hill they could see no civilization; no towns, no roads, no signs of habitation broke the unending roll of tree-covered ridges.

"Why haven't we seen anyone else?" Ailith asked after a short while.

"It's midmorning," Sable answered. "People usually visit shrines early or late in the day, so the folk in the rest of the cars we saw were probably visiting the lake instead." There had been a sign at the trailhead directing lakegoers in the opposite direction, which she belatedly realized was entirely in Japanese. Satisfied, Ailith contented herself with kicking at the rocks on the trail and looking for interesting wildlife as they continued downward.

Ten minutes later they approached a wooden gateway to the side of the trail. "Ah, here it is," Sable announced, indicating the archway before them. Ailith stopped dead in her tracks.

"That's it," she whispered.

"This is the trail you saw?" Sable asked, crouching down in front of the girl. Ailith nodded. "Do you remember anything else from your vision? Anything about the danger you sensed?" Squeezing her eyes shut, Ailith shook her head, lips pressed together. Sable rose and addressed Adem, who had drawn close to his daughter and placed a hand on her shoulder when she stopped. "I think you two should stay here. If there's someone–or something–waiting for us up there–" she indicated the path that wound up to the next ridgeline–"I'll let you know and you can get the heck out of dodge."

"That leaves you alone against a threat we know nothing about," Adem countered.

"Mr. Ozturk–Adem–I've faced many, many threats alone," Sable replied, feeling her lopsided grin spread across her face. "None have bested me yet. Ailith needs protection, and for that she needs you. Besides, I'm far better equipped to deal with whatever I might find up there without having to worry about nearby collateral damage. Trust me." Hitching her duffel higher on her shoulders, she turned toward the trail and its archway. "Be ready to move out if I give the signal–I'll let you know if it's all clear," she cast over her shoulder. Then she disappeared beyond the archway and around a bend, and all of a sudden she was alone again for the first time in days. It felt strange, but familiar, if emptier than before.

Sable approached a second gateway that confirmed she was still on the right track. Continuing up the trail, she noted that the further she got the more overgrown the trail became. *Maybe we haven't seen anyone because nobody visits this shrine anymore.* That would be highly unusual for a shrine this large. She added another tick to her "this doesn't add up" board and started trying to put its pieces together as she walked. They didn't quite fit together; she felt she was missing at least one.

Another gate passed and a wash of power ran over Sable. *Ah ha.* That last spell would have turned away any but the most desperate–or powerful–of visitors. *Luckily I'm the latter.* It seemed Tsuna didn't want visitors, which was very unlike the Tsuna she'd known long ago; something must have happened in the intervening centuries. She completed the journey down the now-overgrown path to the shrine's entrance with greater caution than before. Moss covered the tops of the stonework outside, layered thick over the shaped pillars and steps. The woodwork behind it showed signs of rot and a lack of structural integrity that was not encouraging to Sable. Birds had nested on the cracking lintel for years and still perched there, covering it in a layer of feces. The overall effect was one of abject disuse and abandonment.

Despite the condition of the shrine, Sable bowed deeply at the final gateway before entering the grounds. Just inside the gateway she found a small pond with a running spillway over the top and an old, decrepit ladle set on the stonework surrounding it. Taking the ladle in her right hand, she poured water over her left, then her right, then filled her left hand and brought the water briefly to her lips before rinsing her hand once again. She let the last of the water run down the handle of the ladle before replacing it on the stone nearby. Casting a wary glance around the overrun garden before her, she kept to the left side of the path as she approached the main structure and the mildewed rope hanging to one side. Steeling herself, she pulled the rope a single time and a loud, low chime filled the clearing. Wind sighed from inside the structure, peppering Sable with loosened moss and dirt, then receded as she neared the structure itself. She drew a bottle of fine sake from the duffel bag and placed it in the decrepit box at the front of the shrine, then bowed twice, clapped twice, and bowed once more, leaving her hands in the prayer position. *Tokugawa Tsuna, I come seeking your aid and guidance.* Sable sent her will into the surrounding area in search of her friend.

One by one, the natural sounds of the clearing ceased. Lifting her head, Sable turned to look behind her. The light flowing through the trees had dimmed to the level of twilight and she found she had to strain to make out the figure moving toward her. It lifted its head and regarded her, solidifying as it did so and shining with an ever-brighter inner light. Before long the outline of a kimono appeared along with a matching fan of bright gold. An elaborate hairstyle topped the figure as a pale, feminine face emerged from the coalescing figure. She smiled at Sable and spread her arms wide. "My friend," the figure spoke, her familiar voice echoing through the clearing. "It has been too long."

Smiling, Sable approached the spirit. "Tsuna," she replied, embracing the now-solid figure. "I've missed you. Apologies for not visiting; I was trying to break a curse."

"I understand," Tsuna replied. "And did you find your cure?"

"I found one," Sable replied ruefully, "but I'm starting to think it might not be worth the trouble." Shaking her head, she continued. "I'd love to spend more time catching up, but I'm afraid I need your help."

"You may ask, but my powers are limited," Tsuna replied, her ghostly voice tinged with sadness. "Since I was forced from my home I have had to make do here, and as you can see, it is not an ideal location." She swept an arm across the ruined building before them.

"It's not your powers I need, but your knowledge," Sable replied. "There is a youngling under my protection who is a powerful seer, like you, but who has no family to teach them. Would you be willing to speak with them and impart whatever knowledge you can? I'm not certain how long we have, as we're currently on the run from pursuers unknown."

A breeze stirred the silent clearing once again. "A youngling, you say?" Tsuna asked, peering about intently. "And a seer?" Sable nodded. "There must be something very special about this girl for you to take her into your protection."

Sable's eyes narrowed. "I don't recall telling you it was a girl." The wind picked up as Tsuna regarded Sable. "Tsuna, why did you leave the coast? I thought you said you would never leave Kametaro's grave, so it surprised me when my dowsing lead me here."

"I was forced away from my home," Tsuna replied, raising her voice in anger as the wind whipped at Sable's clothing. "Two hundred years I had spent near his side when *she* arrived." She spat the pronoun as if it were a curse. "How she did it I cannot tell, but I know she was responsible for the earthquake and tsunami that broke the reactor nearby, poisoning the land and forcing me to leave and find this place." The wind was a howl that nearly stole the breath from Sable's lungs as Tsuna continued. "But even then, I wasn't free of her. Even now she haunts my thoughts, bending them to her will, forcing me to do what I would not." She reached toward Sable, who stepped back, almost tripping on the uneven ground. "Leave this place, Sable Montgrief, and do not return. Leave now, before she takes over and I have no choice in my actions."

"Who, Tsuna? Who has this hold on you?" Sable screamed into the maelstrom.

"She is known as–" Tsuna's voice was cut off as another, deeper female voice took over–"Zaurizl." As her voice changed, Tsuna's expression hardened into a look of pure malice. "I know your face," she continued, her accent broadening into a west African note as she switched to speaking English. "You are the one who has kept my master from acquiring the girl. How pleased he will be when I bring him your head." Tsuna's face grinned menacingly as Sable stood, planting her feet.

"I think you'll find that difficult, as I like it attached to my shoulders." Lifting her chin, Sable faced the visage of her friend. "Now let go of Tsuna."

"She has proven most useful; I think I'll keep her." The winds died, leaving a roaring silence in their wake, then slammed into Sable full force. It was all she could do to throw up her arms in time to create a shield and hold her ground. "Her powers within this shrine are far less modest than she let on." Vines began to creep along the ground toward Sable's feet as she fought off the wind, wrapping themselves around her ankles and calves as she fought to stay upright. With a yelp she was yanked to the ground, then pulled up by her feet, hanging onto the duffel for dear life. "It makes me wonder if she is truly your friend at all." As Sable hung before her, upside-down, the vines on her legs began to blacken and burn through her clothing, leaving trails of acid burns in her skin. She screamed and flung out her arms, shoving Tsuna's spirit away with the sheer force of her will. The vines unwound and dropped her to the ground, where she forced herself to her feet as quickly as possible. Without warning or preamble, she reached out and grabbed Tsuna's hand, jerking her roughly forward, and for a moment her form separated into two distinct figures: the Tsuna Sable had known, and another female figure that was tall and lithe and wore decidedly more modern clothing.

Seeing her opening, Sable reached toward Tsuna's forehead and whispered, "Forgive me, old friend," as she touched the spirit and sank into her mind. The twisted storm of emotion and knowledge she found there threatened to carry her away before she planted her feet as she'd done moments before in the physical world, steeling her mind against what didn't belong to it. Beyond the surface thoughts—what Buddhists would call the monkey mind—she could feel the dark undercurrent of the interloper who had stolen Tsuna's will. It played a dangerous game of cat-and-mouse with her around her friend's psyche, tossing emotions and memories backwards at Sable as she chased the other consciousness toward the gate she knew to be lingering somewhere nearby.

Suddenly a gate was there, just as she'd seen in Ailith's mind, and the dark presence within Tsuna hurtled toward it, screaming in protest. It fought and clawed at the air around it in a futile effort to slow its passage, but to no avail, and in seconds it disappeared into the darkness beyond. Sable waited for the gate to recede before picking her way out of her friend's psyche and back into the physical world.

The first thing she realized was that the wind had stopped. Shortly thereafter she heard Adem's voice calling out from nearby—*What on earth is he doing here?* she wondered, and cold fear shifted her body up and away from the stunned spirit before her as she searched for the sound of his voice. Before she found Adem, she saw Ailith suspended between the doors of the gateway to the shrine, her eyes shining with a white light and her arms spread outward. Her feet hovered a foot off of the ground, and Adem stood a few feet behind her, calling her name. As Sable watched, the girl's eyes rolled back into her head and she crumpled to the ground, folding herself onto the grass as gravity faded back in.

Safe in the knowledge that Adem would care for her, Sable turned back to Tsuna's spirit, which was still frozen where she'd left it. She approached with caution, searching for any sense of the other presence that had been nearby—*Zaurizl, was it?*—and finding only her friend. With a light touch on the shoulder she woke the spirit, who shook herself from head to toe and regarded Sable with a saddened expression. "Sable," she began, "I cannot apologize enough. That woman–that thing–had a hold on my mind like I have never experienced."

"No apology is necessary," Sable answered. "Are you whole again, my friend?"

Tsuna nodded slowly. "I think so, but she–it–rifled through my mind. I cannot be sure everything is still there, or that I can find what is. How can I repay you for freeing me if I do not know my own mind?"

"Let's cross that bridge later; for now, I want you to meet some folk." Sable gestured to the gate, where Adem sat on the ground next to Ailith's unconscious form. "This is my charge, Ailith, and her father, Adem." He nodded in greeting as Sable waved, though they spoke Japanese. "I have a suspicion Ailith is the one you should be thanking right now, not me." Tsuna cocked her head and studied both of them, then stepped closer to Ailith's prone form. She ran a semi-corporeal hand over the girl, then drew back and addressed Sable.

"You are correct in that she is a seer, but that is not her primary purpose," Tsuna explained. "There is much more to this girl than the sight. Is her mother living?" Sable shook her head. "Did she die in childbirth?" Sable's brow furrowed as she nodded slowly. "Then there is a good chance she is a gatekeeper, one responsible for guarding the pathways between life and death. They are always children whose mothers die bearing them, though I've never known one to be a seer as well." Tsuna studied Ailith as she fell silent.

"A gatekeeper, eh?" Sable reached back through the extensive annals of her memory for a meaning she knew she'd run across before. It came to her after a moderate amount of rummaging: they were, indeed, said to be keepers of the natural pathway between life and death. They were also responsible for returning the undead where they belonged, which she suspected was why she'd been able to best Tsuna's possessor as quickly as she had; Ailith had sensed the presence of an evil spirit and had instinctively responded to it–or something else had moved her in the right direction to bring her abilities to bear. Sable didn't like that line of thought. "Haven't heard of a gatekeeper being born for centuries," she mused instead. "I wonder why now…"

Tsuna turned to regard Sable. "Those who are chasing you, are they connected to this presence that invaded my mind?"

"Sounds like."

"Then you must be prepared to face one who thinks he is a god." Tsuna turned toward her shrine, away from Adem and Ailith. "Please understand, I cannot help you or the girl. You must find the records of the other gatekeepers to understand Ailith's full purpose. They each keep a record of their duties and how they are fulfilled." Sable nodded, her mind already working furiously. "Thank you for freeing me, old friend," Tsuna said with a smile as she took Sable's hand. "It is good to see you again. Perhaps this will not be the last time. Now if you will excuse me, I have a shrine to maintain." Bowing low, she glided over to the ruined structure before them and disappeared, leaving a trail of budding flowers in her wake.

Recalling that she had never finished her prayer at the shrine, Sable approached it again and clapped once, bowing low, before retreating down the left side of the path to the gate where Adem and Ailith waited. She bowed once more at the gate, then turned to check on her companions. Ailith's eyelids fluttered once, twice, then opened to show her hazel irises. "What happened?" she asked as she sat up.

Sable chuckled, but it sounded strained even to her ears. "A lot happened, but I think for now we'd best be going," she answered, casting one last look over her shoulder at the shrine. Was it a little less run-down than it had been when she'd arrived? She shrugged with one shoulder and led the way back down the path toward the car. "Whatever you did, Ailith, it likely caught the attention of whoever is after us since you banished one of his henchmen beyond death's gate." She chose the easiest path down the poorly-tended slope, wincing as a bush brushed at the wounds on her legs. She'd forgotten about them in the adrenaline rush of the fight, but now that things had calmed down she was intensely aware of the searing pain in her shins and ankles. *No time. We have to move.*

"Sable." Adem's voice cut through her internal monologue. "What happened to your legs? Those look like chemical burns."

Sable didn't ask how he knew what chemical burns looked like, instead opting to answer with the truth. "Tsuna's spirit was possessed by some sort of undead being that turned some vines she attacked me with to acid," she explained. "I don't have the time or energy to heal it right now, but as soon as we get back to the car I'll take care of it."

"You'll move faster if they're bandaged," Adem replied sensibly. "It won't take long; I have everything we need in my pack." He patted the backpack he'd been carrying since they met.

Sable rolled her eyes and sat down right in the path. "Give me the gauze and bandages," she sighed, holding out a hand. "I'll at least make sure the wounds are clean."

"You clean; I'll bandage." Adem rummaged in the backpack and produced rolled gauze bandages and a small pair of blunt-tipped scissors, which he used to cut away the damaged lower portion of her jeans before she could protest. *How did he get those through airport security?* Reaching down, Sable produced a small amount of water in her hand, then directed it up and down each leg in turn, washing off any vestiges of acid left by the vines. Adem wound gauze around each leg as she finished, practiced fingers wrapping and tucking as he went. Sable was impressed with the swiftness and thoroughness of his ministrations. When he'd secured the last bandage he looked up, catching Sable's eye and holding it in a measuring gaze. "Ready to move?" he asked.

Sable nodded, not trusting her voice. Between seeing Tsuna and learning more about their would-be captors, then finally identifying what was different about Ailith, she was off balance and refused to admit it. Adem's nearness wasn't helping, and she realized this was the first time he'd touched her since putting a hand on her shoulder at the cabin. She'd been the one to link arms with him in the airport, not the other way around. *Maybe he's trustworthy after all.* Adem returned her nod and stood, offering her a hand, which she took. He pulled her swiftly to her feet and Sable noted the feel of the callouses she'd only guessed were there. Congratulating herself on being right on at least one thing that day she released his hand and started back down the hill. She had to admit, it was easier to move with her burns bandaged.

They took much of the trail at a jog and made it to the car in much shorter time than they'd taken to get to the shrine. Thankfully the parking lot was no more full than it had been, though Sable still changed their car's appearance once more after they turned the first corner just in case. On the way back to the main road they passed a white maintenance van that made both Sable and Ailith shiver as it passed, but it seemed to take no notice of them, and they continued on to the highway.

"Where to now? And what happened back there?" Adem asked. "It's hard being the only one who can't see what's happening unless it's people flying through the air."

"Remind me when we stop and I'll fix that for you," Sable replied. "And for now, let's head west, toward the coast." She was still turning over the encounter with Tsuna and Zaurizl in her mind. Turning in her seat, she pinned Ailith with a stare. "Ailith, what made you follow me up that trail given what you'd seen last night? I gave no signal, but you arrived just in time to provide exactly the help I needed, which in my line of work is never coincidental."

Ailith shifted in her seat, echoing her father's nervous habit. "I dunno," she answered. "One minute I was standing at the bottom of the trail, watching the wind bend the trees at the top of the hill, and the next I was standing in front of the last gate. I saw the vines drop you, and then you got close enough to that spirit that I couldn't see what you did, but everything froze and I got pulled toward the other side. Then I knew what I had to do." She shrugged. "That other spirit didn't belong here. I just sent it home."

"Is that the first time you've sent spirits home?" Sable asked quietly. She watched Ailith squirm under the weight of her implacable scrutiny.

"No," she said finally. "One of the times they sent people after me there was one who felt like that spirit we just saw, only not quite as powerful." Adem's grip on the wheel tightened. "I sent him home, too. But before that I'd never done it, I swear."

She held both hands before her in supplication.

"And you didn't think to mention it to me?" Adem asked sternly.

"I didn't think you would understand," Ailith grumbled. The car went silent as all three of its inhabitants breathed deeply for a moment in an attempt to rein in emotions.

"Next time, please give me the option of trying," Adem replied, sounding tired. Ailith nodded and blew out a breath.

"So am I in trouble?" she asked. "I know I wasn't supposed to do any of what I did, but I don't know what happened–none of it was intentional." She sounded close to tears.

"I believe you," Sable replied, having mulled it over. "I don't think you had any choice in the matter, and that's what I'm trying to work out: whether that was because of who you are… or because of who I am." She stared down at her hands without seeing them. "You both know that I'm cursed," she began, and they nodded. "Without getting into too many of the details, the entire purpose of that curse is to keep me alive as long as possible. Sometimes, like today, that means saving my life when it's threatened, and it will use any means necessary–and I mean any means–to do so. Up to and including using the people around me." She hung her head, feeling heat creep up her neck. "It's one of the reasons I holed myself up in the middle of the woods for eighty years. If I didn't have any human connections, it couldn't use them." There was more to it than that, but she wasn't ready to go into all the details just yet. She'd be lucky if they still trusted her as far as they could throw her after this conversation–though looking at Adem, she bet he could get her a pretty good distance.

Adem's grip on the wheel was white-knuckled against his tanned skin. "You knew this and you didn't think to mention it?" he demanded, his voice taking on a dangerous tone.

"Not until now," Sable admitted. "I've had trouble getting back in swing of things, so to speak." She trailed off, wishing there was more she could say to explain herself and knowing there wasn't.

"Mom knew." Ailith spoke up from the back seat. "She had to have known when she sent us to Sable. She knows so much, but there's a lot of it she can't tell us because she's on the other side. If she was willing to take that risk, I trust it was the right thing to do." Having said her piece, she leaned back against the seat once more, looking more sure of herself than she had all day. Adem ran a hand through his already-mussed hair and inhaled again, his eyes never leaving the road in front of them.

"Is there anything else we should know about you that might endanger us?" he asked with forced calmness.

Sable considered before replying. "That's the big one," she said after pondering for a minute. "Of course, there are folk out there who don't much care for me who also happen to have the power to try to do something about it, but hopefully we won't run into any of those. They probably think I'm dead, anyway." *Kind of wish I were in so many ways right now, but that's neither here nor there.* "Look, I owe you both an apology for not telling you sooner. There is a very selfish side of me that took over for a century or so, and while I'm doing my best to get past it, a hundred years is a long time to build poor habits. I would appreciate your patience and grace as I attempt to break those habits, but I understand if that's a bit much to afford me right now. I haven't done much to warrant it." On the one hand it chafed Sable to apologize; after all, they had come to her seeking aid and had ruined her chances at death for another eighty plus years. But when she glanced back at the frail-looking girl in the backseat, all her arguments seemed to fade into inconsequence. The girl needed her help; it was that simple. She would give it however she could, for as long as she could, and she would do her best not to endanger her companions in the process.

"You came with us," Ailith said simply. "That counts for a lot. Right, Dad?"

"Yeah," Adem agreed, deflating. "I suppose it does." His anger defused but dormant, he relaxed into a tired expression and went back to scanning the road around them.

"In all fairness, you haven't been entirely forthright with me this whole time, either," Sable pointed out, and the rest of Adem's anger dissipated. "So what say we give this another go, this time with an attempt at more openness, honesty, and trust?"

Ailith nodded from the back seat, and Adem nodded slowly before finding his voice.

"Agreed," he said, glancing at Ailith in the rear view mirror, then at Sable with an inscrutable expression before returning his attention to the road. "But first I need someone to tell me where the hell I'm going. 'West' could constitute literally anywhere that's not here."

"Well, anywhere west of us," Sable retorted, "which if you go far enough includes what's east of us, as well. I'm thinking we need to get out of Japan as quickly and quietly as possible. Tsuna was my best hope for help here, but she did give us a jumping-off point: the gatekeepers." Pulling out her phone, Sable furiously tapped at the screen, searching for something. "Last I'd heard there was a…yep! There's a ferry that crosses over into Russia from the northernmost tip of Japan. They might be watching it, but it's less likely to be under heavy surveillance than an airport. I think those are dead to us for a while. How does that sound?"

"What about crossing the Sea of Japan and heading into China or South Korea instead?" Adem asked. "Where are we more likely to find more information about these gatekeepers?"

"I don't know." Sable chewed her bottom lip in thought. "But I can find out. Next chance you get, pull over or find an exit; it's about lunchtime anyway, so might as well grab some food while I dowse."

"What's dowsing?" asked Ailith. Adem cocked an eyebrow as he searched for an exit sign he could read that looked like it might have food available.

"It's a way of letting the universe tell you where something important is," Sable answered as she scanned the road signs. "Ah ha–donburi!" She pointed at a sign covered in kanji as they passed. "Let's stop here and grab some food, then once we get back in the car I'll do some dowsing while we eat." Adem obligingly slipped into the exit lane and followed Sable's directions into a small town just off the freeway. The narrow streets were well maintained, but some of the buildings crowding in on either side showed signs of their age. Climbing vines sprouted new leaves as they found their way toward the sun along the walls of homes and businesses. Poking out from behind one such tuft of greenery was a sign containing a bowl heaped with food and a set of chopsticks poking out. Pulling into a tiny parking space, they headed inside just long enough to grab to-go bowls, then popped back into the rented sedan.

Adem cranked up the engine and let it idle as Sable pulled out her phone once again, then rummaged in the duffel for another crystal with a cord wrapped around one end. Pulling up the map on her phone, she zoomed out far enough that all of Japan was in view, then set the phone across her lap and dangled the crystal above the screen, swinging it in a narrow circle. Ailith and Adem watched, fascinated, as it began to lean one direction–until the phone's screen dimmed, then went dark. "Stupid screen timeout," Sable muttered as she unlocked the phone and turned off the idle timeout. Ailith snickered in the backseat, and the ghost of a smile pulled at the corners of Adem's mouth as Sable swung the crystal over the map once more. It pulled to the left, past the boundaries of the visible map, and Sable used her free left hand to zoom out until the crystal hovered between two points, then dropped onto the screen. "Ah ha! China it is." Winding the cord back around the crystal, she dumped it back into the duffel and peered at the location it had indicated on her phone. "Guilin, to be exact. A bit inland, and a place I haven't been in hundreds of years. Might be able to dig up some of the language, though."

"No need," Adem replied as he polished off his bowl of brown rice and chicken with vegetables. "I've got that covered as long as we can get there. Any ideas for that? Or what, exactly, we're looking for?" Placing his takeout box back in the bag it came in, he put the car in gear and started back toward the highway.

"Let's head for Niigata and see what options we have there," Sable answered as she started in on her own lunch. Tofu and rice with vegetables–a perennial favorite for her. She thought back on the street food she'd gotten the last time she'd visited Japan, which mostly consisted of hot noodles, and realized how far the country had come in the fast food department. *The US needs to take some notes on fast food from these folks.*

Back on the highway, Sable buried her nose in her cell phone, researching travel options. Train was out; it was too easy for someone to get on while they weren't looking and get the drop on them, plus it was predictable as to where they would go. Car was too slow for long distances and wouldn't even get them across the Sea of Japan, much less the East China Sea. Air was their best option, but they already knew the airports were being watched by people who could see through her glamours. Time was not on their side, either.

"Do you think air travel is worth the risk?" she mused quietly. Ailith had put her headphones back in as soon as the car started moving, so she was oblivious to the conversation. "We can't drive across the sea."

Adem considered for a moment as she studied him sidelong. Sable could almost hear the wheels turning as he calculated risk versus reward. After a moment he sighed. "I don't think we have a choice," he answered. "Niigata isn't as well known an airport, but they do know we're in the general area, so there's a good chance they'll be watching. How much of the check-in can we do online before we get there? Maybe we can reduce the amount of time we spend at the airport."

"I'll look," Sable answered as she tapped furiously on her phone. "Looks like most of it," she replied, "with the exception of the security check as we're not Japanese citizens. Shouldn't take long for that, though, and I can do a more subtle glamour this time. Might let us fly under the radar, so to speak."

"Has anyone told you you make the worst puns?" Adem asked, cocking an eyebrow at her. She grinned in response.

"Literally everyone," she replied. "But that's never stopped me." Her grin faded as she thought through their next steps again. "We need an if-everything-goes-to-shit plan. Last time we flew they weren't actively looking for us and they still found us. They've had days to figure out who bought that last flight and put a watch on my credit card, plus there's no telling what they were told by that spirit Ailith banished." Frowning, she racked her brain. "There might be one option we can use, but only if it's the last option we have, and I'm not sure it would get us all the way to our destination. Still, it's good to have in our back pocket.

If you're good, I'll go ahead and buy us tickets; it looks like there's an international airport in Guilin proper, though we'll have a short layover in Shanghai." Adem nodded as if he didn't see much choice, and she grudgingly bought the tickets. "We should have just enough time to get there and get checked in."

Thirty minutes later they were leaving the sedan at the car rental location at the Niigata airport. Sable had returned it to its original seeming before they pulled in so that it would match the description of the car they'd rented, then settled the bill and headed into the airport while whispering words in a strange, fluid language. Ailith and Adem noticed that despite the busy nature of the airport, no one seemed to look their way. The crowd flowed around them like water around a stone, never acknowledging their presence. "Is this your doing?" Adem leaned over and muttered.

"Yep," Sable replied, then went back to mumbling as they crossed to the check-in desk for their airline. She stopped mumbling long enough to speak with the woman behind the counter and get them checked in for their flight, then continued as they headed into the terminal and toward the security check.

Ailith stopped abruptly, pulling on Sable's sleeve. "Sable," she whispered. "We need to go. Now." She pointed at the checkpoint, which was operated by workers in matching suits with name tags and round hats. Still muttering, Sable followed Ailith's gaze until she saw the flash of a tattoo on the hand of one of the guards. She nodded and tapped Adem on the arm as she and Ailith turned, parting the crowd conspicuously in the other direction as they moved upstream.

A shout from behind them whipped Sable's head around to see two security guards pushing their way through the crowd toward them. "Here we go again," she whispered, then grabbed both Ailith and Adem by the hand. The dichotomy between them was striking; Ailith's small hand was cold and thin in her grip, while Adem's was reassuringly warm and strong. "Time for Plan B," she said, catching Adem's eye. "Be ready to catch me after we get through, and whatever you do, do not let go." He and Ailith both nodded, one looking determined, the other afraid, as Sable drew power from the depths of her psyche and shoved it into the space just ahead of them, bending the universe to her will. The air shimmered and a narrow cobblestone street wavered before them with high stone walls on either side. "Come on," Sable grunted, pulling her companions toward the image as it stabilized. As one they stepped into and through the picture–and their feet landed on the uneven cobbles below. The shouts behind them sounded tinny, as if they were transmitted across a long tunnel through which they reverberated. Then the image behind them shrank to a pinpoint and disappeared, leaving all three companions standing in an alleyway.

Sable wavered on the uneven stones before her eyes rolled back into her head. The last thing she remembered before losing consciousness was something lifting her off her feet before she hit the cobblestone roadway.

What Has Been Seen...

Sable awoke propped up in a comfortable bed with the feeling someone was staring at her. Cracking one eye through the splitting headache that was ruining her chances at further rest, she saw that the dimly-lit room was well appointed and that Ailith was sitting on the foot of her bed, watching her intently. As soon as she noticed Sable twitch her eye she leaned sideways and shouted, "Dad! She's awake!" Sable winced at the volume and shut her eyes to block out some of the sensation.

Footsteps she recognized approached the bed and a weight settled onto one side of it. "How are you feeling?" Adem asked more quietly, mindful of her delicate state.

"Like I just folded space and time over a thousand miles," she answered, her words sounding thick. Her mouth felt as if she'd been chewing on cotton balls in her sleep. "How far did we make it? And how long have I been out? Do you have any water?" She cracked her eyelid once again to peek at Adem, who was smiling with relief.

"You're almost as bad as Ailith," he said by way of answer, then turned to his daughter. "Can you go get a cup of water for Sable?" he asked. She nodded and jumped off the bed, heading toward a short hallway that led to a bathroom, judging by the sounds of running water that followed. "As for where we are, this is the Yellow Moon Hotel in Guilin, China. You've been out for half a day." With a practiced hand he reached out and checked her pulse on her wrist, then asked if she could open both eyes and look toward the light. It was painful, but he seemed satisfied and let her close her eyes once again. "I see no signs of a concussion," he pronounced, "but I bet you're in need of something to eat. We had dinner brought up; you interested?" Sable nodded and attempted unsuccessfully to swing her feet over the side of the bed, managing only to tangle them in the sheets before a wave of dizziness hit. Adem helped her untangle them, then steadied her as she stood and headed for the bathroom just as Ailith appeared with her water. She nodded her thanks and stopped shuffling long enough to take a sip before handing the cup back to Ailith and trudging the rest of the way to the restroom under her own power.

Ten minutes and a few ablutions later, she emerged from the bathroom feeling steadier. The room they'd rented was of a decent size, with two beds and a small table that contained the remnants of their meal. Sable wondered how she'd failed to notice the aromas wafting through the room; she picked out spicy Hunan sauces over vegetables with rice on the side. The smell of the stewed pork next to it left her mouth watering. Seating herself without preamble, she served a to-go plate with most of what was left and began to fill the burning void that was her stomach. She'd forgotten how much energy it took to travel that way, especially over such a distance.

Adem and Ailith sat nearby, waiting with poorly-hidden impatience for her to get partway through her meal before asking questions. Sable hid a smile and ate slower, savoring the food as it sank comfortingly into her belly. After a few minutes she took pity on her companions. "You're wanting to know how I did that, right?" she asked without looking.

"How did you do that?!?"

Chuckling, Sable wiped her mouth and turned to face them. Ailith's eyes were alight with curiosity and wonderment and it made Sable both excited and uncomfortable. "The boring answer is 'magic,' but the less-boring answer has to do with physics I don't know if you've gotten to in your studies yet."

"Try me." Ailith crossed her arms and tried to sit back before realizing she wasn't sitting in a chair. Adem muffled a chuckle at her expense and settled in to watch.

"All right, heard of Einstein?" Sable began, picking up another mouthful of food while she waited for an answer.

"Duh," Ailith answered. "Theory of Relativity, et al."

"Bonus points for the Latin, though I give extra if you know the full phrase and its meaning. Anyway, if you're familiar with it, you can explain to me his theory of general relativity, at which point I can interject where the magic comes in." Sable crossed her arms in a mirror of Ailith's pose, leaning back against the chair she occupied.

"Einstein's theory of general relativity relates an object's mass to its gravity within space-time," Ailith began with her nose in the air. "The more mass an object has, the more space-time is warped by it. A perfect example is the Einstein Cross, a quasar that exhibits the lensing effects present around supermassive objects." She flashed a self-satisfied grin.

"Very good," Sable replied, nodding. "And what does Einstein have to say about folding space-time?"

"Uhh…that it's theoretically possible?" Ailith ventured. At Sable's encouraging nod, she continued, "But he didn't know how it could be done?"

"He hadn't found a type of matter that could create a Minkowski wormhole," Sable clarified, "which is where the magic comes in. Magic is a force that shapes itself to the will of its wielder, so all I did was use it to form a mass that would create a small Minkowski wormhole we could walk through. Problem is, that takes a whole lot of energy, so it's not practical to do on the regular or at much larger scale." She paused to take another bite of the vegetables and rice, which she'd mixed together on her plate. The food worked wonders on her mental state, and by the time she finished the meal she felt almost normal.

Once the rest of the food was cleared away, Sable pulled out her favorite crystal and her cell phone in an attempt to divine which direction they should head next. Ailith, who'd been working quietly on translating the seer manual on her bed, peered over curiously. Closing the book, she sidled over to where Sable sat at the small dining table and peeked over the older woman's shoulder.

"Can you teach me that?" she asked just as Sable lifted the cord holding the crystal. Exhaling sharply, Sable turned and looked at Ailith for a long moment, then seemed to come to a decision.

"Adem?" she asked politely.

"Hmm?" His eyes never left the news broadcast he was

watching on the small television in the room.

"Is it all right with you if I teach your daughter the basics of divination?"

"Yeah, sure. Go ahead."

Sable nodded. "Then yes, I can teach you how to dowse, though I should warn you, it's oftentimes a bit tricky. Sit down." Without waiting for Ailith she reached into the duffel and produced four more crystals of varying colors attached to black cords. "These are my dowsing crystals, though you could use just about anything. I just happen to favor these." Laying them in a row on the table between them, she added the crystal she'd been ready to use, running a hand across them. "You're going to pick one of them to use tonight based on how they feel." Sitting back, she watched Ailith pick up the leftmost crystal and stare at it with narrowed eyes. "Close your eyes," Sable instructed, "and let your feelings and what you see with your third eye guide you. This has very little to do with physical sight." Ailith nodded, closing her eyes and running her hand across the row.

"They all feel the same…wait." She stopped, her hand hovering over a smoky gray crystal. "This one feels like it's vibrating."

"Then it has something to tell you. Pick it up." Without looking Ailith slid her dainty hand up the length of cord and picked it up at the knotted end. "Now, focus on that vibration you felt and swing it around in a circle over the map on my phone." Opening her eyes, Ailith dangled the crystal over the screen, slowly starting it gyrating around Guilin. Her face took on a look of intense focus as she watched it circle the map for a good twenty seconds before sighing and looking at Sable.

"It's not doing anything," she complained.

"That's because you're trying to force it to," Sable answered. "You know how when your dad tells you you have to do something, it makes you not want to do it?" Ailith nodded. "This is sort of like that. The universe knows what it needs to tell you. Let it." Nodding again, Ailith took a deep breath and let it out slowly, keeping her eyes closed this time and swinging the crystal over the map. This time its orbit elongated, settling over the site of the Jingjiang Princes' Palace. Opening her eyes, Ailith squealed with joy when she realized she'd successfully worked out their next destination. "See? Good work." Sable high fived her pupil, who hopped up to share her success with her father while Sable researched where they were headed. It was a historical site built in the 14th century for the ruling Ming dynasty, which meant whatever they were looking for definitely wasn't recent. They might have to find more creative ways to narrow their search if its subject wasn't immediately obvious.

Ailith bounced back to the table and sat down, laying the crystal she'd used in front of her. "Can we do it again? What else do we need to look for?" she asked in rapid succession. Sable chuckled.

"What is the crystal telling you?" she replied. Ailith picked it up, then set it back down.

"It's not doing anything."

"Then there's nothing else we need to know at the moment." Deflating, Ailith picked the crystal up by its cord and attempted to hand it back to Sable, who pushed it back toward the girl. "Keep it; you never know when it might come in handy." Ailith beamed. "Besides, I think that one likes you better than it does me." Sable watched the girl hang her new acquisition around her neck, slipping it beneath the front of her shirt.

"Thank you so much!" Ailith squeaked. "This is so cool." She wandered off to find her phone and headphones, as per usual, while Sable continued her research.

Some time later she heard the television switch off. Without looking up from her phone she asked, "Anything on the news we need to know about?" Adem's footsteps drifted over to the table and he settled himself across from her, leaning back in his chair.

"Nothing trustworthy," he replied. "The news here is so carefully curated it's barely usable." Leaning forward, he peered over the table. "I hear Ailith discovered our next location. Any details?"

"It's a historic site from the 14th century that's open for tours," Sable replied, sliding her phone across the table. He picked it up and scrolled through the information she'd been reading. "Closed at this hour, but if we get up first thing tomorrow we can catch it just as it opens and have a look around. Might be difficult to find exactly what we're looking for without a bit of help, though." Adem passed her phone back across the table and pulled out his own, presumably to continue researching. Sable considered him for a moment, recalling her words from that morning. "You still interested in finding out what it's like to be able to see what Ailith and I do?" Her quiet words snaked across the table and snapped Adem's head around to regard her.

"Yes," he responded without hesitation. "Is that something you can do?"

"I can, but not until you fully understand what you're asking." Sable's steely gaze bored into Adem as she explained. "Everyone is born with the ability to perceive the things we consider part of the occult: spirits, energies, auras, and the like. Few are born with the ability to process it. Ever walk past a graveyard and feel a chill? Or feel like you're being watched despite being completely alone?" Adem nodded. "That's because your brain doesn't understand how to process what it perceives and can't show you where or how it relates to you in what we call the real world. It can, however, be taught how these things relate, which is where I come in. I can teach your mind how to process what it perceives such that you should be able to 'see,' for lack of a better term, what we're doing and more of what we're up against." Sable hesitated, in part to allow for questions, and in part to steel herself for what she would need to do.

"Whatever it takes, I accept," Adem said as he straightened in his chair.

"I'm not finished," Sable replied. "The results of this process vary a bit person to person, so I can't guarantee what you'll see or how much. It's like any other sense in that some people have more or less innate physical ability, and I can't guarantee how good your 'vision' will or won't be. Also, the resulting change is permanent; trying to reverse it could cause significant damage to the subject. What has been seen cannot be unseen." Adem nodded resolutely. "Now, given what I know about you so far and the situation we're in I'll skip the usual admonishments about the psychological effects of being able to see the bogeyman in favor of emphasizing the challenges in the process to get you to where you can. In order to do this I will need to make a temporary connection between our minds, like I did with Ailith to bring her back from beyond the gate at the cabin. What that means is that during the time it takes me to train your brain, so to speak, I will have a very personal amount of access to everything you know, think, or feel." She paused to let this sink in and watched microexpressions flit across Adem's face before continuing in a softer voice. "It also means you will have the same access to mine, though I've had centuries to learn how to block people out from what I don't want them to find. I will do my level best not to pry, but I cannot guarantee success. Likewise, I would ask of you the same." Swallowing, Adem nodded. "Are you ready?"

"Yes," he replied. Sable nodded and moved over to the bed where Ailith sat, tapping her on her shoulder.

"Ailith, I need you to take off the headphones for a bit and keep an ear out," she said, earning a nod. "I'm going to make it to where your dad can see what we see, but while I'm doing that we're both going to be paying a lot more attention to what's going on in our minds than on anything out here, so if something happens, come shake one or both of us on the shoulder. Can you do that?" Ailith nodded again, looking worried. "Good girl. Won't take long." She patted her pupil on the shoulder in what she hoped was a reassuring fashion and crossed the room to take up the chair closest to Adem. "Ready?"

"As I'll ever be." He sat straighter in his chair, all his focus on Sable. She met his gaze and reached out a hand to touch his forehead right between his eyes—and dropped into a flat plane that stretched as far as the eye could see in any direction.

"Adem," she called, "I need to be able to find you to do this." The scene jumped and suddenly he stood beside her, dressed as he had been and staring straight ahead, a blank expression on his face. "I need you to think back to the hilltop where we met Tsuna." Again their surroundings shifted and they were standing just below the hilltop, watching as Sable was lifted into the air and Ailith approached the gateway to the shrine. "Hold it right there." Everything paused, and Sable reached out before her, a paintbrush appearing in her outstretched hand.

As she swept it across various portions of the scene colors and shapes leapt into focus; she hadn't realized herself that Tsuna had not physically manifested, or that Ailith's aura was that shade of red tinged with black when she fulfilled her gatekeeper's duties. As she finished illuminating Adem's memory he looked around in wonder, melting from his half-frozen state and sweeping Sable into a strong sense of unsettled curiosity.

"This is what you see?" he asked, striding closer to the hilltop while the scene remained frozen.

"I see less, actually. It seems you have a proclivity for it." Sable followed his gaze to his daughter, where it lingered.

"What is that around her?" he asked as he circled his child.

"Her aura," Sable replied. "It's a manifestation of many things; her personality, her abilities, how she's feeling at any given moment. We all have one, though some are stronger than others." She squinted up at the image of herself dangling upside down. It always disconcerted her to see herself through someone else's memories. "I actively suppress mine, as you can see." Adem turned to study her image and Sable felt his anger and frustration at his inability to assist her.

"Will this–" he indicated their surroundings with the sweep of a hand– "be present in all my memories now?"

"The information has always been there," Sable answered as she turned to leave. "Now you can see it. But I must warn you–" Her next words were lost as the world tilted around her, picking her up in a mad Rolodex spin as Adem searched his memory for a certain time. The cries of a woman in childbirth echoed around them as a hospital room clicked into view. A brown-haired woman lay on the bed in the room's center, pushing for all she was worth. Her heart-shaped face carried fine features etched with determination as she worked to birth her child, and her deep green aura pulsated with her contractions. After a few short minutes the child's first cries resounded through the room, declaring her unhappiness with her new environs, and Sable felt a ground-shaking depth of love and care flow out from Adem, followed by equally significant loss and despair. As the child cried, her mother lay back on the bed, smiling, as her aura faded and the monitors began to tone.

Adem froze the memory and frantically searched the room, mumbling to himself. Sable let him process what he'd seen, then spoke into the silence. "Adem." Without looking up, he shook his head.

"There has to be something here," he said desperately. "The doctors didn't know what killed her. It had to have been something we just couldn't see." Sable let him cast about the room until he'd searched it as thoroughly as possible before repeating his name. This time he stood and passed his hand over his face, looking more haggard than she'd seen him. "There has to be something. A reason. Anything."

"It looked to me like her reasons were her own," Sable answered. "I saw no foul play." Adem sat down where he stood, sadness marring his features as he surveyed the ruins of the life he thought to have. Sable walked to his side and placed a hand on his shoulder.

"You have lived lifetimes," Adem began after a moment, "and buried more people than I can fathom. My pain feels insignificant in the face of what yours must be, but I still cannot shake it." He tilted his face to regard Sable, who could still feel the depth of his sorrows as he lived them once again. "Thank you. You have given me a gift, and while I wish it carried more answers, I am grateful." For a moment Sable's guard slipped as Adem's pain reminded her of her own loss, and his hazel eyes darkened to brown as his face morphed into a different shape. It was intimately familiar to her, painfully so, and she recoiled from his side. His dark, heavy brow furrowed and a different voice uttered, "Sable?" But the name was wrong; that wasn't her name, was it? He'd never called her that. His face went slack as her memory drew him in, building the rest of the world around them as the hospital room faded from view. Wooden-walled buildings topped with thatch lined the dirt street on which they stood, facing one another as they had so long ago. "Dagomarus?" The name escaped her lips before she could stop herself.

He started to speak, then stopped as Sable realized where they were and froze the image. "Time to head out," she said as she wrenched her heart and mind back to the present and out of both of their minds. It hurt, and she realized she'd overextended herself doing this so soon after the large working she'd done earlier in the day. Still, it was worth it for Adem to be able to perceive all the threats around them.

Opening her eyes, Sable found herself staring into Adem's penetrating gaze, and a single word escaped him at a whisper: "Carata."

Sable's blood ran cold. "What did you just say?" she whispered, feeling the power behind the word.

Adem blinked and the spell was broken. "That word—what does it mean? I heard it spoken in your memory, but I didn't recognize the language."

Sable wrapped her arms around her middle and stood. "You wouldn't," she cast over her shoulder as she walked to the window. "It's been dead over a thousand years." The heavy gold curtains were drawn, their ornate tassels dangling to either side, but she stood before them as if she could survey what was behind them. One deep breath became two, then three, and she let her arms drop to her sides as she relaxed into her normal demeanor. "I'd appreciate it if you didn't use that word again, especially in the company of others," she said as she crossed the room and rifled through the duffel for pajamas. "It's of…special significance to me, and it could give an enemy a disastrous edge over us." She pinned Adem with a dire expression and he nodded, looking tired. "Now, I'm going to put on my pajamas and fall over into that bed right there." She pointed at one of the two double beds in the room as she pulled soft-looking shorts and a comfy t-shirt from her bag and headed to the bathroom to change.

When Sable returned, Adem still sat at the table, staring at the deep red interior wall without seeing it. She put her day's clothing back into the duffel, then crossed the room and laid a hand on his shoulder as she had during their sojourn into his memories. "You'd better rest," she suggested. "You've been through a lot today, and your mind needs to recover. I've set wards; you should be able to see them now." He swiveled his head, picking out the locations she'd used as borders for the wards.

"If I can see them, can't anyone?" he asked.

"Only if I attune the wards to them," Sable explained. "These are attuned only to us. Now get some sleep; we can figure out the rest in the morning." She patted his shoulder in what she hoped was a supportive fashion, then turned toward her bed.

"Who was he? The man from your memories?"

She stopped without turning, and she knew he could hear the small, sad smile on her face as she replied. "Dagomarus? He was my Irene." Crossing the room, she slid under the blankets on her bed. "Good night, Adem. Sleep well, Ailith." Turning away from both, she squeezed her eyes shut and forced her exhausted body to relax. Minutes later she was asleep.

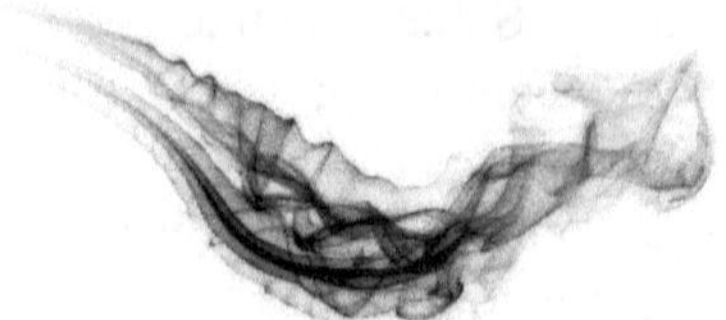

WHO IS SHE?

A hriman." The voice wafted through the shimmering gate as the tall figure leaned his forehead against it once more.

"Zaurizl," he replied. "Who has done this to you? Who has sent you beyond the gate?"

"The gatekeeper," came the creeping reply. The voice drifted closer to the surface, its tendrils of sickly sound reaching just across into hearing. "She is coming into her power faster than we thought possible. You must find her quickly."

"I know!" He banged a balled-up fist on the archway bedside his head, careful not to damage his host's manicured nails. He wondered briefly why he cared, then shoved the man's thoughts aside. "But where have they gone?"

"After the records of the last gatekeepers," the sibilant voice answered. "As they have always done in the past."

"I know that, but which one?"

"Liu Zhi's is closest."

Fingers tapped a staccato rhythm on the stonework that echoed across the gate as he thought. "Do we know where that one is in particular?"

Silence stretched from the gate for long moments, then: "It is likely at the Princes' Palace, in Guilin."

"You are almost more useful on the other side." The gate's glow faded as he stepped away from the arch and strode out of the room. Down the hall he entered the room with the dais and chair where a small gathering genuflected at his entrance. "Where is Sawarl?" His voice shot through the silence as he swept into his armchair.

"Here, my lord." A woman with tanned skin and raven hair stood immediately, bowing her head. Her high cheekbones and dark eyes were cast fervently downward as she replied. "What do you wish of me?"

"You will go to Guilin with all haste. Use the jet, use whatever you need, but you must get there overnight. Be at the Jingjiang Princes' Palace when they open for tourists tomorrow. Look for the girl and her father–and whoever this upstart woman is who's chosen to help them. I want her dead and the girl here in time for the ritual. Her father you may do with as you wish." The woman called Sawarl nodded once.

"As you command." Without waiting for dismissal she turned smartly on her heel and left through the double doors at the rear.

"As for the rest of you," he continued, his gaze grating across the rest of the assembly like sandpaper, "I want to know who this woman is. I want to know what she can do, where she comes from, and what leverage we can use against her."

"Yes, my lord," came the chorus of replies.

"Now go." The rest of the chamber's occupants bowed, then dispersed, leaving only the figure on the dais. His body sank into the deep cushions of the velvet chair as his mind sank into deep thought. He'd never expected this kind of trouble getting his hands on an eleven-year-old girl. Yet here they were, over three months into their pursuit with nothing to show for it. *Sawarl had better not fail.* He had other, stronger servants he could call upon, but the others were less subtle with their approach. *Still, if I must...* He stood, stretching, and went to find the closest bed. His human form was so fragile; he'd forgotten how much humans slept and ate. *Soon I will need to do neither.* The thought warmed him as his host fell into a dreamless slumber.

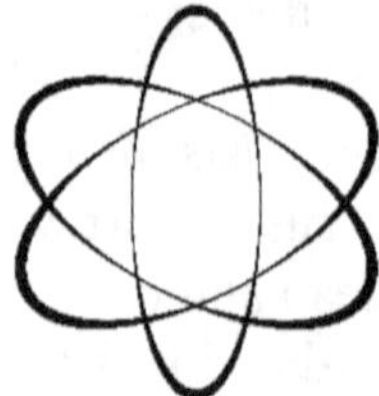

Physics or Magic?

They faced the golden archway and tiered rooftops of the Chengyun Gate on the south side of the Jingji-ang Palace grounds looking like a group of eager foreign college students. All three carried their backpacks in case there was a need for a quick getaway as they wandered the grounds. Adem habitually went first as they entered, eyes scanning the crowd, with Ailith next and Sable bringing up the rear. She had to admit Adem was coping well so far with his newfound ability to perceive the things around him; he'd only startled at something once since they'd left the hotel.

Through the gate they strode down ancient stone pathways lined with decorative hedges as they approached the palace proper. A two-story yellow edifice with orange columns and red doors and windows peeped cheerily between the trees in the manicured courtyard as they neared the building. Painted balustrades lined a second-floor balcony with a perfect view of the gate far beyond. They stood before the steps for a moment, considering their next move.

"It's not in there," Ailith said. "There's something here, but it's not in that building; it's somewhere outside, past it."

"How do you know?" Sable asked, cocking her head to one side.

Ailith shrugged. "I just do. Can't explain it, but there's something…pulling at me, sort of like when I get sucked to the other side, but different."

"Then let's go find it. Lead on!" Sable gestured toward the pathway around the building, then followed her pupil as they explored the grounds further. As they rounded the corner of the palace proper a massive rock formation dominated the visible landscape, with scrub bushes and vines clinging to its sheer sides. A small staircase wound upward around the rock face and etchings could just be seen within the facets of its stone.

"There!" Ailith pointed toward the rock. "It's up there." She tried to take off at a run, but Adem's iron bar of an arm caught her across the shoulders before she made it two steps.

"Take your time," he admonished.

Something tickled at the back of Sable's awareness. "Maybe we shouldn't take too much time," she conceded. "Something's not right." She turned a circle as if looking for a landmark, but saw nothing amiss despite her growing discomfort. "There's someone else here, someone very powerful. I can feel it."

Adem took Ailith's hand under mild protest. "Then let's get moving," he said calmly as they strode toward the base of the hill. Ornate buildings and gazebos from the Ming dynasty passed by them unnoticed as they hurried toward whatever lay ahead and above. As they reached the foot of the staircase up the hill Adem turned toward Sable. "That itching right at the back of my mind–is that what you're referring to?"

"It feels different for everyone, but yes," she answered as they began their ascent. "This one is strong enough I can get an idea of how far away she is and which direction she's heading, which–spoiler alert–is right toward us. Ailith, how close are we?"

"Close!" the girl answered breathlessly from up ahead. "I think it's just around this next–" She cut off as she turned the corner, transfixed by something etched into the rock face there. Rivulets of morning sun flowed around the group as they caught up and stared at the ornate calligraphy carved into the rock face before them. Ailith's jaw went slack and her eyes glazed over as soon as she saw the writing and Adem had to move her gently out of the way to clear the space before it. He pulled out his cell phone and snapped a photo, checked it for clarity, took one more for good measure, then shoved the device back into his pocket.

"We've got what we came for," he said. "Time to go."

"Too late," Sable replied, pointing to a black-haired figure running up the steps behind them. "Up! Quickly!" Adem grabbed Ailith and started running up the stairs at top speed,

Sable trailing behind to throw up a temporary barrier in hopes of slowing any pursuit. As the woman drew closer Sable felt a sense of ennui and despair overcome her. How could they continue to escape whomever was after them? She couldn't fold space every time they needed to travel, could she? It had been too long since she did so many workings in such a short time frame. She was weak and slow and would only drag her companions down; she should give up, give in to the will of the huntress behind her. It would make things easier for everyone.

"Sable!" Adem's voice called out like a whip crack above the oppression of her mind and she shook off the fog that threatened to drag her right into the clutches of the enemy. *This old dog still has some tricks.* Drawing energy from the mountain below her, she channeled it into her legs, pumping them as fast as she could and putting more distance between her and the black-haired woman.

"Keep going!" she shouted. "I'm right behind you!" The earth lent her speed as she caught up with Adem and Ailith just at the top of the stairs. The height was dizzying as they cast about for another way down, finding none, while the presence at their back pressed closer.

"Should we hide in that pagoda?" Ailith asked, her fear written on her face as she pointed to the large building in the center of the peak.

"She doesn't need to see us to know we're here," Sable pointed out grimly. "Looks like it'll be a fight. Prepare your minds; whoever she is, she did something to me that made me want to give up and be captured, so she has some serious mojo." She smiled, a lopsided grin that gave her face a dangerous cast as she cracked her neck and stretched out her arms. "Lucky for us, so do we."

A head appeared at the top of the staircase, its high, black ponytail bobbing as it climbed the last few stairs. "I am here for the girl," she called out, her smooth, dark voice booming across the space loudly enough that the few tourists they'd passed shuddered and ran past her to the stairs. "I am also here to be your doom." She pointed at Sable and a wave of emotion threatened to bring her to her knees. She didn't want to fight; she wanted to submit, to be conquered. There would be nothing better than to give her life over to this woman.

But this time, she was prepared. Latching onto the wave of projected emotion she climbed it with her thoughts until she reached the mind of its originator and struck out savagely. The woman turned her cheek as if slapped and narrowed her eyes at Sable. "You will obey me, witch!" she screamed as she redoubled her efforts. Meanwhile, Adem stowed Ailith in the shadow of a building and crept around to the woman's side, using Sable's retaliation as a distraction. Just as she began her second attack he bowled into her from the side, knocking her to the ground and pinning her on her stomach under his considerable weight.

Her head turned a full hundred and eighty degrees, and she regarded him as a cat would a fly. "I was going to keep you, but perhaps you'll share the same fate as your friend." Adem's determined expression faltered as she pushed herself off the ground and twisted, throwing him to the dirt before exerting her will over him. "You will crush her and then throw yourself off the cliffs." Adem's hands flew to his head as he fought her influence, struggling to stay on the ground as she forced his body upright.

"No!" Ailith screamed from her hiding place in the shadows. "Dad, don't do it! Fight her!" The sound pierced the veil she'd woven and left Adem his own master once again. He growled, a deep, feral sound, and launched himself at the woman once again just as Sable found an opportunity to lash out with a spell. Invisible ropes tangled info the woman's limbs just as Adem grabbed at an upraised hand, twisting it behind her. The sickly pop of her shoulder as it dislocated rebounded off the building and Ailith winced.

"Ailith! Send her home!" Sable shouted as she fought to keep the magical bindings on the writhing creature before them. Stepping out from behind the building, Ailith's eyes glazed over and she reached out in front of her toward the scuffle.

"No! I will not be sent back!" A fresh wave of anger and oppression rolled out from beneath the morass of limbs and bindings, overwhelming Adem and dropping Sable to one knee.

Ailith advanced, unblinking, with her hand outstretched as her father rolled off of his opponent. Sable's weakened bindings kept her from complete freedom, but she turned her head to regard the child. "Come with me," she commanded as Ailith approached.

"Don't listen!" Sable ground out from beneath the crushing weight of the mental onslaught. "It's a trick!" But Ailith was already in range of the woman, taking her hand.

"You come with me," Ailith said as their skin made contact, and both of them froze. The wave of oppression ceased, leaving Adem and Sable on their knees and gasping for air. Instantly Sable shifted her perceptions to see what was going on beyond the physical plane just in time to see both Ailith and a shadowy figure disappear hand in hand across the shining gate before them. In the physical plane the dark-haired woman crumpled, unconscious.

"Ailith," Sable called as she watched the girl drawn deeper beyond the gate. "We need you back. Your father needs you." Ailith turned her head, then was sucked backwards the way she'd come. She and Sable both began to move again and Adem rushed over to his daughter's side.

"Are you all right? What happened?" he asked, placing his hands on her shoulders. She sagged in exhaustion.

"I'm fine; I sent it home." Ailith leaned on her father, who put a protective arm around her and led her away from the scene of the fight. Sable studied their erstwhile opponent where she lay but could not discern anything beyond her hair and skin color—and the mark on the back of her neck that looked like it had been burned into the woman's flesh. It matched Ailith's drawing from the cabin. Sable inched close enough to snap a picture of it before joining her companions in the shadow of the large pagoda tower atop the hill.

"We need a way down," Adem said as he scanned the mountaintop for another exit. They could hear the whistles of the approaching security guards as they rushed across the grounds. "You have any more tricks we might can use?"

"A few," Sable replied coyly. "Would you rather float down to ground level, invisible and blind, or fly a decent distance before floating down to ground level, invisible and blind?"

"Distance seems like a good plan." Adem shifted closer to the building as the whistles grew closer.

"All right, then grab hands, Ailith in the middle, and face the cliff." They linked hands and Sable could feel the connection between them as she began her working. "We'll aim for that peak on the outskirts of town," she announced as she pointed out the tallest peak visible outside of Guilin. "When everything goes dark, we run for the cliff." Ailith nodded uncertainly, looking to her father for reassurance. Adem nodded and set his jaw, eyes fixed on the peak before them, then squeezed his daughter's hand. "Ready? Now!" The world before them blacked out as Sable's spell snapped into place around them, bending the sunlight so that they appeared not to exist. She knew Adem and Ailith could perceive the energy she manipulated into a flat-bottomed bubble around them with wings extended to either side as Adem led the charge down their makeshift runway, and just before their feet left the ground they heard Sable mutter "áel." A wind they could only hear picked up their ephemeral conveyance and bounced it along as they felt the distance below them yawn into a drop of hundreds of feet.

"Dad, this is scary!" Ailith yelled over the wind.

"I know," he answered. "It is for me, too, but do you remember what being brave means?"

"Being scared, but doing what you should anyway."

"That's my girl." Sable felt Ailith's grip loosen a bit.

"Keep ahold of me," she advised, and the grip tightened once more. "Hang on, I'll open a window." A slot appeared in the darkness directly ahead of them, the light blinding to their straining pupils. Through it they could see the tops of the nearest peaks—and that they'd blown off course from their original target. Reaching out with her will, Sable manipulated the winds until they were floating directly at the largest mountain in view. She could feel Adem watching the energies as she deftly arranged them in the shape she desired. "I could teach you both to do this, you know," she said as she directed the bubble. "If you can see it, you can influence it. But don't try it right now," she blurted as she felt both father and daughter begin to pick at the energies she'd so carefully arranged. "Unless you want to crash, that is." Both kept their proverbial hands to themselves and they drifted along safely in relative silence for a while, decompressing.

"So, what did you find?" Sable's too-bright voice shattered the peace as they neared the mountains.

"A poem," Ailith answered out of a half-dream state. "But I don't know what it says."

"I can translate it for you," Adem offered, "since I got a picture of it."

Adem dug in his pocket for his phone and pulled up a well-framed image of the rock face they'd passed. On it was a square section containing chiseled characters arranged in artful rows, as if some calligrapher from a bygone era had possessed the power to copy words from paper onto stone with the nib of their pen. Adem squinted at it, holding the phone further from his face to get a better look as they glided toward their destination. After long moments of consideration he shook his head. "I don't recognize some of these characters," he said with a furrowed brow. "This must be very old. The ones I can read mention something about the flow of a river, the change of seasons, and balance." Handing the phone to Ailith, he glanced over at the concentrating Sable. "Is your Middle Chinese passable? I could use some help with it."

"I'll have a look after we touch down," Sable ground out through gritted teeth. Nature had decided to spoil her plans with a rogue crosswind, which she fought to keep from swamping the aircraft. "Bit busy at the moment." Just as she finished speaking a wall of air slammed into them, shoving the bubble off course toward a shanty town at the base of the mountains. "Stupid downdrafts," she muttered as she pitted her willpower against nature and the laws of physics, hoping it would be enough to get them to their destination in one piece.

Just as she began to flag, warmth surged through the linked hands binding them together for the trip. Ailith went up on her toes as it arced through her small body and sent shivers through Sable. The unexpected boost of energy allowed her to right their craft and direct them up the nearest mountain to settle gently on a craggy outcropping. Light flooded their senses as the bubble dropped, and all three fell to their knees as they fought exhaustion and worry to revel in the fact that they were alive–and together.

School is in Session

The hilltop was pleasantly warm in the midmorning light, with a stiff breeze providing enough cooling to make them comfortable as they sat beneath the stubby trees to stare at Adem's phone. Adem and Sable squinted at the image it contained, zooming in and out as they discussed the finer points of ancient Chinese characters. Ailith wandered the small ledge they inhabited, studying the flora and trying her best not to get too close to the sheer drop mere feet from where she stood. After a few minutes Sable pulled a notepad from the duffel and wrote as Adem dictated, stopping every so often to correct a word before crowing triumphantly and holding up a sheet of paper. "We've got it!" she cried, her eyes locking with Adem's for a moment as they shared their satisfaction in having successfully translated the difficult piece. He gave a Cheshire cat grin in response, and Sable felt her innards do a small flip at the sight. *Nope. Not doing that again. Put a lid on it, old lady; he's way too young for you.* She turned to Ailith just as her neck began to warm. "Want to hear it?" she asked.

"Yeah!" the girl cried, skidding over to where they sat and crouching down next to Sable.

"You were right; it's a poem," Sable began as she held up her notepad. "Here's how it reads:

As the seasons flow, one into another,
So too flows life into death.
Like the Li, whose direction never changes,
This sequence of events must pass.
For each spring, there must be autumn;
For each summer, winter's cold.
Such is the balance of nature, of the world.
To flaunt this balance is mankind's greatest folly,
For to tip it one feather to either side

Would doom us all.

It's signed Liu Zhi, Gatekeeper." Sable handed the paper to Ailith for her perusal and stood, dusting off her jeans. Her hand brushed against the bandages on her lower legs and she winced, recalling the burns she'd sustained and then neglected one day prior. Had it only been a day? So much had transpired in such a short period it was hard to believe it hadn't been more like a week.

"So then, what's next?" Adem asked as he drew himself up from the crouch he'd maintained for too long. "You said there are more of these records hidden all over the world; do we look for another? This one sounds very Taoist, which makes me think it's at least Song dynasty, but it doesn't elaborate over-much." He blew out a breath and shuffled closer to Ailith, who was reading and re-reading the poem. "Does it mean anything in particular to you?" Adem asked, and Ailith shrugged.

"It talks about the balance across the gate," she answered, "which is something I can feel. Sometimes it's pretty even overall, but lately it's felt like it's tipping toward the other side. I think that's what he's talking about."

"She," Sable corrected as she joined them. "Zhi is a female name. So who wants to dowse this time?" Her companions were rapidly acclimating to her abrupt topic shifts and looked at each other.

"I did it last time," Ailith said. "You wanna try, Dad? It's easy; all you gotta do is let the universe talk through you." She smiled brightly.

He chuckled. "I'll leave the divination to the seer and the professional," he answered, moving off under a tree in search of shade.

"You're not off the hook," Sable called after him. "You're helping set our wards tonight." She grinned mischievously at his shocked expression before turning to Ailith, who already had her phone out and the map open and was reaching beneath her shirt for her crystal pendant. "I see you're prepared," Sable commented as Ailith began to swing the pendant in lazy circles over the phone. This time it took very little waiting before the stone's arc changed and Ailith scrolled around the map until at last the crystal dropped. She stared down at the phone, attempting to decipher where they were in relation to the target the stone had marked.

"Where's Palembang?" Ailith stumbled over the unfamiliar word.

"Sumatra," Sable answered. "South of Singapore, if you know where that is." At Ailith's owlish blink she elaborated. "South of here? Indonesia?" Finally the girl recognized a place name and nodded. "Good heavens, what do they teach in schools these days?"

"I missed a lot of this past spring semester," Ailith admitted, hanging her head. Sable ruffled her hair good-naturedly.

"Then we will have to make up the deficiency." Nodding to herself, Sable scanned the horizon. She could almost make out a buzz of activity atop Solitary Beauty Peak behind them and was glad they'd managed to put a bit of distance between them and the commotion; someone was bound to have seen something, and they didn't have time for local authorities. Without turning, she called to Adem. "What do you think: do we camp here for the night or do we push on to Sumatra today?"

"Is that an option?" Adem crossed the small ledge to rejoin them.

"If you're willing to find me a place to land for a few hours on the other side," Sable answered. "It's at least as big a jump as the last one I made, if not a bit bigger."

"Is there any way we can help?" Adem's brow lowered in contemplation or concern–perhaps both. "Can we, I don't know, lend you strength?"

Sable shook her head. "You'll need everything you've got in case someone is waiting for us. Maybe once you've gotten used to handling magic a bit more, but for now I don't feel comfortable either borrowing power or doing a joint working. We could all end up ass over teakettle, and then where would we be?" She tapped her chin in speculation. "It does seem the safest way for us to travel is instantly, but I think it's worth pausing for the rest of today and camping up here so we can be at full strength tomorrow. Besides," she grinned wolfishly, "it gives me time to show the two of you a thing or two about magic."

Adem cocked his head to one side as he considered. "All right," he conceded. "But where are we going to get food? We're stuck on a cliff. Do we float down the way we got up here? Won't we risk exposure going back into town to eat?"

"O ye of little faith," Sable replied, reaching for the duffel and rummaging in its depths. "I don't keep a lot of premade stuff on hand," she began as she pulled ingredients out of the zippered opening, "but I do keep canned soup as a general rule. I like it for an easy lunch sometimes." Three cans of various types of soup sat before the companions, who studied them hungrily. "I can definitely recommend the lentil vegetable, but they're all good."

"I'll take the chicken noodle," Ailith cut in almost before Sable finished speaking.

"I'll leave you the boiled rabbit food in favor of the vegetable beef," Adem quipped, grabbing the appropriate can and studying it as if willing it to give up its contents for consumption. Their latest two narrow escapes and subsequent revelations seemed to have loosened some long-borne restraints within Adem, and Sable found the man beneath them fascinating. His burly exterior belied a sharp wit and keen understanding of the world around him that was fed by his insatiable curiosity and constant situational awareness. It was a combination she had rarely encountered and planned to use to their advantage whenever possible.

Turning to the final can–the lentil vegetable, she realized with relish–she pulled a can opener from the duffel and handed it first to Adem. "I have bowls around here somewhere, but it'd be easier to just eat it out of the cans." Adem nodded and helped Ailith open hers before popping the lid on his own and handing back the tool. "I'll show you how to heat them once we have hot mitts," she continued as she peeled back the lid on her meal. It looked a bit like runny dog food, she admitted, but it was the tastiest of the bunch. Sable produced three worn hot mitts whose scorch marks largely obscured the mismatched floral designs on them. She handed out two and kept the last for her own can, then closed her eyes with the tin held in front of her. *Excite the molecules and...*a waft of steam rose from her meal as it heated to a comfortable eating temperature.

Adem narrowed his eyes at his now-open soup can. He blinked them closed as he concentrated on his task, feeding a trickle of his own energy into the food. He was rewarded with a sloppy popping sound and flecks of brown on his shirt as the soup bubbled once. Opening his eyes, he scowled before determining that he'd still managed to heat his meal, albeit in a messier way.

"Good!" Sable exclaimed. "Most people have trouble with the bubbling, just like in a microwave. There's a trick to it." She turned to Ailith, who was frowning at her soup as if the power of her pre-teen angst alone could make it edible. Sable chuckled. "With that face you'll sour it instead of heating it," she admonished.

"What is the deal with this?!?" Ailith huffed, her frustration painted on her face.

"Remember your physics lessons?" Sable asked. "How do you generate heat at a molecular level?"

Ailith considered a moment, then began rubbing the bottom of the can on the leg of her jeans to create friction. Sable watched as she felt for the tiny amount of heat generated, then fanned it into a warmth strong enough to suffuse the soup. "Ha!" she cried as the liquid steamed without bubbling.

"That's one way to do it," Sable nodded. "There are as many ways to do magic as there are people in the world. Each one of us used a different method to heat our soup, but all of us managed it." Gingerly, she sipped at the thick soup, letting it trickle down to fill the growling emptiness in her stomach and taking a moment to feel grateful she was alive and free once again.

Sable's mind wandered back across the last two days, in which she'd metamorphosed from an elderly recluse into…what, exactly? So much had changed so quickly it left her head spinning as she stared across the city laid out before her. Across the valley more peaks like the one on which they sat reflected the sun's rays with vibrant greens and grays, stone and plant both reaching toward its warmth. She lost count of the peaks as her gaze ringed the town and came to rest on their makeshift camp site. Adem and Ailith were talking quietly as they drank their soup, the ghost of a smile flitting around the edges of the conversation, and Sable swallowed a bit of unfair jealousy at their closeness. Downing the last of the soup in one gulp, she tossed the empty can back into the duffel before standing to stretch. Without a word she made a circuit of the ledge on which they sat, describing a semicircle in the soft gray dirt with her foot. It began and ended at the rock face behind her as she stood in its center, facing the town and squinting in the midday sun.

"What's that?" Ailith's voice beside her made Sable jump. *Girl's half wraith if she's anything.* "Or what's it gonna be?"

Sable regarded her pupil sidelong. "What do you think it's going to be?" Without waiting for an answer, she moved to one side of the line by the cliff face, picking up a convenient stick along the way. A clearer line appeared behind it as she dragged it meticulously beside the first at a precise distance.

Ailith shifted from foot to foot. "A rainbow?" she ventured as the second line appeared.

"Nope." Sable completed her semicircular circuit and started backward, inscribing a complex pattern between the first two lines. Intricate knotwork began to form at the end of her stick as she moved with purpose across the dirt. Ailith and Adem looked on in silence as Sable's brow creased in concentration. The third pass took much longer to complete, but when she was done a work of art stood before them, drawn humbly in the stone-gray dirt. It resembled ancient carvings and paintings from the Celtic world, with simple lines dancing across one another, weaving in and out as they passed such that the work had no beginning and no end.

"Definitely not a rainbow." Ailith's awed voice cut through the quiet of the plateau.

"Nope." Sable plopped down at the apex of the pattern, legs crossed, hands resting on her knees. Her eyes closed and the rest of the world slipped away as she plunged her awareness into the mountain below them. Thousands of years of stone greeted her as she sent her perception down into the heart of the hill on which she sat. She reached the place where the mountain's heart rested, where it was anchored to the bedrock, and she reached out, creating a connection with it. Power surged around her as she anchored herself in the mountain's heart, then pushed off and retreated back the way she'd come, up and up until she reached the cliff side where her body rested. A thread followed her, then attached to the unbroken inscription at her feet, flooding the pattern with energy. Sable felt the pattern fasten itself to the mountain, creating a well-defined starting point for the working she would need to do the following morning.

She opened her eyes, regretting it instantly as the midday sun poured into her vision. Even in the blinding sunlight the markings on the ground were visible, swimming with radiance as the mountain's essence ran through them. Nodding in satisfaction, Sable retreated to the shade of a small tree nearby to recover and consider their next move.

Ailith joined her beneath the sparse branches. "What was that?" she began. "It was awesome! I saw you did something with the mountain itself, like, way down in the deep parts of it, and then bam! Your drawing lit up." She folded herself down next to Sable, who was digging in her duffel for a snack despite having just finished lunch. "What did that do? I can still see that weird energy kind of flowing through the tracks in the dirt…" Ailith reached toward the inscriptions in fascination.

Sable's hand shot out. "Don't touch it," she said as she redirected Ailith's hand into the girl's lap. "If we break the lines it's useless. Remember what I said about traveling point to point?" Ailith nodded as her mind retraced their conversation. "This sets up a location to be one side of that wormhole we talked about. Makes the whole shebang easier to do with less energy—which means I just might be able to stay conscious tomorrow morning when we skip over to our next destination." Smiling, she pulled a package of peanut butter crackers from her bag and tore into them with abandon.

Adem joined them, sinking gracefully into a cross-legged seat across from Sable. "All right, so what do we do with the rest of our day?" he asked, checking to be certain he hadn't disrupted Sable's working when he'd seated himself. Sable leaned back onto one hand and munched the first of her crackers before responding.

"We wait," she said simply, popping another cracker sandwich into her mouth as if daring anyone to contradict her. To her surprise, Adem shrugged, then made himself comfortable against the trunk of the tree under which they sat, closing his eyes. Ailith rolled hers and pulled out her phone, plugging headphones into her ears and laying flat on her back on the single tuft of grass that graced the ledge.

They spent the rest of the afternoon vacillating between companionable silence and bursts of conversation in which Sable learned a few random oddities of her companions' personalities. For one, Ailith's art skills extended beyond simply copying things she'd seen; the sketchbook she carried contained detailed, realistic renderings of landscapes that only existed within the realm of her imagination. At Sable's expression of how impressive her work was Ailith shrugged, mumbled something self-effacing, then shoved the sketchbook back into her backpack. Adem, on the other hand, she caught humming a haunting melody under his breath as he lay in the late afternoon sun. Not wanting to give the impression she was listening, Sable continued to stare at the book on her lap, though she found herself re-reading whole paragraphs on the page before her as she strained to catch every bit of the song. As she opened her mouth to inquire about it, Ailith piped up to ask the same question, saving Sable the awkwardness of having felt like she was eavesdropping. Adem grunted something about a song he'd learned as a boy and blushed–actually blushed–before getting up to survey their surroundings for the fifteenth time that day.

They shared a simple dinner of peanut butter and jelly sandwiches as the sun sank below the mountains, its orb an orange maw with a row of jagged teeth on the bottom. Sable produced two cots as she instructed Adem on how to set the wards, then settled herself onto one of the makeshift beds, comfortable without a blanket in the early summer warmth. Ailith occupied the other and was soon asleep in the way that only growing children can manage, one arm slung over her face, the other hanging haphazardly over the edge of the cot. Sable tossed and turned to get comfortable before rolling up some spare clothing she'd pulled from the bag to use as a pillow and curling up on one side facing away from the cliff. Thus situated, she allowed her mind to drift, touching first on the sleeping child nearby, then on the girl's watchful father, who sat with his back to the cliff on first watch. An unreasonable sense of security swept over her as she surrendered to unconsciousness.

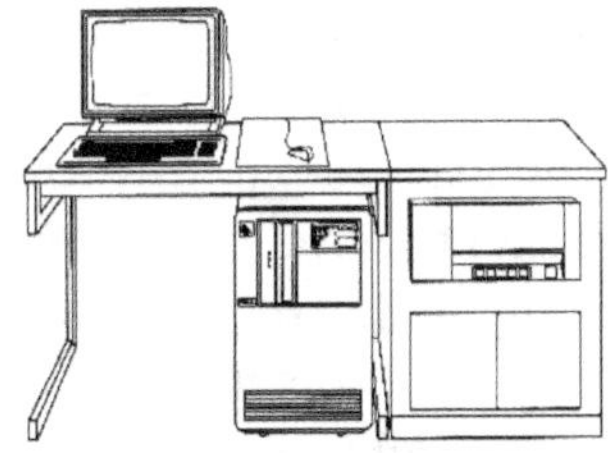

Always Clean Up Your Internet History

"What have you got for me?"

The man sitting in front of the yellowed CRT monitor jumped at the voice behind his shoulder, pushing his glasses up his nose to hide his embarrassment. When he took in the speaker's face his eyes went wide.

"M-m-mister Arcos, sir," he stammered, wiping his suddenly sweaty palms on the thighs of his slacks. "What can I do for you?"

The shaven-headed man behind him pointed at the screen. "What have you found? Anything useful?"

The younger man shook his head. "The machine still works, so I was able to get to everything off the hard drive, but it looks like it's full of, um, interesting videos and that's about it. None of them appear to have been recorded by its owner. Thank goodness." This last he tagged onto the end sotto voce before he continued, relaxing as he warmed to his subject. "I was, however, able to pull up a web browser history." He swung back around to face the ancient keyboard attached to the dinosaur of a computer before him, tapping a few noisy keys and clicking a folder on the desktop. "Combined with the Internet Archive it shows us a bit about her interests from 20 years ago. Seems she posted regularly on various so-called mysticism forums as BoudiccasRevenge. From what I can tell she was well respected within the community, if you can call it that."

"I take it you don't believe in the occult?"

The man shook his head. "Hokey ancient religions, blah blah blah. Still, it gives us some insight."

"Any other names given? Identifying comments or remarks?"

"Not that I've found so far, but I'm only partway through my list." A notepad on the desk contained a handwritten list of web site titles with about a third scratched through. Its owner shrugged self-consciously. "It was easier to write them down than find a dot matrix printer to hook up to this monstrosity. Anyway, I'll keep at it and let you know if I find something."

"See that you do." The bald man straightened from where he'd hunched over to better view the screen, rolling his shoulders back and down as he did so. The effect was that of a large cat stretching before a hunt as he raised his eyes to scan the room before him. A small group of his top programmers sat at tables pushed into a rough rectangle with the one he'd visited first at the bottom short end. Each had a monitor and some form of computer on which to work; most had headphones on, but had removed them or hung them around their necks when he'd entered. Directly opposite him stood the wall containing the Arcos Multinational logo, and seated in front of it was the woman he wanted to see. Striding around the group he watched them shiver in his wake. He revealed in their subconscious fear for a moment before alighting next to the dark-haired woman at the other end of the setup. She turned her near-black eyes upward to regard him coolly as she gave her report, unfazed by his presence. He made a mental note to consider bringing her closer into the fold.

"I was able to find information on the credit card holder from the plane tickets," she began, pulling up a browser window on her computer. "The name on the card was Annabelle Lee, though I'm positive it's a pseudonym. Address listed is somewhere in Oregon. It's been used infrequently over the course of the last five or so years for various purchases online, but none in person, so I'm unable to give an idea of geographic location for the cardholder beyond the likely false address provided." Pulling up another program on her machine, she continued. "I've fed the data I found to the latest version of our profiling engine, which will aggregate all the related information that we have access to—which is a lot. We should have more information in the next few hours, especially if she uses the card again." Pushing back from the desk she turned to face her employer. "If you'll excuse me, I'm in need of a restroom break; it's been a long morning."

She brushed past him, their arms touching briefly, and he felt himself respond with interest. *I forget sometimes this body has needs other than sustenance.* Nodding, he followed her out of the room with his eyes, appreciating the way her full hips swayed, then turned and stalked back through the silent double doors to his left. A short hallway led to his receptionist's desk, who didn't even look up as he passed.

"Mr. Arcos." He nodded, the dance of acknowledgments familiar and comforting as he passed into his outer office and straight through to the single heavy door behind his much-un-used desk. Nowadays the company was set up to run itself while he continued his important work in his inner sanctum. The business had never been more than a means to an end anyway.

He entered the room with the dais and chair, crossing it in a half dozen sure strides as its occupants dropped to one knee at his passing. He ignored them as he disappeared behind his armchair throne and down the hallway toward the gate room. The space lit up at his command, the lights flashing to life as if they, too, feared his power. Palm outstretched, he slowed as he approached the archway, considering his actions. He stopped with one hand hovering just out of reach of the arch's magic and reveled in the tingling sensation on his skin as the glow on the surface of the stone reached for his fingertips like an eager lov-er. In response he brought both hands forward and laid them on either side of one of the large stones before pressing his fevered forehead between them.

"Where is Sawarl?" he asked. "She has not yet returned."

"Here, my lord." The reply came rapidly; she had not been beyond the gate long. "This woman who travels with the gate-keeper is both wise and powerful. You would do well to take every precaution before encountering her again."

"But who *is* she?!?" Ahriman banged his fist against the stone, sending an unpleasant vibration through his own skull. "And how did she best you so easily, if you are now beyond the gate?"

"I will consult the spirits," Sawarl answered, her voice fading into the distance as her energy flagged. "We will send word." As he felt her recede Ahriman did the same, drawing away from the gateway before him in thought. *I need to know who we're up against. Without that knowledge all my careful planning could fail, and I will. Not. Let. That. Happen. Again.*

Determination straightened his host's spine as he strode from the room.

Friends in Holy Places

The sun woke them early the next morning. They broke camp, such as it was, had a light breakfast, and prepared for their hopskip journey to Indonesia. Sable hitched the duffel securely over her shoulder and looked to Ailith, who slung her backpack onto her back and nodded. Adem picked up his own pack and moved next to Ailith. Taking this as a sign, Sable rubbed her hands together. "Here we go!" She reached down and touched a finger to the edge of the drawing she'd made the day before, activating the anchor side of what was to be the bridge to their next destination. It glowed brightly in the early morning light as she closed her eyes and pictured the location she'd chosen for their landing zone. She could feel it, miles and miles distant, and she drew out some of the power from the mountain to reach out, stretching her mind toward the specific point in space-time she needed.

A dense copse of trees appeared before them. "Come on!" Sable grabbed Ailith's hand as the girl grabbed her father's and they stepped as one through the disorienting gap, their feet landing on soft, damp earth. Warm, dense air slapped them in the face as Sable severed the connection from her end and they took stock of their surroundings. Rough markers made out of wood and stone sprouted from tufts of rampant grass as far as the tree line opposite them. Running water could be heard nearby, and the woods around them teemed with raucous life.

Ailith sagged between the adults. "Sable…I…" Her eyes rolled upward and she went limp as Adem reached down to catch her.

"Hang on, I'll bring her back," Sable grunted as she took stock of where they were.

"Show me how." Adem sat down where he stood, cradling

his unconscious daughter. Sable checked their surroundings, then unslung the duffel and sat across from him, facing the trees.

"The path to the in-between must be shown the first time by one who knows it." Reaching out, Sable took Adem's hand, the one on which she'd written the pentacle. "Don't let go until you know the way back." Closing her eyes, she concentrated on where their minds needed to go, then opened her eyes to the monochrome of the plains. The gray-green grass was waist high here, but they had little trouble spotting the gate; it was always close where death was near. They could see Ailith just beyond its stones, walking down a gravel path lined with spectral figures. She appeared to be talking with some of them as she passed.

"Ailith!" Adem's voice rang out through the stillness and she stopped, turning. He beckoned her with his free hand and she waved, turning to say a final goodbye to the figures around her. By the time she reached the gate Sable and Adem had pushed their way through the tall grass to meet her. Sable slowed near the gate, but Adem continued on as if to cross it before Sable drew him up short. "Nope, that's not somewhere we can go. Not yet. Not ever, in my case." He stopped, studying the swirling, transparent barrier before him as Ailith pushed through.

Just as her body cleared the gate a large shadow appeared behind her and grabbed her ankle, letting out a snarl as she tried to pull it through. "Come with me, gatekeeper," it hissed. "I will keep you until he needs you."

Sable thought fast. She dropped Adem's hand, grabbing Ailith's and connecting the points where she'd drawn the anchor marks as she held their hands together. "Pull!" she said as she grabbed onto the girl's shirt and yanked. Adem did likewise, and between their efforts and the magic of the anchoring spell they freed Ailith's foot, which popped over to the right side of the gate with a sucking sound they felt more than heard. The creature howled in disappointment and prowled back and forth just be-yond the barrier, studying them like a predatory animal. "You are just delaying the inevitable," it spat as they picked themselves up from where they'd tumbled into a heap. "She will be ours, and you will burn for a thousand years in the fire of our retribution!"

"Yeah, yeah, heard that one before. Still here." Sable waved a hand behind her as she trudged toward the exit to the in-between. "Save your breath, or whatever it is that makes you talk. C'mon, you guys. Ailith, help him get home; it's his first trip, so he'll need a guide."

They passed through the exit to the in-between and opened their eyes to the blinding sun of midmorning. Ailith blinked and sat up, then crawled out of her father's lap after giving him a brief hug. "You might want to stay close to him," Sable warned as the two of them stood up, dusting off their clothing. "Holding his hand might help, too, since that's where I put the anchor points." Sable stretched and sagged, feeling the exhaustion of having jumped them hundreds of miles set in as the adrenaline wore off. *At least I'm still conscious.* A hand appeared in front of her face and she took it, glad of the assistance as Adem hauled her easily to her feet.

"Where to?" he asked. "For that matter, where are we?" The group swatted at insects as they conferred.

"We should be right next to the Musi River, which will take us into Palembang." Sable wandered toward the sound of running water, careful lest she stumble onto an unexpected slope. Before long the trees opened directly onto the swollen river, which carried mud and other detritus downstream in the wake of the rainy season. "Just need a boat…" Sable muttered as she cast about for any fallen logs or driftwood. Luck was with them; a tree trunk had lodged in a bend of the river nearby, and she ambled over to it, feeling almost as old as she was despite outward appearances. Adem and Ailith followed hand in hand. "Come help me with this." Sable dug her phone out of her duffel and tapped the screen a few times, searching for something in particular. "We're gonna make ourselves a boat. I'll need the both of you to assist; I don't have the energy to do it myself after getting us all the way here, but I can direct things a little." She held up an image of a small canoe-like vessel just big enough to fit the three of them and their packs. "Hold this image in your mind; we're going to shape this log into one of these. Now follow my lead." Sable stepped into the shallow edge of the river, sloshing around until she could lay her hand on the wood. It was waterlogged, but hopefully the transformation would help dry it out enough to float. Adem and Ailith followed suit, watching Sable as she ran her hand across the bark. The wood began to shift, creaking as it took the shape she'd chosen beneath her hand.

Adem flung his pack onto the bank and made his way to the deepest part of the semi-submerged log, cradling it in both hands and concentrating. A prow formed where he passed his hands over the bark and he smiled, pleased with his progress. Ailith stayed in the shallows and formed the tail, then moved to the center, where Sable struggled to flatten the bottom of the canoe. Where Ailith passed the boat turned black as it molded itself into the shape she wrought. Sable let go and simply watched as father and daughter completed their work in a seamless dance.

Sweat beaded Adem's brow as they finished and Ailith sagged a bit as they surveyed what they'd made. The canoe was two thirds black, one third driftwood, with a flat bottom and two small benches. It was just large enough for the three of them to fit. "Good work," Sable grunted through her exhaustion. Simply standing against the current of the river was wearing her out. "Now all we need are paddles. Think you could do the same with a couple of branches now that you have the knack?" They nodded and went in search of more deadfall.

A fluttering sensation tickled Sable's calves. She reached down to investigate and watched the bandages from her acid burns float down the river. *Damn. I keep forgetting about those.* She made a mental note to heal them up first thing after she'd had a nap.

It wasn't long before Adem and Ailith returned bearing passable oars and looking quite proud of themselves. The trio sloshed their way into the canoe and pushed off from the bank, letting the current carry them toward their destination. Adem raised his eyebrows at the open wounds on Sable's legs now exposed to the air, but she had neither the energy nor the inclination to discuss it, instead folding herself into the bottom of the boat and falling asleep to the gentle rocking of the river.

When she awoke they had beached their canoe on a bustling shoreline on the outskirts of Palembang. It was lined up next to a multitude of small vessels painted every color imaginable and against the riot of their hues the monochrome dugout stuck out like a piece of coal in a flower garden. Sable unfolded herself, feeling a throbbing in her legs she could barely ignore enough to move them. She stumbled unceremoniously onto the beach next to her companions, who waited on shore to help her onto solid ground.

"Where to?" Ailith asked, bouncing on her toes as she took in the sights.

"Someplace quiet with food." Sable trudged toward the nearest road, hoping to find both before she lost the little energy she'd managed to reacquire with her nap. It was lunchtime, so the streets crawled with humanity as fisherfolk brought in their catch and sought a meal. Small businesses selling clothing and handmade wares of all sorts lined the roads and Ailith's eyes went wide as they passed window after window filled with brightly-colored cloth and trinkets. Adem kept a firm hold on Ailith's hand as he followed Sable through the crowd; the woman's dark hair blended in with the local population, which made it difficult to differentiate if she got too far ahead. Finally they found a restaurant with indoor and outdoor seating and ducked through the low door.

Five minutes later the group was seated inside with Adem facing the door. None of them spoke Palembang, but the proprietor spoke enough English for them to order food and drinks without much difficulty. Sable chose two entrees for herself knowing the calories would help her recover faster.

"So what's our move?" Adem asked as soon as the man had retreated toward the kitchen. "Find a hotel? Set up a short term base of operations to find the next piece?"

"No time," Sable replied. "We'll have to make do with whatever we can manage on the go. So far our enemy's only sent one of his henchpeople at a time at us, but I think that's about to change. He knows what we're after–how else would he have been so close behind us in Guilin?" She paused as their drinks arrived at the table, thanking the waitress before continuing. "No, I think we figure out where to go and head straight there this afternoon, then find somewhere to hole up until we can hop on to the next place. Staying ahead is our best option, short of finding a better way to travel and hitting our destinations in a different order."

Adem's brow furrowed as she spoke. "You had a way to make the trip easier this time that seemed to work," he began, the wheels in his mind almost visible as they cranked through an idea. "If we can do that every time, that increases our lead time by a full day. And if Ailith and I get to where we can help, we could increase it even more—or could we use that to travel greater distances? Maybe skip the next closest location and head to a further one?"

Sable considered. "It's possible," she admitted as ideas began to flit through her head. "Though much of it will require prep work and maybe a little ritual to pull off. Plus we need to identify all the locations we'll need to hit in order to plan things out better. Up until now we've just been looking for the closest one."

Ailith reached into her bag for her phone as she pulled the crystal from beneath her shirt. "I can do that!" she offered. Sable placed a hand over the girl's to keep her from fully removing her necklace.

"Only if you want a lot of weird looks and questions," she said quietly. "And I'm not sure something that looks a lot like witchcraft is going to be welcomed most places in the world." Ailith's mouth opened in an *O* of understanding and she tucked the crystal back in her shirt. "We'll find a quiet, safe place to do that as soon as we can. But first, lunch!" Their food arrived faster than expected and they fell silent as they enjoyed the first real meal they'd had since breakfast the day prior.

Sufficiently stuffed, they decided to find a public park with a quiet corner to do some dowsing. The heat of midday was even more oppressive when they left the restaurant than it had been when they entered and all three were soaked with sweat by the time they walked the few blocks to the closest park. Its grass was lush and green, having benefited from the recent rainy season, and stands of trees provided shelter from the irrepressible sun. Clusters of students from a nearby university had spread out blankets for picnics and study groups. The gentle hum of their conversation made for excellent white noise as the trio pulled out a world map from Sable's duffel and prepared to make a list of destinations. She handed Adem a piece of paper and a pencil, then nodded to Ailith to begin her search.

As soon as the girl began to wave a skinny arm around the map a pattern formed. The crystal hovered over first Palembang, then India, then Egypt and Sudan. From there it skimmed over the Mediterannean to Turkey before flying across the Atlantic to Peru, where it stilled. "You get all that?" Sable asked as Adem scribbled furiously on the paper.

He nodded. "I think so. It looked like a town in India, then Cairo, then somewhere close to Khartoum, then Istanbul, then somewhere near Cusco. Is that everything?" Sable nodded as he finished writing and looked up. "Shame we can't reverse course and start at the far end from here. We'll just have to go quickly." It was Sable's turn to nod. "Now can we get a closer look at where we need to go here in Palembang?"

Sable let the others pull up a map and laid down for a moment in the grass. The shade took the edge off the heat, but it was still oppressive when combined with her full stomach and the taxing morning she'd had. Before long she found herself dozing as Adem and Ailith spoke in low tones about where they should head next. Ailith's high-pitched voice brought her out of her half-sleep. "Sable? You awake?"

"Mmnf," she replied as she sat up. "Long morning. Did you find where we're going next?"

"We think it's a mosque," Ailith replied with excitement.

"Well, then we'll have to attire appropriately," Sable replied, looking around at the students on the green. The university nearby was a Muslim university, so she took cues from the garments and demeanor of the students on the green when deciding how to configure their next appearance. "It's probably safest to play family again," she said as she ushered them up and past a set of bushes close to where they sat. When they exited the brush both Sable and Ailith wore a hijab and loose-fitting clothing in bright colors while Adem wore loose pants and a long-sleeved shirt that reached past his hips. "Lead on," Sable gestured to Adem. Looking uncomfortable, he started down the street closest to their destination. Sable used the same trick she'd used on the plane to speak directly into Adem's ear.

"Don't worry; I'll let you know if we fall behind or something happens." This time he simply nodded as if to himself and kept walking.

They passed the university itself and two or three bustling bazaars before reaching a residential area full of low-slung houses. The minarets of their target were visible above the rooftops as they approached, keeping watch over the population in its shadow. Adem's feet moved unerringly in the direction of the arched front gate and before long they found themselves staring up at the imposing edifice. "We'll likely be separated once we get inside," Sable whispered to both Adem and Ailith. "Adem, you have a better chance of getting access to what we need. I can watch over Ailith. Sound good?" He nodded imperceptibly and murmured back.

"It'll have to be."

"If something happens, do I have permission to reach directly out to your mind to let you know?" Sable made it a rule never to enter a mind without permission except in times of great need. She was pretty sure something happening to Ailith would constitute "great need," but it was polite to ask.

They stopped before entering the mosque and Adem turned to face Sable. "You have my permission," he answered, as if he understood the seriousness of the question.

"His name was Aalim," Ailith said faintly, her eyes unfocused. "He lived during the Majapahit period, and this was his mosque. He left a scroll." Her small hands pantomimed rolling up a piece of paper and placing it on a shelf or other resting place before blinking and looking at the group. "Wow, this place is old."

Sable chuckled. "Pretty sure I still win the age contest there. Now come on." She took Ailith by the hand and the group split off as they entered the mosque, Sable and her charge heading toward the women's section while Adem met the imam, a shorter man who greeted them at the door. They exchanged the traditional Islamic greeting before falling into conversation in fluent Arabic as they walked toward the building ahead, and Sable knew they'd made the right choice in splitting the group.

She and Ailith walked sedately toward an adjacent wing

next to the main hall. "This is the women's hall," Sable explained as they walked through arched double doors into a room that was smaller than the main hall, but still well appointed. They shucked their shoes at the door and their sock-covered feet made little sound as they padded across a concrete floor painted a uniform white. Narrow pillars soared into a vaulted ceiling fifteen feet high painted a vivid blue to rival the sky, with gold trim outlining the moulding where earth met heavens. The space felt like a pictorial representation of the sacred balance of earth and sky, and it took Sable aback to find such symbolism in a mosque. She turned to Ailith to ask her a question only to find the girl had wandered toward a door at the back of the hall, where a woman had emerged.

Sable snapped herself free of her musings and hurried to join her charge, catching up just as the girl and the strange woman met. "As-salaam alaikum," the stranger said, inclining her head. Her hijab was a radiant shade of gold, pinned meticulously at the sides to fully cover her hair before flowing down to her shoulders. There they met a long-sleeved overcoat that hung past her knee over loose pants gathered at the ankles, both in shades of deep red. Her face was timeless; she could have been thirty or sixty, though her expression belied great wisdom. "How can I help you?"

"Wa-alaikum-salaam," Sable replied. "We are visiting the city and wished to see the mosque as we passed by—it looked so beautiful from the outside. My husband also had some questions for the imam about some research he's doing." She gestured vaguely in the direction Adem had gone. "Is it permitted? We do not wish to trespass."

The woman smiled broadly in response. "It is encouraged," she replied, slipping her arm into Sable's as if they were old friends. "Please, this way—I will show you what I can and answer any questions you may have." Ailith took Sable's free hand as if to make certain the stranger could not abscond with her friend and followed them as they turned to view the room. "This temple was built in the thirteenth century by some of the earliest Muslims in the area. The room you see before you is the original portion of the building, where prayer services have been held continuously for seven hundred and fifty years." Pausing for effect, the woman turned to her companions to gauge their reactions. "These days it is too small to house everyone, so we use it for women's devotions." Turning toward the door through which she'd emerged she ushered her charges into a dimly-lit hallway broken periodically by ornate wooden arches. As the door clicked shut behind them Sable's view of the hallway flashed, showing her a glimpse of oil lamps hanging from the apexes of each arch before being washed away as she blinked. Ailith's hand tightened around hers and she knew the girl had seen it, too. *Something isn't right here.* They slowed as they followed the woman, who had slipped her hand out of Sable's elbow to open the hallway door and now preceded them soundlessly toward a door at the far end, her bare feet making no sound on the concrete.

"Sable." Ailith's voice was the barest whisper, but felt loud in the near-perfect silence.

Sable shook her head, gesturing for Ailith to stay close as they followed. They passed through another plain-looking door and into a comfortable sitting room, complete with fireplace, overstuffed chairs, and a coffee table set with a tea service. "Can I offer you refreshment?" their hostess asked graciously.

"Thank you, no; we just finished lunch," Sable replied as she checked the room for other exits. There were no windows, and the only entrance seemed to be the door through which they'd come. She opened her mouth to ask a question and was forestalled by the woman before her, whose expression remained placid.

"We may speak freely here, without fear of prying eyes or ears," she began, leaning on a small table in one corner of the room. "I apologize for the need to bring you so far before intro-ducing myself. I am Khaleeda, and I know why you have come." Her gaze shifted to Ailith, who leaned closer to Sable.

"You're not alive," Ailith whispered, "but you're not dead, either. And you're not actually speaking English; our brains are just translating for us."

"Very perceptive," Khaleeda replied with a grin. "You are correct; I am no longer alive, nor am I dead; I exist in between as I await the fulfillment of my purpose." She approached her guests, leaning down in front of the girl to look her fully in the face. "Allah has spoken to me through many signs, and he has told me of your coming. You seek information, a record of the gatekeeper who once lived here, do you not?" Ailith nodded, swallowing, while Sable held her breath, ready to yank her charge backwards out of reach if necessary.

Khaleeda straightened and gestured at the chairs nearby. "Then let us sit and talk, for I know much about him." She sank gracefully into the single chair on the opposite side of the fireplace, leaving Sable and Ailith to the adjoining ones across from her. It was not lost on Sable that she had placed her guests within easy reach of the door. *Perhaps she means no harm. Still don't trust it, though. Stay sharp, old woman.* For a moment she considered calling Adem, then decided to wait and see how the rest of the conversation went. If Khaleeda truly did have information they needed it was worth the risk, and she didn't want the massive stir Adem would cause if he interfered. On the heels of that thought came the mental image of him bursting through an adjoining wall with a yell in the manner of an old television commercial and Sable had to stifle a hysterical chuckle as she turned her full attention back to the conversation.

"His name was Aalim," Khaleeda began in an eerie echo of Ailith's earlier words, "but it was not always thus. He was born to a humble Buddhist family not three kilometers from here during the reign of Ranawijaya, who later called himself Girindrawardhana." She paused as Ailith squirmed into a more comfortable position, then continued. "His mother died giving birth to him, so his father raised him with the help of his family. They were craftsmen, and Aalim found he had a particular talent for carving, like his mother.

"At the age of sixteen he met a girl, the daughter of a merchant who traveled these parts, bringing brightly-colored cloth and spices and leaving with decorative carvings and different spices to trade with the other port towns. Traditionally these stories say that he was struck by her beauty or that her piercing eyes ensnared his soul, but the truth is that they were at odds from the moment they met. Both had been educated enough to debate, and she was Muslim–so they argued at length about God and Buddha and the path of the righteous person." Here she smiled a secretive smile that warmed her eyes as she spoke. "In time, their arguments ran in circles, and they realized that where each had first intended to win the other to their side they now enjoyed the discussion more than the conquest. By the time Aalim was eighteen he had fallen madly in love with her, and she with him. With the blessings of their parents he converted to Islam and they married.

"Aalim was an avid student of his new faith and thirsted for the knowledge and understanding that could be gained from the Quran and its scholars. His wife had been raised in the Sufi tradition and helped guide him on his path to enlightenment, sharing the secrets she had been taught and helping him grow in his understanding of the word of God. Yet this was not enough for Aalim. He desired a place for her to worship, to record the knowledge they shared, and to teach others as they had been taught. There were no mosques within easy distance of their home–and so he built one." Khaleeda spread her arms to encompass the room they occupied as she paused for questions.

Ailith sat, transfixed, as Khaleeda completed her monologue. As the woman finished she cocked her head to one side, looking for all the world like a curious bird. "He built all this for you?"

Khaleeda chuckled. "You are very perceptive for one so young. Yes, he did."

"Why did he leave you here all alone for so long if he loved you so much?" Sable winced at the girl's bluntness.

"Because I asked him to. You see, I loved him very much in return, and when Allah blessed him with a vision that someone would need to stay behind and fulfill a specific purpose, I volunteered. Aalim could not stay himself; as a keeper of the balance between life and death he knew he must move on when his time came or risk the safety of the world."

"So we can't break the rules–whatever they are–or it throws things way off balance."

Khaleeda nodded."As a keeper of this balance, it is given to you to know instinctively how to uphold it. Trust your feelings and they will not lead you astray." With this their host rose and made her way to a shelf lined with cracking parchments. One in particular occupied its own cubby near the top of the unit and she floated upward a foot or so to reach it. "Never could reach that shelf," she remarked with a self-satisfied grin as she resumed her seat. "Aalim left this for you." Khaleeda extended the ancient scroll to Ailith, who leaned forward and took it awkwardly.

"I saw this," she replied. "When we first got here I saw this scroll. Dad's looking for it with the imam." She looked at Sable, her expression belying her worry that she'd said too much.

"I think he'll be just fine regardless," Sable answered with a wink. "How does time work in this little pocket of the universe, Khaleeda?"

"It passes normally when I wish it to. How would you like it to pass?"

"Normally is just fine." Sable rose slowly, not wishing to give offense. "But I'm afraid we should be going. Can't stay in one place too long."

"He said you would be pursued," Khaleeda said as she rose to follow them to the door. "Unto the ends of the earth."

"Did he say whether or not we'd win?" Ailith asked hopefully. Khaleeda chuckled, the dark, rich sound putting them at ease despite the gravity of the topic.

"I'm afraid that's not how his vision worked," she explained. At Ailith's crestfallen expression she laid a hand on the girl's shoulder. "But he would not have left you anything if he did not have hope that you would."

Ailith stopped short of the door. "What will happen to you now? Is your job done?"

"Almost." Khaleeda opened the door and leaned through it as if listening for something. "It is time for you to return to your world—and your father. He will be looking for you soon, as will others, and we must make sure you are all well clear of here before they come." She ushered them through the doorway and back down the hall they'd traversed earlier. There was a gentle urgency to their host's steps that made Sable think their pursuers might not be far behind. Moments later they were back in the large chamber they'd originally entered. A few women had trickled in while they were gone in preparation for afternoon prayers, and Khaleeda visibly relaxed.

"Thank you for your help," Sable began, but was shushed quickly into silence.

"It is I who should thank you," Khaleeda replied, bowing at the waist. "You have allowed me to fulfill my promise to my husband and ensure his legacy lives. Now I have but one more task to complete, which I will do when those who follow you find where you have been. You will be safe for a few more hours after you leave, but you should continue on your journey as soon as possible. Stay ahead of them."

Ailith surprised both women by throwing her arms around Khaleeda. "Thank you," she whispered against the woman's chest. A beatific smile crossed the older woman's features as she hugged Ailith back. "And tell him thank you for us when you see him. It won't be long now."

"You have my word." Khaleeda extricated herself gracefully and propelled them toward the door. "Now go, and may Allah go with you!"

"And with you," Sable replied–only to find their host gone.

Another Hop, Skip, and Jump

Dad!" Ailith bounced up and down and waved at Adem from the other side of the courtyard as he exited the building, still conversing with his host. He looked up and around in alarm, scanning for danger before turning back to the older man beside him and bidding him a warm farewell. It didn't take long for him to cross the courtyard to meet them, brow set in concern.

"What happened?" he asked as he took in Ailith's bursting-to-share expression. "Did you find something? Did something find you?"

"Yes," Sable answered for them both. "And we need to get going; we have a few hours at most. Talk on the way." She gestured for Adem to lead on as they passed back through the entryway and into the street beyond. For a moment Sable saw a flash of the surroundings as they were in Khaleeda's time, with low-slung houses and horses in the streets, and she marveled at the woman's tenacity. *I finally find someone who might can relate to my situation and she's gone before I can get to know her. Par for the course, as they say.* She fought back a wave of disappointment verging on despair as they traversed the thoroughfare. Ailith's voice cut through her melancholy and brought her back to the present in more ways than one as the street morphed back into its modern state.

"Where are we going now?" the girl asked from next to Sable's purse.

"You tell me." She handed Ailith her phone with the map already open.

"What, here? In the middle of the street?!? You said not to do that!"

"You're going to have to learn to do things under duress before long. Now's a good time to practice."

"But walking will make the necklace sway. How am I going to figure out where it's pointing?"

"By telling it to behave and show you what you want to see." Sable winked at her young pupil, who looked back at her dubiously but fished the crystal necklace out from beneath her shirt. Dangling it over the phone's screen she let the motion of her gait swing the crystal in a rough oval around the map. Her heart-shaped face drained of emotion as she focused all her spare energy on determining what the item had to tell her. Adem and Sable feigned innocent contemplation as they continued down the street in an attempt to look casual, but Sable still felt off from their encounter and could feel it bleeding into her countenance as she met the eyes of passersby. "It looks like it's in…Raja… Rajas…Rajasth…"

"Rajasthan?" Sable supplied. "In northwest India?"

"Yeah, Rajasthan." Ailith still stumbled over the unfamiliar word. "How do you know how to pronounce literally everything?"

"Study. What part?" Sable leaned over the phone's screen to peek and followed the crystal to its point, which sat directly on top of…nothing. Sable sighed theatrically. "Of course the thing is in the middle of BFE, rural India. Couldn't be someplace with, I dunno, running water and a hotel, maybe?" Reclaiming her phone with a perfunctory swipe, she caught Adem's eye as he scanned the crowd. "Time to find an exit." He nodded and led them to the northeast, away from the river and the center of town.

Another half hour of walking deposited them at the edge of town. The dirt road they'd traveled on foot continued into the distance with barely a shoulder on either side, and with vehicles passing them every few minutes it didn't feel safe to walk beyond the boundaries of the city. So they waited for a break in traffic and ducked into the thick undergrowth on the south side of the road, passing through into the edge of a fallow field lined with scrub palms and brush. Ailith collapsed onto the ground almost immediately, complaining about her legs and feet and all the walking.

"Best not get too comfortable," Sable said with a raised

eyebrow. "Gonna need you to help with some crop circles here very shortly."

"Uuuugh, can it wait five minutes?" The girl fell backward into what she thought would be a welcoming pile of springy branches and finding instead that they were vines with tiny thorns just big enough to pull at clothing. "I hate this place," she grumbled under her breath.

"I'm not much of a fan, either," Sable opined as she sized up the field. "Lucky for us we're getting out posthaste. Think you two are up to helping with the gate this time?" Ailith perked up at the mention of learning how to gate and sat up straighter. Adem drifted over from his brief survey of their surroundings to listen in. "I'll take that for a yes. All right, remember the hilltop on Guilin where I drew all the things in the dirt?" Both helpers' heads nodded. "We're going to do something similar here, only by stomping down the grass. Here's the pattern we'll use." A few taps on her phone screen brought up a symbol that looked like a stylized number three with a flowing cape and hat.

"That's Om," Adem said, pointing at the screen. "Does it help because it's a sacred Hindu symbol or is there something else about it?"

"It does help that it's a symbol for the cosmic absolute," Sable answered, "but mostly it's just something I associate with India. Gate rituals can be set up one of two ways: either as a way to anchor one side, like I did last time, or as a way to call the desired destination. This is the latter." She began stomping down the tall grass and vegetation nearby, referring to the pattern on her phone every so often for accuracy. The burns on her legs complained with every jarring motion Sable made. She was pretty sure exposing them to the water in the river had been a bad plan and that infection was setting in. *Yeah, well, at least you know it won't kill you. No fever yet, so there's still time.*

Adem joined her, thickening the lines they left. "Won't that leave our pursuers a major clue as to where we went?"

"I'm pretty sure they already know the locations of all these relics," Sable replied as she ground at a difficult root in her way. "Or at least an approximate location, which is why they've been able to anticipate us to an extent. So we won't be giving them anything they don't know. They know we can only gate so far at a jump and that we're looking for the same pieces of the gatekeeper puzzle they are, ergo they already know where to find us."

Adem tilted his head to one side in acknowledgment. "I suppose that makes sense," he admitted, "though I don't like it. We still know very little about whoever is following us, and I hate being at an intel disadvantage."

"You and me both," Sable replied. They completed the rough outline of the Om in relative silence, the rhythmic crunch of the grass beneath their feet calming their thoughts. Ailith took the most joy in the work, making a dance out of the turns and twists as she jumped from side to side to widen the lines, and Sable smiled despite herself. *Can't be doom and gloom all the time, however dark things may be. Almost makes you understand why people have kids in the first place.* Her smile faded. *Now now, no time for that,* she chided herself as she made a more comfortable spot to sit in the exact middle of the piece. *Head in the game, old lady.* She beckoned to Adem and Ailith as she pulled up a satellite image of the exact location they were headed. "Here's our destination," she announced as she tilted the screen so they could view it. Grainy images of yellow sand dotted with rocks greeted them between long, barren stretches of single-lane roadways. Jutting upwards in the middle of the screen was a pile of rocks that looked more intentional than the haphazard formations elsewhere and Sable zoomed in on this chunk of the map, pointing as she did. "My guess is that it's underneath whatever that is. So here's how this is going to work: I'm going to hold that image in my mind as our destination. I want each of you to sit on either side of me with a hand on my shoulder so we don't get separated and lend me whatever strength you can. I'll let you in on my thought processes enough to see what's going on and help all of us focus, but whatever you do, ask before you try anything or we could all end up as cosmic paste. Got it?" Two nods met her statement, both far more trusting than Sable felt she deserved. "All right, let's kick this pig!"

Adem turned to face her as they sat down. "Should we try to find out what we're walking into? In case they're waiting for us where we land?"

Sable shook her head. "No time and not enough energy. We'll need everything we've got to make this jump, so we'll have to make it blind and use the element of surprise to our advantage." Adem grimaced and produced a knife from somewhere on his person, then sat down in a defensive position, ready to stand and fight once they arrived, his unarmed hand resting lightly on Sable's shoulder. On Sable's other side Ailith folded herself into the ground, all knees and elbows, then placed a hand on Sable's other shoulder and nodded. She looked frightened, but determined, and for the first time Sable could see the girl's father in the set of her jaw as she steeled her nerves.

Sable took one last look at the image on her phone then put it to sleep, shoving it back into her duffel. Holding their destination in her mind, she reached out first to Ailith, then Adem, and felt each one of them waiting at the edge of her mind. Her last thought before plunging them into the cosmic maelstrom was a desperate plea to whoever might be listening that they would get there before their enemies.

Then they were gone.

A PROMISE MADE, A PROMISE KEPT

The crowd of worshipers flowed around the tall, dark-haired man on their way to afternoon prayers. No one saw him, but they all felt him; his presence bled into the minds of everyone around him as they entered the mosque. Laughter turned to malice as neighbors cast mistrustful glances at one another before kneeling to pray. As the crowd settled uneasily into their places he strode silently across the main courtyard, sniffing the air like a dog hunting a scent. There it was–traces of those he sought, over by the women's mosque. He made a beeline for the smaller building and slipped through the double wooden doors into the women's area.

"Can I help you?" The voice startled him; no one should have seen or heard him enter, much less been able to speak to him. Turning, he was met by a well-dressed Muslim woman in dated garb resplendent with gold chains and medallions. Her smile was grim as she regarded the man before her. "She's not here, you know. The one you seek."

"You will tell me where to find her," he replied in a raspy voice dripping with ill intent.

"I will do no such thing," Khaleeda declared, "and you will leave my temple and its followers alone."

The man slanted his head to look at her like an owl regarding its dinner. "I must find the girl. You will help me. And your followers…are sheep. My mere presence is enough to make them want to do horrible things to one another. Shall I show you?" He beckoned with one finger to the closest person, a middle-aged woman with two teenagers daughters at her side, and she wandered toward him in a trance. "See? This one wishes she were free of the burden of motherhood." He handed her a wickedly curved knife hilt first and watched as she turned toward her daughters, raising the knife high above her head.

"Stop! I will help you," Khaleeda cried. "Please, just let them go. They've done nothing. Your quarrel is with me."

The knife hovered for a moment in the woman's grip, then clattered to the floor in front of her as she rushed to embrace her children, ushering them off to one side of the room away from Khaleeda and the evil presence she could feel but not see beside her. He gestured for her to lead, then followed as she made her way across the room full of worshipers, neither of them making a sound as they passed. They went through the door at the back of the room that led to her sitting room and the man stopped, staring at his surroundings with mistrust.

"I led them here first," Khaleeda said as she beckoned him further down the hall.

"I do not like this place. You will tell me where I can find them and go no further." The man planted his feet and crossed thin arms across his narrow chest, dark brows lowering above black eyes.

"Ah, but I cannot help you if you do not humor me," Khaleeda said, smiling a cat's grin as she sized up the man before her. "It is not much further." She called his bluff and turned, walking further down the hall. Again the fixtures and decor seemed to flicker back and forth between modernity and antiquity, this time in a menacing gleam of firelight penetrating through the ages and into the lamps above them. Shadows danced a macabre jig as they both stalked down the hall with mismatched shadows dogging their steps. Before long they reached the door to her study, which Khaleeda opened and entered. "Come in and I will show you where they are," she said, gesturing at one of the comfortable chairs before her.

The man hesitated. "I see nothing of use in that room. Come out here and show me or I shall return to the hall and find more of your people to torment." He took a step back to illustrate his point.

"Oh, I don't think you will." A gust of wind set the hallway lamps swinging as it buffeted the man. One of them fell behind him, setting the drapes across the nearby alcove ablaze where it landed, and he took an involuntary step forward. "You'll be coming with me," Khaleeda said, her voice deepening to a low growl as she reached through the door and yanked the surprised intruder into the study. The door slammed shut behind him.

"Who are you?" he asked as he picked himself up off the floor.

"I am Khaleeda, wife of Gatekeeper Aalim and protector of his temple!" A ghostly wind toyed with the ends of her hijab as she raised her arms heavenward. "You have brought evil into the temple he built to house the word and teachings of Almighty God. You have threatened my people with violence and ill will, and you seek the only one who can save the world from eternal damnation." She raised her eyes in supplication and the man before her stirred, seeking to use her distraction to his advantage—only to find himself unable to move. He struggled ineffectually, his mouth hanging open in an unheard scream of frustration. His captor continued undisturbed. "Allah, I call upon you to judge this creature, for he is not of this world and has no claim to life. Return him to the depths of the abyss from which he came! Hold my oaths fulfilled so that I may also rest in Your glory! Allahu akbar!" As she completed her prayer the room began to shake, bits of plaster raining down from the painted ceiling onto their heads and scrolls tumbling off shelves. One wall collapsed and was sucked outward to reveal a stacked stone archway covered in an oil slick sheen. The air between the stanchions shimmered like summer heat over hot pavement, rendering the view beyond it watery and inscrutable. Khaleeda wore an expression of beatific peace as she watched her would-be captor sail across the room toward the exposed portal, clawing for any hold he could find against the suction that claimed the room's contents piece by piece. He latched onto one of the gateway stones and braced one foot against it in an effort to shove his way free of its pull. For a moment it looked as if he would win his way free—until Khaleeda paced across the maelstrom, wind snapping the hem of her dress back and forth until it tore, and gently peeled his fingers from the gate. "It is time, Akoman," she said gently as the man's last foothold slipped and both were propelled deep into the world beyond the gate.

Behind them, the remaining scrolls and loose papers in the study fluttered to the floor.

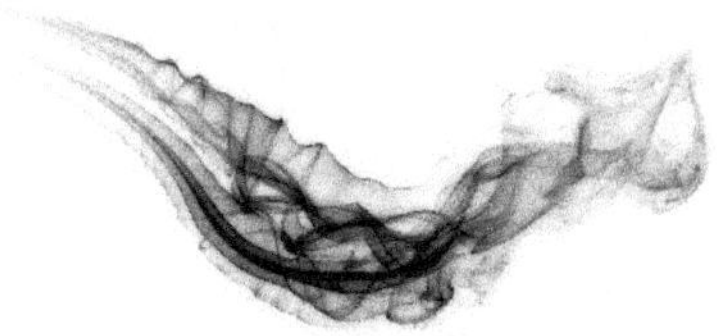

Attrition

"What has happened?" Ahriman's voice held barely-restrained notes of fury as he cast his question across the crowded room. "I sense the passing of Akoman beyond the veil. I need to know why–and how." Silence draped the room as no one dared to speak up, afraid to admit their ignorance. "Have you nothing to say?"

"My lord." A voice rang through the quiescent crowd before him. Ahriman acknowledged the speaker, a young man of average build with dark hair and brown eyes, with a nod. "If I may, I think I speak for all of us when I say that we're at the limit of our resources. We just don't have any more avenues of information." He shrugged in defeat as heads nodded around the room.

Ahriman regarded him with contempt. "Then find more avenues. There are always more places to look."

"With all due respect, sir, we haven't found anything new since we got that old computer."

"And you have no leads from it? Nothing useful from what we found in the house?"

"Nothing beyond some very strange kinks and an interest in the occult, sir."

"What about her credit card history? False addresses? Patterns that may emerge from the data?"

"Our AI is digesting it all, sir, but in the meantime we don't have anything else to go on. It's like this woman had a life decades ago and then just disappeared."

"Perhaps that is what she did." Ahriman leaned his head on one hand, his boredom obvious. "You say she had an interest in the occult; I think you'll find it's more than a passing one given her actions so far. I suggest you start looking for ways she's accomplishing whatever feats she's managed. You may use my personal library for research, as I doubt you will find what you need anywhere else. Now go, and do not return until you have answers." The young man bowed and backed out of the room, followed by the rest of the crowd.

Ahriman rubbed his throbbing temples. Human hosts were always so fragile and inconvenient, but they allowed him to stay in the realm of the living longer than he could otherwise. *This body needs something. What is it?* He walked through his morning routine, recalling that he'd forgotten to feed upon waking. Eating was one thing he felt humanity had gotten right, and the thought of finding a good meal enticed him out of his armchair. Perhaps by the time he'd finished eating he'd have an update from his researchers; if not he might have to consider replacing a few. In his experience workers found it motivating to see their kin crushed before them for their failures.

Smiling, he pressed the elevator button to take him to the top floor.

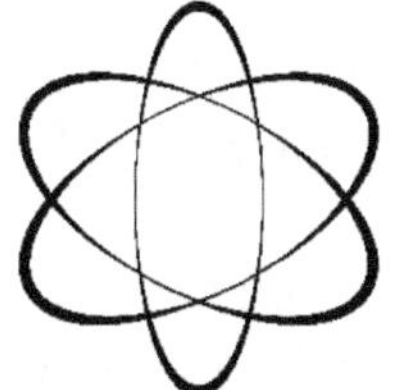

Don't Pick Fights With Physics

It was interminably bright where they'd landed. After the absolute darkness of folded space-time anything would be blinding, but this was particularly painful; the way the sun reflected off of every surface in sight without reprieve kept all of them blinking tears out of their eyes for a full half minute before they could take stock of their surroundings. Adem was the first to recover, declaring their immediate area clear of obvious danger before helping first Ailith, then Sable to their feet. Cursing herself for her lack of foresight, Sable reached into her duffel bag and produced sunglasses for all three of them, donning hers and sighing in relief as the terrain around them revealed itself. They stood on a flat sand-covered plane dotted with rocks and occasional desert scrub. In the distance she was just able to make out the thin ribbon of a road running west to east, but no cars were visible in either direction.

"Well," Sable croaked through parched lips, "looks like we're not far from our destination." She pointed at a rock formation a good hundred yards to their west that was too regular to be natural.

"You call that 'not far?'" Ailith asked as she cast her eyes sidelong at Sable, who snorted in response.

"When you fold the universe in on itself to get us somewhere and get us within even a mile of where you're going you can give me crap about accuracy. Until then, be glad this is all you have to walk." Producing a bottle of water from within the duffel, Sable handed it to Ailith, then offered another to Adem, who accepted it with a gracious nod as they set out toward their destination. "Speaking of locations, Ailith, what do you see about this one? Anything we can use?"

The girl's eyes unfocused and her steps slowed as she considered before responding. "Not yet," she replied hesitantly, "but there's something about those rocks we're walking toward that's familiar." She turned to glance behind them and slowed even more, taking her father's hand to keep from falling. "It gets colder out here at night, doesn't it?"

"A bit, yes," Sable replied offhand as she pulled a scarf from her bag to wrap around her head. The sun beat down on her dark hair and gave the impression it was trying to bake her brain like a potato in a jacket without a head covering. Without being asked she pulled a second scarf from her bag and handed it without comment to Adem, who took it and wrapped it around his head in a practiced fashion, leaving his neck covered as well. "Why do you ask?" Sable pulled a third scarf from her bag and draped it over Ailith's head as she backtracked to check on the girl.

"Because that explains why they're wearing long sleeves in the dark." The words sent chills up Sable's spine. Ailith turned and started back toward the ruins they planned to search as if nothing were out of the ordinary, leaving Sable and Adem up catch up.

"You mean tonight?" Adem asked as he drew alongside her.

"Yeah," Ailith answered. "Pretty sure it's tonight. Three of them are supposed to watch us and see if we find what we're here for."

"Are they armed? What did they look like? Do you know what time they'll arrive?" The questions peppered Ailith in rapid succession and she struggled to keep up.

"Yes, like people walking in a desert with a lot of clothes kind of like us only with robes instead of jeans, and no. Just after dark sometime." She thought for a moment, then added, "I think one of them can do magic."

"Lucky for us all three of us can, though I'll admit to being pretty bushed," Sable answered as they approached the first stack of wind-battered stones that signified prior human occupation. They were darker than the surrounding sand and worn smooth by centuries of sandblasting. Ailith ran a hand over the surface of the topmost stone and had to reach out to Sable, who was closest, for support.

"This place is really old," she said as she caught her breath and steadied her legs. "Like, probably older than you."

"Depends; I'm pretty old," Sable replied. "You okay?" Using her second sight she surveyed the area to see what might have drawn the girl in. The veil between worlds was thinner here, but not due to death or trauma; it was simply what Sable referred to as a thin place. They cropped up around the world and usually were harmless beyond generating plenty of ghost stories and cautionary tales.

"I'm good." Ailith dusted off her pants and skirted the stack of stones, casting about for something. "I know it has to be here somewhere…" She bent down and brushed at the sand next to the rocks with her bare hands until a long, flat piece presented itself. "Ha! Knew it was here."

Adem, who had been on high alert since Ailith's earlier vision, peered down at the dark-colored stone through his sunglasses. "Magic takes the shape of the wielder's will…" he mumbled, crouching down over the elongated stone taking shape beneath the sand. "What's under here, Ailith?"

"Dunno. All I know is it's important and really, really old." She looked sidelong at Sable, who chuckled at the implied humor.

Adem stood as if he'd made a decision. "I want to try something," he declared, "but I'd feel safer if both of you stepped back a bit first."

"What's your plan?" Sable asked warily as she and Ailith backed up.

"I've been reading a lot lately about ground-penetrating radar as an archaeological tool," Adem explained as he trod a circle around the rock post. "I bet it would be helpful here, but we obviously don't have thousands of dollars of specialized equipment on hand. What we do have is magic." He ran a hand through his hair. "It still feels really strange to say that."

Sable ruminated, head tilted to one side and lips pursed. "Should work," she announced after a moment, "though you'll have to be careful not to put too much juice into it or you'll risk damaging whatever's down there." Adem nodded, then focused inward as he faced the stones, laying a hand atop the small pillar and lifting one foot. He brought it down hard on the sand just behind the elongated stone they'd uncovered and Sable watched a wave of force travel through the ground, vibrating the smallest rocks on the surface as it passed. What followed was a radar pulse of information revealing a chamber just past where they stood–the long stone was the lintel of a long-buried doorway that bordered a short staircase down to the main opening. It wasn't large, and one whole section of the stairs was covered in rubble that would need to be cleared before they could safely pass.

Adem turned around with a look of boyish triumph. "Did you see that? Tell me you saw that." He bent down to brush more of the sand off the lintel.

"That was wicked, Dad!" Ailith exclaimed as she bent down to help.

"Well done indeed," Sable chuckled. Her mind strayed back to when she'd first mastered her understanding of the power she carried and the intense satisfaction that came with success. *Still never gets old watching other people find that, too.* "It seems you have something of an affinity for working with the earth, Adem. Which means I should also point out that you're doing that the hard way." She pointed out their slow progress on uncovering the rest of the door lintel.

They stopped abruptly. "What do you suggest?" Adem asked as he considered the yards of earth between them and their goal. The sun was fast dropping toward the horizon, putting a damper on the jovial atmosphere of accomplishment they'd discovered.

"You did well coming up with the ground-penetrating radar idea; what else is in that big brain of yours that might work?"

Adem stared at the ground before him as if his gaze alone could bore a hole through it. "I have an idea," he said finally after a few minutes of poking about. "But you'll definitely want to step back for this one. The ground could get unstable as it shifts."

"A word of caution for you," Sable warned. "I'm still pretty low on energy from gating us here. Ailith is a hair's breadth from slipping back to the other side where we stand right now. If you overextend yourself on this we won't be able to help much, so you'll have to be very careful." He nodded, swallowing, and turned to his work as Sable and Ailith moved clear of the area.

Sending one more small radar pulse through the earth Adem began to shift the sand, piling it up in a growing dune behind the entrance to the stairs as they revealed themselves. The stairs matched the lintel in color and smoothness, giving the impression they had been worked and placed at the same time. As the door frame appeared they could see that it was still structurally sound despite–or perhaps because of–its time buried in the desert sands. Hope that the rest of the tunnel downward was just as well built bloomed in Sable's chest as the space was emptied of its contents; the brightness of the afternoon penetrated far enough into the growing hole that they could see supports placed down its length all the way to the pile of rubble close to the entrance of the chamber at the end.

Adem paused his work to inspect the tunnel and declared it safe to traverse down to the rock pile blocking their way. Sable and Ailith joined him, the three of them poking cautiously at the blockage. "It looks intentional," Adem stated as they surveyed the ceiling above them. "This corridor was sealed at some point. That should mean the roof will be stable once we remove the blockage, though I don't trust it given the age of the structure."

"Mm." Sable nodded in agreement. "Best be prepared to catch it just in case. You want us here in the tunnel so we can help if we're needed?"

"I don't much like it, but yes," Adem replied. "This is definitely work, and I can tell I'm starting to tire. If we group up we're less likely to get separated if anything does go wrong." Ailith scooted up to her father's right side and under one arm while Sable stood as close as possible without actually touching him; she had no desire to be an unfamiliar distraction in any way as Adem learned to use powerful forces he'd just discovered. The stakes were too high.

He blew out a deep breath. "Here goes nothing." One by one the smaller rocks began to tumble out of the wall before them, sliding up and out of the tunnel of their own accord. Bigger and bigger rocks followed until two waist-high stacked boulders were all that blocked their path. Adem dripped sweat despite the coolness of the tunnel as the boulders before them shifted, rolling ponderously up the stairs one at a time to join their companions in the desert heat above. Sable and Ailith craned their necks and were able to see past them into the circular room beyond as the way cleared just enough for them to see and light trickled in through the openings.

A cracking sound shot through the tunnel as the final hallway support buckled, unused to supporting its own weight after centuries of help, and the boulders stopped rolling as Adem threw a hand upward to stop it falling atop the group. "Get inside!" he shouted at Sable and Ailith, who scooted past the boulders and Adem and into the room beyond. Debris was sifting through the ceiling tiles and onto the floor in the small cavern they entered.

"Not sure this is much more stable," Sable called over her shoulder. "Might want to shift focus if you can and shore this up!"

Adem's hands shifted, the boulders forgotten on the staircase as he turned toward the room beyond. "If I drop this support the whole thing will come down," he panted as the sand stopped floating down through the ceiling. "It's connected to the room. I have…to fix…both…" Grunting, he fell to one knee under the weight of the earth above him.

Sable dropped to her knees in front of him and placed a hand on either side of his face, fingers pressing into his temples. "Let me in," she commanded, waiting for his nod before plunging herself into the forces at work around them. A distant sensation screamed at her that she was still overtired from gating, which she summarily ignored as irrelevant. *Can't let this curse kill Adem and Ailith just to keep me alive. I. Won't. Let. It.* This last thought echoed through both of their minds as she traced through Adem's working to find its weak points.

"Stop fighting physics and go around it!" she declared, shifting the working so that it would change the form of what it affected instead of moving it. "Sometimes the answer is reshaping something into the form you need, not just bullying it into doing what you want." Understanding dawned in Adem's mind and he changed his focus to reshaping the stone before him, finding it easier to manipulate it into a different pattern. Sable opened her eyes and watched the ceiling tiles fuse into a smooth, curved plane above their heads that swept down to the floor and attached to it, creating an elliptical bubble that distributed the weight of the sand above it across its surface. It was a brilliant engineering shift, and she mentally applauded his idea as he thickened and reinforced the stone that now encased the room. *Have to keep them safe.* Sable wasn't sure if the thought was hers or Adem's as she realized she still shared his mind—and that he had severely overextended himself. As the last of the stone fused and went still he turned into a rag doll, pitching headfirst into Sable, who caught his head before it hit the unforgiving cavern floor.

Everything went dark, and at first Sable thought she'd also overextended to the point she passed out, but she realized she could still feel the stone beneath her. She shifted herself so that Adem's head was in her lap and reached into the duffel she still wore, digging around and cursing until a flashlight appeared beam-first; apparently the bag was feeling more helpful than usual. Shining the light around the space revealed that they were in an enclosed cavern roughly the size of an average hotel room that contained a stone table fused to the floor in the middle. One wall was covered in ancient paintings that still bore bright pigments despite their age and Ailith was drawn to it as a moth to a flame, ignoring her father and Sable as she stood before the mural in contemplation. Sable could see there was something different about it but was too tired to study it for long. Besides, she had larger problems, such as the boneless sack of stubborn masculinity occupying her lap.

She managed to get Adem's unconscious form untwisted to the point where he wouldn't wake up stiff and sore—or at least not any moreso than passing out on a stone floor allowed—and opted to leave his head resting in her lap out of a desire to keep tabs on his breathing and pulse. Even overtired as she was she could check his vitals with a thought if she was in physical contact and she was concerned she might need to intervene if he'd pushed himself too far. Ailith was still engrossed in the mural dominating the room, so it was up to Sable to take stock of their surroundings and determine their next steps. She started with herself, gauging her own reserves and physical state before moving on to the room around them. *I'm still pretty drained, and these burns just won't quit.* The constant pressure of Adem's inert form and the sandy conditions had aggravated them to the point where they were throbbing, but Sable had no energy left to heal them. *Sure would be nice to have some kind of spiritual battery I could use or something.* An image of a small, stylized snake painted on the mural before them caught her eye and brought to mind the goddess of healing her people had worshiped centuries before. *Maybe she's still around; I could really use her help right now. I'm pretty sure these burns are infected and it's a matter of time before fever sets in.* It might have been wishful thinking, but the slow thrumming of pain in her legs seemed to lessen as she sent up a silent prayer.

Sable turned her attention to the rest of the room they occupied. They had the gear they'd brought in, their own clothing, the duffel, and a bare stone table. *Okay, that's not too bad given that I still have my bag.* Outside was an unforgiving desert for miles in every direction that would contain hostile occupants come nightfall. *At least they'll have a devil of a time getting inside here. Maybe we can hole up long enough to get out before they manage to get in.* Sable decided she didn't have the strength to do much about what was outside and focused her problem solving instead on the immediate problems of food, water, and clean air. The room was completely sealed; she judged they had some hours' worth of oxygen before they started the decline into hypoxia. Judging that to be the most immediate threat she started searching through her bag once again. Leaves tickled her hands. "Very funny," she grumbled as she tried to reach past them to the rest of the bag's contents. The leaves got thicker. "Now is not the time for lessons in decor," she snarled, yanking at the branches of what turned out to be a medium-sized potted ficus tree. As it cleared the bag she realized the duffel was trying to help buy them time and immediately felt bad about snapping at it. *Don't know why; it's just a bag, after all.* But the bag had gotten her through some very tight scrapes in her time, and she felt guilty for not showing it more gratitude over the years. "Sorry," she grumbled at it as she shoved the ficus toward the closest wall. "I know you're just trying to help. Would be nice if you had some oxygen tanks or a path to fresh air in there, though." In answer the hair around her face began to float in the slightest breath of wind. "I'll be damned," she said softly. "We may make it out of this yet." Turning as much as she was able she called to Ailith, "What do you see?"

"Nothing yet except the pictures in the painting, but I know there's more–I just have to find it. How's my dad?" She didn't even turn Sable's direction to respond.

Sable checked in on the patient. "Breathing's a bit shallow, but pulse is good, as is heart rate. Blood pressure is a bit high and he'll have one hell of a headache when he comes to, which won't be for at least another hour, best guess."

"Mhmm." Ailith continued her study of the wall.

"You don't look too concerned," Sable added when nothing else was forthcoming.

"That's because I know he'll survive."

"How do you–oh. Dumb question." After a moment, Sable's curiosity got the best of her. "How often do you See things about us?"

"Not often. Sometimes." Ailith turned an uncanny gaze on Sable that went right through her. "Usually general things, like whether or not we make it out of a situation or who lives and who doesn't." She shifted her focus to her father and her expression softened before returning to Sable. "Sometimes it's just a feeling without anything specific. Ah ha!" She turned back to the wall and scanned it with a finger, tracing an outline across multiple images. Figures stood around a table similar to the one in the room that contained a human who was strapped down and bleeding. The background was split and painted solid, one side white, one side black, and one of the figures held a wicked blade in one hand that dripped with blood. "Nine figures…one sacrifice…" The girl mumbled under her breath as she studied the image further.

With Ailith occupied and their ability to breathe oxygenated air taken care of, Sable turned next to food and water. It occurred to her that processing either one would result in a less livable enclosure if they didn't find a way to keep things clean. The ever-helpful duffel produced an old chamber pot, which

Sable freed herself up long enough to use and incinerate the contents before resuming her vigil over Adem. She was pleased to see that his vitals were normalizing faster than she'd expected with the amount of energy he'd expended and hoped the bag could provide at least a bit of sustenance when he awoke. She played back the events of the afternoon in her mind. He'd held up the entire structure they were in after clearing dirt and debris and using his abilities to find the cavern, all of which put together would have been too much for every experienced practitioner she'd met in the last five hundred years. *Who are you really?* she wondered as she studied his profile from her current vantage point. With his features relaxed he looked years younger, and Sable wondered what he'd been like before life had sent him down the path he trod. There was a wonderment in him that so many people lost as adults; it was what allowed him to solve problems in such creative ways, but it was easily crushed under the weight of life's burdens. She'd seen it time and again: the brightest almost always burned the shortest. A fierce desire to spare him that fate stabbed at her soul, etching a mark there she could no longer ignore. *What are you getting yourself into, Sable? Everything with people always ends in heartbreak. You know this.* But she laid a hand on his shoulder nonetheless as he shifted fitfully in his sleep and watched him relax back into restful slumber.

Across the room Ailith smiled as she went about her work.

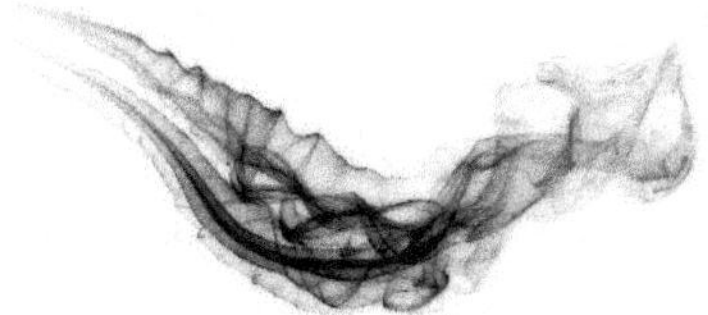

Watchers

A rickety truck sped down the desert road toward the deepening sunset carrying three men and their gear. The driver, a broad, swarthy man in his mid-30s, squinted his eyes as the sun crept below the visor. His only companion in the cab was a man of medium build with a similar dark complexion and black hair. This second figure appeared average in every way–average height, average build, a face neither ugly nor attractive–which combined with the studiously blank expression on his face generated an unsettling impression. But it was their third companion who truly set people on edge. He reclined in the bed of the truck, back to the cab as his bright blue eyes surveyed the road behind them. In these parts he stuck out like a sore thumb; few tourists made it this far into the Thar Desert despite the multiple historical sites available to visit, and it was painfully obvious he was no local. He cared not for people's opinions, but it did make it harder to keep a low profile when he was the only pale-skinned person in sight. Besides, his unusual appearance wasn't what bothered people, though most attributed their discontent to his counterculture clothing and rotating hair colors. Nor was it his slouched bearing and devil-may-care attitude that in anyone else his apparent age would be passed off as part of a rebellious phase; no, they sensed a far greater influence at work, though none of them could perceive it.

He recalled the last conversation he'd had with their master before leaving for this mission, combing through it for any hidden meaning or possible leverage. "My Lord Ahriman," he'd begun, "how may I be of service?" He knew why he'd been summoned, but he wanted to hear it in the other man's words.

"I want you to keep watch," Ahriman answered as he paced back and forth in his office, hands behind his back. "The girl and her father are being helped by someone, a woman of some power, and she is making it difficult for us to procure what we seek. I'm sure you know we've lost three warriors beyond the gate." He'd paused for effect before continuing. "I see no reason to continue throwing resources at a losing prospect. They will eventually acquire what we both need–and then they will come to us of their own accord. Until then, I want them watched and every piece, every scrap of information that can be found passed on to me. Do you understand, Nanghait?"

"I do, my lord." Before bowing his head in deference he'd seen a calculating expression flit across his master's face. "I will not fail you."

"See that you don't. I have faith in your competence –and your restraint." He'd been dismissed then and left immediately for India, where they knew the next piece of the puzzle to be. *But there is more to this. I know there is.*

"Nanghait!" A fist banged on the half-open back window of the truck to get his attention. "Where are we going? You haven't told us where to stop yet."

"A bit further," he replied as he reached out with his senses. They were getting close; he ought to be able to feel it by now. There–southwest of their current location he picked up a strange sensation that pulled at him. "Turn off within the next half mile. Go south."

"There's no road," complained the driver. "We'll get stuck!"

"Let me worry about that." Nanghait shifted both of his manicured hands from their position atop his knees onto the bed of the truck as they left the packed earth roadway. The tires started to dig into the softer sand before miraculously gaining enough traction for steerage as they struck out off the beaten path. After a few minutes the road they'd left behind was a ribbon in the distance as they approached a small hillock of freshly-piled sand. "Stop here," Nanghait instructed from the back, dropping the effect that kept the tires free and allowing them to bog down into the dunes. He hopped over the wheel well before they'd fully stopped and surveyed the scene before them. To the east and south was a vast wasteland with little to define it; no vehicles or beasts of burden were visible, which matched with what he'd been told about how the group had been traveling from location to location. Three sets of footprints appeared heading west, directly toward the odd rock formation he could just see in the distance. It stood next to the miniature dune they'd fixated on as their landmark of choice, but there was no activity that he could see nearby. Still, the footprints lead straight to it. *And now we wait.* Nanghait swung himself back up into the truck bed where his backpack waited. "Get comfortable for a while," he ordered the other two, who were just getting out of the vehicle, weapons in hand. "And put those away; we're just here to watch." *Unless someone does something extremely rash, of course.*

Digging through his bag produced a small bag of mixed nuts, which he snacked on as his companions joined him in the truck's bed. The sun had just touched the horizon, painting the sky a myriad of colors to contrast the monotony of the desert sands below it, and the three of them sat in silent contemplation of it for a long while. As the last rays of sunlight sank below the horizon Nanghait produced a pair of night vision goggles for each of them so that they could keep watch through the hours of darkness. A chill crept into the air as they waited, illustrating why everyone around them wore long sleeves and head coverings—it wasn't just to keep the sun off of hair and skin, though it worked for both purposes. They settled in for the long haul, taking turns on watch as the others made themselves comfortable and waited for their prey to make a move.

Evil Has a Name

Sable could feel the day slipping away from them despite the lack of sunlight. Her flashlight had started to die, so she'd replaced it with a globe of soft light as her ability to channel power without pain returned. Ailith was in the process of drawing an annotated copy of what was on the wall before them and as best Sable could tell was doing a bang-up job of it; the girl was talented, no doubt about it. Adem had fully stabilized and she was beginning to wonder how much longer he'd sleep when he stirred. She'd extricated herself as soon as his breathing and blood pressure had regulated themselves out of a desire not to feed whatever was going on with her unstable emotions. Her plan after this was still to disappear from the world again in hopes of achieving her goal this time, so close connections were a no-no. Still, sitting alone on the cave floor felt much emptier than she'd thought it would. *What do you expect? You've been alone for eighty years. Any human contact is going to feel really nice, but you can't get used to it.*

"How's it coming?" she asked Ailith by way of distraction from her current chain of thought.

"Good. I think I've worked out how they plan on doing the ritual; it looks like someone else tried this before a really long time ago. See this?" She pointed at the knife dangling from one of the figures' hands. "It's not just any knife; it's made of one of the gate stones, and I'm pretty sure this guy–" she pointed at the bound figure on the table "–was a gatekeeper." She shuddered.

Sable unfolded herself from where she sat and walked over to Ailith, placing a hand on her shoulder. "We're not going to let that be you." Swallowing, Ailith nodded and turned to throw her arms around Sable's neck. *I forget she's only eleven sometimes.* She reached around the girl's dainty shoulders and held her for a moment while she regained her composure. *It's not just Adem worming his way into your heart, is it?* Looking up she caught Adem watching the two of them as he pulled himself upright, finally conscious. For a brief moment the three of them felt deeply connected in a way Sable hadn't experienced in centuries and she was keenly aware that the pain of their eventual loss was written on her timeless features. Closing her eyes against the ache in her chest she let Ailith pull away from her and averted her gaze from Adem's now-penetrating stare. Sable drew herself upright with effort and strode across the room to her bag. "How's that head?" she asked Adem without looking at him, her voice sounding rough even to her own ears.

"It's been better," he admitted, rubbing at his temples. She shoved a water bottle at him along with a package of peanut butter crackers and continued to dig around in the duffel with purpose.

"These will help." He took them bemusedly and she heard the packaging crinkle as he opened it. "Where on earth, or wherever this thing keeps stuff, is that bowl? I know I haven't used it in a while, but it should be…ah ha!" Reaching in with both hands she drew out a wide-mouthed stoneware bowl polished to a gloss on the inside. "Right where I left it."

"What is that?" Adem asked around a mouthful of crackers.

"A scrying bowl." She pulled another bottle of water out of the duffel and dumped its contents into the bowl, setting it on top of the stone table behind them. "It's high time we started figuring out what's really going on here." Placing her hands on either side of the bowl she leaned over the top, clearing her mind of everything but her burning desire for information and focusing on the area outside of their current shelter. The reflection in the bowl shifted with pleasing alacrity to show the terrain they'd crossed to get there. The sun had dropped below the horizon, and in the twilight they could see the outline of a truck sitting bogged down in the sand a half mile from their location. Two men were visible in the bed, one prone and possibly sleeping, one sitting up and alert with a pair of night vision goggles. A third sat up in the cab looking bleary-eyed. Sable zoomed in on the figure sitting up in the truck bed to get a better feel for who he might be. Something about him made her uneasy even through her scrying, and she almost dropped the connection before getting a good look at his face. He wore long-sleeved robes like the other two figures, but his features and skin tone were fine-boned and pale, with striking blue eyes visible even in the dim lighting as he pulled the goggles from his sight–and looked straight at Sable.

"That's him!" Ailith exclaimed next to her, almost startling her out of her scrying. "Man, he's way hotter than I thought."

"The dangerous ones usually are," Sable replied ruefully. "Adem, I need your brain and that book I lent you." Her gaze never shifted from the scrying bowl as she heard him shuffle around the side of the room to dig in his pack.

"I gave it back to you," he answered after coming up empty.

"Then it's in the bag," she said as she watched the stranger watching her in the reflection, studying him for identifying marks or actions.

"But…that's your bag." Adem's uneasiness was clear in his voice.

"Oh, it knows you well enough by now to behave itself, don't you, bag?" It opened itself in answer, leaning toward Adem. "Good…thing." He reached gingerly into the bag, feeling around until something was shoved into his hand. A piece of clothing emerged that looked like a short corset with bows on each shoulder strap. "He does not need early nineteenth century lingerie, thank you very much," Sable growled without even looking up. "He needs a reference book. What has gotten into you?" Adem cast the corset aside with two fingers and reached back in with more purpose. This time his hand emerged with the book she'd lent him on the plane mere days ago. "Find the section on daevas," she instructed as the figure in the water smiled and her gut twisted in unintelligible ways. She heard Ailith's breath catch next to her and gently shoved the girl further away from the bowl. "Let me handle this one, Ailith." Pages rustled to her left as Adem searched for the correct section and Sable's unease deepened. She could feel the stranger's influence pulling at her emotions; desire, inferiority, unhappiness at her current situation, and a host of other feelings clamored for her attention as she stared at him through the water.

"Got it–what do you need?" Adem's voice cut through the emotional assault, snapping her back to herself.

"Start reading names and descriptions. Keywords only, if you can manage it."

"Okay…let's start with Akoman, daeva of evil thought." Sable shook her head. "Indar, daeva who freezes the minds of the righteous." Another head shake. "Nanghait, daeva of discontent."

"That's him." She was certain of it; the unease, the strange smile, all of it fit too well to be anything else. Adem joined her by the bowl and glared at the man, committing his features to memory. Sable could feel Nanghait's influence start to seep through the connection again and closed it, stepping around Adem and emptying the bowl on the floor before putting it back into the bag. "Ailith, what's our next location?" She handed the girl her phone, map at the ready, and turned to finish packing up the few things they'd gotten out since arriving. The ficus didn't want to fit back into the bag until she fussed at it for giving her something living she didn't want to just leave in a desert. By the time Ailith returned her phone with a location marked the cave was just as bare as it had been when they started.

They clustered around Sable's phone and stared at a highly recognizable title written in both Arabic and English: The Museum of Egyptian Antiquities. "Cairo–I may have some contacts there," Adem exclaimed. "It's been a few years, but if they're still in the area I'd trust them with my life."

"Let's hope you don't have to." Sable tapped a finger on her chin. "I take it that means you've spent some time there?"

He nodded. "Spent a few months there in the service."

"Think you can give me a good feel for a place to gate us that's safe?"

"I think so, but we'll need to land outside of town and work our way in." He gave her a measuring look. "You sure you're up for it this close together? I'm not sure how much help I can be this time."

"It helps that you have a recent connection there, in relative terms. And yes, I'll be fine." She brushed off his concern and rolled her shoulders, cracking her neck before turning to face Adem for the first time since he awakened. "Ready?"

"As I'll ever be," he said resignedly. Sable reached toward his temple, waiting for his acknowledgment before touching it lightly. As she did she slammed her own mental walls into place to keep her recent revelations from filtering in along with her surface thoughts. Risking her own heart was bad enough; she didn't want to drag him along through the emotional morass that was her very long life. He must have noticed a difference because he narrowed his eyes and tagged a question onto the end of the information he sent her. *:We're not going back to hiding things, are we?:* The openness of his own mind to her was an accusation in and of itself. Knowing she couldn't lie to him directly she cut their connection and turned to look for her bag. He caught her by the wrist before she could take a single step. "I need to know what we're walking into." *:And I need to know how far you're willing to go with us.:* The thought bounced around the echo chamber she'd left open at the forefront of her mind. *:You're already planning on leaving.:*

:I am with you to the end, whatever form that takes.: Sable let the force of her conviction slip through before shuttering her mind again and pulling her wrist from his grasp. "You probably know better than I what we're likely to find where we land," she said out loud.

He chuckled. "More sand." Sable reached out for Ailith's hand and loosened her death grip on her emotions just enough to keep the girl from picking up on her current state of mind as Adem linked hands with his daughter. Ailith looked back and forth between the two of them with questions in her eyes as Sable channeled the full force of her angst into twisting the universe into submission once again. She had to admit it felt good to have a purpose, especially a non-selfish one, and she chose to focus on that as she flung them once again through space-time.

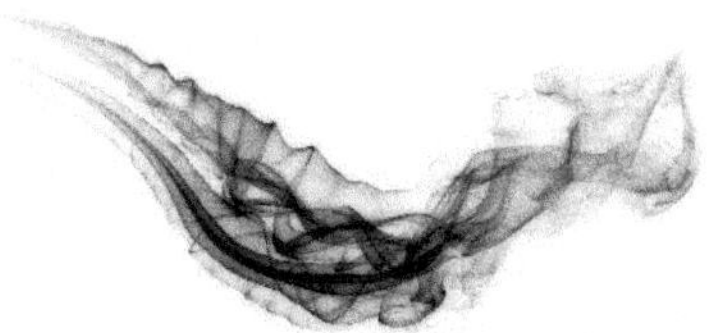

Nanghait folded his goggles and shook the sleeping figure beside him awake as he pulled out a cell phone. "They've moved again," he spoke into it as soon as the call connected. "Get me eyes in Khartoum, Cairo, and Lima." He paused. "No, don't let on that we're watching. Do not engage." He hung up and cuffed the still-waking man next to him to get his attention. "Get us back to the main road."

"How do you know they've left?" the third man asked from beside the truck.

"I no longer feel their presence." Nanghait settled back down into the truck bed, placing his hands on the rusting metal. "We'll catch up to them wherever they're headed. They'll need to hole up for a while after this." He held on as the truck sped off toward the nearest town.

MORE SAND

They landed in the middle of a barren gorge walled on either side with sandstone. The sun hadn't quite dipped below the horizon here; they'd shifted far enough west to chase it down. Its warmth suffused the rocks and sand around them as they searched for stable footing. Sable dropped to a knee, feeling sudden exhaustion set in once again. *Felt that way far too often lately.* Adem offered her a hand up, which she ignored in favor of pulling energy from the sun-warmed rocks around her to help fuel her muscles. She also ignored his frown as they got their bearings. "Where to from here?" she asked.

Adem squinted at the sun. "Northwest," he replied, turning down the broad, well-traveled trail before them. Ailith glanced back and forth between them once more with a quizzical brow before following her father. She slipped her hand into his as Sable stumbled along after them. After a quarter mile or so of looking back every few steps Ailith dropped back to walk with Sable. "You okay?" she asked as she shortened her stride to match.

"Yep," Sable replied, concentrating on putting one foot in front of the other. Even the strength she could borrow from her surroundings was fading fast. They continued in silence for a few moments before Ailith tried again.

"Dad's worried," she pronounced. "He hasn't said it, but I can tell. I think he's worried about you."

"I'm a big girl." They were starting up a mild grade and Sable saved the rest of her breath for the climb. Ailith stayed with her until they reached the top, then skipped ahead to catch up with Adem, who had pulled away during the last few minutes. She tugged at his sleeve and he glanced backward, doing a double take as he realized how far behind Sable had fallen. He stopped and waited for her to catch up.

Sable was breathing hard by the time she topped the gentle

slope. "Keep…going," she said as she leaned over to catch her breath. "I'll catch up…eventually."

Adem sighed. "It's a two mile hike to the trailhead from here," he said as he sat down on a large rock. "And we have another half mile of walking after that." He pointed at another nearby rock and indicated she should sit down. Deciding discretion was the better part of valor, Sable plopped herself down and allowed herself a rest. An awkward silence stretched between them as she racked her brain for ways to speed up her progress. Unfortunately, overextending oneself was like drinking too much; the only true way to feel better was time. She'd need some physical assistance to help her get by.

Wind scythed down the gorge as it had since they'd arrived, only this time Sable took notice of it. She reached into the bag and produced a long board with wheels, then a pole, and finally an odd-shaped triangular cloth. "Is that…" Adem began with an eyebrow raised.

"A sailboard," Sable finished. "Haven't used it in years, but it ought to work just fine." She struggled to screw the pole into the board until a larger set of hands took it and secured it properly, hanging the sail as they finished. "Should be plenty of wind for it," she continued as if nothing had happened. Adem tested its sturdiness by stepping on and bouncing up and down.

"Seems solid," he pronounced. "Hop on." Ailith took his hand and jumped onto the craft while he held the sails in check. Sable took her time getting on, notably without an offer of assistance. All three took hold off the center pole as Adem let the sail unfurl—and the craft jumped forward, nearly dumping Sable off the back. A hand shot out and grabbed her wrist at the last moment from around the pole and pulled her close enough to wrap her arms around it. "Can you hold on?" Adem called over the sound of the wind rushing past.

"I think so," she answered as she held on for dear life. *I don't recall this being quite so harrowing last time I did it.* Adem kept one hand on the mast as he skillfully steered the craft using the angle of the sail and his weight. "I see you've done this before," Sable remarked.

"It's been a while," he answered as they dodged large

rocks. "Seems it's like riding a bike." They went quiet as the gorge sped past, Adem focusing on driving and Ailith and Sable doing their best to stay on board. As the trailhead appeared around a curve Adem cast about for something to stop them. "Where's the brake?" he yelled over the wind.

"There isn't one," Sable answered. "Just stop the wind! Or reverse it, if you're in a hurry." She watched as Adem dropped the sail and struggled to find a way to stop the forces pushing the craft forward, managing to redirect them for a moment before losing control. *Looks like he'll need help with this one.* Sable grabbed the hand that was still attached to the center pole and shoved information at him rapid-fire; winds were something she'd grasped intuitively from a young age, and while she was good at manipulating them, she was awful at teaching people how. In response he simply let go and let her direct his will. It was an odd thing, being both in her own body and mind and in someone else's, and it threw her; no one else she'd ever met would have done something so rash and so trusting. *Shut up and get us to safety, woman.* Using Adem's abilities she slowed the winds pushing at the sails, telling him when to turn them and when to drop them, and for a few brief moments they worked as a seamless team to slow their progress. Not thirty yards from the trailhead the sailboard rolled to a stop and Sable wrenched herself out of Adem's mind. Even working magic through someone else's will was tiring, and as she stumbled off the craft she sat down heavily, Ailith plopping down next to her, beaming.

"That was awesome!" she cried as she bounced up and down on her knees. "Dad, can we get one?"

"Maybe one day," he answered as he took down the sail. "But Sable's going to have to teach me what she did with the wind first. I didn't follow any of it." He shoved the pieces of sailboard unceremoniously into the duffel, which yawned wider to accommodate them before snapping back closed, for all the world like a hungry hippopotamus.

"Right," Sable answered. "Affinity for rocks, difficult with wind." She fell backwards to stretch out on the sand. "The exact opposite of me." The darkening sky above her was dotted with a few early evening celestial bodies as the sun relinquished its hold on the view. "Maybe I'll just sleep here; it's nice out tonight." She closed her eyes in exhaustion.

"Nope," Adem replied as he dusted off his hands. "Gotta get up. There's an old safehouse not far from here–or at least there used to be. We can sleep there tonight and go the rest of the way in the morning." He offered Sable and Ailith each a hand and pulled them to their feet.

"As long as I can trudge there." Sable's feet didn't want to lift very far as she walked toward the trailhead and the road beyond. "I think trudging is all I have left."

They made their slow way across the busy street and down a side road a short ways to a nondescript one-story building made of stucco. It was painted cream and red and bore a faded logo on one wall that gave it an air of disuse. Adem led them around to one side of the building to look through the windows for signs of occupation. "It's empty," Sable assured him without looking. "Feels like it has been for quite a while." Nodding, Adem pulled a set of lockpicks from his pack and set to work, popping the padlock off of the door in under fifteen seconds.

"Whoa, Dad, you have got to teach me that!" Ailith's jaw was in danger of scraping the inch-thick layer of dust off the floor. The room beyond looked like an ordinary abandoned automotive garage; equipment dotted the painted concrete floor and tool chests on casters were scattered throughout the area, drawers half open. It looked as if the employees had simply walked out one day mid-shift. Adem closed the door behind him, setting the deadbolt before turning to survey the room. He made a beeline for the office and Ailith and Sable followed. Locking that door behind them as well, he stepped behind the desk and pushed a button mounted to the bottom. Next to a defunct file cabinet in the corner a floor tile opened on silent hinges to reveal a ladder.

"Let me go first," Adem whispered as he peered down the poorly-lit opening. "It looks like this place hasn't been used in years, but just in case…" Sable nodded.

:You know how to reach me if something goes pear shaped,: she sent directly to his mind.

Satisfied, Adem lowered himself down the ladder into the

murky depths of the basement level without making a sound. For long moments they heard nothing. Then there was the squeak of a hinge and the sound of a loud switch and the tunnel downward was flooded with light. "Come on down," Adem called softly. Sable waved Ailith ahead of her, then followed her ten feet down the ladder and into a small bunker underneath the office and storeroom. Adem pressed a button on the wall and the trapdoor above swung closed just as silently as it had opened, leaving them shut off from the world. "I wasn't sure this was still here," he said as he set down his pack on a nearby workbench. "Let's hope the water is still on, too." A small bathroom was visible to one side. Ailith pushed past them both, calling first dibs on the restroom as soon as she saw it. A flush not long after confirmed the presence of running water.

Sable found a set of cots folded and propped against a wall on the other end of the room. Next to them was a locker containing blankets and travel-sized pillows that weren't terribly dusty–not that she cared at this point. "Can you set wards?" she asked Adem as she dragged a cot out from the wall.

"Can you let someone else help you for once?" he retorted as he unfolded the cot for her.

"Nope," she answered as she fell face-first onto the cot. "Been alone too long. Gonna be alone again soon enough. Self sufficiency is paramount." Gods and goddesses, being this tired was like being drunk. Had she actually said that? No matter; she could feel sleep taking over her mind and she reached for a pillow, stuffing it under her face and giving thanks for a young body that could sleep in any position it wanted. A blanket found its way over her and she wiggled into its scratchiness. Just before she fell into oblivion she felt wards go up around the basement and the mental equivalent of a blanket being drawn over her mind, reassuring her she was safe.

Trust But Verify

Sable awoke in a cold sweat to pitch darkness around her and the wards jangling in her mind. Flipping on her night vision, she glanced over at Adem and Ailith to see them blinking in futility and remembered she hadn't taught them that trick quite yet. Given the lack of floor space in the bunker their cots were in a row with Ailith in the middle, so Sable reached out and touched the girl's arm with a reassuring squeeze as she showed her how to see in the dark. Ailith, in turn, touched her father's arm and silently passed it on. All three went still as the soft click of the trapdoor echoed off the bare walls and steps sounded on the ladder. Adem padded on silent feet to the corner the intruder would have to turn and waited.

As soon as the shadowy figure cleared the corner he snaked out a hand and snatched the interloper against his chest, one hand over their mouth. They struggled for a moment before Adem let go as if burned and flipped the lights on. The abrupt change to brightness blinded them for a few long seconds, during which there was a surprised gasp.

"Adem?" said an incredulous female voice.

"Charlie!" he answered, and they all relaxed. "They've still got you looking after this place?"

Definition faded into their field of vision and the source of the voice resolved itself into a black-haired woman of medium height with olive skin and deep brown eyes. Her features were plump and curvy, but beneath them Sable surmised she was solid as steel based on her bearing and coordination. The newcomer glanced around the room, finding questions everywhere she looked.

"Yeah," she answered as she turned her attention back to Adem. "It's my full-time job these days. I retired early and they offered me the post on contract–figured I couldn't beat the pay for living in a town like this." She looked past him toward Sable and Ailith "Where's Irene?"

"She passed away when Ailith was born." The words dropped over the conversation like a dark sheet and the woman's face fell.

"I am so sorry," she said, placing a hand on his arm. "You guys were so happy."

"Thanks. This is Ailith," he indicated the girl, who waved, "and–"

"Constance," Sable interrupted as she stepped forward, extending a hand. "Nice to meet you." Charlie took her hand in a firm grip and shook it with purpose as the two women's eyes met. *Sparky one, this.* Sable didn't make a habit of reaching into people's minds except in extenuating circumstances, but she read the woman's aura as they greeted each other. It writhed with conflict; desire warred with sadness and excitement, all with a well-buried undercurrent of fear and nervousness. Releasing Charlie's hand, she smiled her best trustworthy smile and stepped back to let Adem do more of the talking.

"What brings you back to Cairo?" Charlie asked as she turned back to Adem.

"The usual," he answered vaguely.

"I thought you were out of the business."

"I did, too. Guess you never really are." He ran a hand through his hair self-consciously. "Listen, is it all right if we hole up here for a day or two? We could use a break."

"Of course," Charlie replied, laying another hand on Adem's arm. "Take as long as you need. Is there anything I can bring you? Save you a trip outside?"

Don't take anything from this woman. "You wouldn't happen to have a car we could borrow, would you?" Adem asked, wincing. *Dammit.*

"Sure–you can use mine. I'll leave it behind the shop here tomorrow." Charlie squeezed Adem's arm before letting it go. She craned her neck to look around the room. "Did I restock the toilet paper? I don't recall; mind if I check?" Adem waved her on and she brushed past Sable and Ailith to get to the restroom. After a few moments of digging she reappeared and set a few travel-sized toiletries on the counter. "Thought you might be in need of these, too." She brushed her hands against the sides of her pants as she sidled toward the ladder. "I guess I'll leave you to it, then. My number is on the dry erase board on the wall if you need anything. Constance, Ailith, pleasure to meet you. Adem…it's good to see you." Casting a long look at him as he waved and thanked her, she turned and disappeared back up the ladder, closing the door behind her.

"Who is she?" Sable asked after she felt the woman leave the building.

"We served together," Adem explained as he sat down on his cot and pulled out one of the MREs stored in a nearby crate. He offered one to Ailith and Sable. "She was attached to the special forces group we worked with here. Knows more about local everything than the locals and speaks five languages fluently."

"Hah, amateur." Sable couldn't help herself; she disliked the woman more by the minute. *Has absolutely nothing about her coming onto Adem, noooo sir.* Adem gave her a quizzical look. "Last count I'm up to around ten, eight if you don't count dead ones." He rolled his eyes and went back to his MRE.

"She your contact you'd trust with your life?" Sable inquired as she started into her own meal.

"No," he answered, "but she's likely the only one left here at this point."

They ate in quiet contemplation for a time. Sable decided that turkey tetrazzini wasn't the worst thing she'd eaten and that modern field rations far surpassed the ones she'd experienced in times long gone. Ailith downed her spaghetti in short order and pronounced that she was getting a shower since it appeared they were "hanging out for a while," grabbing her clothes and heading for the restroom and closing the door behind her. At some point while she was eating Sable realized that her legs no longer ached, so she looked down to check–and sure enough, her burns had healed. *I'll still have scars, but I'll take that over sepsis any day. Thank you, Lady Sirona.* Once she'd finished her meal she strode to the duffel and produced her scrying bowl, ducking into the bathroom long enough to fill it and earning a howl as the running tap turned the shower cold.

Deciding a stack of crates would have to do, she placed

the bowl on top of them and dragged her cot close enough to sit on while she worked. Adem sat across from her to watch. Sable reached two fingers into her pants pocket and withdrew a single black hair, which she held in the upturned palm of her hand as she looked over the rim of the bowl. Charlie's figure swam into view as she walked purposefully through the streets of Cairo, head swiveling back and forth as she searched for her next turn.

"What are you doing?" Adem's voice sounded harsh in the relative quiet and held and edge she didn't like.

"Trust but verify, Adem," Sable replied as they watched Charlie duck into an alleyway. "Trust but verify." She walked halfway to the next street when a woman appeared from the shadows of a doorway. Charlie tensed, then greeted the woman warily; scrying gave no sound, but body language spoke volumes if one could also read lips. Turning the view this way and that revealed the second woman's face.

"That's the woman from Tokyo!" he exclaimed.

"Mmhmm. Looks like she has some kind of hold over your friend." Adem swore beneath his breath. "Hey, can you read off the list of daevas again? I'm getting a feeling from this woman…"

Without consulting the book Adem began. "Sawarl Sarvar, daeva of oppression."

"Nope; we beat her in Guilin."

"Taurizl Tawrich, daeva of destruction."

"No, and I really hope we don't meet that one."

"Zaurizl Zawrich, daeva of plant poisoning?"

"Who would send them to a desert? Though the Nile valley is pretty fertile…keep going."

"We're back to the top. Akoman, daeva of evil thought."

"Not quite right, but closer." Sable could feel a strange, still sensation emanating from the woman.

"Indar, daeva who freezes the minds of the righteous."

"Yes! That's her!" Sable pumped a fist triumphantly. "Two identified. Now to figure out the rest…" She dropped the connection and rose to empty the bowl. "By the way, any cameras in here that you know of?"

"Good question," he said as he started checking the room

for wires and cameras. "There didn't used to be, but I'm starting to wonder." The two of them combed the room while the sound of the shower provided a deceptively calm backdrop for their efforts. "I'm coming up empty on cameras or mics," Adem admitted after a thorough search.

"Me too." Sable sat back down on her cot, still tired after the sleep interruption. She checked her phone; it was 7:00 AM. *Twelve hours of sleep and I'm still tired. I'm too young to feel this old.* "Wait–she went into the bathroom while she was here…think there was a reason for that?"

Adem shoved his way through the bathroom door without answering. The shower was still running, but Sable realized she heard none of the usual sounds of someone getting clean, which Ailith had desperately wanted to do. She peeked around the corner just in time to see Adem freeze in place just past the doorway. "Hang on," she said in a tired voice, hoping her eye roll wasn't audible. "Let me find what's causing it." Without getting too close she reached out with her senses to look for the source of the spell. There it was: an unassuming packaged toothbrush sitting on the small vanity that exuded the same energy Indar projected. "Found it–give me a second," she called through the doorway. Thinking furiously, she decided melting the toothbrush was her best bet. It was the work of a moment to excite the molecules around it enough to superheat the air and melt the cheap plastic, and she was rewarded with an audible hiss as the spell attached to it fizzled.

"Dad!" Ailith screamed immediately from inside the single-stall shower.

"I'm right here," Adem answered as he unfroze and knocked on the shower door. "Go on and get out as quickly as you can."

"Okay." Her voice shook as she turned the water off and reached for a towel. Adem pulled the door almost closed to allow her some privacy while also keeping an eye out for other suspicious activity.

Sable was already packing up the few things they'd gotten out. She handed Adem his pack and stuck Ailith's through the door so she could grab clothing as soon as she was dry."What's our plan?" she asked Adem as he kept an eye on the ladder.

"Depends on where we're going," he answered. "Do we know where the next piece of this puzzle is?"

By way of answer Sable shoved a hand into the duffel and produced a crystal on a string. The universe was on their side; before she could even swing it, it shot across the map of Cairo and landed on the Egyptian Museum. Chucking the crystal hurriedly back in the bag—*it's going to be mad at me for that one*—she stood as Ailith appeared in the bathroom doorway, hair still dripping onto her clean outfit. "Tahrir Square," she replied as she helped Ailith into her pack and hoisted her own. The girl seemed to be struggling with more than just the load on her back and Sable resolved to ask about it as soon as she got a chance. *As soon as we're away from here, anyway.*

Adem considered. "Tahrir Square is northwest of our current position by a decent amount. The metro doesn't come out this far, but if we can get to it we could use it to get to the square…or we could try a cab, but I wouldn't trust anyone not to be under the influence of who knows what."

"Why don't we just rent a car?" Sable asked. As Adem opened his mouth to argue, she continued. "They obviously know we're here, so it won't give away anything else about our position." She held up her index finger to count off points. "It'll get us there faster," one more finger, "and it'll give us a way out when it's time to go that most importantly doesn't involve me exhausting myself. Again." A third finger joined the first two. Adem deflated in the face of her verbal onslaught, conceding the field with a nod. He pulled out his phone and searched for the nearest rental place as Sable and Ailith stacked up next to the ladder. "Upstairs is clear, best I can tell," Sable offered. "Ailith, can you see when they'll be back to check on us?"

The girl's eyes glazed over in the now-familiar expression they'd come to know as searching the future. "About two minutes," she answered as her attention shifted back to the here and now.

Adem hit the ladder after shoving his phone peremptorily back into his pocket. "I've got point. Sable, you're rear. How are you in a fight?"

"Seen more wars than you have," she answered as she watched Ailith start up the ladder. "I'm no operator, but I've done my share of fighting." She climbed the ladder close behind Ailith and emerged into the dim office above. The sun had risen just far enough to send a few rays into the maintenance floor beyond that offered scant illumination where they stood. "Which way from here?"

Adem looked to Ailith. "Which way will they come from?" She pointed at the back door they'd used to enter the previous day. "Then we go out the front. We're heading west about a quarter mile–there's a rental place just down the road. Ailith, you stay between me and Sable no matter what, okay?" She nodded as Sable drew another illusion over them to cover their appearance. Moments later three English tourists strode out into the brightening day.

Five harrowing minutes later they stood outside the rental shop, waiting for it to open. Sable took advantage of the few minutes of inactivity to check in with herself and inventory her energy levels. The past few days' constant ups and downs were wearing on them all, but given the good night's sleep she'd just had Sable was feeling surprisingly energetic. *Or maybe it's just the adrenaline.* Adem was on high alert, as always, and still looked ragged around the edges; he'd been operating this way for months before they found Sable. Ailith looked curious, but was too worn down to take in much of what she saw.

"Hey." Sable nudged the girl with her elbow. "Guess what?"

"What?" Ailith managed to keep most of the sullen tone out of her voice.

"We've finally found some stuff that's older than I am."

Ailith narrowed her eyes. "How old are you, anyway?"

"Ailith, that's not polite," Adem rebuked automatically as his eyes roved about the street.

Sable chuckled. "Figure it out if you can. I've given you a few clues, and there are more if you know where to look." Ailith's face screwed up as she struggled to remember which clues she'd been given. "Don't hurt yourself. I'll give you hints if you get stuck."

Just then the lock clicked open behind them and the front door to the rental company cracked open. A middle-aged man with light brown skin peeked out, took stock of their appearance, and said, "Tourists?" Adem nodded and the man ushered them inside. Five minutes later they pulled out of one of the many parking spaces in a nondescript silver sedan with a tree-shaped air freshener hanging from the rear view mirror. Adem was once again driving, with Sable in the passenger seat and Ailith clearly visible in the middle of the back seat.

Sable broke the ice. "So, Ailith, what's eating at you?" she asked without preamble. The girl at least had the grace to look surprised before grumbling out a response. "I'm sorry, grizzly bear isn't a language I speak. Can you repeat that, please?"

"I said I can't tell you." Ailith's voice broke on the last word.

"Why not?" asked her father. "Remember, we all agreed: no more secrets." He glanced at Sable, then turned his attention back to the road.

"Because Mom told me I couldn't say anything or it might change what happens." The temperature in the car seemed to drop despite the warmth of the morning. Sable and Adem exchanged a wary look and came the nonverbal agreement not to push harder on that particular subject.

"Have you learned anything else that might be of help?" Sable asked in the gentlest voice she could muster around her own frustration with prophecies and foresight. *She's just a kid. No kid should have to carry that by themselves.*

"Loads," Ailith replied, relieved. "The last place we went showed how the ritual works that whoever this is wants to use me for. If I'm right it's some sort of breaking ceremony, one that tears down the barrier between this world and the next. The spirits would take over our world."

"And they need you because you're a gatekeeper?" Sable guessed.

Ailith nodded. "You have to sacrifice–" her voice cracked again–"someone who belongs to both worlds in order to do it. I'm the only one in the world who fits that description right now."

"Well, we're not going to let that happen, right, Adem?" Sable declared. He nodded as his grip on the steering wheel tightened. "What else have you learned?"

They spent the next twenty minutes of the drive discussing the Taoist philosophies outlined in the text they'd found in Guilin and correlating them with what Adem could translate on the fly of the scroll they'd gotten from Khaleeda. Both contained recurring themes of maintaining balance, particularly between the world of the living and that of the dead, but Khaleeda's scroll (as Sable had come to think of it) hinted that the balance could be damaged both by invasion from the beyond and by intrusion from the here and now. Something about that nagged at her, but she wasn't able to sort it out before they pulled into the underground parking garage off of Tahrir Square. It was fuller than she'd expected at this time of day, but they found a spot without difficulty and made their way to the closest exit with their heads on swivels. Sable didn't sense anyone nearby who was paying them any attention, but it didn't hurt to be cautious.

A broad set of stairs opened out onto an even broader pedestrian thoroughfare heading north toward the museum. Raised flower beds and light poles separated the sidewalk from the busy street to their right as they made their way past a broad expanse of concrete dotted with trees. The museum's facade rose up from the flattened landscape before them, drawing the eye to its arched entryway despite the larger buildings to either side and across the street. It wasn't just the building's bright color that made it stand out; it had an aura of age and mystery that garnered more attention than its physical seeming. Sable found her feet drawn to it as a moth to a flame.

"Wow," Ailith breathed as the building loomed into view over the horizon. "Can you feel that?"

"I can," Sable replied warily, "and I don't trust it. Be on your guard."

"You always sound so old-fashioned," Ailith said as they walked. "It's weird."

"You're weird," Sable retorted.

"I will put you both in time out if you can't get along," Adem chided from in front of them. They could hear the smile on his voice as he continued to scan their surroundings, ever vigilant.

Before long they encountered a police checkpoint stating that all bags must be searched before entering the museum. Adem and Ailith had left theirs in the rental car, but Sable blithely presented hers for inspection, waiting patiently as the trim, stern-faced guard pawed through what looked like her purse before passing it back to her. She winked at him through her disguise and was rewarded with a smirk as they traipsed off toward the ticket office. They bought their tickets, then passed through the gates and onto the circular walkway that would take them up to the front steps. Halfway down the walkway Ailith stopped and turned to look left. "It's not in the museum," she whispered as she took a few tentative steps toward the garden to their west. Adem pushed past her to lead the way in case of ambush–*ha, since there are literal bushes.* Sable couldn't help chuckling to herself before following both of her charges.

Ailith walked forward in a trance, passing two red granite sphinxes and walking around a statue of Merneptah that looked like it strode toward them as they approached. The massive antiquities around them barely registered as she made a beeline for the shining white limestone memorial alcove tucked off to one side. A large, rectangular tomb sat atop a semicircular dais, flanked by a rounded wall with alcoves set into it at intervals. In each alcove sat a bust, some made of grey stone, others of bronze. On top of the tomb itself stood a life-sized bronze likeness of its owner with his arms crossed and a scroll unfurling in one hand.

Something about the whole setting made Sable's sixth sense itch. "Wait," she told Ailith as she tucked the girl behind her and reached out with her senses. She could feel something around the tomb; it was as if the veil between worlds was so thin it could be parted with the slightest thought. Taking the girl's hand she led them both up the steps and onto the platform before them. Adem had already made a circuit of the area and joined them as soon as they reached the top of the steps.

A deep, male voice boomed out of the tomb before them. "Ça n'est plus," it began, the tone belying a great sense of loss and grief. "Détruit. Le malotru Italien est tombé dessus par hasard et l'a fait exploser. J'étais censé le trouver, merde. Censé le sauvegarder et le protéger pour qu'il puisse être retrouvé lorsque besoin. Maintenant, tout peut être perdu." A great sigh gusted past, carrying a dry breeze with it that ruffled their hair and smelled of frankincense. "Tu dois retourner à Méroé. Trouvez ce qui reste. Je ne peux qu'espérer que cela suffise." With the last word the breeze died and the energy seemed to flow out from the area, dispersing into the ground.

The three of them were silent for a long moment before Ailith piped up. "Was that French?" she asked.

"Yep," Sable answered. "New French, so I'm not a hundred percent certain on my translation, but I'm pretty sure whoever that was just told us to go to Sudan."

"Sudan?" Adem asked, clearly confused.

"Yeah. Seems some Italian blew something up that this guy was looking for down in Meroë. He wants us to go see if there's anything left of it."

"Who is 'he?'" Adem asked.

"Auguste Mariette," Ailith answered. "The first director of the Ministry of Antiquities. This is his tomb."

"How do you know that?" Sable demanded.

"It's written on the side of it." Ailith pointed to a sign proclaiming same in multiple languages. Sable rolled her eyes at her own inattentiveness and turned to Adem.

"Good thing we rented a car," she said as she started down the steps toward the rest of the garden and the exit.

"Wait! Dad, please can we at least go inside for a little bit?" Ailith grabbed onto Adem's wrist and pulled as he moved to follow Sable. Her large, hazel eyes pleaded her case as she gazed up at him from ribcage height, her soul in her eyes. It melted even Sable's lonely heart just to watch.

"We can't afford the time," Adem answered reluctantly. Ailith deflated, dropping his wrist. "But I promise you, when this is all over, we can come back and look until your little heart's content."

Ailith perked up as she bounded down the steps to catch up with Sable. "Okay, gotta solve this puzzle, then! I wanna see mummies!" She almost took off through the garden, but Sable grabbed her by the back of the shirt to slow her momentum.

"Whoa there," she said as Ailith skidded to a halt. "Remember, your dad goes first." Nodding, Ailith waited for Adem to precede them back the way they'd come and out the front entrance to the museum, casting a few longing looks at the building behind them as they went.

This time they walked around the other side of the block back to the garage as it was closer to the exit they'd used. Tall buildings thrust up on either side of the well-used street, imposing masses of steel and concrete and glass, and they found themselves hurrying along like everyone else trying to get to their destinations. Before long they were back at the stairs across from Tahrir Square. *Strange that they call it a square even though it's round, but I guess "Tahrir Round" doesn't have the same ring,* Sable pondered as they descended the wide steps into the parking garage. Adem had chosen a spot near the entrance but tucked into a corner where he could see all the possible approaches from inside the vehicle. What he hadn't realized was that it left blind spots on their return.

As Adem rounded the last vehicle between the stairs and their rental car he froze in place. Two men in loose-fitting black pants and tunics approached him warily despite his apparent inability to move. From behind their car the brown-haired woman they'd first seen in Tokyo appeared, her teeth bared in a smile.

Sable stopped, trying to place Ailith behind her, and noticed the girl was as frozen in place as her father. *Time to test a theory.* "Indar," she said aloud as she edged closer to the men flanking Adem.

The woman inclined her head. "Indeed. It seems you have me at a disadvantage; you are…?"

"I really don't, given the fact that you got the drop on us instead of the other way around." *Keep talking…* She sidled two steps closer to her targets. *Another ten feet and I'm there.*

A wave of power slammed into her, bidding her to freeze where she stood. Instead of fighting it she stopped in her tracks. *Here's the bait.* In response the woman ducked around the rental car and made her way over to Ailith, trailing a finger across her pale cheek. "So young…yet so powerful." She walked a circle around the girl, taking her measure as she did. "Not much meat on those bones, but I'm sure she'll hold up long enough. Hesham, come bind her hands and gag her." One of her henchmen left Adem's side and strode toward his mistress–directly past Sable.

At the last second a large, ornate dagger appeared in Sable's hand and she shoved it through the man's throat. He gurgled, both hands coming up to grasp at the ruin she'd made of his neck as he fell to his side to bleed out on the concrete. Before his body hit the ground Sable pelted past him and smashed both feet into the left kneecap of the second guard near Adem, following up with a driving stab to his chest that tucked the end of her dagger neatly under the bottom of his sternum. She removed it and sprang back to avoid getting entangled as he joined his compatriot in death.

Sable turned to see Indar grab Ailith around the shoulders and place a small knife to her throat. "Stay back," she ordered, and the command filled Sable's mind, trying to find a foothold like ice creeping up the branches of a tree. *Remember the main reason you're here, woman.* Sable shook off Indar's influence and slowly stepped forward.

"You won't hurt her," she said as she stalked forward, blood dripping from the dagger in her hand. "You need her."

"I said, stay back!" A second wave of magic came and went as Sable moved inexorably forward.

"No."

Indar shifted her blade closer to Ailith's throat. "Not another step," she demanded as a tiny bead of red appeared at the knife's tip. Ailith didn't flinch, still frozen in place by Indar's influence, and as Sable closed one more step of distance she felt her opportunity snap into place. She winked out of existence for the barest moment and reappeared right next to Indar, extending her left arm to break the woman's surprisingly strong grip on the girl. The knife left Ailith's throat as Sable's dagger slid around the other side of Indar's neck in a backwards mimicry of the hold she'd had on the girl. Without a word Sable shoved the blade up through the soft spot beneath the taller woman's jaw and through the roof of her mouth. She collapsed in a heap as blood gushed from the wound.

Sable laid Indar on the ground as Ailith and Adem awoke from their frozen state. "Ailith, send her home!" Sable yelled as she freed her weapon, casting about for reinforcements. Ailith nodded and slipped across the barrier between worlds without question while Adem caught up to Sable.

"Sitrep," he demanded as he turned to watch her back.

"Indar and her two goons are down and Ailith is sending her past the gate," Sable answered. "If you've got this, I'll go watch her back."

"Go." He turned to keep watch as Sable followed Ailith into the in-between. She and Indar had just reached the nearest gateway and were passing through as Sable caught up.

"Quickly!" Sable shouted, earning a nod. Ailith extended a hand and guided Indar across the metallic sheen of the gate just as a translucent hand reached from beyond it to snatch at her wrist. Cursing, Sable snatched at the spectral thumb holding onto Ailith and was rewarded with a howl from the other side of the gate. Ailith jerked her arm back and looked to Sable. "Time to go!" They grabbed each other's hands and ran back through the barrier between worlds.

In the parking garage nothing had changed. Adem was on high alert and Sable could hear other patrons moving around nearby. "We need to go," he stated calmly.

"One second." Sable flicked the last of the blood from her dagger before sending it back to its hiding place with a thought. Pointing at Indar's body, she spoke a single word in a flu-id-sounding language and smiled in grim satisfaction as the body charred to ash in seconds. She repeated the exercise with the other two bodies, then pulled wind from the stairway to dissipate the last of the remains just as the first pedestrian appeared from around the corner.

Adem was already at the car. He nodded, then got in, check-ing to see if Ailith had fastened her seatbelt. Sable slid into the passenger seat and buckled in as the car eased out of its parking space. "Everyone okay?" Adem asked.

"Fine," Ailith answered. One hand floated up to the pinprick on her neck.

"All fine here," Sable replied.

"What happened up there?" Adem asked. "I couldn't see anything from where I was, and it was like my mind refused to work. I couldn't even think."

"Indar freezes the minds of the righteous, remember?" Sable dug in the duffel for a snack and handed an apple to Ailith, who took it gratefully. "She used her mojo to freeze everyone. Well, mostly everyone."

Adem's brow furrowed. "You weren't affected."

"Nope," Sable replied a little too brightly. "I'm not a righteous person. I'm here to keep from getting stuck in a never-ending life of hell on earth, not to save the world or anything like that. Don't forget, I'm a selfish old bat who's looking out for number one." Feeling more than seeing Ailith's sadness at her words, Sable added, "No more lies, remember? Doesn't mean I don't like you; it just means you're not my primary reason for being here."

"You're still going to leave when this is all over." It was a statement, not a question, and she was surprised to hear it from Adem instead of his daughter.

"Yep." Sable sighed, the weight of her life settling on her deceptively young shoulders. "If I want any chance of crossing through that gate, I have to."

"What if we could break your curse?" Ailith blurted out. Sable chuckled, her bitterness making a mockery of Ailith's question.

"You think others haven't tried? I've spent hundreds of years with the most brilliant and capable minds I've known, and none of them could break it. I've got to meet its conditions." Her eyes narrowed as a thought occurred to her. "You don't happen to, y'know, *know* something about it, do you?"

Ailith squirmed in the seat behind her. Her feet pushed into the back of Sable's seat as the girl tried to arrange herself so that less of her was visible in the rear view mirror.

"Ailith, have you Seen something?" Adem demanded. "Our no more lies policy applies to everyone in this car, especially to you. Sable has been honest with us," he glanced over as they entered a freeway heading south, "and I've told what I know about Cairo from my time here before. It's your turn."

"I told you, I'm not supposed to tell!" Ailith finally said in a rush after picking at her fingernails for a tense minute. "Mom said it might change things if I tell people, and I don't want to change what I Saw." *Oh.*

"I think we need to make an exception in this case," Sable acknowledged quietly. "It's hard enough to bear those secrets. We shouldn't penalize her for following instructions." Adem nodded, swallowing any further admonishment. "Have you Seen anything you can tell us about?" Sable asked gently.

"Not since the last time I did," Ailith answered, relief evident in her voice. Sable's mind churned on what she'd just learned until Adem broke the silence again.

"So Indar froze us, and then…?" he prompted.

"Then I faked being frozen right along with you and waited for an opening." She related the rest of the tale to Adem as he drove them southward on the freeway. He stopped her once or twice to ask questions, mostly about how she'd managed to take out Indar without harming Ailith and how she'd moved so quickly.

"I borrowed some strength from the ley lines nearby," she answered, "and did a very small version of the space folding trick we use to travel long distances. That's actually how I figured out the distance travel thing years ago–first thing I ever used it for was combat at short to medium range, like today. I figured out I could be consistently accurate at a distance of ten paces."

Adem chewed on this information. "And where did you get that dagger? I haven't seen you use it before."

"Oh, this old thing?" It appeared in Sable's hand at her silent command. Two hands long and half a hand wide, it had a steel blade with a bronze handle wrapped in well-worn strips of leather. There was no crosspiece, only a widening of the blade's profile that tapered back down to a comfortable breadth for the grip and had a slight flare at the bottom for better stability. "Had this thing since…well, since the beginning, I suppose. Only get it out when I really need it." It winked back out of existence.

"Can you show me how to do that?" Adem asked with a

glint in his eye.

"Probably, but we'll need something to store one in." Sable indicated the golden torc bracelet she wore. "Mine lives in here when I'm not using it. Takes a few materials and some time to set up, too, and I don't know as we have access to the right stuff around here to do that." Her brow furrowed in an unconscious mimicry of Adem's thinking face as she considered. "Let's wait on that until after this is all over, in fact." He looked disappointed, but nodded.

An awkward silence settled over the group. "How long until we get there?" Sable asked, craning her head to see the screen of Adem's smartphone for the GPS directions. It sat in his lap and had slid down far enough between his legs that she couldn't see beyond the case. *Lords and ladies, woman, eyes on the phone…the phone…* She squeezed her eyes shut and waited for his answer.

"Phone says two days," Adem answered grudgingly.

"Two days?!?" Ailith exclaimed from the back seat. "Do we even have two days?"

"Nope." Sable pursed her lips. "But I may know a way to get us there faster." She dug around in the duffel, muttering as she did. "No…not that…come on, you useless–no, I didn't mean that. I'm sorry. I'm just looking for some incense I know is in here, and I know you know that's what I'm looking for, and it's incredibly frustrating when it takes this long for you to just hand me what I need." Sable's voice rose steadily through-out this soliloquy until at last she produced a small triangle of resin from within her purse. "Thank you," she sighed. "Adem, if you would pull over the next time you have a spot? It doesn't have to be on the shoulder."

"But if I pull all four tires off, we'll get stuck in the sand," Adem pointed out.

"Where we're going that won't matter," Sable answered. Adem pulled the rental car off the road and put it in park. The doors unlocked automatically and Sable stepped out of the pas-senger side, incense in hand.

Adem opened his door to follow, but Sable motioned him back into the vehicle. "I'll just be a minute," she said lamely as she crouched down in the sand. She built a tiny mound for the cone of incense to sit atop, then lit it with a thought and concentrated. *I hope you hear me…hell, I hope you're still here.*

Instantly the ground began to rumble. The sand beneath the incense shifted, splitting into two smaller peaks and swallowing the tiny offering whole. Loose rocks and shale bounced by the side of the road in a crazy dance as the ground yawned open before Sable, spitting out a figure cloaked in brightly-colored robes. It lifted itself to its full height and looked down at Sable as she stood, unafraid, gazing at what she'd summoned.

"Nulwa?" a quizzical, but deep voice queried from beneath the frayed hood of its garment.

"Dedun." Sable nodded deferentially. "It's been long years."

Without speaking the figure threw back its hood, revealing a man with ruggedly handsome features and tightly twisted, shoulder-length hair. His eyes were the color of the sands on which they stood, and Sable watched his irises swirl with the wind just the way she remembered them doing. The overall effect was even more intoxicating than she recalled. *Or your body is just way too young again. Probably both.* Before she could comment further the man stepped forward and wrapped both arms around her.

Adem was out of the car and over the hood before Sable realized what was happening. "It's all right!" she exclaimed, her words muffled against a too-familiar chest covered in linen. "He means no harm." Returning the embrace briefly, she pushed away from Dedun to introduce the rest of their party.

"Dedun, this is Adem," she began. The shorter man turned to regard Adem, taking his measure before extending a hand.

"I am Dedun," he said simply, as if his name alone were explanation enough of who and what he was.

"Adem." They clasped hands unnecessarily hard. *Oh boy. Looks like testosterone wins again.* Sable patted both of them on the shoulder and Dedun let go, turning to regard her ardently.

"It has been long years," he said, his hand straying from his side for a moment before dropping. "You are still so young– younger than last I knew you."

"Such is the way of my curse," Sable replied with a sigh.

"So you still have not broken it?" Dedun asked. His accent straddled a line between French and Arabic with unrelated undertones.

"Not yet, but right now we have bigger problems." Sable indicated Ailith, who sat wide-eyed in the backseat of the car, staring at the newcomer.

Dedun took a step toward the car, peering in the window. He looked at Sable, then Adem, then back at Ailith. "She does not resemble either of you," he said finally. "Except maybe him." He pointed at Adem, who raised an eyebrow.

"Adem is her father," Sable explained hurriedly. "She's not mine. You know I've never had children–I'd never break the curse if I did."

"Ahh, that's right," Dedun nodded as he retreated from the vehicle. He stared at Adem for longer than was strictly necessary, then asked, "What is your need? I assume you would not have called me unless it was great, and while I do enjoy your company, I get the impression you are in trouble. As usual."

"A bit," Sable hedged. "We need to get to Meroë in less than the two days it would take to drive there, and we need to do it discreetly."

"Ah, my old–what do you call it? Stamping grounds?"

"Stomping, but yes."

Dedun nodded. "I can do this for you, but I will ask something in return." Adem's expression darkened.

"What would you ask of us?" Sable replied, giving Adem a pointed look.

"I wish to make an entrance when we get there." Dedun drew himself up to his full height, somewhere between Sable's and Adem's, and seemed to grow as he did so. "The people here have forgotten me. The Abrahamic god has long ruled this region, and he leaves no room for the rest of us." A hard look entered Dedun's eyes as he gazed beyond the group before him, back through time to a place where he was revered and worshiped. His clothing shifted, revealing a white garment similar to an Egyptian royal kilt, but with a crossed leather bandolier covering half of his well-muscled chest. A lion's mane sprouted from his neck and shoulders.

Sable's eyes sparkled. "I think we can arrange that," she replied, elbowing Adem in the ribs. He nodded, narrowed eyes relaxing into wariness as he took in their new companion's transformation.

"Wonderful! Then let's get moving." Dedun resumed his former mien and approached the driver's side of the sedan. "I'm going to have to drive," he announced as he looked around for the keys. "Where we're going none of you can navigate." When Adem hesitated Sable plucked the keys from his hand and tossed them to Dedun. She climbed into the backseat with Ailith and watched the sparks fly as Adem took up the passenger seat.

"Sable," Ailith whispered before the rest of the group could get settled. "He's not human! I think he's some kind of spirit of the dead."

"God of the dead," Sable corrected as the menfolk slid into the car. "He's been around a very long time, shepherding souls to their final resting place."

"We are not that different, gatekeeper," Dedun replied from the driver's seat. "In fact, I may can teach you a thing or two while you are visiting my lands. What is your name, child?" His voice gentled as he addressed her.

"Ailith," she replied sheepishly.

"Well, Ailith, we are going to visit a few places you may recognize—and even more you certainly will not." Dedun cranked the car and revved the modest engine a few times. "These modern machines are wonderful, are they not?" With that he threw the car into drive and stepped on the gas. Despite all four tires sitting on the dense sand the car leaped forward toward an opening that yawned in front of them, ramping downward into darkness. "Buckle up!" Dedun yelled belatedly before the car disappeared into the depths of the desert.

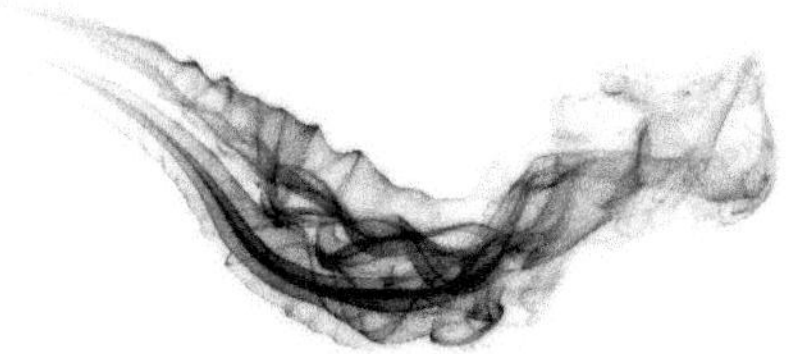

Office Politics

Nanghait stalked into the parking garage, nose in the air as he scented for his quarry. They had come this way, of that he was sure, but he couldn't track their scent beyond the parking spot nearby. There were no bodies, no clues his mortal senses could find as to where the girl and her companions had gone. So he slipped between, into a land of grey fields and uncertain time. Here he could see traces of blood dripped from grievous wounds leading him to a stone archway. He followed the trail right up to the gate and laid a hand on its cold stones.

"Indar." His voice in this place was a rasp of discomfort against the peace and quiet of the fields. "Where did she take you?"

"I am here," a voice whispered from far beyond the gate.

Nanghait chuckled, a deep, throaty, coughing sound. "Got yourself caught, did you? How utterly predictable." His yellowed nails trailed down the rock as he traced the ever-changing runes on the gate's surface. Here he could not hide his appearance behind a mortal shell; here he was truly as hideous as he thought himself to be. "What made you think you could capture the girl yourself?"

"Was it not our master's will that I do so?" came the faint reply.

"My last orders were only to observe," Nanghait replied as he stalked a circuit of the archway. From behind it looked exactly as it did from the front–until one crossed through it into the lands beyond, from which there was very little chance of return. "What were yours?"

"To apprehend," she replied in a whisper. "You told me…"

"I implied that capturing the girl would bring the favor of our lord," Nanghait interjected. It was so easy when Indar's voice was clouded by distance and the magical shield between them. "I think you'll find I never gave any orders to do so, especially not in his name."

"You…traitor…" The words came as whispers upon the wind, and Nanghait savored their discontent. When no more followed, he turned and strode back out the way he'd come, reappearing in the parking garage.

Three down; one more to go.

FRIENDS IN LOW PLACES

The sedan sped through tunnels of sand as they appeared, always one second, one turn away from being lost to the oblivion that surrounded it. Dedun grinned like a jackal throughout. Adem's right hand gripped the armrest, white-knuckled, as he attempted to push his right foot through a brake pedal that wasn't there. Ailith and Sable reached up and grabbed the handles above the rear set of passenger windows and hung on for dear life as they rocketed down into the desert's bowels.

As suddenly as they'd entered them the tunnels spat them out into a familiar field of grayscale. Stone arches flashed by as they continued though the grass at speed before reaching a vast plain that was planted with reeds and rushes. No river was visible, and the monochromatic color scheme made it difficult to determine the details of the terrain, but as the car slowed they noticed figures moving between the stalks. Small yurts came into view, the figures flitting between them and the fields like bees working near a hive.

"It is far more colorful here if you are a spirit." Dedun's voice made the rest of the car's occupants jump. "We are almost to my home. You can rest there a while before continuing on your journey."

Adem looked as though he would protest, so Sable jumped in. "We would appreciate the respite," she said, catching Adem's eye in the rear view mirror. He scowled slightly in response. "Especially since time is more fluid here," she continued with a pointed look at Adem.

"Indeed," Dedun confirmed. "I get the feeling you need a safe place to plan your next moves." Adem's scowl took on a more neutral cast. "I can give you that space without affecting your timeline."

"And what would you ask in return?" Adem asked, clearly skeptical. He crossed his arms as they parked outside of a larger yurt and turned to face their host.

"Only that you prevent what your opponent is planning." Dedun met his stare with the shifting sands of his timeless gaze and Sable could feel the moment Adem realized the extent to which their host was beyond human. The air in the cab released its stranglehold on the occupants. "Come, let us speak of these things inside." The click of the door handle set Sable and Ailith into motion as they followed Dedun and Adem through the leather flap that served as the hut's door. Judging by the stiffness of Adem's posture Sable had a feeling the rest of the conversation wouldn't be particularly restful.

"What's with Dad?" Ailith whispered to Sable just before they entered. "Can't he see that this guy is on the level?"

"He doesn't see everything we do," Sable replied with a sigh. "And Dedun has an effect on people sometimes." She hesitated, but chose to keep the rest of her theories to herself.

Dedun's home was exactly as she remembered it. Finely-wrought chairs carved from extinct woods held bright cushions that were just as vibrant as the last time she'd seen them hundreds of years prior. Wall hangings woven into scenes from Sudan's history separated the rooms and gave an illusion of privacy as they wandered into the heart of the structure, which contained a modest kitchen and a well-appointed bedroom draped liberally with cushions and blankets in every shade of red and orange imaginable. The sudden influx of color after the grayscape outside was dizzying.

"Please make yourself comfortable," Dedun invited as they passed a settee and two larger chairs next to the kitchen. "Are you hungry? I can prepare something to eat if you would like."

"I'm starving," Ailith admitted. Adem's persistent scowl turned on his daughter and she added, "If it's not too much trouble."

"Not at all!" Dedun chuckled and pulled a large pan down from its hanging place on the kitchen wall. He disappeared into a previously unseen pantry, reappearing with an armload of ingredients that were foreign to everyone in the group except

Sable, who rushed over to help him carry the heap of vegetables and spices. "It is good to see you again, Nulwa." Dedun pitched his rich baritone voice for Sable's ears only. "I did not think you would return when last we met."

"I didn't intend to," she answered in kind, "at least not while I still live."

He chuckled good-naturedly. "It seems fate has different ideas for us than our intentions support. Have you reconsidered my offer? It still stands if you are interested."

Of course he would bring that up. "I have not," Sable answered, tension knotting her shoulders. "I cannot spend eternity like this, Dedun."

Their host sighed. "I thought that would be the case. Still, if you change your mind…" He trailed off as he finished cutting up vegetables for the dish he was preparing. Sable lit the fire under the stove, eyes flicking to where Adem and Ailith sat with their heads bent together in quiet conversation. "Your thoughts stray to another," Dedun said as she returned to his side. "Does your heart as well?" He sounded resigned, but not heartbroken, and it gave Sable the courage to speak her mind.

"He doesn't know," she replied. If there was anyone who might understand her conundrum, it was a god of the afterlife who had seen millennia of human interaction. "He can't know. As soon as we finish saving the world, I'm leaving."

Dedun frowned. "Why?" There was genuine curiosity in his voice, as if her reasoning was unclear.

So much for not having to explain. "Because I was almost free," Sable lamented. "I was minutes away from finally moving on when they found me. And if the only way to get that back is to turn my back on the world for another eighty years, then that's what I'll do. I can't…" She hesitated, then decided giving voice to her thoughts might expiate them. "I can't lose them. Either of them. Not the way I've lost everyone else." Sable stared at the table before her without seeing it. That was the crux of the matter, wasn't it? It had been a full lifetime since she'd lost anyone. Faces paraded across her memory, some young, many old, all familiar. She could recall each of them in perfect, excruciating detail. The last one lingered, his brown eyes, mousy-brown hair, and kind smile ripping what was left of her heart to pieces. *Keep it together, woman, or they'll figure out what's up. You don't want this to hurt them as much as it does you, do you?* She felt Dedun's hand at her elbow.

"I'm afraid you cannot avoid that," he said gently. "The question is, will you let yourself enjoy the time you do have, or will you spend it in misery?" He patted her hand for all the world like a wise grandfather. "Go sit down. I can finish this. But think on what I've said, hmm?" Sable nodded, unable to speak, and shuffled to the seat furthest from her companions, curling into a ball and resting her head on her knees.

A few minutes later Dedun joined them in the sitting area with steaming bowls of spiced vegetables. The aroma lent an even more exotic air to their surroundings as they waited for their food to cool. "So, you seek to right the imbalance between life and death that is trying to take over both worlds," he began. It was a statement, not a question, and mistrust crept back into Adem's expression. "I am a god of the afterlife, Mr. Ozturk," he explained, deliberately using Adem's surname since he hadn't given it during introductions. "I can feel when things are out of alignment, and I can see that you are on a path to right them. It may seem like you, Ailith, are the key to defeating this foe, but if any of you fall, the world will be lost." Dedun paused for effect or comment.

"We have information from multiple sources that we need to interpret," Sable offered into the stillness that followed. "Accounts of other gatekeepers, mostly. Ailith, will you share what we've found?"

They spent the next few hours poring over the pictures, parchments, and other pieces of knowledge they'd gleaned. Some of it was of little use; it was either too dated or too specific to circumstances outside their realm of concern, so they compiled it into a new notebook Ailith titled "The Handbook" and set it aside. The rest they began to compile into a list, which Adem recapped once they'd gone through everything.

"Okay, here's what we know: there is a ritual that can be done that will open a permanent gateway into the afterlife, which would allow spirits to return into life without being summoned.

There would be no way to stop them and life as we know it would end, as the dead outnumber the living by an innumerable measure and in some cases bear ill will toward us." A chorus of nods confirmed his statement and he continued. "In order to accomplish this, whoever does the ritual needs a gatekeeper, whom they will sacrifice–" his voice caught before he plowed on–"in order to make the gateway permanent." More nodding. "The most effective time to do this would be at the changing of a season, like the summer solstice, as the barrier between worlds is already thin during transitional periods."

"I've felt it getting thinner for at least a week," Ailith confirmed. Dedun nodded his approval.

"The question is, where will the ritual be held?" Adem asked as he lowered the written list they'd been working from.

"Ailith, do you want to take this one?" Sable asked. The girl shook her head, unsettled by the thought of using her own power to divine where someone wished to make her a human sacrifice. "All right, where'd you put that map you used to have, Dedun?" From beneath the table where they sat he produced a rolled-up piece of vellum that, when stretched to its full length and weighed down at the corners, covered its entire surface. Inky black outlines of the continents appeared and filled in as they watched, first with the rambling borders for countries, then dots for cities. Once the contents were established the entire image drew itself toward the ceiling and below the tabletop to show the topographical details across the world. Ailith's eyes grew more and more round as she watched the world take shape before her.

Sable pulled her second-favorite dowsing crystal from her bag without looking. *Things must be serious for the bag to behave itself.* Swinging the crystal over the map before her she concentrated on the image Ailith had drawn days before, mentally tracing the lines as she flipped the image right-side up in her mind's eye. The leather thong holding the crystal snapped taut and hovered, quivering, over the west coast of South America.

"Peru?" Adem asked.

"Lima, then Machu Picchu," Sable replied, knowing

without thinking about it that she was correct. It took an effort to retrieve her crystal and she wondered for a moment if it had anything else to show her before stuffing it back into the bag. There would be time later for it to speak to her again.

"But we still need to go to Meroë?" Adem confirmed.

"All signs point to something there that will help us interrupt the ritual," Sable answered, "something that at one point resided in the pyramid of Amanishakheto and is still available there. Through some means."

"Ah, Amanishakheto," Dedun sighed. "What a woman. You would have liked her," he told Sable as he walked the path of his memories for a while. "A kandake–a queen–like no other. She was fire incarnate and a wonderful advocate for her people."

"Do you have any idea what she might have to do with all this?" Adem asked, indicating the notes and map spread around the room.

"She had her hand in many, many things," Dedun replied. "I was a bit…distracted during that time in my people's history, so I didn't keep as close a watch on her goings and comings as I might have." He seemed unwilling to elaborate, so Adem moved on.

"So we still go to Meroë and see what we can find in a pyramid that was blown up almost two hundred years ago," he stated uncertainly.

"I can help with the pyramid," Dedun replied cryptically.

"Then we have a plan in the short term," Sable said as she reclined into her chair. "I'll take some time to attempt a scrying session on our final destination since I've had a bit of a breather."

"Can I help?" Ailith asked.

"Are you sure you want to take a chance on seeing whatever is there?" Sable queried. "It might not be pretty."

"I saw what was in that cave in the Thar Desert, didn't I?" Ailith raised her fine-boned chin resolutely. "I wanna help. I think…I think if I face it, I can handle it and it'll stop bothering me so much." Her face fell, and Sable wanted desperately to put a hand on either side of it and tell the child it would all be all right. Instead she nodded in recognition of the girl's resolve and pulled out her scrying bowl. Adem folded himself onto the floor beside his daughter where he could witness the goings-on.

Dedun fetched a ceramic pot full of water and filled the bowl, careful not to spill a single drop. "What do you know about quantum entanglement?" Sable asked her pupil as she trailed her hand across the surface of the water, watching the ripples reach the bounds of their container and turn in on themselves.

Ailith's face screwed up in concentration. "It's something to do with shaking a particle in Australia and making another one vibrate in England or something, right?"

"Sort of," Sable replied. "And close enough for our purposes; what we're doing is only loosely based off of it anyway. The concept that objects in this world are connected even at atomic levels–and that those connections can be influenced, even manufactured where they don't exist–is the basis for scrying." Ailith nodded eagerly as she watched the water in the bowl settle. "It's easiest to scry things and people that are close to us–things with which we already have or can easily build a connection." With a thought Sable showed them a live image of themselves centered on Ailith and was rewarded with a gasp of surprise from her student. "Now you try. See if you can show us your dad." Ailith squinted at the water's surface, brow furrowed in a mimicry of her father's.

A form took shape in the basin. Adem was barely recognizable, his face battered and bruised as he lay, bleeding, atop a pile of rubble. Pink bubbles accompanied his labored breathing, and though there was no sound they could make out the words "I love you" before his face went slack and his breathing stilled.

Ailith screamed and buried her face in Adem's shoulder. Sable stared at the water uncomprehending. "Dedun, what kind of water did you put in this bowl?" she asked, numbed why what she'd seen.

"The same I water the fields with," he answered. "From the aquifers fed by the Nile."

Sable pondered as Ailith sobbed beside her. "Ailith isn't just a gatekeeper; she's also a seer. Do you think she could scry the future? I've never known anyone who could, but there's a first time for everything, and she's incredibly powerful."

Dedun considered for a moment. "It is possible," he acknowledged, "though I too have never known a human with the ability to do so." Adem's quiet shushing seemed to be helping; Ailith sat up and sniffed, ran a sleeve across her eyes, and took a few deep breaths.

"Is there somewhere I can lay down?" she asked in a small voice. It tore at Sable's heart to see her so wounded, but she knew it was bound to get worse before it got better. Sable herself was deeply disturbed by what they'd seen.

Dedun waved a hand toward an opening that appeared in the wall hangings behind them. "Of course, child, though I'm afraid you'll have to share; while I have some latitude with regards to how large I can make my home, it does have limits." Ailith nodded and disappeared behind the drapery.

"Remember that what Ailith sees are possible futures, not deterministic ones," Sable said quietly. Adem nodded and swallowed. "I'm going to see what I can learn about our enemy. You in?" He nodded again, his strong features set in an unreadable expression. Determined not to study his face any more than she could help, Sable turned her attention back to the bowl before her. She called forth once again the image of the name she'd seen written in Ailith's sketch pad and scrawled on the skin of their enemies, breathing a single word:

"Ahriman."

The water in the bowl boiled. In the steam rising from its surface peaks began to form, outlining a tall mountain range. The perspective dipped down to skim the flattened top of a ridgeline, then plunged into the ground beneath, diving through rock and mud and arriving at a chamber hewn into the bones of the mountain. It was dimly lit with four small braziers on pedestals at each corner of the room. In the center sat a huge stone archway of familiar build and hue that felt glaringly wrong. It was obvious even through scrying that it was not meant to be in the world of the living.

"Is that…the gateway?" Adem asked.

"Has to be," Sable replied. "Nothing else could feel that awful from this far away."

"There should be an altar somewhere nearby," Adem pointed out, "based on the drawings we've seen."

"Let's look." Sable sent her perception floating about the room, which held other odds and ends, most notably a heavy bronze bowl on a pedestal. It reeked of blood magic. "I bet he's going to use that instead," she pointed out. "I don't think it matters whether or not you have the altar if you have a way to catch the blood." Sable shivered and fought down nausea despite herself. Adem's rage next to her was palpable; it radiated from him in waves that set her teeth on edge.

"Can't we just destroy that place from here? Nuke it from orbit, as it were?" he asked through gritted teeth.

"I wish it worked like that," Sable answered. "We can only see, not change."

"Then show me how to get in." Nodding, Sable found a door in the underground chamber and followed it down a long hallway with clinical lighting. The hall opened into a throne room of sorts with a dais and sumptuous armchair that sat empty. As they watched a single figure opened the door at the far end of the room and approached the dais. It was tall and lithe, and something about how it moved was unnerving; it was as if there was more than one consciousness controlling the body that walked up the steps and onto the platform. It managed to fold itself into the armchair before looking directly at Sable.

"You." The word reverberated through her skull. "You who would interfere with my plans, you who so smugly thinks she can play her own game and still win mine. Such hubris." He chuckled, the sound grating across Sable's mind despite the distance. "What you don't know is that even without the girl I can unleash hell on this planet. The solstice thins the barrier between worlds enough that I can free the spirits for one night to wreak havoc upon the earth. They will bring her to me so that I can complete the ritual and seize control of the living and the dead. And there is absolutely nothing you can do about it." This time his laugh held menace and the promise that a slow death was not a mercy he would give. Steam began to rise once again from the scrying bowl until Dedun grabbed it and hurled its contents out of the tent via the kitchen door.

"A horrible spirit, that one," he said as he replaced Sable's bowl in her bag and dried his hands on a nearby towel. "Every so often they come out of the woodwork. I think I've met this one before. Ahriman, you say?" Sable nodded, unable to find her voice. "Ah, yes, the Zoroastrian embodiment of evil. Have you run across his henchpeople?" Another nod. "All of them?" Thinking, Sable shook her head.

"I think we've defeated three," she answered, "but we haven't seen hide nor hair of Taurizl Tawrich, daeva of destruction. Nanghait is the only other one left after we sent Indar back across the gate earlier today. Dear gods, was it really just today?" Sable yawned, suddenly exhausted.

Adem stirred from where he sat, still as a stone, staring at the spot on the table the scrying bowl had occupied. "I didn't see an entrance," he said flatly, and Sable wondered what must be going through his mind. He'd just seen a vision of his own death followed by the seat of the ritual that would end the world with his daughter's blood if they didn't succeed.

"We didn't see anything truly useful," Sable answered, shifting in her seat. "I think that was intentional. Ahriman could've shut down my scrying at any point, yet he chose to let us see the worst of what he had planned without giving anything away."

"It's under Machu Picchu." Adem's voice carried an unnamable emotion.

"Which part? And how do you know?"

"I recognized the ridgeline it was on as part of the trail connecting it all. Irene and I hiked it on our honeymoon." He took a deep breath before continuing. "That particular spot is called Phuyupatamarca and once contained some sort of bath house, if I recall correctly. It still has running water." He fell silent as soon as he realized he was rambling.

Sable pondered. "Could you get us there by sight or memory? Maybe gate there from close by so that we're not exhausted when we arrive?"

"I think so, but how will we get into the mountain itself? Did you catch which direction those hallways went in relation to the outside? Don't get me wrong, I'm all for opening a gaping hole in a world heritage site if it saves the world, but it doesn't exactly seem subtle."

"We can dowse for an entrance when we get there," Sable suggested. "Or see if Ailith knows anything else that might help. It's possible she'll have a vision, or that there's already something in her notebook about it."

"She's been through enough for one day, I think." Adem's fatherly tone brooked no argument, but Sable deemed their situation desperate enough to take her chances.

"Agreed, but I don't see as we have a choice. We need information she may have somewhere in that powerful psyche of hers."

"She's a child." Adem's anger at their situation found an outlet in his voice. "I won't put her through more of these visions unless it's the absolute last option." He crossed scarred forearms over his chest and leveled a stare at Sable, who sat up straighter on the cushioned chair she occupied.

"Look around, Adem." She indicated where they sat. "We're about out of intel. The enemy has us on our back foot and we've exhausted most of our resources. Unless you have some sort of deus ex machina in your back pocket, things are looking pretty grim from where I sit." She crossed her own arms in a mimicry of Adem's pose. "These are desperate times calling. It's time for desperate measures."

"If I may," Dedun interjected, pulling a smartphone from somewhere beneath the comfortable robes he'd re-donned once they'd arrived at his home, "I believe there have been recent geological surveys done in and around the location you've described." His fingers flew across the screen as the tension in the room transformed into curiosity. "Ah! Here it is–there was a group that used ground-penetrating radar to look for hidden entrances to underground chambers thought to exist in the hillside." He turned the phone around to share his findings with his companions, who stared at him slack-jawed. Dedun shrugged. "What can I say? I enjoy documentaries."

"Can you send that to me?" Adem asked, pulling out his phone.

"Certainly," Dedun answered. Adem rattled off his phone number and awaited the buzz of the message notification. Sable took a moment to wonder at the incongruity of a god of the underworld exchanging phone numbers with a perfectly normal human. Seeing the two side by side, bent over their phones made the entire situation feel bizarrely commonplace, and Sable felt the calmness of familiarity settle into her soul. She closed her eyes against the scene lest it take root too deeply.

"Sable?" Adem's voice reached into her reverie and shattered it completely. Feigning tiredness, she waved off his questions and rested her head on the arm of the chair.

"Shh, let her have a moment," Dedun said. She heard him stand. "Come with me, Adem Ozturk, and we shall talk." Sable heard Adem rise and listened as both of their footsteps retreated through the kitchen door and into the bleakness outside. She wondered what they could be talking about before true exhaustion overtook her thoughts and drowned them in the waters of unconsciousness.

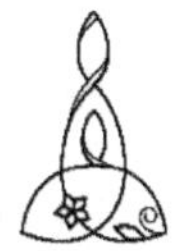

Some Wounds Never Heal

She awoke some time later to someone shuffling into the sitting room. "Sable?" Ailith's uncertain voice was small and sleepy, much more fitting for her eleven years than it often sounded.

"Over here," she slurred, lifting her head.

"Where's the bathroom?"

Sable blinked sleep from her eyes. "There should be a chamber pot somewhere in the room you were in," she answered as she untangled her limbs. Some thoughtful soul had thrown a light blanket over her while she slept, and before she noticed its presence it lassoed her arms together. Cursing, she untucked it around the edges and took another stab at standing. Ailith giggled.

"I have installed an outhouse for guests," Dedun called from the kitchen. "It's out here if you need it." He indicated the outer door behind him.

"Can you come with me?" Ailith asked Sable.

"Only if you hurry," Sable answered as she realized she, too, needed to use the facilities. She scooted out the kitchen door, followed closely by an indignant Ailith. Protests followed her all the way to a squat clay building with a wooden door, which she opened, motioning Ailith inside. "You first." The girl slipped through the door and Sable heard a small bolt close. After a moment Ailith's voice floated through the door panels.

"Where's the TP?!?"

Sable chuckled. "We didn't always have it, you know. Let me find you some." Dedun met her at the door to the hut, roll in hand.

"I forget to stock it most times," he said by way of apology. "Visitors in the land of the dead are few and far between." Sable thanked him and delivered the toilet paper to her charge.

Once they'd both answered nature's call they rejoined Dedun and Adem, who were hard at work finishing dinner. *Guess I slept for a while. At least they're friends now.* Indeed, it seemed the two men had reached some kind of accord; they worked seamlessly, one retrieving plates as the other finished the cooking. Sable wondered if she should be worried.

Ailith hovered at the edge of the kitchen as far from the table in the sitting room as she could get. Sable's scrying bowl was put away, but she could tell the girl was still avoiding the space. "Do you guys mind if we eat outside?" Sable asked. "We've been stuck indoors or in cars so much it would be nice for a change of pace." From the corner of her eye she saw Ailith deflate in relief.

"A fine idea," Dedun replied as he piled heavily spiced meat onto four plates. Flatbread followed, along with the leftover vegetables from lunch.

"I have to admit, I've missed your cooking," Sable acknowledged as they filed out the kitchen door. Chairs she didn't remember seeing before sat facing each other on a packed earth patio. Dedun took the closest, with Sable on one side and Adem on the other. Ailith sat across from him and kept looking up from her food to snatch glances at him when she thought he wasn't looking.

"Ah, but you'll remember that breakfast is my specialty," Dedun replied with a wink. Sable rolled her eyes. "Of course, you will all find that out in the morning," he continued, plowing straight through the double entendre just as it registered on Adem's face. "I hope the sleeping arrangements are to your liking."

"They're super comfy," Ailith answered around a mouthful of bread she'd piled with meat. "I didn't think it was going to be, but man, was I wrong!"

Dedun chuckled. "I'm glad to hear it, little gatekeeper. Of course, if the rest of you require more space you are welcome to share my quarters…except you, young one." Ailith's face fell, then turned red as she figured out what he meant.

Sable opened her mouth to answer, then gaped. "You sly dog! I turned you down, so you proposition him instead?"

"I think you'll find I propositioned you both." The heat in Dedun's expression took in both Adem and Sable and had nothing to do with the desert in his irises.

"I, um, am flattered," Adem began, "but my, ahem, tastes run along different lines, I'm afraid." He turned all of his attention to finishing his food as color crept up his neck and into his ears.

"And I'm doing my best to focus on the tasks at hand, but I appreciate the invitation," Sable replied with more practice and aplomb. Ailith, meanwhile, sat watching the proceedings with rapt attention, her food forgotten in her lap. "You should probably eat that before the flies do," Sable pointed out despite the distinct lack of insects in the underworld.

The rest of the meal was more lighthearted; they spoke of times gone by and shared in human and not-quite-human companionship. The conversation and ease of manners within the group was like a balm on Sable's soul, so much so that for a moment she allowed herself to consider what it would be like not to go back into hiding. She could have this as a regular part of her life again. There could be laughter and sharing and trust and the communion of like minds…so much possibility for happiness.

On the heels of that came the realization of eventual grief when it was ripped away from her by time and the natural order of things, and she closed her heart once again.

After dinner they held council in the sitting room. Ailith went on to bed, citing exhaustion, while Dedun, Adem, and Sable sat up with the map to plan their approach. Sable's notebook came out of her bag along with a pencil so they could list out assets and risks to get a feel for what they had at their disposal.

"Let's start as we would in a survival situation," Adem suggested. "What do we have on our person? I have three knives, a multi-tool, my wallet, and that's about it." As he spoke, he laid each item on top of the map. One of the knives was obviously meant for combat; the other two were smaller, but all three were well cared for.

"Have you had those the whole time?" Sable asked, eyes narrowed. Adem nodded. "How'd you get them through airport security?" He smirked, and Sable realized it was the most playful expression she'd seen on his face. For a moment he wasn't a harrowed refugee running from danger, and it threatened to melt Sable's heart all over again to see him relax.

"Get us through this and I'll show you. Your turn." He gestured at the table.

"Do I get to count things I can summon?" Sable asked.

"Would we be here all day?"

"Probably not, but it may take a minute."

"Start with what you actually have, then," Adem suggested. "We can list out the rest next."

Sable shoved her hands into the pockets of the tan cargo pants she'd pulled out of the duffel the night before. "Not sure when I wore these last…let me see…" Digging around in her right hip pocket, she produced a yellowed copy of the Farmer's Almanac, a small length of copper tubing, two silver coins of indeterminate denomination, a few rusted nails, and a small bell. "I'll be damned! That's where that went!" Sable picked up the copper tubing, which had acquired a few dents in its erstwhile home. "Must've been on my way to fix the still last time I wore these. Probably for the best I didn't." Reaching into the left hip pocket, she produced some dried herbs, a package of peanuts well past their expiration date, and a dusty piece of Werther's hard candy still in its wrapper. "Gotta keep the snacks and edibles separate," she said by way of explanation as she rummaged in the right cargo pocket. Dedun and Adem watched with curiosity as she produced a small hand augur and some feed corn that shimmered suspiciously before reaching into her left cargo pocket.

"How big are your pockets?" Adem asked incredulously.

"As big as I need them to be. Ah ha! Yep, this is the fun pocket." Two bundles of dried marijuana leaves joined the rest of the table's detritus along with a handful of mushrooms. "Don't eat those unless you want to have a very interesting sixteen to twenty-four hours," she warned as Dedun reached for the pile. Adem narrowed his eyes at her. "What? I lived by myself in the middle of the woods and had arthritis, not to mention boredom."

"You've been carrying drugs this whole time? Around

Ailith?"

"I'd forgotten they were there," Sable admitted sheepishly. Mollified, Adem watched as Dedun reached for the pile.

"If it's the same kind you used to grow, I'll keep it safe for you," he said, winking. The weed and mushrooms disappeared into a drawer close by.

They stared at the eclectic mix of supplies before them in silence. "So, next step: what do we have easy access to?"

Sable picked up her duffel. "Pretty much anything," she replied, pulling out a matched set of lamps it produced for illustrative purposes. "It doesn't seem to provide weapons, but it's given me everything else I've ever needed. Food, water, clothing, a place to store stuff, sometimes things I didn't even think I needed but were extremely useful." She handed the lamps to Dedun, who found tables to set them on, muttering in wonderment about how he needed more light in the room.

Adem looked in his backpack. "I have two sets of clothes and some snacks, plus a water bottle. Not much, and not very useful for infiltrating a compound." His face regained the sobriety it had worn since they'd met as reality crept back into their brief respite.

"Did you guys find anything on the geophys?" Sable asked a little too brightly. She winced at the brittle edge to her own voice.

Adem perked up. "I never finished checking it," he answered as he pulled out his phone.

"Allow me." Dedun waved a hand and gray sand filtered through the door flap beyond, gamboling across the floor to suspend itself in the air above the table. As soon as the images loaded on Adem's phone the sand coalesced into a perfect, three-dimensional mimicry of the geophysical data, complete with silhouette of the surface above.

Adem whistled. "Now that's useful," he said as he circled the new planning map. "There has to be something…here." He stabbed a finger at a point where the surface almost touched a tunnel that drove into the mountain paralleling Phuyupatamarca's ridgeline. "We can open up that tunnel for ingress, then slide along it until we reach the main chamber." His finger slid along the shifting sands until it reached a large space just down the tunnel. "It looks like there's only one way out of that room: the tunnel that leads to the chamber underneath Phuyupatamarca itself. Think that's where we'll need to go?"

"You said it still has running water?" Sable clarified. Adem nodded. "Then yes, that's where the ritual will be. Running water makes it easier to cross over into the space between." The three companions stared at the small chamber on the 3D map as if it could regurgitate more details about what it contained. "One more question," Sable ventured. "What do we do with Ailith?"

Adem looked at Dedun. "I cannot keep her safe," their host said, hands raised in supplication. "With the ritual this man is planning, I must defend the spirits under my protection so that they may continue their afterlife in peace. Besides, the in-between is not safe for Ailith. She is better off with you."

Adem harrumphed. "I don't like it," he admitted, "but I think we have to bring her with us. We can hide her outside the entrance we make and do our best to get in and out quietly, or at the very least keep her close." Sable nodded, unable to come up with a better plan, but also unhappy with the necessity of bringing their charge closer to harm.

"Well, it sounds like you have the beginnings of a plan," Dedun exclaimed as he stood, "but you both know it will not go quietly. Have you fought together?"

Adem looked at Sable. "Not as such," she answered for them both as they rose. "Mostly separately."

"Then let us train together before turning in for the night," Dedun replied, motioning them out the back tent flap and into the yard beyond. The unyielding grayscape before them set a foreboding backdrop for the task at hand and Sable felt tension begin to knot her back. *Dedun is right, old woman. You need to know your allies' strengths and weaknesses, their moves, how to not get in each other's way.* With an effort she pulled her shoulders down from where they'd crept up toward her ears and waited to see what their host had in store for them.

Choosing a clear spot not far from the hut Dedun stopped and changed appearances. Instead of the robed figure they'd grown accustomed to there stood a sinewy, graceful figure clad in a white royal kilt with a gold collar around his neck. Leather sandals wrapped muscular feet and ankles as he took a balanced stance before them, a curved stick that mimicked a sword appearing in one hand. "You are welcome to use any weapons you find comfortable," Dedun invited. "Whenever you are ready."

"Is he serious?" Adem asked, looking at Sable with raised eyebrows.

"As the grave," Sable replied. "Got any more practice sticks?" she called to Dedun. A smaller, straighter stick appeared on the ground before her and she picked it up, hefting the weapon to feel its balance. "Yep, this'll do nicely."

Adem looked around. "I prefer guns, but if you're wanting melee weapons I could use the equivalent of a Ka-Bar." A wooden dagger seven inches long appeared on the sand at his feet and he picked it up, wrapping his hand around the grip. "So, how does this work?"

"You try to take me down, two on one," Dedun answered with an open-armed gesture. "If that proves too easy, I make it more difficult."

Sable rolled her eyes. "I've got this," she said, sauntering forward toward their antagonist in a relaxed gait until the very last moment, when she feinted with her stick and struck a passing blow to Dedun's ribcage as she ducked past his reach. "Ha!" she yelled triumphantly—only to find his weapon reversed in his grip and pressed against her neck. "Damn, you've gotten craftier," she ground out through gritted teeth.

"And you have gotten slower and more predictable. Have you not practiced since last we fought together?"

"I've been busy trying to die," Sable answered testily. "Adem, you care for a go?" She turned to look at him only to find the space he'd occupied empty. By way of answer he appeared behind Dedun and snaked an arm around the shorter man's shoulders in an attempt to put him in a rear choke. In the blink of an eye he was on his back in front of their host with a foot on his throat, coughing as the wind returned to his lungs. "Ooh, probably should've warned you about that," Sable winced. "He's a lot faster than you or I. Hand to hand is kind of his forte." Dedun grinned and offered Adem a hand up. Instead of taking it Adem grabbed the man's ankle and yanked, pulling him down to his level where he proceeded to try a series of wrestling and judo moves for ground control. Sable watched with interest as the two men rolled through the silvery sand. *There are plenty of people who'd pay good money to watch this. Hell,* I'd *pay good money to watch this.* She grinned, crossed her arms, and settled in to see who would come out on top. *Either way, I win.*

Before long Dedun emerged victorious after pinning his opponent with an arm bar. "Do you yield?" he asked, not even breathing hard. Adem nodded, caught his breath, and got up as Dedun let him go. "Alone, the two of you cannot defeat me," Dedun began, "but together I do not think I could best you both. Sable I have trained with enough to know her ways, which makes her easier for me to defeat, but though she is small she is strong. She is also smart and much faster than most give her credit for. Adem, you have both strength and intelligence on your side, and it is obvious you are trained to use both. Now, how can the two of you complement each other well enough to win a fight?"

"Depends on who we're up against," Sable answered.

"In this case, me."

"All right, then let us huddle up for a minute and figure it out."

"You don't have a minute," Dedun answered as he lunged at Sable weapon-first. She parried and riposted, earning a grunt as she tapped him in the ribs using a style she hadn't called to mind in centuries as her mind whirled.

"The whole point of this was for us to figure that out," she panted as Dedun changed tactics, going instead for heavier swings that forced her to tighten up her technique.

"There is a far faster way of doing that," Dedun replied as he dodged Adem's attempt to take him from behind, dancing to the side to face a single opponent at a time.

"No." Sable swung harder than was strictly necessary and cracked a shot onto Dedun's knuckles. "I am not linking minds with him to do this."

"Why not?" Barely keeping his weapon in hand, Dedun turned to parry Adem's latest advance before returning his attention to Sable.

"Because I can't," she answered lamely as she shifted directions to find a weakness.

"Can't–or won't?" Sable caught a kick to the gut that knocked the wind out of her.

"Won't, and you know it." Feigning disability, she used the opening it created to spring at Dedun's back while he engaged with Adem. Before long she found herself staring up at their host from the ground. Adem was likewise situated not far from where she lay and was wearing a thoroughly confused expression. Dedun offered each of them a hand up, which they took, dusting themselves off. The ubiquitous sand fell from their clothing in a strange argent mist that left none clinging to them.

Sable was the first to find her voice. "I appreciate the help, Dedun, really I do, but I'm not the same person I was last time I came through here. I've seen too much, experienced too much, and been dragged through too much to put myself deliberately in the way of more heartache. We'll have to find another way."

"Bullshit." Steel flashed in Sable's eyes as Dedun leveled his own implacable gaze at her. "You are the same headstrong, unstoppable woman I knew so long ago. Stop finding excuses not to be and step in where you are needed. That girl–" he pointed toward the hut where Ailith slept–" is the key to saving both our worlds. The woman I knew would not let her down by giving in to her own doubts and fears."

"Do you have any idea how many people I have lost while doing exactly what you've just asked of me?" Now Sable was toe to toe with their host, their audience and surroundings forgotten as anger roiled through her.

"Yes." Dedun's answer was soft and full of regret. "I know every one. I am a god of the dead; these things are mine to know." The fire of Sable's indignance was snuffed out by the compassion in his voice. "I cannot fathom how that must feel, especially for one with such a soft heart, so you know I would not ask this of you except in the direst of need."

Sable hung her head. "I can't go through that again." Without meeting the eyes of either of her companions, she shuffled off toward a log that sat nearby and settled herself on it to think, head in her hands. The screams of the dying floated up from her past to plague her thoughts as her mind dragged her back through experiences she'd thought long buried. Lost in her reverie, it startled her when someone settled onto the log beside her, close enough to reach but far enough not to intrude.

"Want to talk about it?" Adem's voice floated across the space between them, quiet and undemanding.

"No." Sable didn't even look up.

"You have PTSD."

"Is that what they're calling it these days?" Sable answered bitterly. "It was shellshock last I heard."

"Same thing, different century." Adem leaned over to rest his forearms on his knees. It brought him closer to her level, though he still didn't look her way. "I can't say I fully understand it, but I've watched more friends than I care to consider work through what they've seen and experienced, so I've gotten pretty good at listening. Every one of them said it helped to talk."

"Had any of them been in solitary confinement for eighty years? Fought off legions of Romans to try–and fail–to protect their homeland? Watched their homes burned and their people subjugated?" Sable shook her head as her fears warred with her need to put words to them, then plowed forward. "I spent decades–centuries–avenging my people, only to find it an empty cause when the empire fell through no effort of mine. I'd learned tactics, strategy, every fighting style I could get my hands on, anything that might give me an edge–all for nothing. Didn't want to waste all that effort, so from there I decided to spend some time as a mercenary. Eventually I found someone who taught me more about magic. By then I was so far removed from the start of my whole ordeal I could stomach the thought of using it, so I learned how to use magic and martial arts together.

"I remember the first time I linked minds with someone to coordinate combat. It was during one of the Umayyad campaigns; I forget which one. Fought in most of them trying to help the Hispano-Romans and then the Franks keep, then retake their territory from the Moorish invaders. We were running a night op against an encampment to try to break the Moors' morale–sneak into camp and take out supplies, steal horses, kill the guards and leave before the camp realized what was happening. Since it was dark we needed a way to coordinate the two wings of the assault so that we hit the camp at the same time. I'd been working with one of the other officers long enough to trust him with the knowledge I was a witch, as they called me, and he trusted me enough to link up with me so we would know when to attack. What we didn't know was that they were waiting. Alaric gave the signal to move in–and was run through by a Moorish sword. They knew we were coming." The feel of steel sliding underneath her ribcage and into her lungs and heart returned unbidden. "I felt him die. I felt the steel pass through his organs and stop his heart, and I was with him when his spirit fled." Sable swallowed against her suddenly dry throat. "Needless to say we lost that particular campaign.

"I was a lot more resilient in those days, and not wanting to throw away a tactical advantage, I took to using mind links for coordination on other quiet operations with small units. Sometimes it worked; sometimes it didn't. It helped more than it hurt, but each life I watched slip away left a mark. Eventually I gave up martial campaigns altogether and decided to throw myself into peaceful pursuits, uprooting every decade or so in order to avoid the inevitable witch hunts that would follow if I didn't. For a while I was able to set aside what I'd seen, heard, felt…it's been hundreds of years. But it's never left me." She hugged herself in hopes that the nausea her recollections brought up would go away.

Adem sat in silence for a moment, waiting to see if more was forthcoming before answering. "That's a lot to carry on your own," he ventured.

"Nobody else to carry it for me." Sable's loneliness replaced the feel of the blade that took Alaric, settling into its familiar space in her chest. "Hasn't been for two thousand years."

"You've had friends throughout that time, haven't you?"

"Lost every one of them."

Adem contemplated in silence, unable to refute her point.

"Have I explained to you the terms of my curse?" Sable queried.

"No, but I'd like to hear them," Adem replied.

"When everyone I have ever known or loved is dead and gone, and everything I've created turned to dust or uselessness, my soul can finally rest." Sable sat upright against the sadness and ennui that threatened to bend her body to its will. "Those were the words Cantismerta spoke the day I killed her in retaliation for the death of my beloved." A tear formed at the corner of Sable's eye despite her valiant attempt not to let her emotions leak out. "She was young and powerful, and we desired the same young man. But Dagomarus and I had been in love since we were children growing up in the same village. I was his other half, the portion of him that knew before he did when he would speak and how he would feel. He knew when I was hurt and how to make me happy. We had agreed to wed with the blessings of our families—and the day before our handfasting, *she* appeared at our doorstep, demanding to see the groom-to-be." Sable's face twisted into a rictus of hatred. "We let her in, being the good hosts we were. And when his back was turned she ran him through with a knife rather than let him bind himself to me. In my rage I grabbed a harvesting tool from the wall and stabbed her with it until she fell to the ground, choking on her own blood. Her last words were the death curse that has haunted me ever since." Tears trailed down her cheeks as the source of her grief was traced anew through her recollections.

"He was the one I saw in your memories," Adem stated. Sable nodded, not trusting her voice to respond. "That is a grief I can speak to," he continued. "It's been eleven years since I lost Irene, and I've spent most of them angry. Angry at fate for taking the love of my life, angry at whatever god might exist for denying my daughter her mother…I've railed against it all. But most of all I've missed my other half." He shifted on the log in contemplation of what to say next. "I've never dated, you know. Since Irene. I've never wanted to; instead I threw myself into being the best father I could be to make up for Ailith not having a mother." He trailed a toe in the sand, drawing a semicircle in an absent gesture, then ran a hand through his dark hair. Adem's discomfort softened Sable's bitterness as she considered the bit of context they shared while hating that they'd experienced similar loss.

"It gets easier over time," she answered as she wiped at her own eyes. "Never really goes away, though."

"Did you ever find anyone else?" Adem's voice sounded smaller, more vulnerable, and Sable reached out to rest a reassuring hand on his shoulder.

"I moved on, yes," she answered, "but I've never replaced him. That isn't possible. What is possible is finding happiness in different ways." She started to slide her hand from his shoulder and was stopped as he covered it with his own. He gave it a squeeze, then let it drop as they resumed their own sides of the log, a strange, new openness occupying the space between them.

"So," Adem began after a long moment, "where do we go from here? We know where we're supposed to end up, but how do we get there? And what do we do when we find this place?"

"Well, first we go to Meroë," Sable answered as she regained some of her usual composure, though she could tell something had shifted between them. "Ailith's visions tell us there's something there we need to know, and we did promise Dedun we'd head there and help him make an entrance." She grinned despite herself.

"Were the two of you…"

"Involved? Yes, hundreds of years ago," Sable answered, "but that's ancient history even to the experts. He's a great guy, but it wasn't meant to last." She stood and stretched her stiff muscles, wondering at how tired she was despite the nap she'd had earlier. "Come on, let's get some rest; I have some ideas on how we can help Dedun out, but we'll need our strength to pull it off." She took a few steps toward the hut, then stopped. "And thanks for listening." Without turning around Sable made her way back to the room she shared with Ailith and crept inside. The girl was fast asleep, curled around a large pillow and taking up a good two thirds of the space on the padded floor. Sable settled in on the third that was left, choosing a pillow for her head and allowing herself the small comfort of one to hug as she drifted off to sleep.

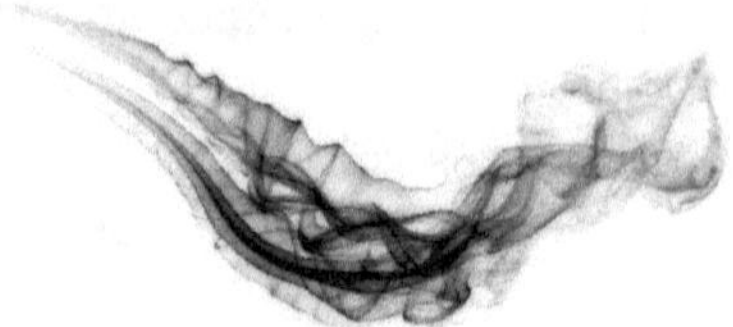

The Chess Board is Set

The tall figure seated on its red velvet cushions chuckled to itself. *All is happening according to plan.* Less than two days until their plan would come to fruition and the final players in the game were heading straight into his arms. He'd fed them just enough information to know where to find him, but not enough for them to know how to thwart him, and based on their behavior thus far he had no doubt they would rush in to try to stop the ritual. If he was lucky they would be flying blind with no knowledge of how to accomplish their goal. But this enemy was resourceful; there was a good chance they already knew what was required. Still, all he had to do was bide his time and set the trap. It was already baited.

"My lord?" A lightly accented voice broke Ahriman's reverie. "You called for me?" The voice belonged to a tall, burly man with blond hair and eyes the color of ice.

"Yes, Taurizl," Ahriman replied. "I am in need of your expertise."

"You have but to ask." Taurizl bowed stiffly from the waist.

"You are the final piece of my puzzle." Ahriman stood and circled his underling, taking in the breadth of the man's shoulders with an appreciative gaze. "Beautiful destruction contained in an equally beautiful shell. You always choose the best vessels." He sighed and trailed his hand across the man's shoulder blades, watching him shudder. "You will be my protector, the deliverer of my will to these interlopers once I have the child. I want them crushed, destroyed beyond recognition, and I don't care what you have to take with them to do it as long as the ritual remains unimpeded."

"Please, master, allow me to find them and deliver your justice now." Taurizl stood, a cold fire in his eyes.

"No. It's too risky." Ahriman resumed his seat on the dais, beckoning Taurizl to sit on the step before him in order to stay below his level. "You will remain here and set up whatever you need to spring a trap on the Ozturks and their companion." *Whoever she is; I still wish we had more information on that one. She's trouble.* "You have all of my considerable resources at your disposal."

"I will need at least twenty loyal followers who can fight."

"You have twenty five."

Taurizl nodded and stood. "Then I have what I need. We will hold this room at all costs, and if it falls we will destroy the hallway beyond and seal the chamber with the gate. By then you will have the girl?" Ahriman nodded. "Then with your leave I have many things to arrange."

"Dismissed." Taurizl bowed low, backed away, and strode from the now-empty room.

Ahriman paused an extra half minute after Taurizl disappeared before speaking. "Nanghait, I know you've been eavesdropping," he drawled, and the daeva in question wavered into view at the edge of his vision. "You know your part in this game, do you not?"

"The girl is as good as mine," Nanghait replied. "They will bring her with them, and once they've arrived I will find my opening."

"Be certain you do not wait too long and miss your window of opportunity." Ahriman stretched, then stood, staring down his body's long nose at his minion. Nanghait sketched a mocking bow, then wavered back out of existence. *I've never trusted that one.* Sighing, Ahriman slid around behind his chair toward the hallway behind it. Of late he'd spent many of his waking hours close to the arch, feeling the veil between worlds thin and communing with his allies on the other side of the gate. He'd ignored the insects buzzing around the office building he'd attached to this location via a permanent gate. They asked too many questions about things that would soon be inconsequential. It was useful taking a host who had power and funding, but the tedium of managing them was never something he enjoyed. *Paul Arcos of Arcos International. Shame you were always so selfish.* A buzz in the back of his psyche reminded him that his host still inhabited their mind, but he swatted at it as he would a troublesome fly and felt it recede once again. Soon enough he wouldn't need a body.

Soon no one would.

How to Make an Entrance

Sable rose before everyone else, stumbled to the outhouse, then went in search of coffee. Some thoughtful soul had rigged a serviceable coffee maker with a filter and ground beans, ready to start at the push of a button, but Sable knew this kitchen, and a few moments of rifling rewarded her with a handled copper vessel, which she filled with water and set on the stove. Another moment's search revealed a container of finely-ground coffee from which she took a measure and added it to the pot. The click of the gas stove cracked through the hut as the mixture began to heat. She added cardamom, cloves, and cinnamon, then sat back to wait as the contents came to a boil.

Three minutes and a search for mugs later Sable poured the foaming result of her chemistry into chipped earthenware that might have seen the fall of the Kushite pharaohs. As she took her first appreciative sip a disheveled head appeared around the corner of one of the bedrooms. "Is that what I think it is?" Adem asked.

"You like yours sade, az şekerli, orta şekerli, or şekerli?" Sable asked as she ambled back over to the stove.

"Orta şekerli, lütfen," he replied, pulling on pants as he cleared the door. It was obvious he'd slept in the wrinkled shirt he wore. As Sable refilled the cezve–adding sugar this time, per his request–Adem settled onto the single stool nearby and snuck a surreptitious sniff of Sable's cup. "What did you put in yours?"

"The three C's: cardamom, clove, and cinnamon," Sable replied as she brought a second cup to a near boil. This time she spooned off half the foam into a second cup before letting the mixture finish cooking. The resulting cup was more stylish than the one she'd made herself, and she set it down in front of Adem. "It's how I make my chai, too." She watched as he took the first sip of his coffee.

Adem's eyes closed as he savored the warmth of the beverage. "I haven't had real Turkish coffee in years," he said, leaning back on the counter behind him.

"Me neither." Sable reached just past him to save her own cup from its precarious position at his elbow, leaning just far enough to reach it before retreating to a less distracting distance. "Figured you might could use something stronger than normal for today's shenanigans."

"And here I thought you were actually starting to like me." She couldn't see Adem's expression behind his cup, but she could hear the smile in his voice. He sighed. "I've missed this stuff. My mom used to make it every morning."

"I grew up without coffee." Sable sipped at her own cup appreciatively. "Still not sure how that worked, but we survived. Somehow."

"So, you have a plan?" The potent drink was already threading its way through their systems and both looked more awake.

"I do." Sable grinned. "Even Dedun's going to like it."

"Going to like what?" Their host stepped out from his own bedchamber and stretched despite the fact that it was obvious he'd been awake for some time. He emerged wearing only a pair of silk boxers in a rich red that set off his skin in a very fetching way. Sable rolled her eyes. He grinned back boyishly and turned on the coffee pot, making sure to lean closer than was strictly necessary to both of his guests as he moved around his kitchen.

"I've concocted a way for us to make your entrance–or rather, re-entrance–when we get to Meroë." Sable pointedly ignored Dedun's posturing in favor of seating herself in the sitting room. Adem followed suit with alacrity and took up the closest seat to Sable, one eye on Dedun all the while. *For someone as well traveled as he is, he's sure as hell prudish about some things.* Sable stopped herself hoping the prudishness didn't go too far. *We've got to make it through the next few days,* she reminded herself. *Then I can reevaluate my life choices. Again.* Once Dedun had the coffee pot going she outlined her plan, earning a mischievous grin from their host and a nod of approval from Adem. Ailith appeared just in time to hear that she had a role to play and was excited for the first time since they'd seen the Egyptian Muse-um. All three adults breathed a sigh of relief at seeing her smile again after the previous day's trauma.

After coffee came breakfast, and Dedun made good on his word: they had spiced potatoes, roasted vegetables, and thick-sliced bacon to go with their coffee. "I get mine from America," he explained as it sizzled in the pan. "No other country has such a selection!" Once they'd eaten their fill and put up the leftovers there was nothing left to do but head for their destination.

Dedun's driving was less terror-inducing on the way back to the surface; Sable only had to grab the oh-shit handle twice during the trip. She'd relieved Adem of front seat duties in favor of allowing him to retreat from his own awkwardness, which gave her an up-close view of their destination as the desert spat them out west of the pyramids. It was late afternoon of the same day they left Cairo, and with the sun riding three quarters of the way through its journey they were in a perfect position to see the location at its best. The destruction of the impressive structures sank into Sable's heart as a massive waste; none of the visible buildings had retained much of their original shape and the signs of blasting around the largest were obvious. *"Italian thug" is right, Auguste. I'd have called him worse,* Sable thought as she recalled the message they'd heard at the muse-um.

"Wow," Ailith breathed from the backseat. "Are those real pyramids? Like, the ancient kind?"

"What's left of them, yes," Dedun replied, looking wistful. "They were once impressive monuments to the rulers of this land; now look at them." He swept his arm across the eastern horizon. "So much work, all wasted."

"I still think they're impressive as hell," Ailith muttered, earning a chuckle from the driver's seat.

"Just you wait, young one. Just you wait."

"Pull off here." Sable indicated a spot not far from a scant dirt road running north to south through the emptiness around the historical site. "We'll need some space to work. Adem, you're with me; Dedun, you're on wardrobe." Both men nodded as they exited the car. Adem and Sable surveyed the site before them. "That's where we're headed," Sable began as she located the largest pyramid base on the site. "The tomb of Amanishakheto."

"Ah! What a woman." Dedun's voice floated up from behind the car where he stood taking stock of Ailith's size. "Warrior, scholar, queen…she oozed confidence. It was extremely attractive." He pondered a moment, then added, "It might also have been her backside I was infatuated with. You would have liked her, Nulwa." He smiled a Cheshire cat grin at Sable.

"But would she have liked me?" Sable retorted.

Dedun laughed. "She would likely have had you beheaded as a threat."

"Then you're right; I would've liked her." Sable grinned wickedly back, then refocused on their objective. "All right, it looks like we have enough space between this set of ruins–" she indicated the group that held Amanishakheto's pyramid–"and the next set to the north to set up our barrier and not hit anything. Adem, you're on sand duty; you'll be working with me. Dedun, you and Ailith stage behind us so that once we have everything set up we can just roll in." Nods greeted her all around and she realized Dedun had already changed their appearances to match his; all of them looked Sudanese in features and wore some variation of white garment. Sable wore a white sheath dress that hugged curves far more ample than her real ones with gold sandals tied to her feet while Adem retained his usual build and wore a sleeveless white vest with no shirt beneath it and a pair of matching slacks. Ailith looked like a Sudanese boy who was dressed in a white suit that was the smaller twin of the one Dedun wore. The god of the dead himself was clad in a tailored white suit that shone in the late afternoon sun, complete with golden tie and white wingtip shoes. His twisted hair was pulled back at the nape of his neck in a loose, short ponytail, and he carried a black cane topped with a golden lion's head. The overall effect was one of opulence and refinement. "After you." Sable indicated that Dedun should lead. He offered her his arm, which she took as she began to call forth the winds that would bring her plan to life.

Tourists thronged to Meroë to view the ruins as sunset

painted them colors the desert could never match without its help. One such group had just debarked a modest tour bus and stood before one of the southern structures, half listening to the guide as he explained the significance of each building, while other visitors were strung between the pyramids in a loose human chain that draped itself across the available space. Despite the sun's trajectory the light in the ruins began to dim. Shadows faded, then disappeared as twilight took over the central courtyard of the site. One visitor then another reached out a shaking hand to point at the mounting wall of sand encircling the set of buildings they'd come to visit. It extended twenty feet from ground level and was so dense that only the barest amount of sunlight filtered through, casting a pall over the entire area and blocking out all sound but the roaring of the wind.

Blinding light appeared due west of the pyramid of Amanishakheto. A razor-sharp sunbeam illuminated where the door should have been, interrupted only by the four figures standing in a gateway within the whirling maelstrom. They were backlit as they approached the ruins, but as they neared the tourists began to murmur in wonder. Who was this man? And the woman with him—she looked dangerous. One of the tour guides whispered a name and the rest backed away, superstition telling them they were in the presence of one of the old gods. The man behind the pair stood tall even as he sweated under the strain of some invisible burden, and the serving boy with him held his head high in imitation of the man in front. Heavy silence dropped on the courtyard as the group stopped at the foot of the ruins and the woman turned to face her companion. "Rebuild my temple!" she cried, her voice clear and demanding above the sound of the wind. "Let it not languish in this state! Am I not worthy of a greater resting place than this pile of brick and mortar?"

"Indeed you are, Kandake." Dedun's easy, smooth voice gained a booming, otherworldly quality as it echoed through the courtyard and everyone within the bounds of the sand wall stepped back a pace, their feet making no sound. Even the wail of the sandstorm without was muted as Dedun raised his hands. The earth shook, sending bits of debris rolling down the sides of the surrounding pyramids–until the bouncing rubble stopped, rolling backwards as the rumbling continued beneath their feet. Larger and larger stones joined their tiny companions as the ruins grew into a masterpiece of architecture and engineering, their journey revealing every facet of the building's innards before sealing them once again behind a great stone doorway. At a sharp command from Dedun the doors swung open on silent hinges to admit them into the torchlight beyond.

"After you, Kandake," Dedun invited, and they strode through the double doors, Sable in the lead. The stone doors clanged shut behind them with finality, leaving the tourists and tour guides to puzzle over the newly-risen wonder before them as sound rushed back into the plaza and the wall of sand dropped back onto the desert floor.

As soon as the doors closed Adem sagged against the wall. "I hope…that was what…you were looking for," he panted as their disguises dropped, leaving them all looking much the same as they'd left that morning with the exception of his own missing shirt. Sable noted the lack and rolled her eyes.

"Did he tell you that you had to go shirtless for the disguise to work?" she asked, one eyebrow cocked at Adem. He nodded, and she turned her stare on Dedun. "You really are incorrigible, you know that?" She reached into the duffel and dug around for a shirt. Her hand found one, but every time she grasped it something snatched it further away. "Not you, too," she whispered angrily at the bag as they fought. "I've got ninety-nine problems right now, and a shirt oughtn't be one!" A bit of tugging and a popped seam later she was able to free an undershirt from the bag's shenanigans and toss it to Adem, who nodded his thanks as he donned it.

"I cannot help myself sometimes," Dedun chuckled. "He is a beautiful man; you would not begrudge a lonely old god this small entertainment, would you?"

"That's up to the butt of the joke, I'm afraid." Sable waved vaguely at Adem as she continued further down the stairs and into the pyramid. Ailith crept by her side, eyes glazed over but still standing.

"I can see her," Ailith whispered. "They brought her in

and placed her right down…there." She pointed at a decaying wooden sarcophagus resting in the chamber beyond, which was lit with torches that guttered in wall sconces around the room. "She's not there, though."

"She lives in my lands now." Dedun rested a hand on Ailith's shoulder. The mists in her eyes cleared and she looked around the room as if seeing it for the first time. "Yes, I was able to restore the paintings and stela, as well," he chuckled as the girl's eyes went wide. "There's a good chance that's what you're here for, after all."

"How did you…?" Ailith trailed off as she gestured at the walls of the staircase around them. They were covered from floor to ceiling in richly-painted murals depicting the accomplishments of the kandake herself, both military and otherwise. Support beams punctuated the ceiling to keep the tunnel from collapsing and carried carvings and paint of their own. The ceiling mimicked the night sky with a riot of bright stars against a deep blue background.

"You see that color?" Dedun pointed at the vista above them. "Nowhere else in the world will you find it. The painters crushed precious stones into it and mixed it with other minerals they found nearby to keep it bright for all eternity. I did nothing to restore its shade." Ailith's mouth opened in an O of wonder and even Sable raised her eyebrows. "Come, let us find what we came for." He led the way past elaborate scenes of battles and into the burial chamber itself, which boasted the richest images of them all. Dominating the back wall stood an image of two women standing next to a stone archway, one on either side, with the woman on the right clutching a hunk of rock she'd pulled from the structure. The woman on the left plunged a rough-hewn stone dagger into the chest of a tall, vaguely humanoid figure with a neck far too long for its body. Dedun stared at the depiction with the rest of his companions. "So that's what she was after," he mused.

"I guess that answers the question of what we need to do," Sable said. "Hey, isn't that Amesemi on the other side?"

"Indeed," Dedun answered as he walked across the room. "Though the likeness does not do her justice." He reached a hand up to touch the goddess's fierce expression as she tri-umphed over her enemy.

"So we're supposed to find an arch and take one of its stones, then stab something?" Adem asked, doubt evident in his voice.

"Removing the stone weakens him," Ailith answered vacantly. Her eyes had once again glazed over, but she stood upright, weaving back and forth a little as she looked around the room. "Once we have it we can take his mortal form from him and I can send him home." She sat down and sent dust flying up around her in a cloud, her eyes clearing as the air muddied. "But we have to use the dagger he's made on him instead of me. Nothing else will work."

Well, that's new, Sable realized as Adem moved to check on his daughter. *At least she's not slipping back into the in-between when she does it. No telling what's lurking there.* "All right, then, next question: how are we going to get there? By my calculations we have about half a day before the solstice."

"You have one and a half," Dedun interjected without turn-ing. "Time passes as I will it in my realm."

"Okay, one and a half, and thank you." Dedun nodded, still deep in contemplation. "Gating is out of the question; it's too far and too soon to be worth anything when we get there, and we all need to be at full strength. He knows we're coming, so do we just catch a flight?"

"And risk giving them Ailith early? No way," Adem replied. "Besides, we could get stuck somewhere and miss a connection. We need another option."

"I don't know of any alternatives that aren't too slow." Sable passed a hand over her brow, wishing she hadn't spent so long out of the game that she was out of non-financial resources.

"I might also be of service there." Dedun glided across the room to where they'd congregated on the floor next to Ailith. "This place you are going, it had a god of the dead at one point, yes?"

"The Incans called him Supay," Adem answered. "They believed he ruled the underworld and had an army of demons at his command."

Dedun nodded. "Give me a moment; I will return shortly." He took a step away from them and blinked from existence.

"I like him." Ailith's voice echoed across the stillness left in Dedun's wake. She sounded for all the world like a regular eleven-year-old again. *That shouldn't surprise me; she* is *eleven. But I guess both of us are older than we look.*

"Me too," Sable agreed.

"Wait, do you *like* like him, or just like him?"

"What?" Sable's brow furrowed in confusion. "I don't even know what that means."

Ailith shrugged. "Do you, y'know, like him a lot–" she winked twice–"or just like a friend or something?"

Sable rolled her eyes and let it bleed into her tone. "He's a good friend," she answered. "Helped me through some tough times."

"Yeah, but he's totally hot!" Ailith blurted out. She glanced at her dad, who stopped taking pictures of the wall paintings to stare at her. "What? He is! Sable, back me up!" Sable raised her hands and stepped out of the line of fire.

"He's far too old for you." Adem sounded calmer than he looked as he went back to recording the information they'd found on his phone.

"A few thousand years too old," Sable agreed. "Come back in at least ten years." Adem shot her a glance that was only slightly murderous and she winked back at him, earning a head shake and a hefty sigh.

The three fell into companionable silence as they waited for Dedun to return. Adem surveyed the drawings for every ounce of information they would surrender while Ailith stared at them, half in and half out of the world above. Sable made herself comfortable studying the sarcophagus before them. It was brightly painted, showing a strong Egyptian influence while also bearing markings whose meaning had been lost to time. *Much like my own language,* Sable thought. She hadn't thought much of her people–her first people–in a very long time, but found herself wishing she could see her home once more, as it had been. *They say things were simpler then, but really they were just harder.* The effort it took to build a home, or grind wheat into flour, or slaughter livestock and process the parts seemed commonplace when it was all you knew; now she considered the luxuries around her and saw new wonder in humankind's progress. Devices that allowed you to talk over incredible distances, running water everywhere you looked, meat already packaged in neat trays for cooking…she'd started taking it all for granted, and now, sitting in an ancient tomb with torches for light, she was starkly reminded of how things had been when she was young.

"Anything useful on the sarcophagus?" Adem asked from right beside her. The man was a ninja. He could appear and disappear in full lighting without anyone noticing.

"Nope." Sable dusted off her shorts as she stood, doing her best to look as if she'd known he was there all along. "All written in Kushite script, which no living person can read, myself included. It predates even me."

"I can read it if you'd like." Dedun reappeared on her left, leaning in to whisper conspiratorially. Sable glanced to either side of her, feeling keenly the proximity of both of the men beside her. It was cloying.

Lords and ladies, I'm a man sandwich. A manwich, if you will. "If you think it'll tell us anything useful," she answered, stepping back to remove herself from the direct line between the two. A tension developed across the space that hadn't been present before. *Oh, for Pete's sake, this is not the time.* "Otherwise we should be on our way." She shifted toward Adem and Ailith, holding Dedun's gaze as she shuffled sideways and prayed she wouldn't trip over a stray rock. Dedun turned to study the coffin.

"I don't believe any of this has to do with the scene on the wall," he said after a tense moment. "If you have what you need from the paintings, I am ready to relay you to your next port of call."

"And that would be…?" Sable raised a questioning eyebrow.

"Ukhu Pacha. We go to the Incan underworld. From there Supay has granted you passage to the place you seek."

"Thanks to your intercession, no doubt." Sable smiled tightly. "We are in your debt once again, Dedun."

"Only if you fail to prevent this cataclysm," the god replied, a tired look replacing his usually carefree expression. "That is the only payment I require."

"Can you not come with us? We could use your help."

"I must stay with the souls in my charge and protect them from whatever may come." Steel flashed in Dedun's expression and for a brief moment he was fully a god of the underworld, wreathed in a power not seen, but felt. "It is for you to finish this task." This he directed at Ailith, who nodded. "You must finish what Amesemi could not. She was a goddess, not a gate-keeper." Deflating, Dedun passed his gaze around the room one more time, lingering on the paintings before sliding back across the group. "Now, if you're ready…"

"Adem? Ailith?" Both nodded, unwilling to speak. "Then let's get moving." Sable watched as Dedun opened a crack in the wall, stretching it until it was wide enough to fit the four of them before leading them through–and into a portion of the in-between Sable had never seen.

DEVIL'S TELEVISION

Dedun led the way through the fissure, with Adem close behind and Ailith on her father's tail. Sable took one last look around the tomb and gave silent thanks to its occupant before slipping through the gap. She could've sworn one of the paintings on the wall waved as it disappeared from sight. *Maybe that'll mean good luck.*

A path wound a silver ribbon through the ether before them, starting from where they stood and extending out as far as the eye could see toward what passed for a horizon in the dimness of the in-between. It folded back on itself a few times before disappearing into a thick fog. The rest of the group was already making headway by the time Sable made it through and she hurried to catch up. Adem turned with a concerned look as he realized she was missing. When his gaze lit on her figure jogging through the grey landscape he stopped to wait for her, his cloudy expression clearing into one of relief. Ailith looked up at her father, then at Sable, and smiled. She ran back to take Sable's hand as she rejoined the group. "So where are we going?" she asked.

As if I know the answer to everything. "You'll have to ask him," Sable answered, pointing at Dedun.

"To Ukhu Pacha, as I said," their leader replied, striding hurriedly toward the fog. "Supay has agreed to grant you safe passage through his lands." There was an edge to his voice that Sable didn't like.

"What's the catch?" she asked, letting go of Ailith's hand to make her way to the front of the group.

Dedun hesitated. "He has agreed to safe passage through his lands…but I do not know what price he may exact for leaving them." He glanced sidelong at Sable. "Supay is not known for his reasonableness. There is no telling what he will want from you in payment for leaving."

"We'll have to be careful, then." Sable steeled herself for

whatever was to come, her spine straightening in determination. Dedun stopped and turned her to face him.

"Even with care, he may exact a price beyond what you wish to pay." He spoke directly to Sable, his desert eyes boring into her soul. "There may be other options, other ways of getting you where you need to be in time…"

"We're out of options, Dedun," Sable replied, laying a hand on his shoulder. "And so are you if you're even suggesting this one. I appreciate the warning, but we'll have to take what comes; the world–and all the souls who've lived in it–is counting on us." She smiled grimly and patted the solid frame of his arm, ducking out from underneath it. "Besides," she threw over her shoulder as she continued down the path, "I can't die, remember?"

"That is what I am afraid of," Dedun replied, his words only audible to Adem, who had caught up with the pair as Dedun fell behind. He shook his head. "She is far too brave for her own good." They walked in silence for a few steps, both pondering the woman before them. "You will look after her." It was not a question. Adem smiled ruefully in response.

"She seems more than capable of looking after herself," he replied.

"You are correct, but she is fragile. Not in the way that old glass shatters at the slightest touch, but in the way that nitroglycerin must be transported with care. She has seen and experienced more than humans are meant to partake over their short lives, and I am afraid for her mind." Dedun slowed as they approached the wall of cloud marking the edge of Supay's domain. "You have seen her power. You know what she would be capable of if her mind broke." Darkness spread across Adem's expression as he considered the possible repercussions.

"Are you guys coming or do you plan on talking about us all day?" Sable called from ten feet ahead. Both men looked guilty as they caught up to Sable and Ailith, who had run ahead as soon as the grown-up talk began. Sable didn't like Adem's expression as they approached, but it cleared as soon as he realized he was scowling.

Dedun stopped in front of Sable, his eyes narrowed. "You

are certain you wish to do this?" She nodded and he folded her into a supportive hug. "Be careful," he advised as he let go.

"Always," she answered, then disappeared into the fog.

Static-filled gloom closed around Sable, electrifying her skin as she pushed her way through the morass before her. She called out for her companions but whatever material made up the barrier sucked away her words, deadening them into quiet uselessness before throwing them back at her. *Nothing for it, then.* She pushed on with more urgency, hoping they would all emerge in the same place and cursing her lack of forethought; if only they'd bound themselves together before plunging into this cotton-candy jumble…

A small hand grasped Sable's and she nearly jumped out of her prickly skin. *:C'mon. Dad's this way.:* Ailith's voice cut through the static and into her head, and she realized the hand holding her own was familiar, though she couldn't see its owner. It tugged and she followed, shuffling her feet to avoid any irregularities in the path. It proved smooth, and she felt more than saw another figure connect to their chain of humanity in the sea of sensory deprivation around them. With a stomach-lurching pop all three emerged into a wonderland of waterfalls and meadows, forests and streams, all lit by glowing crystals, bright as daylight, growing from the ceiling and walls of the massive cave system they had reached. The pastoral landscape before them was devoid of movement, though the soft rustling of small creatures could be heard at intervals. A graveled path not unlike the one they'd left followed a babbling stream toward a hill in the distance, turning corners every so often to switchback up the gentle incline.

"Is this…" Adem began dubiously.

"Ukhu Pacha, yes," Sable finished. There was something definitely off about the place, a buzz of warning at the back of her skull she dared not ignore. "Let's stay close," she recommended, keeping a firm grip on Ailith's hand. Ailith, in turn, kept an even firmer grip on her father's hand, and the three of them started down the path, gravel crunching under their feet.

Just past the first bend the gravel gave way to packed earth with small puddles here and there. Sable's feeling of unease increased with every step they took and as they passed the first puddle she glanced down into it–and saw the face of a demon grinning over her shoulder, tall horns thrusting from its forehead like an antelope's. Whipping her head around, she thrust out her free hand and met no resistance. Nothing was there. *You're just seeing things, old woman.* But she'd been alive too long not to listen to the small voice in her gut that told her everything was not as it seemed.

They continued around the winding path toward the hilltop, each bend veering closer to the flowing creek until one twist in the gravel disappeared into its edge. Ailith leaned toward the water to peer curiously into its bubbles and whorls and was pulled back by her father, whose grip on her hand tightened. "Don't go near the water," Adem ground out from between clenched teeth. "It's…wrong. Can't you sense it?"

Ailith's face had the blank expression she wore when she was half in and half out of the present moment. "It's exactly what it ought to be," she answered. Adem's grip tightened further, but she made no move to get closer. "This is the underworld, after all." A silent wave of force thrummed from her small frame and threatened to separate the group as the illusion they beheld shattered. Gone was the gravel path and the gurgling stream; in its place they saw a raging river trimmed with heavy bogs and the barest dirt path leading ever upward toward a mansion at the top of the hill. What had previously been a blank, pastoral landscape held a jarring mishmash of tents, hovels, single-family homes, duplexes, and a few sprawling compounds filled with expensive-looking buildings. All of it was occupied by creatures whose visages ranged from grotesque to jaw-dropping and everywhere in between. Humanoid forms darted between the buildings and flitted through doorways, mere shadows in a colorful, vibrant world. "There they are," Ailith said dreamily. "They're the ones who weren't good enough to get into Hana Pacha, but some of them…some just made a bad deal, or were at the wrong place at the wrong time." She began to sag between Sable and Adem, who propped her up between them as best they could. She looked into Sable's eyes as her expression cleared. "We shouldn't have come here." With that her eyes rolled back into her head and Adem caught her, lifting her effortlessly off her feet and cradling her to his chest. She looked so tiny and fragile, and once again Sable cursed the unfairness of time and fate in forcing one so young to bear such burdens.

"We should go," Adem said, the warning in his tone sending a chill up Sable's spine as she cast about for a trail back the way they'd come. But there was no trail; behind them the earth was cracked and barren where the river didn't flow and the current was too strong for them to swim.

"I guess forward is our only option," Sable said grimly as she started forward, taking point so that Adem could care for Ailith.

"Stay close," he warned. "We're being followed."

:I know:, she answered directly into his mind. *:Followed and paced and preceded up the hill.:* She sent images of the flickers of movement she'd caught in her periphery as they continued toward the summit and the giant house it held. The closer they got the bigger it looked until they faced the biggest Frankenpalace they'd ever seen. A central pyramid in the South American style sat amidst every type of architecture imaginable, with flying buttresses supporting a massive wall around the complex and random cupolas and spires peeking over its top. Every direction Sable looked she saw a different type of gaudy architecture. It was imposing in its eccentricity.

Center-most on the wall stood an ornate wrought-iron and wooden gate forged in a different style from its housing. As they stopped to stare at the edifice before them the gate swung open with an ominous creak and a figure appeared in the void it left. Standing well over seven feet tall, the silhouette bore horns that twisted upward from its forehead. Otherwise it looked like a man. It wore a loincloth tied on with golden chains and little else besides thick gold bracelets and earrings that hung down from its elongated ears almost to its shoulders. Thong sandals crunched on the gravel path as it approached the group. "It has been a long time since we saw visitors," it said with a malicious grin. "Please, join me in my hall."

"We are merely passing through," Sable replied in a demure tone. "Dedun assured us you had agreed to safe passage through your lands, Lord Supay. We wish no disrespect, of course." The air around them stilled into a miasma as her words reached their would-be host.

"I agreed to safe passage, yes," the figure before them replied condescendingly. "I did not agree to a safe departure." His grin widened as he took in Sable's narrowed eyes and Adem's brief panic before he hid it behind a stone mask of impassivity. "Come, let us talk while you wait for the young one to wake. We may yet strike a deal." He turned on his heel and strode back through the gate. Adem looked to Sable, who felt nauseous; they'd walked into the trap willingly on her recommendation.

:Do we follow?: he asked silently.

:We have no choice,: Sable replied. She led the way as they passed through the gate and into the stifling hallway beyond. The passage was surprisingly short for running through a defensive wall, and Sable understood why it was outfitted with the flying buttresses they'd seen on their approach: without them a wall that height would never have remained standing. She also had the impression it was meant more to keep things in than it was to keep them out. As they cleared the second gate another jarring mixture of architecture greeted them. Within the courtyard created by the wall lay a pyramid and two outbuildings, each of which sported a different type of ornate design. Grecian columns and frescoes from Italy graced the first, while the second looked like a Frank Lloyd Wright conception. The only common theme throughout the decoration was scenes of torment and destruction: the Italian frescoes depicted war, pillaging, and the rape of both men and women, while the building beside it contained a wall through which flowed scenes so grotesque Sable couldn't bear to give them names. She sent a silent thanks up to whatever gods may be listening that Ailith was asleep as they passed the disturbing sights and followed their host into the pyramid that sat front and center inside the grounds.

"You're welcome," Supay answered. When Sable looked at him quizzically, he explained, "For making sure the child was unconscious before you entered my hall. I have no quarrel with her; in fact, she is my guest of honor." As he strode through the front doors he nodded at a pair of guards, who peeled off to follow Adem, Sable, and Ailith down the hall before them. Their footsteps echoed against the stone walls, bouncing off of stone covered in gold sheet before dancing down the hall. Reflections swam through the brilliant surfaces as they passed. Sable felt her eyes drawn toward the nearest wall and squinted in the dim light, expecting to see her own scrunched-up visage. Instead she saw a small scene with a woman stuck by the side of the road with a flat tire and a cell phone in one hand. A demon stood unnoticed beside her, one finger on her unresponsive phone as she tapped it repeatedly. Further down the hall she passed a man strapped to a bed and evidently unhappy about it while a wicked-looking woman with curved horns stood over him, whip in hand. *That escalated quickly,* Sable thought as her eyes skimmed the rest of the walls. Demons perpetrated every type of torment imaginable on humans going about their daily lives in the world above with none of them the wiser. The group stopped at the entrance to a large central chamber within the pyramid and Sable was still so distracted she almost ran into the closest guard.

Supay followed her gaze to the walls. "Ah, I see you've found my television," he said as he walked backwards toward the throne in the center of the room. It was overlarge and opulent, with elaborately-worked armrests shaped like claws at the ends. The back fanned out behind their host as he reclined into its black velvet cushions and threw a leg over one armrest. "How better to keep tabs on my children as they work?" He smiled as he surveyed the suffering present on every wall. "Makes Daddy proud."

The guards ushered Sable and Adem into the throne room and up to the front of the dais on which the throne sat. Neither was inclined to move any closer than was necessary. "You spoke of a deal," Sable began, but was cut off.

"You, witch, are not to speak unless spoken to." The air crackled with heat as Supay's voice lanced across the space between them and a sharp pain turned Sable's head. Anger rose within her, brilliant and red and hot, and she fought to contain it. *You are severely outclassed and in his domain, Sable. Keep your wits about you. You've had worse.* She dropped her eyes to the foot of the throne and ran through a few breathing techniques she'd learned to help manage the pain and calm her nerves.

"Now, where were we? Ah, yes: we were discussing passage out of the lands of Ukhu Pacha." Supay grinned, showing extra rows of pointed alabaster teeth. "Of course, the young one is welcome to traverse my domain whenever the need arises; she is a gatekeeper, and if I can be of service in helping her keep the balance between the world above and the world below I am happy to assist. I am, after all, a god of both beginnings and endings." He stood with the grace of a stalking cat and descended the single step between them, eyes locked onto Adem. "As for you…your wife's sacrifice allowed your daughter to become who and what she is. She saved countless lives with her own, and I cannot ignore the imbalance that created for your family. You are also welcome to come and go from my lands until that balance is restored as payment for the debt I owe you." At last he turned to Sable, who kept her eyes trained on the throne Supay had vacated as he circled her, his eyes burning a line across her flesh. "You." The single syllable dripped from his mouth like acid. "You have spent far too long in the world above. And for all the years you've lived, for all the lives you've taken, never once have you given life. You have no children to show for all your long years, and yet you come here, to me, to the god of death and birth, and expect me to allow you to pass? The nerve!" He spat onto the polished stone floor, missing Sable's foot by an inch, and the spittle sizzled where it landed. "You I will keep with me until you have paid your debt to the balance."

"We need her." Adem's voice was plaintive, though Sable could hear the steel beneath it. "Without her our plan to beat Ahriman is worthless."

"Time passes as I will it here," Supay replied, his voice returning to a normal timbre. "I can get her back to you before you even know she's gone."

"Where would you take her?" Adem asked.

"To my apartments, of course," Supay answered. His hand drifted up to Sable's hair and he leaned forward to sniff the strands as they dripped through his claw-tipped fingers. "A witch this powerful will give me strong sons and daughters. I need more demons to serve me, and she must pay for her long years with the giving of new life." Sable shuddered as she considered how it would feel to be the brood mare of the god of death. "Come now," Supay cooed, "I am also the god of childbirth. I could make it easy for you if you behave." He laughed as Sable fought the urge to vomit, his visage shifting until he stood barely taller than she. Familiar brown eyes stared at her with an unfamiliar expression. "If you're very good, I can help you pretend none of this ever happened." Dagomarus's face swam between her and the throne.

"No." There was fire in Adem's tone as he stepped closer to Sable. "There must be another option."

"Well…if someone were to settle her debt, I might could let her go just this once." Horns grew from Dagomarus's forehead and his teeth lengthened before he turned to look at Adem, fully the god of the underworld once again. "But who would give up my good favor for one so utterly broken?"

"Don't do it, Adem," Sable warned, steeling herself for what was to come. "There's always a catch."

"Catch?" Supay feigned surprise. "You wound me! There is no catch; I would simply no longer owe said person anything, including safe passage and exit in future. I would, of course, allow them passage this once in light of the matter at hand. You see? I can be magnanimous."

"And Ailith would still be free to leave as well?" Adem glanced down at her supine form, still housed safely in his arms. "All three of us would?"

"One time only," Supay answered.

:He knows something about the future we don't,: Sable shot at Adem. *:Either he owes you big and is getting rid of the debt or you'll need his help in future and have to bargain again. Maybe both. That's how this always works.:*

"I see you've been around the block a few times," Supay chuckled. Sable's eyes widened in surprise. "Yes, I can hear everything you think to each other while you're in my domain. No secrets here, hmm?"

"Do it, Adem." The voice that issued from Ailith's parted lips was not hers; it was much older and very faint. "If you don't, my sacrifice was in vain."

"Done." Adem choked on the word as it left his lips and he stared at his daughter, who lay still once again. "But I'm trusting my wife's word here, not yours."

Supay grinned, his rows of teeth gnashing as he considered the man before him. "Very well," he answered as he spun on his heel and strode back to his throne. "But mark my words: unless you can find a way to right this wrong–" he pointed an accusing finger at Sable–"one day she will still be mine." He waved dismissively at them. "Go out the back. It's the proper entrance for servants anyway." With that, Supay turned to his guards and spoke with them, ignoring the trio he'd dismissed.

Sable's knees were weak, but she managed to steer Adem around and behind the throne, keeping her mind as blank as possible. "Not a word until we're back on the surface," she whispered fiercely. He nodded and they hurried through a small doorway at the rear of the room, Adem ducking under the low lintel. The hallway beyond was nothing like the entryway they'd seen before; here bare worked stone lined their path on each side as the hall became a tunnel which angled upwards. Before long they reached a wooden door that was barred from the inside. Sable shoved the bar away with a thought and they spilled out into green-tinted twilight. She gasped a huge breath, not realizing she'd been holding it until the still, warm air of the jungle hit her face.

"Mmm…" Ailith stirred and Adem set her down on a patch of soft moss. "Where are we?" she asked.

"Phuyupatamarca," Adem answered. "We made it."

"Did Mom give you her message?" Ailith looked worried and hopeful all at once. Adem nodded, a tear forming at one corner of his eye. "Good. She told me it was super important and asked if she could use my body for it. It was weird, but it didn't hurt or anything." Ailith rubbed her forehead. "I don't remember much else."

"That's for the best," Sable answered. She hugged herself despite the warmth of the muggy air. "Glad we got here after the heat of the day," she mused as she took stock of their surroundings. "It must've been a scorcher, even for the beginning of summer."

"Today is the solstice." Adem's voice was flat. "We're out of time."

"Good thing we're already here, then." Sable rubbed her hands together and shoved down every thought that clamored for her attention. *Just gonna lock those up with all the others in the deal-with-this-if-we-survive box.* Pulling out her crystal from the strangely-obliging bag, she lifted it over the map on her phone and watched it drop onto a spot just up the ridgeline from them as if magnetized. "Man, Supay dropped us closer than I'd thought–and with an hour to spare until sunset. Guess he wants us to succeed." Adem grunted in response, obviously not impressed. Sable looked around as a scent assaulted her olfactory nerve. "Do you smell that?" she asked. "Smells like a latrine."

Adem went still, listening. The jungle around them was alive with sounds; birds and insects filled the spaces between the brush with a racket that made it hard to distinguish other noises. *:Move to silent comms,:* Adem advised over a mental channel that encompassed both Sable and Ailith, who nodded their affirmatives. *:Latrines mean people. We may be closer to an entrance than we thought.:* With that he motioned them forward. Sable placed Ailith in front of her to keep an adult at the front and rear and switched all of her senses to full blast. The additional input set her reeling for a moment, but she remembered quickly what it was like to process all five heightened senses at once plus a sixth that fed her information on the movement of energies in the area. *Just like riding a bike.* She filtered out the tiny green pinpricks of insects and animals from the background of teeming plant life, then looked for larger sources. Twenty yards ahead of them her sixth sense was rebuffed by a barrier, before which stood the outline of a human wreathed in an angry red aura.

:Contact ahead.: Sable sent the others a picture of what she'd sensed and felt their reactions shift from confusion to interest. *:Looks like we may have found our entrance. How do we take out the guard?:* She sent an image of herself blinking into existence next to him and sliding her dagger between his ribs,

but Adem shook his head.

:If they can block your senses, won't they also know if one of their own is killed?: Sable considered and scrapped the idea. In response Adem sent an image of himself sneaking up behind the guard and pulling him into a rear naked choke until he passed out. Sable nodded and added herself and Ailith to a hiding spot behind a nearby bush, close enough to help if they were needed. Ailith put little pom-poms in the hands of her shadowy image as if she were cheering on her father. Both adults looked at her askance and she shrugged, then removed them. *:Move as quietly as possible. Ready?:* Sable and Ailith nodded, then headed for their assigned bush through the dimming light. Adem all but disappeared into the thick overgrowth, the negligible sounds of his passage further obscured by the sounds of the forest's waking nighttime inhabitants. Just as Sable settled Ailith into a likely spot she felt rather than heard Adem make his move. A few moments and some shuffling later he joined the two of them, dragging the unconscious body of the guard with him. *:Keys. We need keys and anything else he might've had on him that was used for access.:* The three of them rifled through the pockets of the man's dirty jeans and button-down shirt until they came up with a key card. It looked to fit a small, rectangular spot outside the door he'd been guarding.

:What do we do when we get inside?: Ailith asked. *:I can't see anything from out here.:*

:Me neither,: Sable admitted.

:Does your bag have a snake camera in it, by any chance?: Adem asked. Sable shoved a hand into the duffel and lo and behold, a flexible tube with a USB port appeared in her hand. *Maybe I should just give him the damned bag if it likes him so much. I know I didn't put that in there.* She handed the camera to Adem, who took it with raised eyebrows and turned to the door. A moment's work dug a tiny groove in the packed dirt under the door and they snaked the camera through it until it fed them a black-and-white image of the hallway beyond. It was empty as far as the device could show and ended in a brightly-lit doorway some distance into the mountainside. *:Looks clear,:* Adem announced. *:I'll lead. Sable, you take rear,*

and Ailith, stay in the middle. We'll stop as soon as we can see what's in the next room. Slow and steady and quiet as a mouse.: He rose and touched the card to the reader, then flinched at the beeping sound it made before unlatching the door and slipping inside.

As soon as they crossed the threshold Sable's sixth sense unblocked and fanned out, once again searching for information. *:Hold up,:* she sent, taking Ailith's hand and tugging on the back of Adem's shirt to arrest his progress. *:I can sense them now.:* She shared a mental image of what her third eye told her: that they approached a large chamber containing twenty-five humans and one larger life force that stood out like a funnel cloud on a clear day. They had spread themselves across the space so that no one could pass without being seen or sensed. *:I can't see the exit, though. Can you give us radar and find it?:* Adem's heel tapped softly on the stone floor and they watched as tiny ripples spread through the area, outlining the high ceiling of the room before them–and the hallway behind the raised dais in the middle. *:Bingo,:* Sable thought. *:So, how do we sneak past these folks?:*

:Do you have a way to make us invisible and let us climb walls?: Adem asked, his doubt evident in the tone of his thoughts.

Sable cocked her head to the side as she considered. *:Invisible I can do, but climbing is trickier, especially since we'll be blind. You can come at it a few ways: by reversing your own gravity, by making yourself incredibly light, or by mimicking nature and growing sticky spots on your palms and feet. That last one's probably the easiest.:* To illustrate she held out her hands, palms upward, and concentrated. The skin took on raised lines reminiscent of the bottom of a gecko's foot and she placed her fingers on the wall, where they adhered to the stone. *:Think y'all are up to it?:* Adem and Ailith looked at their own hands and she felt them focus their will. Soon both had rougher, but similar lines in their own hands. Ailith's took two tries before they stuck when she climbed, but she beamed when it worked. *:Better do feet, too.:* Sable removed her shoes, chucking them into the duffel before adding grip to the soles. Her companions did likewise. *:Test it out a bit on the walls–quietly,:* she suggested. Adem took his time, but Ailith scampered up to the ceiling without missing a beat.

:THIS IS SO COOL!: Ailith shouted mentally from her upside-down vantage. Sable winced.

:Keep it down,: she answered. *:Even if they can't hear us, it's painful.:* Ailith sent an apology over the link they shared and Sable was amazed again at how naturally she picked up new things. Emotions tended to either miss the link entirely or bleed through constantly, depending on who was using it, but the girl had already mastered balancing the two. *Makes sense she'd find a way to balance things; she's a gatekeeper, after all.*

:All right, time to go dark.: Sable dropped a light shield on each of them to obscure their visible presence just as she'd done in Guilin, except this time there was no gap through which to look. *:Use all six of your senses to navigate.:* She illustrated by sharing what her own senses told her about their position in the hall relative to the rest of the area and felt them pick up the thread on how to use their own sixth sense to look for energies.

:I'll keep point,: Adem said. *:Ailith, stay between myself and Sable unless things go very wrong, in which case you run and hide wherever you can. Remember everything I've taught you.:* They felt rather than saw Ailith nod. *:Let's go.:* There was barely a scuffing of feet on stone as Adem joined his daughter on the ceiling, Sable right behind them, and they set off blind to cross the chamber beyond.

Pecking Order

Y ou!" Taurizl's outstretched arm shot toward the small group of soldiers clustered next to the chair on the raised dais at the back of the room. "Keep vigilant. One never knows when a crafty enemy will strike." One of the group, a man of perhaps twenty, smirked as he turned away from his friends. Between heartbeats Taurizl appeared in front of him. He didn't have to loom for menace to flow outward from his chiseled body. "I see you disagree. Explain."

Undeterred, the young man shrugged. "We're at the back of the room. You said they would enter from the front. With so many of us between them and the exit you don't need us back here." He met the daeva's icy stare. A flicker of doubt paled the younger man's features as an abyss of destruction stared back.

"I see." Taurizl backhanded him, sending him to the floor as the crack of his hand meeting facial bones reverberated through the bare-stone chamber. "It is not for you to question my tactics, boy." Blood dripped onto the floor as his target tried to pull himself upright and failed. "Remind me of the number of men you have killed." He aimed a kick at the man's ribs, earning a gut-wrenching grunt of pain. "The number of wars you have fought and won." Another kick, another grunt. "Tell me what qualifies you, a snot-nosed whelp, to question an order given by me, the daeva of destruction!" Taurizl's voice rose to a bellow as he slammed the man's now-limp head into the stonework, a sickening crack accompanying his efforts. "Would anyone else care to question me?" He spread his arms wide and turned a slow circle. None of the eyes in the room met his. "Keep to your assigned posts. Stay sharp. And remember: if they get past enough of you I'm bringing the whole place down." Dropping his arms, Taurizl stalked over to the chair on the dais and took up a position to its right where he could see every corner of the room except the one behind him. Hands clasped behind his broad back, he waited.

Rolling his eyes in disgust, Nanghait leaned back against the doorway to the hall beyond the main cavern. *So crass, so wasteful.* He'd never liked Taurizl's methods, but he had to admit they were effective–at least, in the right circumstances. *Now to wait until opportunity knocks, as I know it will.*

PEAR-SHAPED

Sable could feel the unseen distance yawn beneath her as she followed Adem's mental radar ping onto the ceiling of the cavern. Every sense was razor sharp, honed on the edge of her adrenaline until it was painful. Small sounds of occupancy floated up from below and she wondered again how no one had noticed any signs of their passage. *We're invisible, sure, but that doesn't mean we're imperceptible.* Every so often Adem would tap the stone under his hand and let the tiny waves of resonance map out their route above the crowd. By the halfway point Sable's hands were sweating enough she worried about dripping onto their waiting adversaries and blowing the whole operation. Adem stayed focused, but she could sense Ailith starting to flag. *:Hey kid, you need to stop for a second? Catch your breath?:*

:No,: came the strained answer.

:Now's not the time to be a hero.: Sable stopped shuffling across the ceiling long enough to focus on communication. *:If any of us fall we could be mincemeat. Take a quick break if you need it.:* She felt Ailith slow, then stop. *:Let us know when you're ready to move on.:*

A few slower heartbeats later Ailith answered. *:Okay, I'm good. Caught my breath. I just want to be done with this–it's scary.:*

:I know, baby girl.: Adem replied from ahead of them. *:You've been so brave. Just a little longer, okay?:*

:Okay,: she replied, her mental presence stronger this time. They had almost made it past the dark blob of energy Sable associated with Taurizl when a loose bit of rock broke free in Ailith's hand. Sable couldn't watch as it tumbled to the ground, but the answering silence in the cave let her know their enemy had heard the sound it made as it bounced off the stone floor. *Couldn't even*

get lucky enough it landed on that soft chair, could we? The pressure of searching eyes froze all three in place.

"They're on the ceiling!" Taurizl cried from below them. "Secure the girl! Kill the rest!"

:Get back to the entry hall, Ailith, and stay invisible,: Adem ordered.

:Shield yourself.: Sable threw knowledge at the girl to show her how to block kinetic energy from entering the space around her while still allowing her to move. *:You too, Adem. They have guns.:* He wrapped himself in a similar protection as she shoved the knowledge his way as well. *:I'll take the big one if you get the yard trash.:*

:Deal.: As one, they dropped their invisibility and their climbing assistance and fell on their enemies, each still barefoot and brandishing a large knife. Visual input flooded Sable's brain, which worked at a fever pitch to process it all during her short fall. She aimed herself toward the minion closest to Taurizl himself, opting to make herself some room to work instead of tangling directly with the larger man. Adem disappeared from her line of sight as he angled toward the closest cluster of humanity and threw up a hasty wall of stone to cut off part of the room as he fell. She made sure to keep the lines of communication open, but focused on her own task as her dagger slid effortlessly across the neck of her first target. *First blood. Gotta make sure I get the last, too.* She turned to face Taurizl as the woman she'd slain slid to the floor. The body the daeva wore was a head and shoulders taller than Sable and she craned her head to meet his flinty gaze. *:About to be real busy.:*

:Don't die.: Adem's thoughts carried snatches of motion and reactions to attacks as he moved his opponents into better position to fight only one at a time.

:I can't, remember?: Without another word Sable stepped in toward the larger man, dagger flashing in her hand. His arm shot out to grab her–but she wasn't there. He twisted his body just in time to avoid a knife to the ribcage and shoved himself backwards, away from the grinning woman across from him. "I see you are more than you seem," he said as he began to circle to his left, drawing Sable into the beginning of a dance only one

of them would finish. "Unfortunately for you, so am I." As he finished his statement Taurizl shoved a kick at Sable's gut that she barely avoided. Without her kinetic shield she was certain it would have left her doubled over and nauseated, but as it was she was able to recover in time to avoid the follow up kick aimed at her head.

"You think that's gonna work?" she scoffed. "I've been short my whole life. Everybody thinks they can kick me in the head." She punctuated her sentence with a feint to the neck before dropping low to slash at Taurizl's right hamstring. He howled in pain as her dagger connected, not quite severing the muscle.

A gravely sound began in Taurizl's throat. "You think you can render me lame with your tiny pig sticker, witch?" Sable watched as the wound knitted itself back together without even a scar to mark its place. She tucked and rolled to avoid a stomp from Taurizl before repositioning herself with two lackeys between herself and her enemy. *Let's see how much ugly cares about his coworkers.* Bellowing, Taurizl lowered his head like a bull and charged, heading straight through both of the men standing between him and his target.

Guess that answers that question. :Adem, I'm going bowling!: Sable shot her ally a brief plan and got a mental nod in response; he was too busy to answer in words. *:Coming your way first to clear out some space.:* "Hey ugly!" she called as she leaped over Taurizl mid-charge. "Think you can catch me?" Using tiny micro-jumps she blinked in and out of the groups of humans still occupying the room. Adem had managed to wall off about half of the combatants; she could hear them banging on the other side of the rock wall. *Good opener. Hope it sticks long enough.* Just as the thought occurred to her Taurizl did a double take, coming to the same conclusion. He roared and charged directly at the stone wall, which gave way under the crushing weight of the daeva of destruction himself. *:Adem,:* Sable warned.

:I know—busy!: A gunshot cracked through the room, temporarily deafening Sable and everyone around her as a bullet whizzed by and ricocheted off the solid walls.

"NO BULLETS!" Taurizl yelled above the general din. "Not until we've found the girl!" Sable sighed in relief; they hadn't found Ailith yet. *She can be sneaky as hell when she wants to be. Keep it up, whatever you're doing!* Blinking into existence behind Adem, Sable shoved her dagger deep into the chest of a woman who was raising a club at the back of his head.

:Got your six for now.: In response she felt Adem back up until their bodies touched, ready to hold their own in whatever space they could clear. Adem wasn't communicating with her on a verbal level, even mind to mind, but she felt her own thoughts slide into lockstep with his as they fought, becoming a single four-armed whirlwind of death. Sable fought back visceral memories as she blinked them into a better position and they separated to surround an enemy, striking as one and landing blow after blow, slice after slice. Answering hits registered, then slid off their kinetic armor, the air around them shimmering like a heat wave over pavement. The flow state they'd entered dulled emotion and outside thought, reducing them both to efficient, ruthless masters of the battlefield.

Another roar and a sense of movement to their left brought Sable out of her reverie. She shoved Adem backward just in time to take the full brunt of the attack Taurizl had aimed at his chest. It knocked her backward and she felt her kinetic shield explode out from her body, deflecting the energy into everyone and everything within a ten-foot radius. As she picked herself up off the ground, dazed from the slide and stumble that had left her there, she felt a giant hand close over the front of her bloody flannel shirt and lift her off the ground. Taurizl's face swam into view wearing a violent expression. "Your little shields are child's play for me to break, just like your bones," he hissed into her face, his breath hot and reeking. "And now you will tell me where the girl is or I will start breaking those bones one by one."

Sable felt Adem freeze for half a second, then burst into action behind Taurizl. *:NO! I have him where I want him!:* she cried out too late to stop Adem from launching himself at their enemy in an attempt to put him in a rear naked choke while his hands were occupied. Without turning around Taurizl reached out his other arm, hand outstretched and fingers splayed. Adem ran into his hand and was rocketed backward, kinetic shield destroyed. Sable watched him crash into the stone wall, felt his head crack against the unforgiving rock as if her own had been bashed instead. Stars swam in front of a vision she was powerless to stop as Adem slid down the wall trailing blood from the head wound he'd sustained. Their breathing was ragged, and Sable realized he had a punctured lung from the broken ribs that had accomplished his concussion. Something else was bleeding internally, but she couldn't tell what; there was only pain, slowly fading into insignificance as Adem's consciousness faded.

Something fundamental snapped inside Sable's psyche. Hundreds of years of pent-up sadness and rage and grief rushed to the surface as she felt Adem's life slipping away. *Not again. Never again.* The words echoed in her mind and across the chamber as Sable reached into the ground for strength. Bones snapped in Taurizl's hand as she grasped it and twisted it off her shirt, freeing the rest of her body as he dropped her to the ground. She retained her hold on his broken fingers, twisting his wrist around until it, too, snapped. Taurizl grunted in pain, the first acknowledgment of it she'd heard, and she dodged his next snatch at her head as if he were moving in slow motion. Everything around her had slowed to a snail's pace, allowing her to reposition and land crushing attacks before her enemy could even blink. A detached part of her mind realized her curse was allowing her to manipulate time just enough to defend herself, and she let it carry her around and through a sequence of moves that left Taurizl's host body broken on the floor. Both of his arms and one leg were twisted in unholy directions, and the savagery of the scene as she stood with one foot on his back brought her satisfaction in a way she had not felt in centuries.

Sound returned to Sable's awareness as a gurgling to her right pulled her from her detached state. Adem lay on the cold floor in a heap, blood trickling from his head and chest as he coughed and tried his hardest to breathe through lungs filling with fluid. Emotion rushed back as Sable blinked to his side, looking for some way to heal what was broken. *:It's too much,* *even for you,:* Adem sent, unable to speak. *:Go on. Win this. Take care of Ailith. Save the world.:* Sable opened her mouth to speak, but Adem's eyes went blank as his breathing slowed to a stop.

He was dead.

CHECK

Ailith skittered along the wall back toward the hallway they'd entered, keeping the kinetic shield Sable had showed her up and active along with the invisibility and climbing spells she'd learned. She could feel herself start to tire as she reached the coolness of the hall and darted inside. *Gotta be brave for Dad. And Sable.* She worked her way back down the hall until she was about halfway between the door to the outside and the door to the main chamber and sat down, propping her back propped against the wall as she listened to the melee beyond. She didn't dare drop her invisibility long enough to see what was happening, but she knew on a deep, instinctual level that some of the sounds she heard involved people getting hurt in awful ways. *I just hope it's not them. Please let it not be them.* The vision she'd had of her father dead on the floor flashed before her and she squeezed her eyes shut. *He's gonna be okay. He's gonna be okay.*

Discomfort snaked its way into her mind as she sat on the bare floor, listening to the sounds of combat beyond. *Why can't I help? Dad taught me how to fight! I should be out there with him!* She balled up her fists in frustration, just like she always had when she didn't like the instructions he gave. *I'm not a little kid anymore.*

"No, you're not." The voice slid through the hall and into her mind, freeing all of her annoyance and angst at being left behind, treated like a baby. "You're so much older, more capable than that."

"Yes!" She spoke aloud without thinking. "I can handle myself!" She dropped her invisibility with the intent to head straight into the next room and join the fray–and found herself staring into a pair of bright blue eyes set into a fine-featured face she'd once thought handsome. Now they sent chills up her spine as he took her by the hand.

"I'm sure you can," Nanghait answered, patting her hand as he led her into the in-between. "I'm sure you can."

247

"I'm sure you can," Nanghait answered, patting her hand as he led her into the in-between. "I'm sure you can."

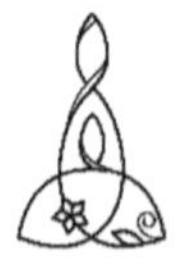

UNACCEPTABLE

That's not possible. I won't let it happen. Sable tried and failed to reconcile the still form before her with the man she'd just fought alongside. *He has to live.* A wind kicked up inside the cave as a niggling thought tickled the back of her mind, trying to remind her of something important she should be doing. *Nothing is more important than this.* Shoving the thought down she went to work healing Adem's body, setting the bones and the broken ribs and bringing down the swelling in his brain. She made his heart beat a slow cadence and expelled the blood from his lungs so they could fill properly again. But it wasn't enough. He wasn't there. She felt overextended to the point of exhaustion, but pushed the thought aside. *The curse won't let me die. I have to keep trying—need more power! Work FOR me just this once, damn you!* Sparks of life nearby caught her attention and she reached her hand toward them, dragging them one by one out of their hosts until she could no longer contain their energy before resuming her work with single-minded determination. Sable's mind and body were seared by the overextension as she channeled more and more power into the healing spell she wove.

An epiphany hit as she continued knitting the wounds in Adem's body. She recalled a ritual she'd seen performed by an entire coven of wise women once to save the life of a child who'd fallen over a cliff. They'd found him mere minutes after his death and had combined their power to re-bind his soul to his body, giving him another chance at life. It had killed the eldest of the women, but she had sacrificed herself freely for the child's sake.

Sable set to work, ignoring the yells and attempts to disrupt her that came from the few surviving followers of Taurizl. The daeva himself was slowly healing his host's wounds; before long he would be able to move again, so her time was limited. The wind she'd called kept his minions at bay for the time it took to draw a crude set of runes around Adem's body with the blood dripping from a finger she pricked, her own body providing the paint she needed. She finished by drawing a pentacle on his chest, then knelt by his side and began to chant, her voice filling the chamber. Everything else went silent as she spoke words of power lost to the modern world and the room faded from view.

Sable was in the in-between, kneeling in a field of gray-scale grass that nearly covered her head. She sprang up, head whipping back and forth until she spotted a familiar figure walking toward a crumbling archway. "Adem!" she shouted as she ran haltingly toward him, her exhausted legs stumbling over every small hillock in the grass. He hesitated, then continued forward. One hand reached out for the iridescent surface of the gate as Sable fell, scraping her knee. *I'll never make it in time. This was all for nothing.*

A ripple crossed the surface of the gate and another, smaller hand pushed through. It was dainty and thin and wore a simple gold band on its ring finger. It moved Adem's hand aside, then laid on top of his arm. He stood motionless, listening, for a few heartbeats that felt like an eternity before turning to look at Sable. The hand on his arm retreated back across the gate as Adem's gaze burned into Sable's mind. His expression spoke of bittersweet emotions; sadness warred with confused hope as he turned to approach the tiny mound that had tripped his would-be savior. Wordlessly he offered her a hand up, which she took. Her legs weren't working well, and she realized it was because she had drained a lot of her own energy just to get where she stood. "I'm sorry," she said, unable to think of anything more to say. "I wasn't fast enough."

Adem smiled ruefully. "Neither was I," he answered. "It wasn't your fault."

"I was hoping I could save you," Sable added, feeling more useless than she had in decades. "But at least this way I can say goodbye."

"I thought you said there was always a third option." Adem cocked an eyebrow as if he knew the answer to their predicament and was waiting for her to catch up. Sable wracked her exhausted brain for the reason she'd plunged herself into the in between. *A ritual…thirteen women…but I don't have a coven here! What can I…oh.* Shoving the sleeves of her flannel up her arms she stood, her full height carrying her nose even with Adem's chest and forcing her to tilt her head at an uncomfortable angle to meet his gaze.

"There *is* a third option," she replied as her dagger materialized in one hand, "but I'm not sure how far-reaching the consequences of it will be. It could fail, or it could bring you back only for a short time." She paused, then plowed onward. "Or it could give you my curse." Sable lowered her gaze from his, unwilling to witness his reaction. "The choice is yours."

"Well, I've been told that if I don't, and I quote, 'get my ass back out there and save the world,' it won't get saved." Adem chuckled. He gently lifted a semi-corporeal finger to Sable's chin, tilting it upward until their gazes met. "I was also told that your idea will work and that if we continue to follow our instincts and stick together we'll see this thing through. So whatever it is you have to do, do it." He tensed, his hand dropping to his side.

Nodding, Sable used her dagger to gouge her thumb until grey smoke began to seep from it. "Here we do not bleed," she explained. "This is a place of souls, not flesh." She held her torn thumb against his chest, moving it in the shape of a pentacle to match the one on his body and watching as the vapors lifted toward Adem's face. "Breathe, and follow me back." Adem inhaled deeply, tendrils of smoke wending their way up his neck and into his nostrils, and he took a tentative step toward the rift Sable had entered from the outside world. The spell hit Sable like a ton of bricks as it took and her knees buckled. Without looking Adem reached down and snaked an arm under her shoulders to support her weight as they slogged through the grass. It pulled at them as they moved away from the archway and toward the world outside. *I need more,* Sable thought as she felt herself weakening. *The curse won't let me die, but it will stop the spell before it's finished if I don't find another source, and soon.* An answering flicker of energy flared to life near her physical body and she snatched at it, surprised she could even sense it from the in-between, but unwilling to look a gift power source in the mouth. Her legs steadied and she felt the spells she'd wrought strengthen as she fed them from the renewed well within her. *Strange; I thought I left a wind spell running,* she mused as they reached the halfway point, then dismissed the thought as inconsequential, or at least lower in priority. Another flicker of energy popped up, then another, then a third, and she drew from all of them, bolstering her strength. More appeared and she continued to draw strength. *No telling what we're coming back to, and I still have to get Adem back into his body.*

Minutes–hours–seconds later–Sable couldn't tell–she and Adem emerged from the in-between. His body still breathed on its own, and he looked down at it with a strange expression. "You have to choose to return to it," Sable explained. "Last chance to go back."

Without a word the now-transparent form of Adem's soul floated parallel to its host, hovered for a moment, then disappeared. Sable shut down the spell that kept him breathing and watched with joy as his chest continued to rise and fall. She was dimly aware of a commotion behind her and turned to see what was happening.

Bodies were the first things that registered in her field of vision. Seven lifeless corpses stared back at her from inside the wind wall she'd created. It was weakening, which was how they'd managed to get through, but they'd never made it to her corporeal form while she retrieved Adem from death; in fact, they'd fed the spell she'd worked to bring him back. *I'll call that a good trade.* Notably missing was Taurizl, who had been prostrate on the floor directly behind the cooling bodies of his followers. *Uh oh.* The wind wall fizzled, dismissed with a thought to reveal a half dozen armed fighters with guns and weapons pointed her way. Taurizl stood behind them on the rubble left from Adem's wall. "You may surrender now if you wish," he called, his voice carrying easily with the room's acoustics.

Sable laughed. "My good man, better than you have tried and failed. You'll have to do better than that to take me out."

:Adem, how are we doing?: Because I'm gonna need some back-up here real soon...

:I feel fantastic! What did you do, give me unicorn juice or something?:

Oh, he definitely got a bit of my soul, all right.

:Will explain later. Fight now!: The world went into bullet time as a wall of lead flew toward Sable and Adem. Instinctively Sable threw up a protective kinetic shield, then felt it curve to catch and reflect the bullets as Adem joined her defensive efforts. *:Did I just change your spell?:* he asked, just as surprised as she was to see the bullets speed back up and accelerate into their attackers.

:Yep.: That was an unexpected side effect...I wonder what else he can do now.

:Hear your thoughts, even when you don't want me to.: Sable's stomach dropped into her feet and she tried–and failed–to set up a mental privacy screen. *:What happened to fight now?:* Half of their assailants had avoided being struck by their own bullets and were charging toward the pair with whatever melee weapons they had at hand.

:Fine, but don't distract me,: Sable answered. *:It's hard enough to stay focused with everything that's in my brain already.:* She got an impression of a wide grin from Adem as the battle joined and she lost track of conscious thought.

The two of them fought like they had trained together for decades, splitting the group so that they could each fight only one person at a time as they led them on a deadly promenade around the cavern. One by one Taurizl's followers fell until at last he stood before the pair, cold fury boring into them through his narrowed eyes. "So you think to pass into the inner sanctum," he drawled, circling to put himself between Sable and Adem and the inner door. A rumbling sound shook the stone around them as Taurizl spoke, sending a jolt of nervousness through Adem and into Sable. *He's going to bring the place down!*

Adem sprang into action. He launched himself at Taurizl in an attempt to tackle the larger man, hitting him hard below the waist. The two grappled furiously for a moment before Taurizl got the upper hand, pinning Adem face down onto the vibrating stone below. It groaned along with Adem as it began to crack. Seams ripped the cavern into three sections, the closest of which split right beneath Adem's face. Against all odds, he smiled. The expression was savage and perverse, and it made the hair on Sable's arms stand on end as she watched the gap grow wide enough to swallow both combatants. As the pair dropped into the yawning gulf Adem took advantage of the moment of weightlessness to slip his opponent's hold on him and shoved both feet into Taurizl's chest. *:Equal and opposite reaction, right?:* Adem's voice rang through Sable's disjointed thoughts as she watched him shoot upward out of the earth's clutches. Taurizl fell at a similar rate as the gap opened, his face a rictus of rage. The air in the room shifted with a pop as Adem clapped his hands together and willed the earth to close once again, trapping their enemy inside. His brow creased and dripped with sweat as he fought the daeva's original spell. Sable caught him with a cushion of air as he dropped like the stone he manipulated, his concentration on his first working shattered by the effort it took to break the spell ripping apart the cavern.

:Around the problem, not through it!: Sable reminded Adem of their last cave encounter and felt light dawn in his mind. Instead of fighting the daeva's spell of destruction he let it be, guiding it back toward its trapped owner before letting it crumble the stone on either side of the rift before him. Boulder-sized rocks tumbled into the gap, followed by smaller pieces that filtered down between their larger brethren to create a rough new floor for the cave.

"That won't hold him for long," Sable called out over the tumbling of more rocks as other parts of the cave settled.

"What will?" Adem asked, exasperated. "Nothing we do seems to take him out for long."

"If we do enough damage to his host body he'll be forced to abandon it," Sable explained. "Even a daeva has a limit to its power, and he's used a lot of his just keeping himself together." As she spoke Sable heard the rocks shift underneath the cave floor. *We're about out of time.*

:That's not helpful.: The thought wasn't aimed at her, but Sable heard it anyway; apparently hearing each other's thoughts

was a two-way street she hadn't realized she was on. She schooled her own mind toward problem solving.

"You know, sometimes brute force really is the answer." Adem sucked in a deep breath, turning his palms upward toward his face. When he exhaled, he turned his hands downward and exerted not only the force of his body but that of his will to compress the pile of rubble before him. Smaller rocks shifted and were crushed into sand as they filtered down into every crevice in the stack. Over the susurration of rock and sand they heard a muffled cry of anger and pain that made Adem hesitate for the briefest of moments.

Sable laid a hand on his shoulder and lent him her strength, renewing the downward force they exerted with fervor. *This asshole has been responsible for the destruction of cities. It's killed thousands and never felt one moment of pity. We need to send it back from whence it came.* Together their righteous anger exerted enough pressure to buckle the new floor. It flattened where they pressed their hands and for fifteen feet in every direction, carving out a smaller, smoother bowl in the depression they'd already created. All sound but the cracking of boulders ceased.

Quiet settled over the cavern. Sable realized that at some point she'd turned on her dark vision instinctively as the electric lights had gone out. Adem had done the same, and they surveyed the settling cave for signs of life. It looked far more primitive than it had when they'd arrived; the once-worked-stone walls were jagged and irregular in shape, their previous facades shaken off with the cave's tremors. Sable couldn't see the entrance they'd taken into the caves from where she stood.

:Ailith?: Adem was broadcasting over the channel they'd established across all of their minds, but Sable picked up more emotion this time than she had the last time they'd all spoken. The girl's lack of immediate response froze Sable's heart as the bottom fell out of Adem's world. "Ailith?" he queried. Silence. "Ailith!" Louder this time, he made sure to project his voice enough to carry into the far reaches of the cave as both he and Sable scrambled for the entrance. *She has to be here!* Sable wasn't sure if the thought belonged to her or Adem, but it roused every protective instinct she possessed. "Ailith!" The echo from

Adem's anguished cry bounced off of all the irregular surfaces in the room, deepening the anxiety he felt as they traveled unhindered throughout the space.

:Dad.: The faintest response tickled their minds before disappearing once again into the darkness. It carried a host of images that slammed into Sable and Adem, bringing both to their knees as they realized where the girl was.

He has her.
The portal is open.
We're too late.

 # CHECKMATE

Ailith's restraints left little room for her usual fidgeting. Her captors had bound her hand and foot and left her chained to the leg of a table inside the deepest room in the compound, right below the bowl they planned to use to catch her blood as they spilled it to unleash the spirits of the dead on the world. She tried not to think about it, but her proximity to the item made that difficult, as did the constant desire to slip back and forth between the physical world and the in-between. Here she could feel the pull of the other side of the gate as a tangible force; Sable had spoken of thin places, but even the cave in the Thar desert hadn't been this thin. Ailith had experimented with slipping back and forth between the physical world and the next to find a way to get a message to her father or Sable, but something blocked her ability to reach out to them in both places. She thought she'd managed to slip something through at one point, but she couldn't be sure.

The tall bald-pated man in charge strode toward her as she tried to shift further underneath the table. Nanghait had bowed to him when he'd delivered her. This must be Ahriman, she realized, and the figure nodded, a broad smile splitting his features. It was neither friendly nor inviting. "Indeed I am, young one," he answered despite her lack of vocalization. "And you are my key to bringing about a new age for this world." He folded his lanky form until he sat on his heels before the table, reaching out to hold Ailith's jaw with two fingers. They were cold, and she shivered at his touch. "It's a shame you'll never reach adulthood," Ahriman mused as he turned her head first one way, then the other. "I'm sure you would have been beautiful. And smart," he added as he dropped his hand to regard her from arm's length. "I know you've been looking for a way to reach your father and that witch he's brought with him. But they're with Taurizl now." He stood in one fluid motion and strode to the stone archway that dominated the room. "I don't think they'll be coming for you."

As he leaned his forehead against the gate Ailith could see the shadowy outline of the spirit that inhabited the body before her. It was even taller than its host, with a grotesquely long neck and spindly fingers that ended in sharp claws. Dark eyes burned in heavy-lidded sockets as they sought something beyond the rippling barrier before them.

"You're wrong." Ailith's high-pitched voice was clear as it bounced off of the worked stone walls. "My dad will always come for me. And Sable will, too!"

"So that is her name?" Ahriman mused. "Sable. I suppose it's fitting given her dark hair. No matter; she and her unusual powers are too late." He pushed away from the archway with effort, smoky eyes lingering on its stones before turning to face his assistant. "Nanghait, prepare the knife."

"Yes, my lord." Nanghait's voice bore no trace of its usual sullenness as he picked up a piece of stone the size of Ahriman's hand. One edge had been chipped away on both sides to create a jagged edge sharp as a razor. To test the blade he held up one hand and used the other to dispassionately cut off his pinky. Blood welled from the wound as the finger dropped to the floor with a wet sound that made bile rise in Ailith's throat. "It is sharp," Nanghait reported before stooping to pick up the missing digit. Within seconds he had reattached it to his hand, the skin and muscles knitting together without a mark.

"You could have left that, you know," Ahriman remarked as he took the blade from Nanghait. "These bodies are no longer of use to us."

"Call it one last vanity." Nanghait stepped back to give his master the space he required. Light flared from the archway as Ahriman spoke a word of power, bathing the room in white light. Ailith noticed for the first time the etchings on the floor surrounding the gate; they were unfamiliar to her, but each thrummed with the same power that contained the spirits within the gate itself. Every instinct within her screamed that this was wrong, that the power Ahriman harnessed was meant to separate the worlds, not bring them together, but she was powerless to stop the spell he'd created. Even her abilities as a gatekeeper could not undo what he'd wrought without breaking the etchings themselves, which she couldn't do from across the room. The light from the archway began to pulse as the seconds marched on toward sunset. Ailith could feel the day dying from within the mountain, and as soon as the sun sank below the horizon light shattered the thin veneer containing death beyond the arch. Ahriman threw his arms into the air and stretched upward, shedding his human skin like unwanted clothing in order to join the host of spirits which boiled from the gateway. His erstwhile host looked around in disbelief, then horror as ephemeral figures surrounded his body, carrying off his soul to join the maelstrom building in the room.

"To me, my children!" Ahriman boomed, his otherworldly voice echoing from every surface in the room. "We must finish the ritual and shed the chains of death!" In response the glowing bodies stilled, taking places around the room from floor to ceiling and creating a path for their master. Ailith recognized the feel, if not the form, of the three daevas they'd defeated before as they took their places near the head of the line. Ahriman stalked toward Ailith carrying the stone knife, and all she could think about was the frieze they'd found in the desert cave. *This isn't how it's supposed to end. Mom said.* She was numb, disappointed, and frozen with fear.

"A mother never tells her child the stories with the bad endings." Nanghait appeared in his true form at Ailith's elbow. He was much shorter, with spikes in place of hair and gnarled fingers and toes. His bloated gut rounded out a squat body that had no trouble sitting under the table with her as his hot, metallic breath brushed past her face. Untying her restraints, he lifted her easily onto the table above them despite her frantic kicking and squirming. "Now now, settle down," he admonished as he forced her flat on the table with her head over the awful bowl. "You don't want him to have to hurt you just to get what he needs, do you?"

Ailith screamed.

Sable and Adem raced down the passageway they'd found behind Ahriman's toppled throne, unwilling to believe that all was lost. Every few feet Sable blinked them both further along until they stood before a sterile metal door with a digital access pad to one side. Adem flung a hand at the door and it buckled on its hinges before slapping into the stone wall behind it. He burst into the room beyond, Sable two steps behind.

Two inhuman heads whirled around to meet them. "Nanghait," the taller one ordered. The smaller, uglier of the pair peeled himself off of the table they'd bent over, revealing the still form of Ailith as he started toward the intruders.

Adem's mind became a blank slate of cold rage. *:I've got the archway if you've got her,:* Sable sent as Adem turned toward the approaching figure. He nodded once, then rushed the stumpy creature. Sable turned her attention toward the stone arch before her and the spirits surrounding it. The room was full to bursting with them. *For once it's a good thing I can't die, else everything in this room would kill me.* Pushing past a variety of spectral forms she located the smallest stone in the arch and ran toward it, shaping a shield onto the front of her hand as she punched at the stone. Spirits crowded her as she moved, their ephemeral forms slowing her progress, but she blinked out from between them and landed a solid blow on her target, shifting it less than an inch. Light pulsed through the room as the stone shifted and she felt Ahriman's attention swing toward her. *Ignore it. He can't hurt you.* He could, but she wasn't about to tell herself that, not while she needed the morale boost. She took another swing at the stone and was rewarded with another inch of movement, another pulse of light. Movement from inside the gate caught her attention as she pulled her arm back for another hit. A face she recognized swam up through the maelstrom and winked at her before sailing through the gate along with another, less familiar face. Sable turned to track their progress as they sped across the room toward Ahriman, who had raised the lanky appendage holding the stone knife over Ailith. Adem had bulled his way through Nanghait, tossing him to the side like a rag doll with strength borrowed from the earth around them, but she could see he wouldn't make it to his daughter in time. His single-minded despair sang across their link as the realization of his slowness hit, followed by confusion as the two new spirits latched onto Ahriman's arm. Recognition dawned as Khaleeda's face drew up in a snarl. She snatched the knife from the larger spirit's hand as her companion–her husband?–grasped its arm to immobilize it. *You've still got a job, woman!* Sable reminded herself as she continued her efforts to dislodge the stone. More spirits emerged from the gate behind Khaleeda as Sable worked. Some were men, some women, many old, some young, and all came from different time periods and walks of life. A woman in Ming dynasty finery floated past, her face serene despite her obvious determination, followed by a man with brightly-colored fabrics draped over his spare form. They joined the throng surrounding Ahriman, each reaching for a different portion of his spectral body. The stone knife clattered to the ground at Adem's feet just as he reached the table and scooped up Ailith. Sable felt his relief as he realized the girl was unconscious, not dead, and her own answering joy at their unexpected aid combined with Ailith's recovery renewed her efforts further. Two more swings of her fist freed the stone from the archway, which settled with a thump before toppling backwards onto the polished floor.

As the gate fell the polarization of the portal within it reversed. Every spirit in the room was sucked backward into the swirling vortex left by the archway's destruction, starting with the ones Ahriman had summoned. Nanghait screamed from where he sat on the floor as energy from beyond pulled him from his seat. He grabbed at anything that might slow his descent back to the world from whence he'd come, his knobbly claws scrabbling at the hard stone, dragging gouges through its smooth surface. Hands reached out from within the jagged tear that had opened up and grasped his limbs, pulling him bodily into the seething mass of spirits within. Nanghait's final scream would haunt Sable's dreams for years to come.

A few feet away Ahriman was locked in an epic struggle with Khaleeda and the spirits holding him back. The stone knife lay on the floor, forgotten, as he fought against their inexorable pull to keep his footing. It was a losing battle. Before long the spectral hands attached to his spindly form dragged him into the pandemonium beyond the portal-that-was. As he sank into the depths of the murk beyond his head bobbed to the surface long enough to utter a single phrase.

"I will return."

With that Ahriman returned to the emptiness from which he came.

Thank goodness that's over. Sable turned to the tear in reality that had digested most of the spirits before realizing that Khaleeda and her compatriots remained in the room. The portal itself showed no signs of collapse; in fact, it looked less stable than it had a moment ago. The gap before her widened as she watched. *Or not.*

Ailith chose that moment to awaken. She tapped Adem on the shoulder and asked him over the wailing of the spirits around them to put her down, which he did, gingerly. Sable felt his reluctance to let her out of arm's reach again, so he followed behind her as she approached the group of spirits standing before the portal. They leaned forward and spoke as one. "Gate-keeper." Ailith nodded, swallowing against her obvious discomfort. "There is still an imbalance between the world of the living and the world of the dead." They turned toward Sable, empty gazes penetrating as they indicated the object of their explanation. "You must right this. It is your duty."

"But it could kill Sable!" Ailith cried. "I can't do that!"

Sable's heart sank as she realized what they'd suggested. *It makes a lot of sense. I should have died long ago.* Before she could spend too long thinking about it she moved to stand before Ailith and laid a hand on her shoulder. "I should have died a long time ago," she reassured. "You and your dad deserve more than the future that awaits if we don't close this portal, and my continued existence is not a worthy trade for any of that. I've had my time and then some. You do whatever you need to do to make this right." She patted the girl on the shoulder and went to stand with the spirits before the gate.

Ailith's eyes brimmed over. "I...don't want to do this," she sputtered.

"I know, honey. We've all had to do things we don't want to do. But I want this," Sable replied as she met the girl's gaze. "There are people I miss on the other side of that gate, and you're the only one who can let me through to see them." Hundreds of faces swam across her mind's eye as memory supplied names to go with them. *Looks like I get to see them sooner than I'd hoped.* The thought felt hollow in a way that it hadn't two weeks ago. An answering tug of emotion pulled her eyes from Ailith to Adem, who stood a pace behind his daughter, his expression saying what no words could. Sable smiled as her heart finished breaking, tears long held back spilling past her dark lashes. "I'll miss you both," she said as she sniffled. "Someone take care of the duffel for me." Removing the strap from across her shoulders she set it down and slid it across the floor toward the pair. "I think it likes you better than it does me anyway." Turning to face Khaleeda, who regarded her with a kind, fierce expression, she nodded. "It's time."

"Speak the words," the voices said in unison. "Make your will into reality."

Ailith took a deep, shuddering breath. "I want to break Sable's curse," she yelled into the void before her. As the words reached the portal they echoed across time and space, reaching into Sable's soul and unlinking it from the torturous spell that had been her bane for fifteen hundred years. A lightness came over her as she turned toward the storm beyond the portal and stepped through into the light that had appeared on the other side. It flashed even brighter–and then there was nothing.

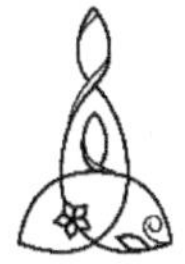

WHAT LIES BEYOND

Sable found herself walking a dirt path through the woods. The colors around her were vibrant and vital, greens and browns and yellows in familiar shades telling her that autumn was near. She'd always loved this time of year, when the earth calmed before going to sleep.

The village was right where it had always been, at the first clearing in the forest. Round huts of wood and moss dotted a central hub where townsfolk met and traded and travelers were welcomed. There was the usual crowding and bustle here and there as the villagers went about their business, but she ignored it; there was only one face she sought, and she knew right where to find it. Turning left at the first intersection of paths she followed the track straight to the door of a familiar hut, one she'd helped build a season before. She smiled and pulled at the solid oak planks, feeling their familiar weight as the door swung open without effort.

The dark-haired man tending the fireplace looked up as the door opened, his face breaking into the most beautiful smile she could ever imagine. "Carata!" he called as he stood, his simple clothing marking him as a woodworker's apprentice. "You're home!" Sable ran into his arms and buried her face in his leather jerkin, tears streaming unbidden down her face. Wiping at her eyes, she looked up into the young man's soft brown gaze.

"Dagomarus," she sighed. "I've missed you." The tears sprang up once again as she spoke and her voice faltered.

"I know," he answered, and the hut around them darkened into nothingness. "I've missed you, too." For long moments they held one another, content to simply exist in the same place at the same time. "But this is not your time," Dagomarus continued as he let go of Sable's arms. He placed his hands on her waist instead so that he could look down into her confused face.

"What was done to you–to us–was monstrous. No one should have to endure as many lifetimes as you have. We aren't made for it any more than we're made to be alone." He reached up and caressed her face, concern evident in his features. "You should have a chance at a normal life. That chance was taken from you against your will, which means a debt is owed that will now be repaid."

"But what about you?" Sable asked, her heart breaking for the second time in recent memory. "I've spent dozens of lifetimes waiting to return to you, and now that I'm here you're telling me I can't stay?"

"All things come here eventually," Dagomarus replied. "This is not the last time we will meet. But you will have changed even more the next time we do." His smile turned sad as he regarded her.

"I've not changed that much," Sable retorted.

"You have. You've grown into a knowledge of the world you would never have acquired had we lived the lives we thought to have. You've learned and done things we never imagined were possible. You are so much more than the lovely woman I wished to marry, and it fills my heart with joy to know that." It was Dagomarus's turn to tear up at this last statement. "But we are not meant to be. Our moment in time has come and gone, and you deserve the chance to find the same happiness we could have shared with another." He started at Sable as if willing her to understand.

Memory rushed back. *Adem.* Dagomarus nodded as he watched realization dawn in Sable's expression. "I will always love you, and I know you will always love me, but there is room in your heart for another if you are willing to let him in.

"And now I must say goodbye for a while longer." He squeezed Sable's waist once, then let her go. On impulse she reached up and kissed him, once, before backing away.

"I love you, Dagomarus."

"And I you, Carata. Now go live the rest of your life." With that he faded into darkness, leaving Sable alone and in tears once again.

Light flashed against Sable's closed lids. She studied
the aftereffects of its passage as green spots floated under her
eyelids. *Wait. Am I awake? Is this real?* She cracked one eyelid
experimentally just as another flash of light shot out from somewhere in the room. Sound rushed in, a great rumbling accompanied by shaking and the sensation she was being carried. *Ah,
there are the rest of my senses. Must've gotten hit pretty hard
that time.*

:*You weren't hit in the head; you were dead.*: Adem's voice
sounded stressed even in her mind, and Sable opened both eyes
long enough to see what was going on. They were moving at
speed despite the fact that Adem had her in a fireman's carry,
blinking forward as line of sight allowed. Sable barely recognized the hallway they'd entered as they sped past the outer
door, which was blown off its hinges. Behind them the mountain belched a cloud of dust and rock as the whole side facing
them collapsed into a heap of displaced trees, boulders, and
ruined architecture. From her sideways vantage point the scene
was equal parts terrifying and comical.

"You can put me down now," Sable croaked through
parched lips. Adem held onto her for a few more paces until
they were in the shelter of the tree line, then obliged. All three
of them watched as a dust cloud obscured the path they'd just
taken. Sable reached for the duffel to find something to drink—
and remembered she'd removed it just before going into the
portal. "Where's the bag? Tell me someone grabbed it!"

Ailith giggled. She sounded a bit unsteady, more on edge
than amused, but she handed the duffel to Sable. It seemed to
cling to the girl's hand longer than was possible according to
the laws of physics, but let go in time to save its rightful owner

an embarrassing struggle with an eleven-year-old. "You told us to take care of it, so I grabbed it before everything went to shit."

"Language," Adem warned automatically.

"Oh, I think she's earned the right to a few choice words, don't you?" Sable chuckled. Her own laughter held a similar edge of hysteria.

Adem studied his daughter in the darkness of the forest. In the three months since they'd been chased from their home she'd endured the onset of new powers unknown to anyone around her and adapted to turn them into an asset. In the past week they'd met the strangest assortment of people, traveled the world, and managed to keep it from turning into a haven for the spirits of the dead. She'd had visions of her father's death and who knew what else. *Children her age ought to be worrying about who to go to the mall with on the weekend, not whether or not they can save someone's life with powers they don't even understand,* he thought.

:She's done beautifully,: Sable answered as she came to stand next to him. They both watched as Ailith squinted into the dusty air in an attempt to see past it. Her eyes went in and out of focus as she shifted her perception easily between the physical world and the in-between to better see what was happening. *She's gotten a handle on that, too.* The girl seemed to be watching for something in particular. "What are you looking for?" Sable asked, breaking the outward silence and keeping everyone's attention on Ailith for the next few minutes. She still had things to process.

"Hang on…" Ailith craned her neck and jumped up and down a few times. "Almost there…" A large boulder skittered down the slope and out into the dust-laden fog to their right and Ailith let out a triumphant whoop. "Yes! I knew it!"

Adem and Sable shared a confused look. "You knew what?" Adem asked.

"That we were going to win!" Ailith did a little dance around the tree next to her. "That was the last part of the vision I had where we beat Ahriman and Sable's curse was broken!" She stopped to stare at Sable in her strange, piercing way. "I didn't get to see whether or not you made it, though. I'm really, really glad you did." Tears sprang up in her eyes and she rushed over to Sable to throw both arms around her neck. "I was so worried I had killed you." Her voice was muffled against Sable's shoulder.

"Even if I had died, it wouldn't have been your fault." Sable felt the last bit of frost melt from around her heart as she took Ailith by the shoulders, holding her far enough away to look her in the eye. "The only person you would have had to blame is the witch who cursed me in the first place, and I have a feeling she's had a bad enough time of it as it is." She dried the girl's tears with the only clean spot she could find on the cuff of her flannel shirt. "So don't you think on it one more moment. I'm here, and I'm free, and it's all thanks to you." Ailith smiled and nodded, looking at her dad with a relieved smile. Adem smiled back, content for the moment in the knowledge that she would be all right.

He turned to study Stable, who was doing her best to avoid looking at him. *I'm not so sure about her yet. She's been through more than all of us.* His concern was a balm on the raw portions of Sable's heart. *I wonder where she plans on going now that she's free to decide.* The question was open ended, and Sable realized that a lot more rode on her answer than she cared to think about. She consulted her own desires and motivations, sifting through emotions she hadn't allowed herself to have, focusing in on what felt right.

"It's been a hell of a week," she began aloud. "I've almost died twice, only once because I wanted to, and now I'm stuck in the middle of nowhere in Peru with the only two people on the planet I know. I have no home outside of a raggedy-ass cabin, also in the middle of nowhere. I have no plans, no aspirations, and my only reason for doing anything at all over the last fifteen hundred years is gone." She paused as the weight of her words settled around them. "I think what I want the most right now is a hot shower and a goddamned drink, in that order."

"I don't think the baths here will be warm," Adem chuckled, glancing up at the hillside above them. "If they're even intact; you did know I was only partly serious about blowing a hole in a world heritage site, right?"

"You were dead serious," Sable retorted, unable to help herself. She met Adem's gaze and held it, leaning into the silent communion that had sprung up between them. She'd shared the stuff of her soul with him; it seemed that cursed or not, they were bound inextricably from this point forward. *:There's no one I'd rather be stuck with.:* He answered her thought with a shy smile and extended his hand. Sable noticed the ring he'd worn was gone. *:Irene took it when I saw her before you saved me. She told me I couldn't keep living in the past.:* The words resonated with Sable as she recalled her own final farewell. *:She was right.:* Sable slid her right hand into his left, shivering at the intensity of the contact. It tingled, but in a good way. A smaller, colder hand slipped into her left palm as Ailith appeared alongside her, grinning like the cat that ate the canary.

"Don't tell me you knew this would happen," Sable warned. Ailith giggled uncontrollably. Sable rolled her eyes and started forward, Ozturks in tow.

"Where are we going?" Ailith asked as she trotted along.

"Anywhere but here." Sable looked up at Adem, who glanced at Ailith.

"Let's go home." Ailith nodded and looked to Sable, who was already preparing herself to make a gate. *That'll be a lot easier with two of us,* she mused. *Probably won't even need much besides willpower.* As one she and Adem reached out and sketched a semicircle in the air before them, which shimmered before resolving into a portal to a comfortable living room. Ailith squealed and ran through it with abandon before either adult could catch her. They dove through behind her and dropped the portal just as the sounds of the jungle began once again, leaving nothing in their wake.

Acknowledgements

I can't count the number of people involved in getting this story out to the world. My husband, my kids, my parents, my uncle, all of my friends...each and every person who has encouraged me to keep writing and publishing has played a part. That said, a few people have gone above and beyond, and I'd like to name them here.

Kate Sinnott was kind enough to give me a French translation for Auguste Mariette's soliloquy on Giuseppe Ferlini's destruction of the pyramids at Meroë. Her care in researching the historical accuracy of the text was humbling, and I am extremely grateful for her help. French is one language of which I know nearly nothing.

The items Sable carried in her pockets were crowdsourced from my social media site. Many thanks to Steven Cortinas, J.L. Henry, Harold Straugh, Sarah Cook, Sarah Timmins, Ashlee McDaniel, Jen Broomall, and Samuel Levine for your submissions! The first three of those names are fellow authors, so please check out their work if you get the chance. You won't regret it.

And finally, thank you. Yes, you. I hope you enjoyed the ride.

ALSO BY
EMILY BARLOW

THE WEATHERWORKER CHRONICLES
SUNCHASER
STORMKINDLER

THE RAVEN'S CHILDREN

Sunchaser

She can bend the weather to her will...but will it help her forge her own path?

A small inland farm and a valley in the mountains are all Glorya has ever known. When she graduates from weatherworking school penniless, she must rely on her ingenuity and determination to make a name for herself. Her resourcefulness earns her a berth on a ship in exchange for protection against the foul weather that runs rampant off the coast.

But the coastal weather–and the people who sail through it–are unlike anything Glorya has ever experienced. Soon she finds herself navigating both extreme weather and new cultures as she struggles to make a place for herself in the world.

Will it be enough? Or will the raw power of nature combine with deadly foes to defeat her before she has a chance to prove herself?

*** Note: Sunchaser is a novella consisting of three short stories that introduce Glorya Sunchaser as she begins her adventures.

Stormkindler

In the shadowy winds off the north coast of Midlands, a sinister plot brews on a ship poised to pounce, threatening the fates of thousands unaware of the danger lurking just beyond their shores.

Enter Glorya Sunchaser, a formidable name across the lands, as she returns to school after years in the field. She accompanies her niece Zayira, a gifted but unconventional student, whom she promises to protect as she attends the only weatherworking school in the realm: Weatherwatch. But as Zayira struggles to find her place, Glorya steps into the daunting shoes of her late mentor, who left behind not only a legacy but a dangerous mystery that could change everything. With time running out, Glorya must unravel his secrets before they fall into malevolent hands.

Can they navigate the perilous tides of magic and betrayal, or will darkness consume them both?

The Raven's Children

An ailing king. Three successors to the throne. A kingdom on the brink of turmoil.

Ambjorg, Asbjorn, and Audolf watch as their father, King Hrafn, wastes away before their eyes. Figures lurk in the shadows, waiting for the right moment to strike and steal the crown. And all the while the three siblings and their father share a secret: an affinity with animals they use to keep their homeland safe.

As tragedy strikes the royal family, reports of attacks by aberrant beasts start to trickle in. The siblings are split in many directions, thrust into new responsibilities that test their resolve and their bonds. It will take every skill and ally they have to best whomever--or whatever--is behind all the unrest. But will it be enough?

Or will they lose both their kingdom and the lives of the ones they love?

ABOUT THE AUTHOR

A software architect by day, Emily enjoys reading, writing, knitting, crocheting, sewing, running, and learning martial arts with her family in her spare time. She is supported by her longtime husband and two wonderful children, who endure her eccentricities with enthusiasm.

For more information and to join her mailing list, visit https://emilybarlowwritesthings.com or scan the QR

www.ingramcontent.com/pod-product-compliance
Lightning Source LLC
Chambersburg PA
CBHW071500110726
47908CB00003B/676